THREE RIVERS

A GATEWAY TO LOVE NOVEL

CHLOE T. BARLOW

THREE RIVERS - A GATEWAY TO LOVE NOVEL
http://chloetbarlow.com/
All Rights Reserved
Original Copyright © 2013-2014 by Chloe T. Barlow

ISBN-13: 978-1497317925
ISBN-10: 1497317924
First Edition Published March 2014

Cover art by Complete Pixels and Eisley Jacobs

Edited by Marilyn Medina of Eagle Eye Reads Editing Service

DEDICATION

To my beloved husband,
You are the hero of my heart, of my life, and of every story
that I will ever tell.

To my incredible mother,
You showed me how to live a life full of passion, courage,
hope, and fierce resolve. Because of you, I will never regret
what I do, only what I do not do.

And, to *mi carnalitas*,
You are the greatest friends anyone could wish for and you
both inspire me every day. Without you, there would be no
Althea, Aubrey and Jenna. *Orale!*

PROLOGUE

Althea's teeth chattered around a muffled curse as icy sleet from a late December storm finally defeated the barrier of her coat and sweater, which were pathetically gaping under the weight of her overstuffed backpack.

She fumbled in the dark for her house keys as quickly as her rapidly numbing fingers could manage, desperately trying to ignore the slushy droplets that were charting a tortuous victory lap down the line of her chilled spine. At twenty-four, she had plenty of years of experience lugging textbooks home, but law school supplies had always been a whole new level of back-breaking weight.

After finally opening the door, she collapsed inside, stumbling in the dark over the mail waiting on the floor of the entryway. She released a defeated huff of breath. Even though she had guessed the house would be empty again tonight, the confirmation of that fact still stung. She didn't know what she hated more: that her husband wasn't home, or that after his weeks of unexplained late nights at work, it no longer seemed to surprise her.

Althea tossed her keys onto the coffee table with a grunt

and dumped her backpack in a chair. She sighed as her eyes scanned their messy living room. She summoned the energy to busy her hands with picking up the usual exam season mess — coffee cups, tissues and protein bar wrappers.

No wonder you're so tired all the time, she thought. *You can't sleep when you're alone, and you keep filling your body with this junk.*

A sparkling Christmas tree softly illuminated the room, even as its cheerful lights and ornaments mocked her frustrated loneliness. She'd decorated it herself after waiting night after night for Jack to come home in time to help her. Finally, she'd given up, poured herself a huge glass of eggnog and put up the ornaments they'd collected during their five years together on her own.

He'd apologized for missing it, had held her close and made love to her in the middle of the night, promising that all his crazy work would be over soon and they would spend a quiet, romantic Christmas together admiring the tree she'd so thoughtfully decorated. Jack had made it all better then, just like he always did.

But that had been over a week ago and nothing had changed. If anything, he was gone even more now, staying late in his shabby research assistant's office at *Carnegie Mellon University*, worrying over God knew what and coming home long after Althea had gone to sleep.

She flipped through the pile of old mail and registered Jack's notation to her on each item, indicating bills he'd paid or issues he'd already addressed. Even as distracted as he was, he still handled every problem that came their way. Usually before she even knew about them. He was a fixer by nature, which was probably why he'd chosen to tinker with robots for a living.

Althea was making her way over to flop onto their couch

when she paused to pull her cellphone out of her pocket. She stared at it as if it were an alien life form for several minutes, reflecting on how she had repeatedly attempted to ask what was bothering him. Despite these efforts, with each week he still became more distant and she felt increasingly shy with each of his tender rebuffs of her questions.

She was furious with herself for not even being able to talk successfully to her own husband about what was bothering him. She'd always hated confrontation, but this was ridiculous. If she couldn't even demand the truth from him, how could she ever hope to be an attorney?

She took a deep breath and called him.

"Hello. Tea?" His voice sounded so tired that she couldn't help but cringe.

"Hey baby," Althea cooed softly.

"Did you get home okay, gorgeous?"

"I did, but it's pretty cold and lonely here. When are you coming home?"

"Soon. I need to wrap up some things, but then I'll hurry home and snuggle you senseless."

"Mmm, that sounds amazing. I miss you baby."

"I miss you, too, gorgeous. How'd your final go today?"

"It was fine. A couple tough spots but I feel good about it."

"Still think you can make top of the class at graduation this year?"

"Working on it. I picked up my last two take-home exams."

"Great! Then you can take a break from having to hang out with future lawyers all day."

"Ha ha, you're married to a future lawyer, watch it bud," she said with a small smile.

"Objection withdrawn, counselor. You are most definitely the cute, sweet, sexy exception to the rule."

"You're forgiven. Seriously though, Jack, please tell me what's going on. I'm worried about you. Whatever you're working on seems to really be wearing you thin."

"It's fine, honey. I mean it."

"Jack, I know you want to look out for me, but this isn't like when we were in college and you'd sweet talk a professor into giving me an extension on a project. Whatever is going on is really bothering you...and it's starting to scare me."

"Please gorgeous, don't be scared. Anyway, your timing is perfect. I actually made a breakthrough and I think I'm on the verge of sorting everything out. I just need to check into one more thing tonight and then we can spend all the time in the world together. I promise."

"Are you serious?"

"Totally serious. I mean, I promised, right?"

"Yeah." Her heart felt lighter because when Jack made a promise — it was for real.

"I can't wait to see you later."

"Me neither. I love you, Jack. Bye baby."

"Love you, too. Goodbye gorgeous."

Althea smiled to herself at the idea that all this would be over soon. They'd married young and Althea reminded herself it was natural for couples to hit spots where work and life got in the way of love. She fixed herself a cup of chamomile tea and curled up under an afghan to watch the tail end of *The Daily Show* while she waited for Jack to come home for some of that snuggling he'd promised her.

Things were finally getting back to normal.

Althea was startled to hear a loud knocking on the door. *Did Jack forget his key again?*

She opened her blurry eyes and turned them to the cable box.

It's 2:31 in the morning! What the hell? I must have dozed off big time.

She picked up the remote and groggily turned off the infomercial about a hip-hop aerobics DVD and slowly stood up.

A second round of banging jarred her as she walked to the door and figured Jack must be freezing out there for him to be so noisy at this hour.

When she opened the door she was confused to see two uniformed Pittsburgh police officers instead of her husband's smiling face.

Her heart started to race a little. Nothing good ever came from the police being at your door in the middle of the night. Althea had lived a pretty sheltered life, but even she knew that.

One was much older than the other, with graying hair, a ruddy face and pot belly, but it was his serious gray eyes that caught her attention. The younger one looked to be about Althea's age and wouldn't stop fidgeting and shifting his eyes away from her. His nervousness ate at her, making her stomach drop to the floor and her hands shake a bit as she white-knuckled the front doorjamb.

"Good evening, ma'am. I'm Officer Arndt and this is Officer Shields. Is this the home of Jack Taylor?" the older one asked. His tone was steady but Althea couldn't help but stare at the tiny beads of moisture on his upper lip. It seemed so odd to her that he could be sweating on such a cold night. She was in a sweater and jeans and still shivering.

Officer Arndt kept staring at her until she remembered he'd asked her a question. "Uh, y-yes," she quavered. "I'm his wife."

"Can we come in?"

"What? Um, has something happened? Please just tell me."

They wouldn't say anything, instead they looked at each other and she felt herself step aside to let them in.

"We think you should sit down."

"Uh no, I'm okay." She wrapped her fingers around the bottom of her sweater and glanced around the messy room she'd never finished cleaning up, before looking back at them. "Can I get you two something to drink?" She may be jumping out of her skin with worry but her southern manners just wouldn't quit for even a moment.

"No thank you ma'am," the young Officer Shields said and she turned back to look at him when she could have sworn she heard his voice cracking. It sounded so loud in the room it almost echoed.

"Are you sure you won't sit down?" Officer Arndt quietly asked, throwing a warning glance at his young partner that made her fingers wrap so tightly into her woolen top she was sure it would tear.

Althea felt her head shake from side to side, the movement coming from somewhere else, surely not from her own body. With each quickening breath she felt more nervous, practically hyperventilating, until their shifting glances and uniformed bodies began to turn into unfocused, hazy shapes in front of her.

The uniformed blur on the left, Officer Arndt, said quietly on a deep breath, "Mrs. Taylor, we are so sorry but your husband was in a car accident tonight."

"What?" She released her sweater.

Car accident? Those happen all the time, right? Hopefully he isn't too hurt, she thought. *Probably drove home when he was overtired. I need to get my purse. Where are my boots? They were right here.*

She started scampering around the room, when she asked over her shoulder, "Oh no, is he okay? Which hospital?" She saw her boots and sighed with relief and went to grab them, but as she felt the leather under her fingers, a horrific realization clicked in her brain.

Althea turned and slowly looked up at the two officers, trying to make out their shapes through tears that seemed to come from nowhere. "Wait, why isn't the hospital calling me? Why are you..."

She looked at the young one and his heartbroken face said it all. It was the first time he'd looked her in the eyes and she was struck by how lovely they were. Almost golden, just like Jack's, but they were red rimmed and his face was so blurry. "Oh my God," she sputtered.

As understanding started to take root in her mind, her knees turned to liquid and the floor began shifting underneath her. The boots slipped from her hand and she heard the impact of them as they clip-clopped onto the floor beside her.

"Ma'am, we are so sorry. Please, let us help you sit down."

Arms reached to her, she saw legs move but they were all so far away, spinning out in front of her. It was so hard to hear their words over the ringing in her ears. It was as though she were underwater and they were trying to shout down to her.

How can everything feel so slow and yet so out of control all at once?

"Oh God, oh God, oh God." Althea lost track of the words coming out of her mouth, her joints felt like rubber, her vision turned to pinpricks. She could no longer see the officers. The only thing she registered was the Christmas tree behind them.

It was lit up like it was on fire, illuminating these two angels of death.

They had descended to her living room to tell her that her life was over, that her chance at happiness was gone, that all her dreams, her hopes, her plans, they had all been for *nothing*.

Yet, through it all, that damned tree kept blinking at her.

Sounds came in and out of her head. She assumed it was the officers talking, but she couldn't focus on anything but the flickering taunts of that tree.

She reached a hand out for support, but there was nothing there and she stumbled a little. Hands were on her elbows leading her somewhere.

Her mouth formed one word. "Where?"

"We think he was coming home, but it looks like he went off course with all this ice on the roads and went too close to the river. He may have fallen asleep at the wheel." That must be the older one talking. His hands were on her right, rough, calloused, and cool to the touch.

"The river?" she whispered.

"Yes, Mrs. Taylor. The Allegheny. We had divers retrieve his body from the water and found his wallet on him, but we're working to pull the car out now." This was the younger one, his smooth hands clammy with sweat. She turned to him, focusing for one moment as the tall blur said, "We're really sorry Mrs. Taylor, but he was pronounced dead on the scene. We need you to come with us to formally identify the body."

And with that, the Christmas tree and the two blurs disappeared and Althea's whole world went black.

Two Weeks Later

Althea threw the pillow over her head and attempted to fall back asleep. Soon her best friends Aubrey and Jenna would be back. They'd tried to order her out of bed, tell her to go shopping, to go out to eat, to start to breathe again. She knew they meant well with all of their pushing, but she wasn't ready to rejoin the world yet.

Maybe later.

Maybe after everything stopped reminding her of Jack and all he did for her every day.

How much he'd loved her.

How much she'd lost.

How she had nothing left.

The first thing to go had been the Christmas tree. Althea had dispatched Jenna and Aubrey to take down all the decorations the first day they'd arrived. She'd tried but couldn't do it herself. Instead she'd blankly stared at the lights through watery, unfocused eyes, seeing red and white turning to screeching tires and metal until she'd screamed aloud.

After that, they took her practically catatonic body upstairs. She'd been in bed pretty much ever since, except for when she dragged her weary bones to the bathroom to throw up from a nagging stomach flu and when they made her get up to change the sheets.

She vaguely understood she couldn't lay in this bed forever, but for now she needed to hide until the pain in her heart eased, or at least until she didn't feel so exhausted and queasy all the time. She stood up to go to the bathroom as a wave of nausea smacked her yet again. She managed to make it to the bathroom before vomiting, but it was still demoralizing.

Some women could make grief look lovely and romantic. Althea was apparently *not* one of those women. She wasn't ashamed to admit that she looked bad and smelled worse.

Coming back from the bathroom Althea stared at their empty bed. She pulled her cell phone out of her slightly torn sweatshirt pocket and pulled up Jack's contact for the thousandth time. She'd set it to a picture of him from their honeymoon in Paris, looking sexy as sin with his broad shoulders wrapped in a striped sweater and his golden tiger-eyes hidden behind sunglasses. He was sipping champagne at the bar on top of the Pompidou Museum with the sun glinting off his sandy blonde hair.

Althea would have given up all the rest of her years for one more minute of the life in that photo.

She stroked the edge of the phone thinking how gorgeous he was — *had been*. She pressed so hard that it fell out of her hands, clanging and bouncing on the hardwood floor beneath her, until it finally stilled and Jack's smiling image on the screen faded to black.

A series of sobs broke through from her throat so intensely that her knees buckled. She let her body fall on the bed and curled up into a tight, tiny ball, clutching her empty hand to her chest as it squeezed into itself, holding nothing.

Jack had been the center of her universe for years. Now he was gone and she was thrown completely out of orbit, spinning into nothingness.

She thought of all the memories they wouldn't have a chance to create: growing old together, children, and grandchildren. *Everything, it was all lost.*

In the times when she would doze off she still imagined, still *believed*, he would come back. In her restless dreams he would open the door and walk in. Kiss her, make love to her and hold her through the night.

But she always woke up far too quickly and the truth would slam into her again that Jack was gone and she was completely alone — left with nothing but the lingering shadows of a life almost lived.

And it had all been her fault.

What kind of woman can't talk to her own husband? What kind of a woman simply believes him when he says everything will be fine? A failure. That's who. A child that can't take care of herself or her man. That's who. And now it is all too late.

She'd created an elaborate daydream about how she could have done things differently during the last few weeks of Jack's life and it played on an infinite loop in her tormented mind.

In this alternate world, she'd had the nerve to refuse to let him keep blowing off her concerns and she'd realized how tired he was. She'd convinced him to take a cab home, or he called her to pick him up. Anything to keep him from taking that deadly drive home by himself.

But in this world? The real one? She'd failed him as his wife and best friend, and simply let her weakness control her until he finally died.

Althea's cries faded to whimpers out of sheer weariness, rather than relief, until she could only open her mouth in silent wails, her stomach cramping and shoulders hunching with each wave of brokenhearted agony.

Her body finally stilled from exhaustion as she stared blankly out of the large window beside their bed. Fat, wet flakes of snow were falling from the sky into the Allegheny River that stretched across below. The river was warmer than the air and the snow, causing the flakes to vaporize and turn to fog over the inky black water on impact in a way that almost hypnotized her.

One flake, two flakes, three flakes.

No matter how much the snow fought, it always gave way to the power and heat of the river as it flowed on.

The leafless trees arched under the weight of the heavy snow, bowing down and offering themselves to its dark power, yet the river cared nothing for their attention either. It was simply hurtling itself to the point where it would join the Monongahela River to form the beginning of the massive Ohio River, where they would barrel forward together, with no concern for the rest of the world — or for one desperate woman's broken heart.

Had the river even noticed when Jack's body drowned in its icy depths? Had it even cared that it stole him from her...or had it just rolled along?

She lay there, desperately trying to get her breathing back under control, when she heard their footsteps coming to her door. Jenna and Aubrey were back. They would be ready with another pep talk and crappy idea of something to do that invariably involved getting out of bed. All she really wanted was to be held until the pain passed. Perhaps she could persuade them to crawl into bed with her to watch a movie or maybe *Sex and the City* reruns. Anything so that they would leave her alone and she could go back to sleep — back to dreaming of Jack.

As Althea gained confidence in her plan, the bedroom door cracked open and she could see them standing, backlit, with a drugstore bag full of what appeared to be oblong boxes.

"Er, it doesn't look like you have popsicles and ginger ale in there," Althea choked out warily.

"No, sorry Tea," Aubrey said.

They walked to the bed. Jenna picked up Althea's cellphone from the floor and carefully placed it on a table before the two lay down on either side of Althea. Jenna faced her and began stroking her hair while Aubrey spooned her from behind and rubbed gentle circles across her back. Their tenderness reawakened her tears, such that the room was filled with nothing but the sounds of their breathing and Althea's almost pulsating misery, expressed every few minutes with her quiet hiccupping sobs.

Jenna finally broke the silence, asking, "Did you throw up again, Tea?"

Althea nodded and looked into Jenna's soft blue eyes. "Jenna, what's in the bag?"

Jenna and Aubrey looked over Althea's shoulder at each other nervously, until Jenna finally broke the silence. "Tea, we need you to take a little test."

"A *test*?"

"You're great at tests, right?" Aubrey whispered uncomfortably. After a pause, she added with a slight tremor in her voice, "It's just...there's no studying for this one, Tea."

CHAPTER ONE

Approximately Five Years and
Thirty-One Weeks Later

Althea looked down at the huge number five candle in her hand and breathed out a sigh. As she stroked its waxy surface, she tried to process that tomorrow would be Johnny's fifth birthday. Each of his past four had been painful experiences for her — bittersweet reminders that another year had passed since his father died, leaving her lost, pregnant and alone. Yet, this birthday was particularly poignant, as Johnny would begin kindergarten in a few days. Another milestone that Jack would never share with her, or his son.

She still loved Johnny's father so deeply that his absence felt like a living, breathing entity inside their home, and these annual reminders only fanned the flames of that pain, making it burn even more brightly.

She and Jack had met at *Duke University* when she was 19 and from the beginning they'd shared an instant passion for each other and for the pursuit of their dreams. Although they had vaguely considered starting a family someday, that step was to be much farther down the road. They had all the time in the world to wait to have kids — or so they'd thought.

It was as though they'd boarded a high speed train to their futures, ticking off one stop after the other — college with honors, grad school, prestigious jobs, a mortgage, next up was going to be savings, then promotions, maybe a great vacation or two. Not kids. Kids were for much farther down the railroad tracks, after the train could slow down and they could enjoy the view and savor their hard work. Kids were for their thirties, of this, they had been sure.

Yet their train had derailed and gone dramatically off course. The night Jack died and she was unknowingly pregnant, Althea's carefully orchestrated life had rolled into a ditch, the wreckage of her plans and security burning alongside the sounds of her own muted screams of agony and loss.

She would get back up and move forward again, but she would never be back on the same train again. Her whole journey had changed. Althea roamed on foot now, clinging to a backpack full of the remnants of a life they had tried to build together.

There were no mile markers or train depots marking Althea's progress on this new path, because she hadn't really made any. She simply marched forward, keeping her focus as sharp as a Prussian military commander on her new goal of keeping Jack's legacy alive. She worked tirelessly at a famous law firm, raised Johnny with determined zeal and helped Jack's mother, Carol, at his family's Italian restaurant, *La Farfalla Viola* ("*Viola*" to the regulars).

Jack's grandparents opened *Viola* after World War II, back when Pittsburgh's Mt. Washington hovered atop an expansive industrial wasteland. What Mark Twain had referred to as "*hell with the lid off.*" Feeding the hungry steelworkers honest Italian comfort food just like their own grandmas used to make. Now that Pittsburgh was a high-tech and medical research based economy with clean rivers and jogging trails, *Viola's* Mt. Washington address, and its stunning view of the city below, was as much a draw as its cuisine.

Althea had made some changes, mainly moving out of her and Jack's cool riverfront condominium in the hip Lawrenceville neighborhood to Mt. Washington to be closer to Carol. At first, the idea had seemed crazy to Althea but once the home she'd shared with Jack had been robbed and turned upside down a month after his death, Althea couldn't fight it anymore. She'd never felt anything but safe in their home, but now it was not only a reminder of Jack's death, but of her loss of security, as well. Drunk on pregnancy hormones and grief, Althea packed up and moved into a cute, albeit tiny old Victorian duplex near Carol and *Viola*, with enough of a view of the three rivers below to soothe Althea's soul at night.

And just like that, this had become Althea's life. Only a handful of miles as the crow flies — it might as well have been a different world, so far from her existence before Jack's death.

Living by her late husband's mother didn't cramp her social life because she didn't have much of one, at least not a dating life. She had friends. Two years after Jack died her friend Jenna took a job at a hospital nearby so she could move to Pittsburgh from Atlanta. Aubrey followed close behind, moving to Pittsburgh from LA, camera equipment in tow. Pittsburgh wasn't their hometown either, but the opportunities were good and Althea knew they'd been worried about her living here all alone with nothing but a toddler to keep her company. The girls lived in a funky apartment near the bars and restaurants in the East Liberty area and were always trying to drag her out on the town. A girls' night in over a glass of wine and maybe an early dinner at *Viola* was the usual compromise.

Althea lived a quiet, small life, but she knew it was what she could handle and as long as she made it to light more candles for Johnny without completely dissolving into grief and loneliness, it was enough.

Sometimes she would try to persuade herself to move on with her life, but that only made her feel the sharp knife wound of Jack's loss in her gut yet again...that, and the guilt. She felt so much guilt — for still being alive, when she was convinced she should have somehow managed to prevent Jack's death.

No matter how much pressure she felt to move on, she always came back to the same question: *How could she start over when she gave everything to one life, one plan and it failed — she failed?*

It was better to stay in the same place and help Johnny and Carol. That she could do.

The screen door crashed shut behind her and Althea jumped in her seat, knocking over her glass of iced tea. "Real slick, Tea," she muttered to herself as she cleaned it up and watched her son bound into their kitchen.

"Hey Mommy," Johnny shouted as he ran toward her. She looked at him, his golden eyes gleaming below his towheaded locks that were styled in the fauxhawk he'd demanded for the last few weeks.

"Can I get a skate boawd?"

"Excuse me?"

"Auntie Bwey said I could."

"Oh, well I didn't realize Aunt Brey cleared this already," she answered sarcastically. "Sorry, honey, but no. You're too young and Aunt Brey is just trying to stir the pot."

"What is she stirring? I just want a skate boawd, I don't need stirring," he asked, clearly confused.

"Don't worry about that, just know that skate boards are too dangerous and I don't think you need one."

"But Aunt Bwey said a punk needs a skate boawd. I'm a punk, so I need one," he said, crossing his arms in defiance. Althea smiled to herself, it was hard to see him as intimidating when he still hadn't quite shaken all the trouble he had with his r's.

"Oh boy. You're a real punk now, huh?"

"Uh, duh," he answered and Althea smothered a giggle.

"So kids still say 'duh,' huh?"

"*Yeeees* mom. Now can I have a skate boawd? It *iiiis* my bewthday."

"We'll see, okay?"

"Okay mommy. Aunt Bwey said to tell you to think about it."

"How helpful of her. Yes, I will think about it."

"Sweet!" he shouted and then used his tiny hands to perform what Althea could only guess was an air guitar riff. "Can I have money for the ice ceam man?" Althea gave him the mom death stare. "Aw, come on, it's hot out there."

"It's not hot, baby. You want to know hot, spend late August in North Carolina every year like I had to. Your sweat will sweat, sugar. This is nothing."

"Gwoss mommy. Come on, pleeease."

"Oh, all right, honey. I guess it *is* your birthday tomorrow, after all." He jumped up, starting toward the direction of the ice cream man's chimes. "But first you need to wash your hands, they're *filthy*," she said with a laugh. He rolled his eyes, but turned to climb a step stool to the sink where she joined him.

She read a note that was taped next to the sink:

Tea, I brought my plumber over, sink's all fixed. Let me know if you need any help getting ready for the party. See you tomorrow. David

Althea smiled, grateful that her husband's former boss still did so much to help her out after all these years. Jack had been David Murphy's research assistant at *Carnegie Mellon*. David stuck by her in the months and years following Jack's accident, supporting her like a father would, when so many others had simply attended the funeral and disappeared from her life. He'd been in a car accident himself the year before, making him all the more sympathetic with her life's upheaval.

When Althea discovered she was pregnant she'd been completely terrified and so alone. By the time Jenna and Aubrey arrived, the support of Carol and David had been the only thing keeping her sane.

The music from the ice cream man outside jarred her back to the present, unleashing a fresh ache in her chest. Jack used to chase the ice cream man down for her, on foot or by car, anything so he could get her a Push-Up pop or some other frozen throwback treat she liked. It meant that every time she heard those chimes go by her heart hurt a little all over again.

A single tear fell down before she could stop it and plopped hard on the counter.

Johnny looked up from the faucet and she wiped hard at her eyes. She tried so hard to hide her pain from him, but sometimes it got away from her.

"Mommy? Are you okay?" Johnny asked, reaching out his tiny wet hand to place it on hers. His comforting gesture tore into her.

She bit her lip and felt her breath catch on a burbling sob in her rapidly tightening throat as she looked up at her stamped tin ceiling, desperately trying to regain composure in front of her son.

Her breathing normalized and she bent forward and through a forced smile said, "Of course baby. It's just allergies. Here's a couple bucks, you better hurry or you'll miss him."

"Thanks Mommy. Bye!" Johnny hopped down from the step stool and ran toward the front door.

Althea silently chided herself. She couldn't afford to get emotional at every reminder of Jack's thoughtfulness or silly romantic gestures, especially not in front of their son.

Instead she took multiple deep breaths and waited for the pain to retreat. It never left, never subsided permanently, just ebbed back, until the next turbulent wave of anguish would swell and crash over her again.

Just as Althea had sat down, Aubrey came barreling into the kitchen with Jenna not far behind. They both collapsed dramatically into kitchen chairs alongside her. Ever since Aubrey and Althea pledged Kappa Mu sorority at *Duke University* their freshman year, they'd been inseparable. Jenna was already a sophomore. When she became Aubrey's sorority big sis they'd quickly become a devoted team of three.

Althea's sadness of just a few minutes before was forgotten for the moment, as she couldn't help but marvel at the physical differences between the three women. Althea had long honey-colored hair that was so thick it sometimes seemed like it needed its own zip code. Her hazel eyes, golden skin, full lips, and slim but clearly athletic build were the result of her mother's more delicate French and English heritage smashed together with her father's solidly Polish stock. It made for a striking combination of strength and sensual gentleness, as though Althea could stir you a great mint julep, right after she finished plowing your field.

Aubrey on the other hand was tall and lean with a short dark pixie haircut that framed her huge caramel eyes perfectly. Those eyes paid Aubrey's rent, having a vision for a great photograph and magazine layout of all forms that had become sought after over the last several years.

Jenna was yet another study in contrast from the other two women, with long blonde hair, blue eyes, and a sharp sensibility, she was the voice of reason of the three. Jenna's trim waist accentuated her rounded hips and full breasts, or as Althea called them, "*Her great rack.*" Raised as the only child of an intense high school football coach in Georgia, Jenna had grown up trying to be the son he'd really wanted. She learned to hide and joke about her very feminine frame, often laughing and saying, "*I don't know if it's a good rack, but I am definitely not built for speed.*"

She eventually came into her own and was now a highly successful orthopedic surgical resident, specializing in sports medicine. Her life growing up around football left her with a love of sports and healing those that played them, which was only surpassed by her distaste for the arrogance of male athletes.

"This cake is great! I love the Johnny Rotten theme," Aubrey exclaimed.

"Yup, you know how my boy loves his punk rock. Oh yeah, and thanks for making him want a skate board Auntie Brey, by the way," Althea said sarcastically as she eyed the lovely dragonfly tattoo on Aubrey's right arm.

They all three had a matching tattoo of three distinct birds intertwined and flying together on their right hipbones, but Aubrey had gone on to get several more. She loved introducing Johnny to punk music and fake tattoos, as evidenced by her contribution to the next day's festivities. "Did you bring

Johnny's punk supplies, tattoos and all, Aunt Brey?" she smirked at her.

"Of course, and you are very welcome. Come on, have a little fun, Tea. I think you should go punk like your son."

"Ugh, I get enough rocker bad boy, emphasis on the 'boy' from driving Johnny around. While every other kid is listening to Radio Disney on XM, my son can't get enough of Liquid Metal and 1st Wave."

"C'mon, my job as the cool aunt is to make sure he takes risks and has fun. I leave it to Auntie Jenna to make sure he graduates college in one piece and with a degree."

"Hey, you make me sound so boring," Jenna protested.

"Aw, sweetie, you're just responsible. I mean, the invisible human gift you got him will be very, um, educational, I'm sure," Aubrey said through a giggle.

"Oh Jenna, is that what you got him, those are gross!" Althea moaned. "What did you get him, Brey? A gift certificate for bailing him out of jail someday in the future?"

"Ha ha. *No.* I got him a drum set," she said with a twinkle in her eye.

"Classic. Well, it stays at your and Jenna's place," Althea decided.

"What? Don't punish *me!*" Jenna wailed.

"Nope, you live with her, you pay the price of no sleep. And while I'm at it, that invisible human organ thingy gift can stay at your place, too. They give me the creeps, yuck."

"I don't want it either," Aubrey proclaimed. "Hot naked men in our apartment — okay. Skinless replicas of men and their guts — not okay. That's officially a new rule." She looked back over at Althea, "So, it's settled, Johnny will be a rocker, not a doctor," Aubrey winked.

"Um, I'm not sure. I still hope it's a phase. I mean at this rate, how wild will he be at sixteen?" Althea asked with a giggle.

"Come on, you knew any kid of yours and Jack's would be cool, right? And the girls love a bad boy," Aubrey teased.

"He already looks just like Jack. I'm not worried about girls being uninterested. I'm more worried about what it will cost me to put up one of those electric fences they use on farms to keep out all the marauding females who are sure to be in love with him."

"Seriously, you'll have your hands full with that gorgeous Taylor man DNA in him. Tea, I swear, you married the only hot engineer out there." Jenna laughed.

"Speaking of Taylor DNA, is Jack's little brother Baxter going to make it to the party tomorrow?" Aubrey asked loudly. "Once I get full of cake, I would like to load up on some of that eye candy, yum!" Aubrey mused, while Jenna rolled her eyes.

"Gross, Brey, he's a baby," Althea responded.

"He's twenty-three! Yes, maybe a little young for me, but just because I can't afford the jewelry doesn't mean I don't like to look in the window." She leaned back and placed her hand against her heart, releasing a theatrical sigh.

"And no, he can't make it. He's still wrapping up his training at that culinary academy in France. So, we may not see him until Christmas," Althea said quietly.

Just the mention of Christmas still made Althea's heart race and palms sweat. It was ridiculous, but the trees, the Christmas lights, every part of the holiday brought back that horrible night for her.

She would do the best she could when it came around every year for Johnny's sake — getting a small pre-lit tree and setting it up in a back room they only used for the holiday. Luckily the girls and Carol would decorate their houses to look like a Christmas display at a department store to make up for Althea's guilt over depriving him of such a huge part of growing up. At least for a few more years she wouldn't be ready for Christmas. If she was honest she knew she may never be.

Jenna must have noticed that Althea was shutting down after bringing up the holiday because she stroked her hand until Althea was visibly calmer. All the fuss they had to make just added to her shame.

Aubrey caught on to the silence and said, "Aw man, gorgeous *and* a French trained chef. He is too delicious!" Althea was relieved that the conversation was now back to lighter topics.

"Delicious or not, I'm looking forward to when he can move back and run *Viola*. Carol deserves to retire. He's got the business training, he's going to be a great chef, we just need him to get here."

"No kidding. And his sexy ass will definitely increase the amount of clientele, female or otherwise. I guess I'll just drool over Doctor Hottie while he chases after you tomorrow. Hopefully he won't talk too much and ruin it for me."

"Wait, Doctor Hottie? Who? Oh no, you didn't invite Curt, did you Jenna? *Seriously?*"

"Yeah, what's the problem?"

"Stop acting all innocent. He's always asking me out. You know Carol will have a fit."

"He's coming as my friend, just chill," Jenna said.

"Besides, Carol needs to stop butting into your life so much. It's not healthy. David's coming, she doesn't complain about him being around," Aubrey pointed out.

"Because Carol knows he's like a dad to me, Brey," Althea said.

"Maybe for you, but not for him. He doesn't look at you like a dad looks at a daughter. You're so blind woman."

"Gross! Why do you keep saying that about David? He's not like that."

"Ease up ladies, let's not have this fight again, okay? Let's address the important matter that I just can't believe little John Edward Taylor Jr. is five years old!" Jenna exclaimed.

"It's crazy. That's for sure. You know, hearing his full name still throws me off a bit," Althea said. "When Carol suggested naming him after Jack I was against it, but he's so much like his father already, I guess it makes sense they have the same name."

"I didn't know you fought that," Jenna said. "Why?"

It's just weird to name your son after someone you had sex with, but then I realized that sadly, I wouldn't have that problem."

Aubrey and Jenna glanced at each other uncomfortably for a moment, until Jenna finally cleared her throat and fixed her gaze on Althea. "Glad you brought that up."

"Brought what up?" Althea asked.

"Well, *Sister* Althea," Jenna continued, "Doctor Curt 'Hottie' Connors asked me how you were doing again and I was thinking maybe you should finally say yes to going out with him."

"Uh, I don't think so. I mean, Curt's okay, I guess, and it makes a lot of sense to have a live in doctor around in case Johnny's inherited my lack of grace."

"You mean your total spasticity," Jenna chuckled.

"Yes, exactly. My spasticity. Doctor Sutherland, could you put that condition in layman's terms please? But it doesn't matter how cute Curt is, I'm just not ready."

"You'll never be ready at this rate," Aubrey huffed.

"Maybe I won't," Althea answered, her chin raised in defiance.

"Don't you *want* to fall in love again?" Jenna asked carefully.

"No, I don't," Althea answered. "Having a relationship? Loving someone? It's just wrong after what Jack and I shared." She breathed deeply, steadying her increasing heart rate, and looked Jenna squarely in the eye. "I already *had* my *'happily ever after,'* my *'love of my life.'* I don't get another. That's not how it works. There's a reason those terms are so final sounding, it's because they *are*."

"That is so depressing! And not true!" Aubrey shrieked.

"It *is* true! That part of my life is done. My book is written. Now I need to keep picking up the pieces while I raise our son. That's my destiny," Althea responded.

"Fine," Aubrey huffed at her. "Then what about sex?"

"What about it?"

"Why not find somebody to get busy with? You know, someone you won't feel guilty about or risk falling in love with," Aubrey commanded.

"Honey, she's got a point. You need to start living your life," Jenna said softly.

"*Start* my life? I have a life."

"You have a job that you work at nonstop, a son you spend every possible moment with, and you have us. But honestly, babe, you know you don't have a full life," Aubrey said diffidently.

"Gee, thanks. Come on, I don't even get this. What's the big deal? I mean, why now? It's not like anything's changed."

"Christ, that's the whole point, Tea!" Aubrey said passionately. "It's been almost *six* years and nothing *at all* has changed. I think we've been more than patient all this time. We thought it was part of the healing process, that maybe it was a fear of moving on, but now, it's settled — you're in a certified rut missy."

Jenna leaned over and covered Althea's hand, which had only recently been moist from tears and waited until Althea looked into her eyes. "Johnny's birthday and all the dates you keep turning down just cemented it for us. We can't sit back anymore. Think about Jack, you know he wouldn't have wanted you to live like this. He always took care of you and now that's what we're trying to do, and that's why we can't sit back anymore." Althea knew they were trying to be nice but their words felt like red-hot pokers to her heart.

"Point is, Tea, we know you're lonely," Aubrey added.

"Well, of course I'm lonely," she said with a lot of *duuuh* inflected into her voice. "I'm a *widow*." Althea couldn't help but wince, "God, I hate that word so much. It seems so old and menopausal, like I should be in one of those clubs with old ladies that wear purple dresses and red hats."

"I thought it was purple *hats* and red *dresses* that those ladies wear," Jenna corrected.

"Whatever. Never mind," Althea blurted. "The point is, you guys need to nip this birds and the bees business in the bud." They crossed their arms and huffed at her in response. "Look, I appreciate your concern, I do. But I'm being proactive. I'm even thinking of getting a rescue dog."

"That's nice and all, but it's your vibrator that really needs rescuing," Aubrey responded.

"Aubrey!" Jenna choked out. "Remember when we discussed 'never says'? *That* was a never say."

"Yes, Jenna," she responded in a singsong voice. "Jeez. Welcome to the no fun zone, party of Jenna," she muttered under her breath.

"Okay," Jenna sighed. "Let's agree that it's at least a 'not now say.'" Jenna looked back to Althea. "How long since you last had sex?" Jenna asked in a soothing voice that belied her great bedside manner.

"You know the answer to that."

"Not since Jack, right? Okay, how about a kiss then?"

"Jenna, come on." Althea thought for a moment. "That dentist Ted and I kissed."

"That lame, closed mouth mess after your one date with him years ago? I'm talking about a real flip your insides over. So hot you need to put your panties in the freezer kind of kiss," Aubrey said.

Althea paused. That sounded pretty nice but she didn't want to admit that to them, "You know the answer to that, too. Besides, I'm okay with my life."

"And 'okay' is not enough. You're a young, hot MILF..." Aubrey began.

"Ugh, please don't ever call me that again. And speaking of the "M" in that ridiculous phrase, Johnny..."

"Johnny is getting bigger, he doesn't need you to sacrifice your whole life for him."

"Bigger? He's five. It's not like he's investing in his 401K."

"You owe it to him to have a life."

"I owe it to Johnny to have *sex*?"

"No, you owe it to him not to give up on having anything for yourself. You and Jack broke records for marathon sex, I'm sure. And now you act like you'll never be a sexual creature ever again. I mean yesterday you wore mom jeans *and* a visor!"

"They weren't mom jeans," Althea huffed. "They were capris," she corrected.

"With the highest waist seen on anyone not fishing for lobster in Maine. Face it, they are gateway pants," Aubrey said.

"But I love those pants," she mumbled.

"They're like a dick vaccine, those pants!" Aubrey exclaimed.

"What's with the new fixations on my lady bits getting action? Is this like a   *sex*-ervention or something?" Althea joked.

"Exactly! So glad you're finally getting it," Aubrey responded.

"Jenna, help me out here." As the most sensible of the three friends, Althea was sure she would take her side.

"Sorry, girl. I think Aubrey's right on this one. How about we start with one night. Baby steps."

"A hot one night stand," Aubrey added. "Like back in college."

"Uh, I don't know if my limited sexual experience in college before meeting Jack really qualifies, guys," Althea grimaced.

"Okay, then like Aubrey in college," Jenna responded with a smirk.

"Shut it, bitch!" Aubrey countered, but she was clearly laughing. "Come on Tea, baby, it'll be fun. We already cleared it with Carol to come over soon and take Johnny for you so you can have a girls' night with us. We will dress you up as sexy as can be and take you out for a night of fun. If you meet a hottie to sweat up the sheets with for one night, awesome. If not, no biggie. I'll pay for the ice cream and lend you my favorite pajamas. No risk, no strings. You can't possibly feel like you're somehow tainting your love for Jack."

"What about my mom? She gets in tomorrow morning, I should focus on that."

"I can't think of anyone who would be more excited about you getting laid than Vivian."

Althea knew Aubrey was right on that point. Her mother, Doctor Vivian DuBois, lived by two mantras: *"Never regret what you do, only what you don't do,"* and *"It's better to ask for forgiveness than permission."*

Vivian had adored Jack as much as anyone from the very beginning, but she also worried about Althea constantly, thinking that her apparent refusal to start a new romantic endeavor was detrimental to her health.

Her mother may be right. If anyone would know it was her. A flamboyant and brilliant behavioral scientist with an alphabet of letters after her name and a slate of paid speaking appearances so full they would make Oprah Winfrey reach for a Red Bull. She specialized in human relationships and no one knew more about life from the intellectual or passionate points of view than she did. Althea often wondered if she found it a personal failing that her own daughter had remained single for so long after losing her husband.

"Okay, but I was planning to maybe make more treats for the party. You know how Carol is about her crazy Pittsburgh cookie tables. How about next week?"

"Uh-uh, no more excuses," Jenna interrupted and raised her hand to stop her protestations. "Doctor's orders. I prescribe dressing you up like the sex kitten you are and taking you out on the town. No complaints, no second opinions."

Althea looked down at the candle in front of her. She wanted to be indignant with them, but the fact was, they were right.

How had she ended up here? She still felt like a child and yet she was a thirty -year-old woman with a child of her own, with nothing changing in her life year by year, except for the number of the candle on a cake.

She took a breath and said, "Okay."

"What?" The girls squealed in excitement.

"Are you serious, Tea? That's awesome!" Aubrey exclaimed.

"One request before I go to my sexecution?"

"Yes, prisoner," Jenna intoned seriously.

"Can we drink margaritas in lieu of my final meal?"

"Of course. We aren't animals," Aubrey said with a smirk. "C'mon, Jenna will blend the hooch while I gussy you up!"

"Well, I guess I can't argue with that. After you," Althea said, dramatically holding her arm out toward the bedroom.

CHAPTER TWO

Nicholas Griffen Tate rubbed his face and gritted his teeth as he drank his *Macallan Gold Scotch* on a stool at the crowded downtown Pittsburgh bar two blocks away from the glamorous *Fairmont Hotel,* which would be his home for the next two weeks.

His mom wanted him to stay with her, but he couldn't do it. Even now that his father was dead and buried all these years, it still hurt to be in that house — the whole street for that matter. If a zip code could be filled with regret and lost opportunities, for Griffen, that was it.

"Need another?" Griffen looked up quickly at the nattily dressed bartender.

"Yeah, a double sounds good."

"Gaht it. Comin' right up." Griffen smirked bitterly into his glass as he emptied it and shook the perfectly square ice cube against the sides.

He hadn't heard the Pittsburgh dialect in years, but it was as distinct as they come. The years away were disappearing for him with each extended vowel he heard.

"Hey, you look familiar," the bartender added as he started to fill a fresh tumbler. "Have you been in 'ere before?"

"No, I, uh, grew up here, but I'm thirty-one, man, I doubt you know me from then."

"Nah, that's naht it. Sorry, but it's gonna bug me all night." Someone elbowed him behind the bar and whispered in his ear. "Oh man, I didn't realize — you're Griffen Tate, the writer! I heard you were from da Burgh, but this is crazy. Though, it looks like you probably don't want any attention, right?"

"No. No, I don't want attention, just the drink."

"Gaht it," the bartender said as he switched out the glasses. "Man, that's so cool though. I love those Cade Jackson movies," he whispered across the bar, his young hands gripping the edge.

"Thanks. You know they were books, too, right?"

"Oh yeah, I read 'em. I just love watching all that stuff blow up for real in the movies."

Griffen winced. Of course this kid would like his Cade Jackson stories. Young males with a love of booze and a desire to live like they were in a video game were his target audience. He nodded at the grinning bartender in thanks for the second round, hoping that getting drunk would take the edge off his shitty mood, and then hating himself for sounding just like his dad.

He sighed, feeling weary down to his bones. It wasn't too long of a drive down from New York, but for him it had felt like an eternity. He'd been filled with dread each mile that he drove closer to his hometown and all that it meant to him.

Everyone raves about the view coming out of Fort Pitt Tunnel into the heart of the city. You emerge from the belly of an ancient mountain to see each of the three rivers and all of the triangular shaped modern downtown area laid out in front of you, as though you're trapped in some enormous snow globe. Yet, for him it had felt like a slow march into a past he'd been running from for longer than he cared to admit.

Christ, man, just drink your scotch and turn down the self-loathing a notch already, will you, he told himself.

Being back here was doing a number on his head. He ran his hand through his wavy dark hair and squeezed for a second. He shook his head, letting his hair flop across his forehead and his hand fall back to his glass. Griffen wasn't a drink snob, but he'd felt like getting from zero to wasted as quickly as possible, and a glass full of the throat burning hooch had seemed like an effective way to start.

Ten years.

That's how long he'd stayed away and it would have been longer if it were up to him.

Forever seemed like a good length of time.

Griffen jerked when his phone vibrated in his pocket. He pulled it out with a grimace. Kevin Stevens texting again: *Glad you made it in all right. The key to your office for the next 2 weeks is with the provost. Thanks again kid!*

Griffen snorted. He definitely wasn't a kid anymore, but he couldn't complain. Coming from Professor Stevens the term felt like a badge of honor, an endearment. Even though his mind was reeling from the rush of old memories that being back in Pittsburgh brought to him, Griffen hadn't hesitated to agree to fill in for a couple weeks to cover the start of Stevens' investigative journalism and non-fiction writing courses at the *University of Pittsburgh* while he finished recovering from his double bypass surgery. In fact, he felt grateful for the opportunity to help him out. Stevens and his high school football coach had been the only relationships Griffen had ever experienced that resembled what someone would have with a good father.

Stevens' heart attack had hit Griffen so much harder than his own bastard of a dad's death. He was still handsome and fit at fifty; no one had seen it coming and it made Griffen feel like an ass that he hadn't visited him during all this time. He owed him the world. He knew that the least, *seriously, the least*, he could do was swallow the painful discomfort of being back in the Steel City and all the rotten memories that came with it — if only for a couple weeks.

Stevens was great friends with Griffen's mom Valerie. He suspected Stevens had wanted it to be more, but he never said anything to his mom. Either way, it was Stevens who'd mentored him when he went to *University of Pittsburgh*, recognized his talent and guided him toward becoming an investigative journalist and writer.

Even after Griffen left school, Stevens never stopped looking out for him and giving him advice. He'd supported his decision to quit football and leave college after his sophomore year and set him up with his first big job with the Associated Press. Griffen always sought out the most dangerous assignments, quickly landing an assistant job on an exciting embedment with an elite Army Rangers unit in the heart of the biggest Taliban insurgency in Afghanistan.

His time with the Rangers inspired "Mountains of Enemies" — his first mystery thriller starring "Cade Jackson." It became a runaway bestseller with the hottest action hero character in the world.

After it was turned into a successful movie, Griffen got restless, then living in Mexico for a year, researching and investigating the Mexican drug cartels. This led to his second bestseller and another movie and a solid reputation as an "*it*" writer. Then came a blockbuster video game based on the books, cell phone covers, ring tones. Whatever crap could be made from these stories, they'd done it.

Christ, last I heard there was some whiskey in Japan name after Cade. Ridiculous.

Now, at thirty-one, he had more money than he could ever spend, he never wanted for female attention and he could finally try to convince himself he was worth something. That he was better than his father. Yet, the moment this city had laid itself out in front of him, he realized just how little pride he really felt in who he'd become.

He took another burning sip, desperate to quiet the painful memories and disappointment that kept rising up with each breath.

Griffen's phone buzzed again in his pocket. He frowned at the screen. Another call from his agent. He hadn't been able to write anything since his second book, instead relying on riding out the fame of his first two novels. His agent and publisher were still breathing down his neck for a new hit, but he didn't have it in him.

Fuck 'em, they can wait a little longer. I've made them all very rich.

Griffen took a deeper drink and thought, *well, if I can't write and I'm stuck in this damn city, I might as well keep drinking.*

As he waited for his next drink, Griffen was finally feeling nicely buzzed and leaned back to observe the crowd, surprised by the hip cocktails and hipper clientele. Chic or stodgy, he didn't give a crap, but this certainly differed from the dive joints he remembered getting loaded in growing up. Several women gave him long, meaningful glances. He smirked back but couldn't get himself interested in that kind of distraction.

Before he could get too wrapped up in the same cycle of guilty thoughts, a lilting female laugh behind Griffen's back jarred him to attention.

After a heartier laugh followed, a throaty but feminine voice said, "Jeez ladies, I think he's a bit too hipster for me. If I hooked up with him, it would have to be done *ironically*. I mean, he's got a beard *and* he's wearing a vest!" Griffen laughed as the bartender put down his drink and he tried to listen in as inconspicuously as possible.

"What about that one?" Griffen heard a louder voice ask. "*Mmm*, what a fine ass, and nice broad shoulders. He's turning around...*come on lucky seven*. Uh-oh, no," she added with a snort. "Sorry Tea, my bad. He's got a hot body, but his face, blech. Moving on."

A third female voice said, "Excellent point. Let's keep looking in a logical manner. I'm not giving up yet. Hmm. He's too big, he's too young, he's too short, he's too...Ugh."

"All right Goldi*cocks*, I think you both have had your shot here. This is the third bar you've dragged me to tonight. It's late, my feet hurt and I think I've been a good sport. Let's move it along now, shall we? How about we just go home? You promised me ice cream and pajamas if this didn't work out — I think it's time."

Aw hell no, Griffen thought, he had to get a look at this woman with the sexy voice before she left. He slowly turned around in his stool and his breath caught and his throat closed right around it. She was fucking gorgeous.

Her friends — Goldicocks one and two he presumed — flanked her. They were lovely in their own right, a blonde and a brunette, but he only had eyes for the honey haired beauty in front of him.

He looked down at his drink pretending not to hear them, when the brunette blurted, "Over there by himself at the bar in the gray sports jacket. Ooh, he's delicious. This Goldicocks says he's *just right*."

Griffen stifled a smile when he glanced at the sleeve of his gray sports jacket. *Oh yes, Goldicock number one, do me a solid with your friend please,* he silently pleaded.

"Uh, girls," the goddess stammered, "a little too perfect, don't you think? Not sure I can afford the stud fee on that one."

Griffen almost choked on his drink as he thanked God that women with a couple drinks in them lost all capacity to whisper effectively.

This pretty little thing finds me perfect, huh? Very far from the truth, but I can let her believe it for now. Maybe this night isn't a total loss after all.

He surreptitiously shifted in his stool so he could take her in more fully.

Gorgeous. That was the only word that kept going through his head. The only word he could say about her. He hadn't wanted any of the other women staring at him from around the bar, but this one was another thing altogether. She looked like exactly what he needed to take the edge off his internal shit storm. He had to have her.

Her hair was long and fell in waves across smooth, lovely shoulders and round, soft breasts that looked like they would fit nicely in his hands — and his mouth, which watered at the thought. It was her eyes that had him transfixed, though. They were wide and almond shaped and the most unique color — hazel, with radiating shades of gold and green throughout, with an outline of jet black around the irises making the unique color even more pronounced.

He stood up and walked toward her. She quickly realized what he was doing and her eyes suddenly turned scared and her cherry red lips parted slightly. She looked like a cornered deer recognizing a predator's scent in the air, but her eyes never drifted from each of his. They were like a tractor beam and he couldn't even feel his legs moving as he walked toward her.

"Hello, I couldn't help but overhearing that you're disappointed in tonight's offerings. I hope you aren't really leaving." She was sitting on a stool, so Griffen could look down at her without releasing her from his gaze.

From behind him he heard her two friends stumble out a flurry of assurances.

"Oh no, we're not leaving. Actually, Jenna and I just saw a friend of ours, right?"

"That's right, Brey, there is that friend over there. Hey...you." Griffen watched as his lovely conquest followed their retreating figures with wide eyes and visibly tensed up.

"Hi," she gulped out, training those beautiful eyes back on his. "No, I guess it looks like I'm not going anywhere for a while."

"Thank God, gorgeous," he drawled at her.

"Uh, what did you call me?" she asked on a gasp, sitting upright quickly.

"What? Oh, I called you gorgeous." He took advantage of her surprise to take her in more slowly. She was remarkably beautiful in a very unique way. Besides the hypnotic eyes that were doing some kind of Jedi mind trick on him, she had the fullest bottom lip with a perfect Cupid's bow on top. Everything about her was a combination of strong and soft — firm legs that were still softly sexy and shapely, a small waist and taut stomach that led up to smooth shoulders and pert rounded breasts.

She was stunning, yes, but what was truly knocking him off course was that although he'd never met her before, something about her seemed so familiar, but also so sad and a little lost. He alternately felt like kissing her senseless and just holding her on the sofa to watch a movie. Griffen had to shake himself back into the present.

Don't scare her man. You've been staring at her eyes and lips for possibly a creepily long amount of time. Get with it.

"Right." He cleared his throat. "I called you gorgeous and since I don't know your real name yet, I will just have to go with that for now, I guess. Unless you want to share that information with me?"

She seemed completely flustered at the endearment, which was adorable but befuddling.

Could she really not know how hot she is?

He leaned in close to her so she breathed the same air as him and he could tell it was setting her off balance.

"Althea," she whispered huskily, looking at him then quickly averting her eyes again. "You can call me Althea."

Holy hell, Althea thought, *this guy is way sexier than is even fair.*

She'd already been totally thrown by his looks, and then he called her gorgeous...she hadn't heard that nickname since Jack and it added to the way this whole experience was sending her neurons into overdrive. She blamed that for the confusing fact that she told him to call her Althea, instead of Tea.

She'd even blinked a couple of times as the name slipped out, seeing as she even used "Tea" professionally. It never felt like *Althea* really fit her. Apparently most people agreed, because no one ever called her that.

For as long as she could remember everyone shortened her name to Tea, or called her by her childhood nickname of "Sweet Tea," because she had always been such a *doggone* nice little thing.

Ironically, she'd been named after her man-eating great-grandmother who'd lived it up in Charleston, South Carolina in the roaring 20's with multiple husbands (some of whom died in mysteriously gothic southern ways).

Althea hadn't felt much like that kind of a vixen in, well, ever. No, that had never been her. She was respectable *Sweet Tea*, after all.

But there was something about the way Griffen stared into her eyes that made her heart stop and had her feeling at once at ease, yet also full of desire. She felt more intense, more daring, more connected to the wild woman that was her namesake.

"I'm Griffen. I would introduce myself to your friends, but it seems they had to be somewhere other than here very quickly." He grinned, revealing two of the sexiest, deepest dimples she'd ever seen. Althea had a sudden desire to dig her nose into one of those cute things and wiggle it around, until she realized she was staring and couldn't help but feel a blush spread across her cheeks.

"Yes, they do seem to have run off, haven't they? I guess it's just you and me," she responded as she tried to turn her head and stop staring at him, but she was pretty sure she just looked like she had some kind of a facial tic.

"That works for me," he said with a twinkle in his eye.

Althea had really just been humoring the girls. She'd never actually intended to hook up with anyone. The plan was to have a few drinks and laughs with her friends, maybe look at some guys, flirt with one or two. Those had been the baby steps she'd really had in mind. Yet Griffen was so exciting and new, while at the same time something about him seemed so natural, that she couldn't imagine doing anything that night except for enjoy spending time with him.

Only problem? She was sitting in front of him completely mute, her mind blank of anything to say, and it hit her — she was totally incapable of talking to men, especially this man, romantically. This would likely turn embarrassing fast and it didn't help that she was so damn twitchy. Now it was her leg that kept jumping up and down erratically.

"Do I make you nervous?" he asked.

"A little," she muttered in a voice she barely recognized.

"Just breathe," he whispered. Althea blew out a huge gust of air.

"Thanks," she said, feeling embarrassed.

"I can't have you pass out on me."

"Sorry, I'm a little out of practice at this."

"At what? Talking to a handsome stranger in a bar? I think you're doing just fine."

"Well, you think highly of yourself, don't you?" she said with a smirk and she noticed his eyes drop to her mouth again.

"Don't you?"

"Think highly of *myself*?" Althea asked confused.

"No," he teased and then let half his mouth turn up in what might have been a smirk or was more likely some precursor to his wolfish plan of eating poor Little Red Riding Althea whole. "Of *me*."

"Puh-leeze," she groaned with an epic roll of her eyes. "You *can't* be serious."

"I'm not, but I did make you forget how nervous you are with me for a moment, didn't I?"

She couldn't lie, it had, but she didn't want to give him too much credit. "You certainly made for a good distraction, I will give you that. Thank you."

Though he'd only helped to distract her from her nervousness. Other than that she was hyper-focused — on him: his impossibly aqua blue eyes (seriously, is that even a real eye color?); his broad shoulders; that delicious mouth; the way his slightly shaggy hair grazed his dark brows. Everything about him was hardwired to excite her on every level. Even the one inch vertical scar next to his left eyebrow, that was the only thing marring the perfection of his masculine beauty, drove her insane. Althea wondered if it would be rude to lick that scar in front of a bar full of strangers...?

She couldn't believe she was thinking this way about a man after all these years, but it was as though he'd been crafted and chiseled to make her do something crazy and she liked the feeling.

"Let's go back to the basics. How about that?"

"The basics?"

"Yeah, the basics. I know your name's Althea. Next up — where are you from?"

"Charlotte, North Carolina."

"Dogs or cats?"

"Huh?"

"Do you prefer dogs or cats?" he repeated slowly with a smirk.

"I'm just a general animal lover..."

"Bullshit."

She gasped.

"Everyone has a preference, spill it."

"Okay," she laughed. "Dogs."

"Good answer. Do you cry at those emotionally manipulative Sarah McLachlan commercials about animal cruelty?"

"Of course! You?"

"Maybe..."

"Maybe?"

"All right, definitely, and I always donate a ton of money every time. I think I've ended up with five subscriptions to their magazine by now. Okay. Back to you. Birthday?"

"June 15."

"See how easy this is? Good, now ask me something."

Althea's mouth suddenly went dry and her palms were sweating. She knew that if she put her hand on the bar, she would leave a steamy handprint behind.

Gross, she thought. *Jesus Althea, come on. Ask him something, anything. Baby steps or not, could you be more boring? IRS agents sound more exciting than you. Maybe you should offer to do his taxes, that'll make his night. At least ask him a question. You're so wound up you've got this guy asking enough about you to fill out a visa application for you to go to Abu Dhabi. Least you could do is ask him something back!*

She was having some sort of flirtation stage fright and it was kind of humiliating. She tried desperately to remember how to do this but God she hadn't really flirted with anyone since flip phones were an exciting technological development. She looked down and glanced up at Griffen through her lashes, feeling incredibly self-conscious and for some reason — like a failure.

She couldn't believe how much she really wanted something to happen with Griffen. They had steamy glances back and forth down but she would have to talk more or they would start looking like they belonged on a show on *The WB* when what she was really feeling about this guy was more in line with late night on *Skinemax*.

Althea felt way out of her league but kept reminding herself:

This is just a baby step — I can do this.

Ha, she thought, *this guy is no baby step, he is a full marathon of hotness, an Olympic long jump of yumminess.*

Maybe I can still go after that slightly chubby hipster. Is he still here? He seems a better way to get back into things. I mean, he may want to discuss his kitschy collection of ceramic diner milk servers, but I can deal with that. I can't deal with someone this irresistible. At least not yet, right?

"Hey, are you still breathing over there?" Griffen asked, stroking his fingers over her hand and resting two on her pulse with a smirk. Althea hadn't realized so much time had passed but his touch burned the delicate skin on her wrist, jolting her very much to the present.

"Oh, sorry, I was just thinking."

"About what?"

"You," she said, barely above a whisper.

"Good," he leaned closer and looked in her eyes. "I like you thinking about me, then I don't feel so alone in the fact that I'm sure I won't stop thinking about you for a while." His eyes darted down to her lips and she wondered if he may kiss her. Instead his eyes looked uncertain for a moment and then he leaned back and picked up her drink. He tasted it and let his tongue dart to pick up a drop that lingered on his bitable bottom lip. "Mmm, a manhattan?"

"Ye-es, they age it in oak barrels for months to develop the flavor. It's my favorite drink." Althea's voice sounded thick and husky to her ears.

"Is that so? Well, then you should be enjoying it more,

shame to let something so perfectly developed go to waste." Griffen looked down her body then back up to her lips and leaned the glass to them. As he tilted it up, she opened her mouth to swallow the smooth but heady cocktail. Griffen replaced the glass on the bar and moved his rough thumb across the swell of her lower lip to collect some of the drink that remained there. Althea gasped slightly. His thumb was delightfully cool, but she felt like her lip was on fire. Without looking away from Althea's eyes, Griffen placed his thumb gently into her mouth. "Don't want to miss this, do we?"

Althea looked back at him and sucked his thumb into her mouth. His eyes widened, clearly shocked at how bold she'd so quickly become, but he smiled in glee as soon as he recovered, dimples in full effect. Althea smiled back and let her bottom teeth scrape the pad of his thumb while she sucked at him with her greedy mouth.

"Althea..." Griffen removed his thumb on a slow groan of her name.

She was so glad she told him her whole name now. Just hearing those syllables on his tongue had her warm all over and embarrassingly wet between her legs, because in that moment he made her feel so sexy.

It thrilled her to think that for just one night she could be someone else — not a boring mom or a lonely widow, but a glamorous, desirable woman who could hold her own with a delectable man such as Griffen. The thought that she could turn him inside out, make *him* want *her*, was more intoxicating than the strong cocktail in her hand.

"So, what do you do?" she squeaked loudly, suddenly overcome by how quickly everything was getting away from her and by the pleasantly warm and thrilling sensation running through her from his touch.

If the rest of him tastes as good as that thumb I need to stop being an idiot and make at least something happen tonight. She grabbed her manhattan from the bar and took a big gulp of it. *Let's do this girl,* she cheered to herself.

Griffen laughed at how the woman in front of him so quickly switched from Jessica Rabbit to Jessica Fletcher, as he quickly gestured for the bartender to come over.

"Another round, man? It's last call."

Griffen nodded and watched his new best friend rush away to make their drinks, as his mind went back to how charming and unpretentious Althea was.

She smiled at him with that sexy half smile of hers and his heart clenched again as she asked, "You know, what do you do — what is your day job? Since I can only assume you spend your nights interrogating other helpless women like myself." She gave Griffen a little raised eyebrow and a smirk and it hit him straight in his crotch. She was starting to open up and he could tell this was just going to get more fun.

"I'm shocked, just *shocked* that you think so poorly of me. You're the only woman I'm interested in interrogating right now, nighttime or not, but as for how I spend my time when I'm not trying to monopolize yours...I'm in town for a couple weeks as a visiting professor at Pitt. Journalism and nonfiction writing."

Okay, it's true for now, he thought to himself.

He didn't want to give her any indication that he was rolling in it. It was refreshing to be around a woman that didn't know who he was or what he had, and he wanted to keep it that way.

"Pitt, really? What a coincidence."

"Christ you aren't a Pitt student are you? Because picking up a Pitt student would *not* be the way to start off on the right foot," he laughed. "Even if it is just a short visit."

"Oh no!" she laughed. "Pitt Law School. Class of '08."

"So, this one's pretty obvious then, but I'll ask anyway. What do *you* do?"

"I'm a lawyer," she grinned.

"You don't say," he said sarcastically. "All right, now, what kind of lawyer are you?"

"I do complex commercial litigation."

"Big firm, little firm?"

"Big global monster firm."

"Exciting?"

"Not really." He quirked an eyebrow at her.

"Everyone pictures Boston Legal," she looked at his slightly confused face and added, "or whatever show about lawyers people are watching these days...but it's really one big company fighting another big company. I get into court and I find it interesting, so it works for me."

When the fresh cocktails arrived they held them up to each other. "What should we drink to?" Griffen asked.

"Baby steps," she said back to him.

"Not sure what that means, but works for me. To baby steps and a beautiful woman in a helluva dress." She wore a cherry red dress that was low-cut and gathered provocatively around her breasts. It hugged all her curves in a way that made his hands itch to do the same. The straps were thick and soft and sat just right on her enticing shoulders. He wanted to bite those shoulders — and soon.

"Oh, um, thanks," she said blushing.

Christ, that blush is beautiful, he thought. He couldn't think of the last time he'd even seen a woman blush.

"Well, it is *some* dress and you look great in it," he said, slowly perusing her red clad frame.

She rolled her eyes. "I would've preferred jeans and a brow-beater but the girls hijacked my clothes too."

"Brow-beater?"

"Calling a ribbed tank top a 'wife beater' is misogynistic — so I say 'brow beater.'"

He laughed. "I never thought of it that way, you're full of surprises."

She winced, "Oh God."

"What?"

"I just realized how bad I am at this. I mean here is this great looking guy talking to me and I can't stop blathering on about stupid stuff like tank tops."

He leaned forward and whispered, "I think you're doing great, gorgeous."

"Yeah, swimmingly," she muttered sarcastically.

"Let me guess. You're not used to this?"

"Is it that obvious?"

"A little. But it's sweet. Adorable."

"Yup. Every girl's dream. Meet a handsome stranger and he thinks she acts like a newborn deer wobbling all over the place."

"I didn't know newborn deer were sexy as hell. Because trust me, Althea, you are."

"Oh. Thanks," she managed to breathe out.

Griffen laughed despite himself and his seemingly never-ending supply of lustful thoughts. The sound was almost foreign to his own ears. He hadn't had much reason to laugh for a long time.

"And trust me, you couldn't do anything to make me not want to rip your clothes off."

"What?" she shrieked.

"Don't get me wrong, you're funny, brilliant and completely charming. Add on that you're beautiful and sexy as hell and I'm pretty much at your mercy right now," he smirked. "I'm wondering if I should be worried about the power you have over me."

"Really? Ah, no, I'm a sweetheart."

"I'll hold you to that, Althea. In fact," he said, placing a hand at her lower back until she gasped, "I would like to hold you to a lot of things."

"Ooh, that's a good line."

"A line?" he asked, his hand leaving her back to rest on his chest, his brow furrowing in a perfect image of false hurt. "You wound me, gorgeous."

"I'm sure your ego will recover."

"I'm not sure, I may need a bit of special attention, just to be sure." She rolled her eyes at him again and he simply smirked right back at her.

"All right, another question. Favorite movie?" he asked.

"Chinatown."

"Come on, *actual* favorite movie, not what you tell people to sound deep."

She giggled. "Legally Blonde."

"And the truth shall set her free," he teased. "Favorite song?"

"*In Your Eyes*, but only in *Say Anything*." He raised an eyebrow and she whispered, "I've always had an unhealthy crush on John Cusack."

"Hmm, now where am I going to find an enormous boom box in this century? Will it get you to come back to my hotel with me if I hold my iPhone over my head and play that song?" He started fiddling theatrically with the music controls on his iPhone.

She choked on her manhattan and almost spilled it down her front. "Go back with you?"

"Ooh, and I thought I slipped that in sneakily enough."

"I thought slipping it in was why you were trying to get me to go back with you," she blurted without thinking. "Oh my God, I just said that out loud. Can we go back to talking about tank tops please?"

"We can, but don't you think this is more interesting? I want you to leave with me tonight, Althea." He wasn't touching her but his nearness was driving her crazy. His lips were right next to her ear when he whispered, "Do *you* want to leave with me?"

"Oh. Well, um." She knew her eyes belied her growing terror and nervousness.

"Althea, I could give you a bunch of bogus reasons. Offer to show you the great view. To make you a signature cocktail or some other bullshit. But the truth is this bar is closing and I don't want to go to another one. I want to be alone with you. I'm just not ready to let you go. So will you come with me?"

He was leaning close to her ear, his breath spreading across her cheek and the warm air sent a rush of heat through her that had her body flushing and her heart racing. She wasn't ready to let him go, either.

The idea of being with him tonight suddenly seemed more than tempting — it was *necessary*.

No one had ever had this effect on her other than Jack. She knew she may never feel this way about someone again.

Can't I just let myself have this? Just one night with no strings. Let myself pretend to be someone else. Someone bold? Someone free?

Can I have just one night without fear and guilt, without crushing loneliness?

Before she knew what she was doing, Althea turned her head slightly so their cheeks touched, sending another rush of electricity straight to her core. The wait seemed to go on for an eternity but her mouth finally said, ever so softly, "Okay."

Griffen lowered his head next to her neck and breathed in deeply. "Thank you. So are you ready to go?"

She raised her head so she could look into his crystal blue eyes, so full of desire and said with more courage than she felt, "Yes. I just need to tell my friends." She looked around and met their gaze. She jerked her head to beckon them to her until their eyes widened and they ran over.

"So, I don't need a ride home," she whispered to them.

"Oh, gotcha," Aubrey smirked at her, then quickly turning toward Griffen with narrowed eyes she asked, "Is our girl safe with you? You aren't a serial killer, are you? Don't lie to me, I can sniff out a liar."

"No. She's completely safe with me."

"Hmm, that *is* what a serial killer would say, but you seem honest. Here, let me take your picture. If anything happens to her — you're toast," Aubrey snapped a shot, looked at it and said, "hmm, can't see your butt in this one. I'm gonna need you to stand up and turn around."

"Aubrey!" Althea interrupted. "I think that picture is more than enough. *Behave.*"

"All right, you know how to reach us," Jenna added. They kissed her cheeks and Jenna whispered in her ear so only she could hear, "You got this girl. We're proud of you and we're just a call away if you change your mind."

After they walked away, Althea turned and stared at Griffen, making no move toward her purse. He leaned closer to her and whispered, "Are you sure?"

"Yes, I'm really ready now." Althea looked at his outstretched hand and slid her long fingers across his palm and resting her hand in his. She licked her dry lips and looked up at him, thrusting up her chin in a dramatic show of confidence she only half felt. "Let's go."

As they walked out of the bar into the warm night air, Griffen placed a light hand to the small of her back and it awakened a world of nerve endings in her that had for too long been forgotten.

CHAPTER THREE

Griffen closed the door behind them and Althea gasped at his suite's panoramic view of the city. She walked slowly toward the back expanse of windows and looked out over its breathtaking view of the city and all three rivers.

Dumbstruck by his palatial accommodations, she turned to him with a smirk on her face, "Some digs, stud. Professors must be doing better for themselves than back when I was in school."

He rubbed the back of his neck nervously, "Uh, yeah. You've got to treat yourself once in a while, right?"

"This is quite a treat. Don't worry, I won't ask. I figure you robbed a bank or something so I probably don't want to know," she said with a wink. If she was going to indulge herself and pretend to be someone else for the night, she couldn't worry herself with interrogating him. She looked back out the window, marveling at the spectacular view of the city and the calming rivers from his suite.

"This is one helluva view." She turned and smiled at him shyly and she could see him swallow in response.

Damn, even his Adam's apple is sexy.

He stalked toward her, his blue eyes trained on her hazel ones, and she actually shivered. He just stood there in front of her and she could barely breathe. Underneath all his playfulness there was the hint of someone intense and only barely contained, and the combination was driving her deliciously crazy.

Finally, he placed his hands on her shoulders and she released a little gasp. He gently slid them down the bare skin of her arms and she leaned her head back revealing her neck more fully to him as her hair fell away from her. Griffen nuzzled his face in her neck so that his masculine scent surrounded her, while his strong, warm hands rubbed purposely up and down her arms causing her insides to ignite like a wildfire. He gently kissed her neck, then teasingly bit her shoulder, and it was as though an electric shock shot straight to her core and she could feel herself becoming wet already.

"Althea, you're incredible, you know that?" he asked as he moved his hands to her waist and pushed more fully against her, until his legs were snugly between her thighs and the cheeks of her ass were pressed against the cold glass. It was a stark contrast to the heat of his body and the intense warmth and wetness in her center. She imagined that if she pulled away there would be a steamy imprint of her back and ass against the glass and it made her feel beyond sexy.

They were already breathing heavily when he whispered, "Looking at you against this glass, the city behind you — now *that* is one helluva view," he groaned against her ear, licking and nibbling her earlobe until she had to lean her dizzy head back against the cool glass for some relief.

"Griffen...Oh! That feels so good," Althea whispered hoarsely, her voice slurring a little — whether it was from the drinks she'd had or arousal — she wasn't sure.

"How drunk are you Althea?" he asked, leaning back, and his surprise growth of a conscience jarred her.

"Excuse me? Don't you want me?" She suddenly felt shy and embarrassed, like her pretense was ripped away and she was just her same old stable self — no Althea, she was boring old *"Sweet Tea"* again.

"Dammit, Althea. I want you like crazy, but I want to know you really want this, too."

"I know what I'm doing, Griffen. I know what I want to do."

"And what's that?"

"You."

Whoa. What brazen hussy said that? she asked herself as his answering groan made the muscles in her stomach squeeze tight.

"Shit. You're so sexy Althea. But you're a good girl. I don't have a lot of experience with good girls. I'm not quite sure what to do here."

Althea smirked at him, grabbing his butt and pulling him tightly against her center. "Something tells me you've done this before."

Griffen laughed, "Yes, that's true. And I definitely have lots of ideas of what I'd like to do to you...with you. I meant I just want you to be sure."

It was bizarre to Althea that this man, whom she'd followed to his hotel room after only just meeting him, could tell so easily that she was a good girl. Because he was right — she was one, always had been.

"Yes, Griffen. I guess I've done my best to be a good girl my whole life. I also try to be a damn great woman. But tonight. Now. Here," she purred, enunciating each word with the scratching of her nails up and down his smooth cotton shirt, brushing his nipples until he groaned. "I just want to be...with you. What do you say?"

"Yeah, gorgeous," he said, lightly brushing the fingertips of one hand down her face. Running them across her lips and resting them there. "We can definitely do that."

Althea poked out her tongue and ran it across Griffen's fingertips. On a growl, he grabbed her ass in his free hand — squeezing hard — then releasing it to slide his hand at a painfully slow pace up to her waist. He clenched her to him for a moment and pushed her up against the window with the force of his body.

She slowly looked up into his eyes and for a moment they were simply entranced with each other. He slid his fingers from her face to her neck and rested his hand there.

Energy was humming between them, as if their blood and souls were reaching across the tiny pieces of air between them, electrifying it with desire, want, and anticipation of what was yet to come.

"Are you just going to stare at me all night, stud?" Althea teased.

"I was thinking about it," Griffen whispered huskily, looking in her eyes as he squeezed her ass again and pulled her up so her warm center rubbed against his erection. Her body hummed all over at the pleasure of the tight pressure, fascinated by how hard he felt against her.

"I can't say I would particularly mind, but first, I need another taste, and I want more than just your fingertips this time." Althea dug her soft fingers into his wavy, dark hair and pulled his mouth to hers.

Their lips met and Althea felt like she was in the eye of a hurricane that had sucked her whole world into its vortex. So many years of denied passion and desperate loneliness spun around her in a frenzy, driving her insane. When suddenly, the sensual storm slowed — narrowing and concentrating itself inside of her, and in the exhilarating moment — to a world that was only the two of them together.

Althea's ears were almost ringing, the intensity wrapping around her as she finally let go and simply descended into the sensations, *into him.*

Althea was so desperate to expand this new and incredible awareness of his body that she ran her tongue over his teeth, and then dove into his mouth, deeper. Griffen growled again, pulling her hair until she looked at him again.

"Wow," she panted.

Griffen smirked and lightly grasped her jaw in his right hand, pulling her lips closer to his again so that his breath was tickling across her sensitized lips.

"Well put," he whispered. Griffen used his hold on her hair to take over the kiss, running his tongue over her full lips. "Christ, woman, you even taste like cherries, how is that possible?" He kissed her again, then pulled back to say, "Perfect," against her lips, as they caught their breath again. "Everything about you is so fucking perfect."

She moaned at his words and the pressure he was exerting against her feverish skin. He tilted her head to the side and attacked her mouth with a ferocity that had her feeling like she might burst from the sensation of electricity coursing through her fingertips, down to her toes, up to her core. His tongue passed over hers and explored her mouth in a way that made her feel she could barely move from the pleasure.

The few brain cells functioning at the moment sent a lazy message to Althea that she should consider being embarrassed because she was probably going to climax right here, on his black slacks, before they even got to the good stuff. Though it was hard to imagine it getting much better than this.

Althea pulled away, gasping for air and hungrily eyeing the sexy man in front of her. "I wish I could look at more of you." She eased off the glass of the window and yanked off his sport jacket, noticing how smooth the linen felt against her hands.

He grinned. "Excellent idea." And with even more force he shoved down the top of her dress, pushing it just below the rise of her breasts, forcing them upward. Her already upturned nipples pointed directly at him. He wrapped his hands around the sides and placed his lips gently across the dusty rose tips. "No bra?"

"Not much room in this dress to hide one. Is that a problem?" she asked with a smirk.

"Absolutely not. I just can't believe I sat across from you all that time and this little scrap of fabric was all that was between me and these perfect breasts." He licked one breast then the other, repeating the motion, but this time sucking and nibbling on her taut nipples.

She gasped and smiled back at him, "Mmm, my turn." Her hands rested at his waist. "What delicious options. Do I look at what I'm sure is a beautiful chest or go right for the gold?" she asked, stroking up his chest then lowering her slightly trembling hands, just barely grazing the top edge of the distinct bulge in his pants until a frustrated deep groan rumbled from his throat.

The masculine sound was so alien to her ears that Althea paused for a second, swallowing hard. She looked up at Griffen's handsome face, his eyelids slightly hooded with arousal.

The reality of her actions began sinking in and Althea's nerves rattled and zinged rapidly through her veins even as her whole body was humming at the deliriously exciting effect of this contact with his.

She breathed in and let her fingers trail back up his hard stomach and taut chest. So much time had passed since she felt like this — sensual and liberated.

Tonight, she could imagine she was a fully realized woman, defined by nothing more than her own needs and desires. Here, in this moment, there was no tragedy, no loss, only two people reveling in the pleasure they could bring to the other.

The thought of losing this chance was more sickening to her than any doubt could be. She couldn't — *wouldn't* — let herself back out now.

"Gorgeous, if you don't make up your mind soon, I might jump your turn," he threatened with a hard thrust of his clothed erection between her legs.

Althea gasped but grappled within herself to regain some of her composure. "We wouldn't want that, would we? I can't let you cheat. I have to keep you honest. I *am* a good girl, after all," she breathed out, letting herself sink back into the experience.

"That's right, you're *my* good girl," Griffen added rubbing his hard cock against the tiny scrap of material covering her pussy, stroking her legs through her dress as she stood flush against him.

"*Your* good girl, hmm, I like the sound of that." And she did, even if it was just this one night, this felt so good, so right. More right than she'd felt for a long time. With that, she tore at his soft long sleeve shirt and pulled it over his head. "Holy shit," she gasped, when she caught sight of his bronze muscular chest, with a dark trail of hair traversing between his perfect pecs down the ripples of his abs into the slacks she couldn't wait to get off his body. "Griffen, Jesus, you're perfect," she whispered, running a finger back and forth under his waistband.

"You're the perfect one, gorgeous," Griffen said, running his hands up her waist, across her collar bones, between her breasts, finally resting them along the sides of her neck, his fingers reaching into her hair. "But, you won't distract me from my turn." He pulled down her zipper slowly, so the cool metal shocked the warm flesh of her back, then slid her dress down until it pooled at her feet. As he pinned her with his hips against the window she gasped at the chill of the cool glass against her overheated skin.

He looked up and down her body, naked but for a tiny red thong. "You're so fucking beautiful." He cupped a hand on her bare hip and the other against her chin, his fingers wrapping around her mouth and whispered, "So fucking beautiful," and he kissed her hard again.

She thrust her tongue into his mouth and he sucked it. He pulled away and she stared at him. She opened her lips, feeling how swollen they were from his aggressive kisses. She shifted her chin slightly, just enough to pull two of his fingers into her mouth, rolling her tongue over them, sucking them in and out of her mouth as she stared into his eyes. It was a sensual promise that made him groan.

Griffen slid out his fingers and trailed them between her breasts down her belly and over her silk covered mound. He slowly moved the material aside and slid his fingers up and down her wet slit.

She grunted anxiously and moaned, "Please Griffen. Please."

"Fucking amazing," he groaned again and knelt down as he put one finger inside of her. The sensations were overwhelming and she unconsciously rocked against his hand.

Griffen suddenly removed his finger from inside of her and she whimpered at the loss of his touch.

"Sorry, gorgeous," he said "but you've teased me till I can't see straight. I need to taste you. Now."

He pulled her panties down. "I love this cherry red thong, baby, but it needs to go." He stroked her smooth skin, "You're hairless, gorgeous. I guess you're not *that* good of a girl. I like that. You're so sexy everywhere." He pushed a finger back in her and twisted it around, curving it into the soft front wall of her vagina.

She writhed and he took one of her legs over his shoulder and stared at her. She knew she was wet and ready for him. "Griffen," she whispered.

"I told you, gorgeous, you're my good girl tonight. And I want to take my time." He looked up at her as he placed another finger inside and then licked up the full length of her slit. He slowed his ascent, flicking his tongue against her swollen clitoris until her legs shook and she moaned from so deeply in her belly that she thought he must feel the vibrations against his tongue. He pushed and pulled his two fingers repeatedly inside her. His own sensual promise of what was to come when he finally put his cock inside her.

As Althea's legs began to quiver faster, Griffen increased the pace of his fingers, curving into her most sensitive area. She was gripping his hair so hard she thought he might have a sore head the next day, but she couldn't stop. His tongue quickly flicked over her clitoris, finally sucking until she screamed his name.

Althea fell apart around his fingers inside her, as his other hand grasped her ass so firmly that she was sure she'd have a bruise there the next day, but she didn't care. In fact she hoped

— *no, craved even* — for him to mark her and leave her with a physical reminder of their one night together.

He pulled her harder against his tongue that was worshipping her clit. She tensed against a pleasure so intense it felt close to pain until all she saw was light as she shattered on his tongue. She came against his mouth and she could've sworn he murmured something about cherries. He stroked her legs, looking up at her as her chest heaved.

"I could look at you come all night, Althea," he said with more than a bit of reverence in his voice.

"Well, stud, you promise to make it feel like that each time, you got a deal."

"I aim to make it even better, gorgeous."

"Oh shit," she gasped and Griffen barked a laugh, hugging around her waist and burying his nose into her warm mound before he slithered up her body, trailing his mouth, still wet with her juices, slowly up her belly and between her breasts. Althea couldn't stop looking down at his sexy face and body. God, he called her gorgeous, but he was beyond anything she could imagine and he'd made her feel so damn good. It was years since Althea had climaxed with another person. It had just been her hand and mechanical friends since Jack died, making it all the more surprising that she'd come so quickly with Griffen. Christ, she almost came just from taking off his shirt.

He stroked her slowly as he stood. Kissing her, idolizing her body with his hands. He'd put on a condom and was poised at her entrance hesitating, until she begged, "Please, Griffen. Yes."

He smiled for a moment before thrusting inside her. She'd barely collected her breath and her brain from her first orgasm, when the force of his thick, hard cock inside her reignited her climax as though it had never abated. She grabbed his hair and thrust her tongue in his mouth. Mirroring the delicious work he'd done on her with his incredible mouth. Griffen lifted her behind her knees and wrapped her legs tightly around him so he could spin her around and sit her butt on the desk next to the floor to ceiling windows. The rivers flowed beneath her as he entered her intensely and repeatedly. He was big and thick — even bigger than Jack, who'd been substantial — and her unused body had to stretch every time he entered.

"Christ. You feel so good. You're so tight," he whispered against her cheek as she leaned her head back against the wall.

"Er, it's been a while," Althea gasped sheepishly as she looked up into his eyes. He slowed for a moment, his eyebrows raised, then smirked, slamming into her even harder, until her back was arched and her breasts grazed his bare chest. She started screaming his name again. He tilted her chin up until he could look in her eyes and tenderly stroke her cheek, a stark contrast from the intense physical pleasure he'd been relentlessly releasing on her below.

"I like that, baby. I want this pussy and I want you to remember that it's mine, that right here, right now, it's mine." He thrust again and Althea felt his possessive words driving her crazy. "You feel incredible my gorgeous good girl," he whispered and kissed her tenderly, even as he slammed into her again. She could feel herself spasming and tightening intensely around his cock.

Had sex always been like this? Althea wondered as waves of warmth crashed over her.

She'd been a pretty reserved bookworm growing up. Not really blossoming until senior year of high school, she'd not lost her virginity until she was nineteen, having had sex with two guys before she met Jack. Bumbling college boys, both of them. One was a sensitive guy who was also an English major, like her, with little to no knowledge of the female anatomy. The second was a short-lived boyfriend from a good fraternity and an even better family who'd bored the hell out of her. Once she met Jack, that was it, there was never anyone else. Until now.

She was indeed Griffen's right then and it felt amazing.

Sex with Jack had been wonderful — sweet, loving and intimate. The safe lovemaking of two people who knew each other better than anyone because they'd grown up together. But there was nothing safe about this. This experience was animalistic and intense, while also protective and warm. Griffen was no boy and her body was acting all woman.

"Christ," she gasped, as Griffen pulled his head up, trapping her with his eyes as he placed his hands under her ass, tilting it up until he went even deeper, hitting some point inside her that made her clench, the warmth turning to ripples of energy throughout her body, and she screamed his name yet again.

Griffen used his other hand to stroke her still sensitized clit. "I feel you tightening around me, gorgeous. You're so incredible." The words, the stroking, the pumping of his hard body and the intense look on his face were all too much. Althea tingled from her core ubiquitously, coming even more spectacularly around him.

"Oh Griffen. Oh God."

"Yes. Yes gorgeous. Fuck, yes."

She came again, as Griffen grew harder and stiffened inside of her, coming right along with her.

"Althea," he shouted. Griffen held her as she stayed seated on the desk and they caught their breaths. He disposed of the condom, then his slacks and boxer briefs, which they hadn't made it to taking off yet.

He picked her up, which gave her a burst of awkwardness, but she tamped it down — like everything else tonight, she would let herself enjoy it. He carried her to the nearby bed with an amount of ease that made her feel downright girly. They were both still lightly panting, kissing each other everywhere they could reach. He placed her gently on the bed and lay down beside her.

"Jesus, Althea, you were amazing," he whispered as he stared at her and ran his hand up and down her body.

"Well, I, uh, do a lot of yoga," she whispered seriously.

He barked out a laugh. "That's not what I meant, but good to know," he said with a smirk.

She laughed and looked up at him as he stroked her hair. "In that case, you aren't so bad yourself, stud."

Althea felt warm and content, yet also exposed, stripped bare and mildly terrified in the best way imaginable. She felt so free, and that was the scariest thing for her.

Maybe the girls were on to something. Break herself in with a sexy stranger just passing through. No worry of seeing him again or him expecting anything. No risk that he would want her to be whole — someone capable of any real future with another person. This was all she could give, and if it gave her so much pleasure in return, it couldn't be bad, right?

But if I want no strings, then why did I love the closeness, his possessiveness? Why did I like being his good girl so much?

She told herself, that's because this was a perfect fantasy.

She'd belonged to no one but a ghost for years — simply living out her life sentence of grief without parole — subject to solitary confinement with nothing but memories to keep her warm in her cell.

But this was real. This was beautiful. She was owned by this stunning man for this tiny safe moment in time, and it had felt wonderful.

They lay together in his bed for some time, kissing and occasionally talking in hushed tones. Althea rolled over revealing her rounded breasts above the sheet and Griffen had to take them in his mouth again.

Pulling up, he rested his face in her neck, whispering, "So beautiful. Althea," as he moved her hair to kiss her earlobe and neck. She moaned and his cock began to harden again like he was a teenager who couldn't be satisfied. "Baby. You keep moaning like that and I'll have to take you again."

Althea turned and smiled wickedly. "You promise?"

She made him as hard as he could ever remember being. Talking to her all night had been stimulating, to say the least, but now he could barely contain himself from thrusting inside her again. It felt good to feel. To be excited about something for the first time in years. Certainly the most interested he'd ever been in every aspect of a woman.

He wanted her so pleased by each part of him that she couldn't forget him. He had no idea why, but he knew he had to mark himself on her and he wasn't going to question it.

Griffen growled and rolled on top of her. He grabbed a condom packet, tore it open with his teeth and had it on in a matter of seconds, so quickly ready to be inside her again. Griffen bracketed her chest with his arms, his shoulders and biceps tense and flexed. He looked down at her, his heart feeling a strange clench.

"Griffen," she whispered looking at him with her huge hazel eyes, green flecks dancing in the dim light of the room.

She stroked a lock of wavy, dark hair off his forehead and he pressed his face into her hand.

He smiled at her and entered in one slow thrust. They moaned and leaned toward each other. Griffen stroked into her, gently this time, slowly bringing her body to another orgasm, even as he kissed her entire face, her eyelids, her cheeks, and her lips. Althea held him tightly as she moaned, curling into his body.

Jesus, she is way too hot for it to have been so long like she said.

It had surprised Griffen how much he'd liked hearing that. He didn't want to think about her with some other guy, even though that had never mattered to him before. The thought of her choosing to be with him rather than anyone else made him even harder inside her. He grabbed her hands in one of his and held them above her head, pushing her back so he could pound into her even more deeply — possessively and intense.

"Griffen!" she shouted as he thrust into her deep, until his balls were flush with her body as they both came again.

He shouted her name like a song and collapsed on her, still semi-hard inside her tight body. "Fuck, Althea, I think I need to chain you to this bed. You're so incredible."

"Hey, you promised my friends you weren't crazy," she laughed.

"I promised I wasn't a serial killer. Never said anything about not being crazy. And you," he said as he brushed his lips against her neck, "make me crazy." He rolled off, and immediately missed the feeling of her body wrapped around him. He tossed the condom in the trashcan by the bed and gathered her in his arms.

As Griffen began to doze off, he pulled her soft body closer against his hard, muscular frame, fitting his legs between hers. She was warm and stunning, but he felt something greater

— joy, perhaps. Though that was one sensation with which he was not very familiar. Especially not here in Pittsburgh.

Something about her was so familiar but also so exciting. He was overtaken by a desire to enjoy that feeling again, like a drug that he knew would get more potent with each hit. He began to work out the possibilities in his head.

Griffen didn't do relationships. It wasn't that he had anything against them in theory, but he'd learned the hard way that committing yourself to someone — relying on them in any way — left you open for a world of hurt. It was better for both parties to know their limits, and for him, his cutoff came at attachment. Maybe if he and his Mom had lived by that code when he was growing up, they could've been spared years of torment at the hands of his father.

But, that didn't mean he couldn't spend some more *unattached* time with Althea. That would certainly make his stay in this place that had been the site of so much hurt for him more bearable — pleasurable even.

In the morning he would propose she help him enjoy his two weeks in town — preferably in his suite, but he was flexible on location.

Suddenly being back in his hometown didn't seem so heart-wrenching after all.

"Goodnight, my gorgeous good girl," he whispered against her hair. "See you in the morning." Griffen felt peaceful and happy, in a way that was alien to him. He pulled her close and fell into a deep sleep.

The morning? What? Oh God. I've got to get out of here.

Althea swallowed dryly around the panic that started to creep into her throat. She'd been almost asleep when those words broke through her consciousness.

Althea knew she couldn't be there when he woke up, that was most definitely *not* the plan. Her heart went from a lazy sleeping rhythm to a frantic pace. She tried to stay calm until Griffen finally seemed to be completely asleep, then carefully slid out from under his arm, intending to shimmy off the bed. Unfortunately, her trademark clumsiness kicked in and she plopped flat on her bottom on the floor. She grimaced and looked up at Griffen in the bed from her undignified perch on the floor. He took a deep breath and rolled over closer toward her face, though she could tell he was still asleep.

She gulped but didn't hesitate to take another long perusal of his handsome body and face.

Way to go Tea, that is one hot male!

She shook off her gawking and found her phone. She made sure it was silenced and texted Jenna to pick her up at his hotel.

After she dressed, Althea sat on the floor of Griffen's hotel room silently admiring him and wishing life was different. He was so good looking, but more than that, he was confident and charming, with a vein of intensity and strength that made her feel at once contented and unsettled. Their lovemaking had been passionate and hot, but it had also been so much fun.

What if she were free enough to stay till morning like he asked? To make love again, shower together, wear a fluffy robe and feed each other room service while planning a fun day in, and out, of bed. The fantasy wrapped around her heart and mind so clearly she could almost smell the room service coffee and pancakes.

She hadn't had this much fun with anyone since Jack died.

Dammit! What about Jack?

And there it was, the guilt. The feeling that she'd cheated on her one and only. He was gone, but it still felt like he would come back the next week from a trip, even after all these years.

The sadness and memories had become a form of comfort to her — they were a partner that would be with her forever, one that would never die.

But she'd felt no guilt while having sex with Griffen, in fact, so many facets of his personality reminded her of Jack's charming strength and beauty inside and out that it made her feel connected to Jack in some way, even if for only this brief time. She hadn't felt the usual sadness or guilt tonight until just now when she'd decided to leave.

She actually felt disappointed, like she was leaving a wonderful vacation and wishing she could buy a home and move there permanently, but knowing she would never be able to afford it.

The light on her phone shocked her back to consciousness.

It was Jenna. "*I'm downstairs. C u soon.*"

Althea stood, grabbed her purse and walked out of the door quietly in her bare feet, ridiculously high heels in hand. She scuttled through the now empty hotel lobby, which was resting until the dawn of a new day, with no hint of the boisterous conversations and antics of only hours before.

As she stepped through the revolving door, her heart leapt at the sight of Jenna. She heaved a sigh of relief and climbed into the passenger side of Jenna's practical Ford Focus.

She looked over and smiled. "Hi girl," Althea said.

"I'm glad to see that phase one of 'Operation Get Tea a Life' appears to have been a success."

"It was. Whew, was it ever."

"And you feel okay? Not entering some kind of Tea shame spiral?"

"I did for a minute there, but I forced myself to stop. I'm letting myself be happy about it."

"Good for you!"

"Now get me home and put me to bed."

"Bossy, bossy! But I am getting details tomorrow."

"Of course!"

Althea leaned her head back and looked out the window as Jenna raced across the Smithfield Street Bridge, adrenaline and pleasure still warming her heart. The dark night enveloped them, but for the lights flickering on docked boats below and lining the elaborate wrought iron decorations of the trestles above them.

The city was sleeping. Even the rivers and streets, the constantly moving veins of the city, seemed tranquil.

"Jenna?" she eventually said.

"Yeah babe?"

"Thank you."

"For picking you up? You think I would drag you out for a night on the town and just leave you to the wolves? Or one wolf in particular?"

"Of course not. No, I mean, thanks to both you and Aubrey for — for everything." Her voice caught in her throat, a gulp of air and emotion lodging inside and choking her lightly. "Thank you for not giving up on me, for pushing me. For being...aw shit..."

"We know, honey, we know." Jenna reached across the console and held her hand. "We're sisters and it's an honor. I love you."

Althea smiled. "I love you, too."

CHAPTER FOUR

Light stretched across Griffen's face and he cursed himself for not closing the curtains before he and Althea went to sleep. He reached over to pull her close.

If I have to be up this early, I might as well get some pleasure out of it, right?

His hand found nothing but pillows and sheets. He pried open his eyes, only to confirm he really was alone.

What the hell?

He sat up and found his room completely empty. No woman, no clothes and — upon further inspection — no phone number.

Her being gone wasn't really surprising, even though he'd asked her to stay, she owed him nothing. No, what was the shocking part was that for some reason Griffen felt disappointed. He had really wanted to see her again and her running out left him more than a bit pissed. He'd specifically asked her to stay and she had snuck out like a...well, like *him.*

Griffen started to work out in his brain how to find her. Pittsburgh was certainly a larger sized city, but in many ways it was still a small town. The remnants of a blue-collar culture and challenging geography of rivers, hills and valleys had created a unique archipelago of self-contained walkable neighborhoods. Each had its own culture, but they were all interconnected, like a family tree. Add into that a rabid sense of hometown pride and the place had maintained a small town vibe. In Pittsburgh there were only two, maybe three, degrees of separation between people and Griffen knew this meant he had a good chance of finding her if he put his mind to it.

He knew a fair amount about her. He investigated for a living, right? A lawyer, young, with a unique first name. Maybe he could find her in his spare time.

Oh Christ Griffen, 'find her in your spare time?' and that is not stalking, why?

Just as frustration really started to take root, he noticed a text from his mother asking him to call her.

Griffen took a breath. She was an early riser, so he might as well get it over with. "Morning, Mom."

"Hey baby. Welcome back to town stranger. What are you up to today?"

"Well, I was planning on going for a run and then working on my first lesson plan."

And maybe trying to track down a hot local lawyer that ran out on me last night, but you don't need to know that Mom, he added to himself.

"Okay, well whatever you do, I need you to be free by noon."

"Why?" He breathed out slowly. "What do you have up your sleeve, Mom?"

"I want you to come with me to Jack's son's birthday party."

"Jack Taylor's son?" he asked as a pain shot through his chest.

"Yes, little Johnny Taylor."

Griffen had heard that Jack's wife found out she was pregnant after he died. The idea of meeting a little Jack was amazing, but Griffen didn't feel like he had the guts to follow through with it. Just thinking about Jack felt like a knife in his gut.

"Mom, I don't know if I can do that. How about I go by and meet him on my own sometime before I leave?"

"Oh no you don't, Nicholas Griffen Tate. You will not blow me off on this. Jack was your best friend since you were little. You meant the world to each other and his mother still asks about you, even though you checked out of his life after high school."

"I didn't check out on Jack, I wanted to move on — from everyone."

"Well, it's been years since he died and you didn't even go to his funeral." Griffen cringed and wondered to himself how such a great night could have morphed into a morning this terrible.

"Christ, all right, I feel like shit now, are you happy?"

"A little. But I will lay off if you go to this birthday party today with me. You need to meet his son."

"Fine, I'll go."

"Great, I'll come pick you up at noon and we can head over together."

"I have a car here with me."

"Oh, no you don't. You'll sneak out first chance you get. I'm trapping you there. I'll pick you up."

"All right. Just call me when you're downstairs."

After taking a shower Griffen wrapped a towel around his waist and walked over to his laptop. Pulling up his email, he opened the folder labeled "Jack."

Griffen's mom hadn't been totally accurate in her scathing description of Griffen's desertion of Jack. They'd kept in touch over the years through phone calls and emails, but nothing like how inseparable they'd been growing up. They'd gone to different colleges and Griffen had been on his location assignment in Afghanistan when Jack married his wife.

He sat on the bed, rubbing his face. He had tried to avoid remembering Jack. Done everything he could not to think of him, but being here in Pittsburgh, waking up in this hotel, all he could do was think about him.

His mind suddenly wandered.

Jack had understood that Griffen needed to get as far away from the painful first part of his life. Other events always came up to keep Griffen away and neither pushed to get around them. From the outside, the world saw that he and Griffen ruled the school; stars on the football team. No one knew how bad things had been with Griffen's dad, not even his mom. Only Jack knew, which is why he never pushed Griffen to come back to Pittsburgh and face down his demons.

His eyes went to the last email from him. If it had been a letter, it would be frayed and torn at the edges from the thousands of times Griffen had taken it out and read it. It was a simple message from Jack to him:

Nick - Are you back from Mexico yet? I could really use your help with something. Call me. Jack.

Even though they were still friends, Jack's cryptic email had seemingly come out of nowhere. Jack and Griffen had both been consumed with work for months. Griffen had just returned from Mexico for follow up research on his second book centered on the violent *La familia* Mexican drug cartel and knew that Jack had been wrapped up in some high priority robotic projects. It had been a huge opportunity for Jack and the book was a breakthrough for Griffen, so they hadn't spoken or emailed in months.

Griffen had gone to sleep that night intending to call Jack in the morning, but he'd gotten so wrapped up in his publisher's requests and final edits that a week had passed before he circled back to calling Jack.

A call from his mother beat him to it.

Jack was dead.

Killed in a horrific car accident the night before.

Griffen felt his mind go back to that terrible morning.

His phone had slowly slid out of his hand. He had sensed himself walk across the room to his laptop. He'd seen words quivering in relief on the screen and thought fleetingly that they looked liked the ones from Jack's email.

He'd known on some level it was his legs that were moving but he couldn't have controlled them if he wanted to. Instead, he merely watched hands grab his computer fiercely and heard a voice growl and scream like an animal. He watched as those angry hands threw his laptop across the room. It broke into several pieces and scattered across the room.

Griffen had suddenly fallen back into his own body just in time to feel his heart break into a million tiny pieces that exploded painfully out of each of his pores. In their place he was filled with rough, fragmented shards of self-loathing and regret.

He eventually bought another laptop but the broken and jagged remnants of his heart never made it back inside his chest.

And Griffen hadn't written a new word since.

Griffen swallowed hard and brought himself coldly back to the present. He dreaded facing Jack's family and finally confronting his own failures head on. It was bad enough being back in this town but now he had no choice but to see the aftermath of his neglect of Jack.

At first Griffen refused to come home because it reminded him of his brute of a father, but after Jack died, this city became even more horrific to him — turning into a living, breathing reminder of what a selfish failure he was. Seeing Jack's family would only drive that home more.

He'd never been any good with feelings. He preferred the cold comforts of denial and instant gratification.

Sex. Great sex always helped distract him from the pain, if only for a fleeting moment. But he didn't want that empty relief with just anyone. No, he needed to lose himself in a certain honey-haired lawyer, even if she was a bit of an ongoing flight risk.

Griffen wouldn't be deterred. He would just need to get through little Johnny's party and then get back on the task of trying to find this woman again.

And he *would* find her — in a completely non-stalker way, of course.

CHAPTER FIVE

Althea opened her eyes slowly and felt a pleasurable soreness she hadn't experienced in years.

Oh yes, nothing like the feeling of knowing you had a fun nighttime workout, she thought with a lazy grin. She yawned and stretched her arms above her head and enjoyed the calm before the storm. Her mother would be arriving soon and Carol would be downstairs preparing for the party like a cyclone.

After she'd showered and dressed she knew she couldn't delay the inevitable anymore. She would have to face Carol. Althea felt more than a little awkward when she walked downstairs and found her scurrying around the house, doing the final preparations for Johnny's party. *Oh please don't let me have missed any beard burn or hickeys. It would kill me if Carol knew I had done something with another man. Ugh.*

"Carol, it's so good to see you. Thanks again for all your help."

"Of course, dear. And don't you look lovely this morning! You must be so excited about Johnny finally making it to five, because you are *glowing!*"

"Oh, uh, yeah, I slept really well. I am relieved to have all this planning done. Yup." *Oh yeah, good cover Althea. Jeez.*

"Tea, honey, where are your rings?"

Althea looked down at her bare left hand. She'd stopped wearing her wedding rings a year ago in an effort to come to terms more with Jack's death, but she still wore them around Carol to avoid just this moment.

"Oh, well, I don't wear them as much anymore. It hurts to see them all the time."

Carol glowered at her and Althea felt horrible. "Humph, well I guess it's up to you if you just want to disregard the symbols of your husband's love, but personally, I don't think it's right."

"Carol, please..."

Carol turned from her and started to fill the goody bags for their young guests. "No, you just do what you want." Her words were cutting and Althea could feel tears come to her eyes.

"I'm sorry."

Carol turned and hugged her. "You can go put them on later, no worries. By the way, sweetie, I invited a couple more people."

"Oh? How many?" Althea breathed in and out slowly to fight off her emotions and started to do a mental catalog of all the food and hoped it would be enough.

"Just two."

"Phew, what a relief. That I can do."

"Good, because I'm so excited for Johnny to meet Nick."

"Who's Nick?"

"He was one of Jack's oldest friends growing up. He left town ages ago, but I was always friends with his mom. I hope you don't mind."

"Of course not. You know, I remember Jack mentioning him. Football, right? I never met him, he couldn't make it to the wedding."

"Oh, that's right. He went to Pitt for a couple years and then left to travel the world. Honestly, I'm not sure if Jack and he ever saw each other after high school, but they were so close growing up. Jack probably showed you pictures."

"Yes, I think so. When we were planning the wedding. God, that was so long ago," Althea's hand trembled around the cheese wrapper she'd been opening up. She felt her heart rate pick up as images of their perfect wedding day invaded her brain and she took a step away from the table.

"Oh honey," Carol reached over and hugged her tight until she started breathing again. "Are you okay, Tea?"

"I'm fine, thanks," she said, pasting a weak smile on her face. "It's just hard, hearing about Jack's childhood friend, thinking about the wedding, all on this day..." She looked away again.

"I can tell Valerie and Nick not to come if it's too upsetting. I just thought Nick should meet little Johnny."

"God no, don't un-invite them because of me. I need to be able to do this."

"Oh good. He really is a total sweetheart. He was a lady killer in high school, just like Jack. Now he's some sort of world-famous investigative journalist writer type but he'll always be little Nicky to me."

Althea tried to act normally, returning to slicing cubes of cheese for the meat and cheese tray. "So just him and his mom, not his dad?"

"Oh no, he died ages ago. Good riddance. He was a horrible abusive drunk, just a general piece of crap. Best thing he ever did for them was dying."

"Gosh, how terrible! Are you still close with his mom?"

"Not as much as when he and Jack were in school. I still see her around some, she lives on the other side of Mt. Washington, but you know how it is. We chat on Facebook and the phone, though."

"Have I met her?"

"Um, well, she went to the funeral, but I don't think you met her."

No, Althea wouldn't remember anyone she met at Jack's funeral. It had been packed with people because Jack had been extremely popular his whole life and so young when he died.

"I talk about you to her all the time, so she probably feels like she knows you," Carol continued.

Thoughts of Jack and his funeral had effectively put a fierce damper on Althea's mood. No more daydreaming about a hot night with a sexy stranger she'll never see again.

It was back to reality for her — the reality of being Jack Taylor's widow.

Hours later Althea was giving herself a mental pat on the back. She had all the food laid out, her cutest little sundress on and sweet tea chilling in the fridge. Johnny was outside in a T-shirt of a punk band she'd never heard of, playing with his best friend. It was a moment of solitude for her in the kitchen before the craziness of a houseful of five year olds descended upon her.

"Ahh, peace. I think you may finally be getting this mom thing down, Tea," she sighed to herself, only to jump in her seat at the crash of Jenna and Aubrey stampeding into her kitchen.

"We have collected your mother from the airport!" Aubrey boasted with arms spread wide, as though she'd made an accomplishment right up there with resolving all tensions in the Middle East.

"And we are back not a moment too soon. Are you talking to yourself girl? Should we be worried?" Jenna added.

"No, just enjoying thirty seconds of peace and quiet. Please tell me my mother is behind you and not fussing with the decorations in the living room?"

"I'm right here Sweet Tea, though I must say you've gone kind of dark for a kid's party, don't you think? I was just going to move some pieces around to make it look more cheery..."

"It's fine mom, please, relax," she said through teeth gritted in that way that only a beloved mother can cause. "Johnny wants the whole party to be punk. I'm not sure what that means, but I know he won't want cheery."

"Thank goodness I had a girl. Boys are too weird," Althea's mother said as she placed a warm kiss on her daughter's cheek.

"Good to have you here Mom. How about a bourbon with a splash of Diet Coke?"

"Gentleman Jack?"

"Of course."

"Perfect. That will certainly refocus my DIY energies." Althea stood and fixed them all something a little stronger than sweet tea. On her way back to the table she saw Jenna catch sight of the rings on Althea's fingers. Jenna pursed her lips and gave Althea a disapproving look.

"Tea, I thought you were moving past wearing those all the time? They just make you sad."

"Carol saw and it upset her. I think I need to keep wearing them around her. It's no big deal."

Jenna, Aubrey and her mother exchanged worried looks before her mother finally cleared her throat and asked, "So Tea, honey, what else is new?"

"Yeeees, what *is* new Tea?" Aubrey asked in a singsong voice, followed by a giggle from Jenna.

"Oh my? Has something finally happened Tea? Please tell me it involves a naked man, because if you tell me you're grinning so wide right now because you took up knitting or some dumb crap like that, I'll be sorely disappointed."

"Keep your voices down," Althea whispered, "I don't want Carol to know. But yes, I followed doctor's orders."

"Wait, now I'm confused. What were doctor's orders?" her mother asked. "Tea, baby, are you sick? That's not your news, is it?"

"No, Mom."

"Don't worry, it was a man all right, Viv. I wasn't there the whole time they were together, so I can neither confirm nor deny that he was naked, but..." Aubrey intoned.

"She wasn't ill, Viv, she was just sick of being in the born-again virgin's club. We took her out to get some no strings attached action and she landed herself a serious Hottie Mctottie! I had to pick her up after midnight! I have to admit, Tea, I wasn't sure you had it in ya," Jenna said with a grin.

"Oh honey, that's wonderful," Althea's mother cooed, as though she'd just come in first place in a piano recital. "I'm so happy to hear that!"

Vivian was always more of a friend than a mother to Althea. She lived from moment to moment, making Althea feel like she needed to be that much more grounded, more secure. Althea plugged her ears to block out the sounds of the three women's squeals. She could tell this would be one of those moments where her mother would bring out her particular brand of brashness.

"Though you really should have stayed till morning. That's when the really hot loving happens," her mother added.

Yup, there it is, Althea thought.

"Eww, Mom, gross. Morning would have been complicated. Besides, I wanted to be home when Carol brought Johnny back today. This was great. I wasn't looking for more than that."

"Why on earth not, baby? You know, evolutionarily we are actually serial monogamists. That is why you see that many of those who lose a spouse are in a new relationship in the first year. At the very least, sex with a new partner after the loss of your last one is appropriate and healthy. Or maybe at least some repeated nooky before you receive your AARP card."

"Thanks Mom," she muttered.

"Though you have an AARP card and no shortage of admirers. Right, Viv?" Aubrey asked with a grin of idolizing glee.

"Yes, you're so right Aubrey darling. I've never let a little thing like menopause interfere with my love life. Believe me!"

Jenna stepped in to the rescue. Left unchecked, Althea's mother would go on for an hour about evolution and the mating rituals of mature humans. Althea would need a pitcher of cocktails before she could listen to that.

"So, point is, did our Tea get her groove back?" Jenna asked.

"Not fully back but definitely a bit more groove going on for sure," Althea answered with a happy smile. "I mean, I must say I do feel better — he was sexy, smart, funny, interesting, sexy."

"You said sexy twice," Aubrey pointed out.

"I know, it was worth repeating..." Althea said with a smirk. "And I'll never see him again, so I don't feel guilty, it was just a perfect one night stand..." Althea stated, standing and grabbing a tray of hot dogs and hamburgers to take to the serving table in the main party area.

Althea paused at the sound of loud voices at the front door. One was certainly Carol and an unfamiliar woman's voice but the gruff masculine voice that shot shivers up and down her spine and into her core was definitely familiar.

"Val, hi! And little Nicky Tate! You look wonderful, both of you!"

"Oh come on Mrs. Taylor," he drawled, "no one calls me Nicky anymore. I go by Griffen now, but I'll let it slide and give you a big hug."

"Griffen? I don't know if I can get used to that, but if it will get me some of your great hugs, I'll manage."

"Mom brought cookies. I'll add them to the pile," Griffen said. "I missed a lot of things when I left, but I think I dreamed of tables full of cookies at weddings and birthday parties the most."

Their conversation continued to float into the kitchen as Althea's chest grew tighter.

Oh God, Althea thought as she started to get cold sweats and shake. The world was slowing down, but her heart was racing. She started to mentally consider methods of escape. *Would Johnny like a private birthday somewhere far away?* she wondered. *Maybe in the witness protection program?*

Jenna jumped forward and steadied the tray Althea was close to tipping forward, as all three of them quickly figured out who was there. She needed support but they all looked stunned right along with her.

"*Griffen,* come and meet everyone. This is Tea, Jack's wife." Althea came out of her stupor enough to cringe. Carol still referred to Althea as Jack's wife. It generally didn't bother her, actually making her feel good — feeding into her feeling that she was always his — but then again, she'd never had sex with his best friend without knowing it.

Oh God, please don't throw up in the kitchen, please don't throw up in the kitchen.

Carol barreled on, "And this is Jenna, and Aubrey. Jenna is an orthopedic surgeon at UPMC — very successful, this one. And Aubrey is a great freelance photographer. Both single, wink wink."

Oh God, Carol actually said *wink wink!*

Althea had thought it couldn't get worse, but she was wrong.

"Tea, honey, are you all right?" Carol asked.

"Oh she's fine. Just worked too hard to wrap up the party plans. *Right* Tea?" Jenna asked pointedly.

"Right." Althea nodded.

"And Tea's mother, Vivian," Carol added. "I'm so glad you could meet everyone. Guys, Griffen here was like Jack's second brother!"

A wave of nausea passed over Althea and she finally looked up straight into Griffen's bright aqua blue eyes. She was relieved to see he looked dumbstruck, as well. At least she wasn't the only one shocked and uncomfortable.

The voice of the woman Althea presumed was Griffen's mother broke through. "Carol, is there anything we can do to help?"

"Don't be silly, but you can come into the living room and see Johnny and the rest of the guests. We're going to put out lunch any second now." With that, Carol started ushering them out of the kitchen, not noticing that Griffen almost broke his neck staring back at Althea as he walked out of the kitchen.

As soon as they'd left the kitchen it exploded with sound but Althea remained silent and continued to stare at where

Griffen used to be. Althea could barely make out that her mother, Aubrey, and Jenna were all trying to sort out the facts. She finally broke in.

"Shh, all of you."

"Do you realize what this means?" Jenna asked.

"It means I slept with my husband's best friend."

"Your dearly departed husband who's been gone almost *six* years. Don't you dare think for a second that you did anything wrong baby," her mother said, steering her into a chair.

"Only me. Only I could finally decide to take one little baby step forward with my life, to have one fun night, and it ends up being with my husband's best friend. I think I'm gonna be sick. Jenna, Aubrey, *FYI,* I'm going to kill you both. And I'm going to make it hurt."

Althea thought that to their credit they also looked mortified, but that wouldn't save them.

"But you were so happy last night. You said you were glad you did it. That you love us," Jenna moaned.

"That was when I was in a post-crazy awesome sex haze and I thought I'd never see him again. *Before* I knew he was the prodigal BFF to my dead husband, now returned!" Althea flopped her head in her hands with a satisfying thump. "What a disaster."

Vivian stepped toward Althea, shuffling away her befuddled friends with two well-placed knocks of her hips. "Honey, please. Just breathe."

"I kind of like sitting here feeling sorry for myself, actually."

"Oh, just stop it, baby girl, that is *quite* enough. Aubrey, Jenna, get this girl another bourbon with a splash of Diet Coke, stat." They started scurrying around the kitchen. Althea had to smile, no one rallied the troops like her mother.

"Look at me Sweet Tea." Her mother pressed her cool hands into Althea's cheeks, forcing their eyes to meet.

Althea suddenly felt like an awkward teenage girl again, being consoled after their father deserted them for his new family two days before her fourteenth birthday. "You were always so serious, sweetheart. Even now you're trying to turn a one-nighter into an existential crisis."

Althea looked at her with big, sad eyes. She could sense in some back part of her brain that she was acting like that overly dramatic teenager from her memories, but if you can't be one with your mom, when can you be?

"You have done nothing wrong," Vivian continued. "Your whole life has been committed to honoring Jack's memory, from raising his son on your own to supporting and helping his mother, this thing with that hunky man in there is something you did for yourself and I couldn't be prouder. I know you want to take that baby step back..." "Why thank you Aubrey," she said as she took the large cocktail from Aubrey's hand and passed it to Althea, "drink up baby girl. I refuse to let you feel guilty because that boy is beyond handsome. Instead, you're going to let us touch up your makeup and you're going to go out there with your head high with a plate full of burgers and hot dogs and you're going to have a nice time. Got it?"

"Yes, Mom, you're right."

"That a girl, now give me a hug." With that, Althea hugged her as tightly as if she were turning five years old herself.

"Come on ladies. Let's get me out there, it's time for another baby step!" Althea exclaimed. The three women responded with a cheer that made her roll her eyes and grin at the same time.

Griffen watched as Althea and her entourage entered the living room, carrying trays of food with deliberately neutral facial expressions. He was just as thrown as they were. How could this woman that was the first — in as long as he could remember — that had gotten under his skin and wouldn't leave, be Jack's widow? Could fate be that much of a bastard? Christ, he'd been hours from hunting her down and making her get to know him just that morning.

He wasn't surprised that Jack's wife was stunning, that part was a given. Growing up, he and Jack had spent as much time having their pick of every pretty girl they wanted as they had studying and playing football.

It was also no shocker that she was charming, brilliant, and driven. That had been golden boy Jack in spades. Jack would have recognized Althea as a keeper right away and wouldn't have let her go.

What *was* surprising, shocking even, was that Griffen had found himself entertaining those same kind of thoughts.

"Nicky, I mean Griffen — sorry, still not quite used to that. How does it feel to be back in the Burgh after all these years?" Carol asked.

"Huh?" He'd barely been paying attention to everyone's chatter, being too busy watching Althea while she avoided his gaze.

"Being back in Pittsburgh? What do you think?"

"It's good, a little surreal, especially since the city looks so different, so much activity going on," Griffen replied, all the while craning his neck to try and see Althea as she walked to the kids' table to check on Johnny and his friends.

"Johnny, come over and meet one of your daddy's oldest friends," Carol said across the room. "Tea, bring him over." Althea's eyes widened and she followed as her little boy ran over. He had some kind of spiked up hairstyle, a wild T-shirt and arms covered in fake tattoos.

"I'm a punk. Do you know what that is?" he demanded.

"I do. I actually like punk rock."

"You do?"

"Yeah. Ever heard of Maddie Hatter?"

"Duh! Of course," Johnny scoffed.

"Well, I know her back in New York," Griffen said, glad he could impress this kid.

"You know *the* Maddie Hatter?" Aubrey exclaimed and looked over at Jenna and Althea's blank faces. "She is only like *the* hottest female punk rocker ever, and she's super cute. How do you know her?" she asked Griffen with a raised eyebrow, that was suddenly mirrored in Althea and Jenna's skeptical faces.

Griffen quickly raised his hands in surrender, "We share a copyright lawyer and she's married to Captain Syringe, so she and I are just friendly acquaintances. Trust me." He couldn't believe how desperately he wanted to keep these women from thinking he was a womanizing jerk, when really, he pretty much was. But he didn't want Althea to see him that way.

"Anyway, Johnny, want her autograph?"

"Yes! Sweet!"

"Now, Johnny, I don't think you need to bother Mr. Tate with that. He's very busy," Althea said slowly.

"Nah, anything for Johnny, it's my pleasure." Their eyes met and something hot flashed in hers for a second before she looked away quickly and went to straighten more trays for the tenth time.

"Cool. Can you get me Captain's autograph, too?" Johnny was jumping up and down at that point.

Before Althea could protest, Griffen quickly answered, "Consider it done," and high-fived him.

Aubrey and Johnny jumped up and down excitedly. Point one for Griffen. Then Aubrey schooled herself and went right to eyeing him warily. And bam, just like that, docked half a point.

"Well, I guess you're okay," Johnny said through narrowed eyes, looking back at his mother and somehow seeming to catch on to her nervousness. "What else do you like?" he added cautiously.

"I played football. I saw you guys have a football over there."

"Yeah! I'm a quarterback."

"Just like your dad, huh?" Griffen had to look away, the words choking in his throat as they came out.

"That's what Grandma says." Griffen's heart twisted again.

This kid had the world's greatest guy for a father but he would only know him from stories and memories. From old football trophies and scholarship awards. He would be like a character in a book to him — only existing through the retelling of another. Jack would never be a flesh and blood man that could hold him. And that made Griffen want to hug this boy as tightly as he could and never let go.

Griffen composed himself and looked back to see that Althea was staring at him with tears in her eyes. He had to clear his throat before he could speak. "Are you on a team?"

"Yeah, but we aren't really good. It's just a small local league."

"He's still not old enough for real pee-wee football," Carol added.

"That's no problem," Griffen said. "You gotta start somewhere, right? How about this? After lunch I take you guys out and show you a few things I picked up back in the day?"

"That would be awesome. Thanks!"

"Uh, Johnny, Mr. Tate probably has a lot to do. Don't you?" She looked at him meaningfully.

"Nope, I've got nothing but time," Griffen answered ignoring her widened eyes.

"Cool!" Johnny said.

"Fine. But you need to actually eat lunch first, Johnny, and don't forget about cake and presents."

"Yeah Mom. See ya later, Gwiff." Johnny ran back over and quickly gave his friends the good news.

Val smiled and glanced back and forth between Griffen and Althea with a look of interest that was not lost on Griffen. "Johnny is so funny. How did he even find out about punk music and tattoos?" Val asked.

"Aunt Aubrey, would you like to enlighten her?" Jenna asked.

Griffen caught himself staring at Althea again. He wasn't sure what his plan was here, except that he wasn't ready to let her out of his sight again. Not yet, at least. She was so beautiful. She was also Jack's widow. How come he didn't feel worse about it? Yes, he was completely thrown when he saw her standing in the kitchen and his emotions had been battling between guilt and lust ever since, but lust and a strong desire to just be near her were winning out handily by the time she'd emerged from the kitchen.

Just when Griffen wondered if he was obviously staring at her, he got confirmation from three sets of male eyes.

The first were Johnny's, looking at him with what could only be the sternest form of suspicion ever to grace the face of a five year old. Johnny looked Griffen in the eye and with two fingers gave him the universal *"I'm watching you"* gesture.

Dammit, I love this kid, he thought. He may like that Griffen could teach him to play football and get a great autograph, but he was still protective of his mom. Good kid. Griffen would need to work extra hard to make sure Johnny was comfortable with him. If only because it meant a lot to him to know Jack's son.

The other two sets of staring eyes were far older and belonged to two clearly jealous men. One was a good looking doctor around Griffen's age, no need to worry about him, he followed her around like a puppy dog but Griffen saw nothing but polite tolerance from her in response.

No, it was the older one that garnered his focus. He'd introduced himself as David, Jack's former boss at *CMU* and he'd not stopped looking at Althea once throughout the party. David was supposedly a friend of Althea's, but there was no denying the possessive frustration that invaded everything he did. Oh yeah, this guy was obsessed with her, no two ways about it. Griffen was sure of it, if not in part because he was rapidly becoming familiar with the condition himself. *Oh boy. This is going to be a long day*, he thought.

"So, Griffen. Carol tells us you like to tell stories," Althea said with a raised brow that was mirrored in her two friends. Griffen jumped a little and then winced at her implication. She thought he was a liar — telling her he was just a professor — not a good start to getting her to feel comfortable with him.

"Oh he's a big time writer. Local boy done good," Carol enthused.

"I wrote a couple books."

"They're movies now! He and Jack used to make up stories all day long. When they were little I had to sew the costumes and they would create these elaborate plots. Everything from superheroes to aliens to cops and robbers. They kept me busy!

Do you still have those stories Griffen?"

"Not on me, no," he chuckled.

"I know that, you're still such a smart butt Nicky Tate."

"Were they scholarly works, your books?" David asked in a snotty voice. Griffen hated him right away.

"Excuse me?"

"I write quite a bit as a professor at *CMU*, I thought perhaps we had that in common."

"No. I write blow 'em up, shoot 'em up type books. I think it's safe to say we have nothing in common." *Other than an obsession with Althea Taylor*, he thought.

"Wait, are you Griffen Tate, the guy who wrote those Cade Jackson books?" This from the doctor.

"Yup, that's me."

"Those are a blast. Real brain candy." Griffen smarted at the comment. He knew he didn't exactly deserve the Nobel Prize for literature but he would rather his books not be compared to completely nutrition-free fluff.

"So great to meet you. I've been trying to get Tea here to watch a movie with me for months, maybe now that she knows you she'll agree to watch one of yours with me. You know, for the novelty of it." Griffen looked closely at him and decided, *yep, I hate this guy, too.* "Whaddya say Tea? Care to blow off some steam with an action adventure?"

Griffen noticed Jack's mother bristle at the question.

"Doctor Connors, Althea does *not* date," Carol said sternly.

"Excuse me?" he asked, visibly surprised by the interruption.

"I'm not sure if Jenna mentioned it, but Althea is married."

Griffen's eyes widened. He'd heard Carol introduce Althea as Jack's wife but he couldn't believe she was so visibly controlling of her.

"Carol!" Althea's mother said with exasperation.

"Uh, I know she was married, but I, uh," Doctor Connors stuttered out.

"She will always be married to Jack. Tea, maybe it's time for cake?"

The room stared back and forth at Carol and Althea. Carol looked totally unfazed and Griffen noticed David looked oddly pleased. Althea, on the other hand, was blushing and looking supremely uncomfortable in a way that made his heart go out to her.

Althea finally broke the silence, saying, "Wow, everyone ate lunch so fast. Carol, you're right. I'd better get that cake out." Minutes later, after hearing a couple small crashes in the kitchen, she emerged with the craziest kid's birthday cake he'd ever seen with a solo number five blazing on top. They'd barely sung happy birthday and Johnny made his wish before she jumped right back up and declared, "Can't keep these kids waiting too long, I mean who can resist eating black icing, right?" And just like that, she was gone again. Another little crash from the kitchen got her two friends to their feet.

"We should go help her, wouldn't want the cake to end up on the floor, would we?" Jenna said uncomfortably.

"No, let me. I haven't gotten a chance to get to chat with her, yet. It's the least I can do," Griffen said quickly. "Carol, sorry to leave in the middle of our conversation, but I would really like to get to know Jack's wife," he cringed at the words but didn't need her interfering with him being alone with Althea.

"Of course! Thanks," Carol said, as she smiled at him in motherly way.

Jenna and Aubrey stared at him blankly until Althea's mother piped in with the sweetest southern accent to say, "Yes, what a great idea. You get in there and help her out, darlin'. That will give us a chance to visit in here and get all these presents set up. Go on now."

Well, at least Althea's mother approved of him talking to her. That was a start. Her friends didn't seem to know what to do with him. Griffen stood and walked slowly toward the kitchen. Behind him he heard Althea's mother coo again, this time to say, "Now, David and Doctor Connors, I think she has more than enough help as it is. That ain't the biggest kitchen in the world. You're liable to knock the whole place down if all four of you are in there. Come over and help me with these presents, would you?"

Another solid from the lovely Vivian, he thought to himself as he pushed his way into the kitchen.

The door opened behind her and Althea jumped, knocking her knee on the table in front of her. "Ouch. Dammit!"

"Are you okay?" she heard Griffen ask quietly from behind her.

She quickly turned around, still holding a large knife for cutting the birthday cake.

"Whoa," he said smirking and raising his hands. "You can have my wallet and my phone, but I don't have anything else on me." She laughed despite herself. "That's better. I thought I was going to have to put you on a respirator if you kept holding your breath around me."

"Right, well, it was a bit of a surprise seeing you," she murmured, her hand shaking slightly as she held the knife. She was unable to figure out where to rest her eyes. She couldn't focus on the cake because she wanted to look at him but that only made her more uneasy. The compromise her body made seemed to be to look shiftily at nothing and everything in the room.

"Let me look at that knee of yours." He took the knife from her hand and gently placed it on the kitchen table before he knelt down in front of her and touched her knee lightly. She jumped again, but not from surprise, this was from the shock of desire that shot through her at his touch. Looking down at his dark wavy hair and tanned hands on her bare leg as he crouched before her, she couldn't help but think back to the previous night when he made her come spectacularly from that same vantage point. She started to breathe in little pants, hating herself for how quickly her body responded to the nearness of him when his voice suddenly broke through the lusty fog in her brain.

"Are you going to avoid me the rest of the day?"

"I am not avoiding you, I'm just..."

Griffen looked up at her with skeptical eyes.

Oh Christ, he's so handsome.

"I am just...regrouping. Putting on a party for a five year old is not as easy as it seems. Professor," she added with a sneer.

Griffen had the grace to wince. "Yeah, about that. Come on, gorgeous, be fair."

"Don't call me that!" She stiffened and shook him off her leg. "I think my knee is fine. You can stop touching me now."

"You know that you're the one that snuck out on me, right?" Her eyebrows rose at that. She couldn't believe that someone as sexy and experienced as he was would have cared that she left. *Interesting.* "I'm not a bad guy. Well, at least not this exact time," he added with a smile.

She sighed. "Dammit, you're right. This would be so much easier if you were an asshole."

"Sorry?" he teased and she couldn't help but laugh.

"But you did lie to me," she said.

He pulled his hands away from her and stood. She immediately missed his fingers on her and was furious with herself for it. "Hey, come on," he said. "All I did was withhold. It was more of an omission, like how you didn't tell me you have a kid." Then he looked in her eyes, rubbing the back of his neck and leaning his head down. He looked at her through his lashes and a wavy lock of dark hair that had fallen across his forehead, the same dark hair she'd almost pulled out at the root. "And I call you gorgeous because that's what you are — gorgeous. So, will you let me explain about my omission, and I'll simply accept yours?"

Althea leaned away a bit, thinking he was so sexy she might have a heart attack right there in the kitchen — next to a punk themed child's birthday cake — *how lurid*. Thinking that she should probably avoid such a humiliating end, she slowly forced herself to begin breathing again.

"Okay, then explain away."

"I am filling in for one of my former professors and mentors at Pitt for the next two weeks in his investigative journalism and nonfiction writing courses. It really is the truth right now. I have a faculty ID and everything."

"You just happened to forget the part about being a famous best-selling author?"

"I haven't written anything new in years, so I don't really feel much like a writer these days."

"Writer's block?"

"You could say that. Tell me, if I'd told you the whole truth about what I do would that have mattered to you? Would you have liked me more?"

"No, that wasn't really possible." Griffen smiled with a full smug grin and Althea rolled her eyes at him. "Get over yourself, stud. I liked you, that was no secret."

"*Liked*, past tense?"

"Okay, liked and considering still liking. Okay? Your 'rock star writer' status probably would have actually scared me off. You aren't off the hook yet, though. It's just, I have a thing about honesty and openness."

"What about it?"

"I like it. I guess you could say I require it. I don't want secrets between me and the people in my life. So, I didn't like finding out in my kitchen from Carol that you hadn't been honest with me. Do you really even go by the name Griffen?"

"Absolutely. It's my mother's maiden name, my middle name, and I've always liked it. Nick was my dad's name, too. Once that asshole died and I left Pittsburgh I wanted a new beginning. A new name seemed like a good idea. Anyone who knew me when I was a kid still calls me Nick, though. How's that for open and honest?"

"It's a start." She looked down and took a breath before saying softly, "Jack talked about his best friend Nick sometimes. I guess that's what he called you?"

"Yeah, Jack and I were pretty inseparable from five years old on."

Holy crap, Althea thought, as it hit her that Jack and Griffen were in high school together. In the same building. At the same time. That seemed like a cruel way to torture teenage girls. Christ it probably was too much cocky hotness for the teachers, too!

"And he talked to me about his beautiful, brilliant love named Tea. You know, you looked so familiar to me last night, I realize now it must be because I saw a couple pictures of you."

"You seemed familiar to me, too. I would never have thought in a million years..."

"Had you seen pictures of me?"

"Yeah. Old shots of you guys playing football. You guys as kids. There wasn't exactly Facebook back then, so just those old pictures Jack had."

"I'm not really the social media type anyway," he said with a smirk. Griffen paused to take her face and body in slowly. "I think you look different from the pictures Jack emailed me."

"Ten years and a baby will do that to you."

He stroked a lock of her hair and she couldn't resist the small shudder that passed through her. On a swallow she said, "I used to color it."

Althea's throat burned with pain at their mention of Jack and the confusion she felt inside being so close to Griffen. She looked up to stare through blurry eyes into Griffen's beautiful blue ones. She was surprised to see what looked like deep anguish had taken hold of his usually playful face. They must have been looking at each other for some period of time because she jumped when Griffen broke the silence. "Althea..."

Althea turned and placed her hands on the kitchen table, trying to regain her composure. She clutched the knife again but couldn't seem to grasp it well.

"Your hands are shaking," Griffen whispered after clearing his throat. She looked down to see her trembling hand holding the knife over the cake. "Here." Griffen walked behind her and gently steadied her hands with his, putting it down on the table while Althea breathed deeply. He'd only touched a small part of her body but every molecule of hers was aware of each of his. She felt the full length of his body behind hers, warming her even though she felt tingly and almost numb in her stomach and toes.

"Of course they're shaking! Jeez, aren't you at all mortified?" she asked.

"Mortified? I don't know. I mean, I was definitely shocked. Jack was like a brother to me. Sleeping with his wife, widow or not, is not on the top of my list of good things to do. But I was also really happy to see you again today. I didn't like waking up and you not being there. That was a real first for me, trust me."

"It was wrong," she whispered, mostly trying to convince herself.

"Why?"

"I was married to Jack."

"Don't do that to yourself, Althea. You have nothing to feel guilty about." She laughed bitterly to herself. *If only he knew just how guilty I feel every day. How I let everything be ruined.* She swallowed and picked the knife up again, clutching it tightly.

Althea leaned forward, away from him, her chest rising and falling as she tried to get herself under control. He leaned forward and she felt his warm breath as his mouth nestled right next to her ear. Her hand started shaking from full-on tremors with the renewed nearness of him.

He finally whispered, "Althea?"

"Yes," she whispered, her back straight as the knife started wobbling slightly in her hand.

"Why don't I cut the cake for you?" She put it down and heaved out the breath she hadn't even realized she was holding. She stepped aside, grateful for the distance from this man. He was even more devastating in the daylight, if that was possible.

He began to cut perfectly straight slices in Johnny's cake and without looking up said, "Well, now that I know you were married to the most wonderful person I've ever met, I guess I feel a little less offended about you running out while I was sleeping. Without even a note, I might add." She only saw some of his face when he looked sideways at her for a brief moment, but she could tell his mouth was playing with a smirk. Althea felt grateful that he was veering the conversation away from her twisting heart and had taken it back to gentle teasing.

"I thought men like you appreciated that kind of consideration from a woman."

"Hmm, and what exactly is a 'man like me'?"

"Oh no, I'm going to plead the Fifth on that one."

He made two passes of the knife, the silence giving her a chance to collect herself as she finally took the chance to lower herself into a chair.

Griffen looked over at her and her heart raced again as he said, "So when you said it had been a while...are you saying I am the first guy you — you know..."

"Slept with since Jack?" He nodded. "Yes."

"Shit!" His hand slipped and smeared a perfect white piece of skull shaped icing into the black icing below. He quickly smoothed the piece over and Althea trained her eyes on the now gray blob of frosting rather than look at his face. "Sorry," he said quickly. "Seriously, though, how could it have been that long?"

"I don't know. I can't believe I'm talking to you about this."

"You can tell me anything. I did love Jack, too, I want to help you," he said and something in his eyes, and the way the playfulness turned to a sorrow she recognized too well from her own mirror, made her trust him.

"I know I can't love anyone else like I loved Jack."

"So, no dating or sex?"

"Well, so far I've been on a 'no anything' policy. But, most definitely, no relationships. I had a couple of first dates after

Johnny was born. Not sure if you recall but Pittsburgh is still a pretty family-oriented town."

"Yeah. Fiddler on the Roof had less obsession with matchmaking and getting hitched."

Althea giggled and leaned back a bit. Something about talking to him soothed her. "There were definitely a lot of mothers and best friends of single guys pushing them my way — good girl like me, right? And I was already vetted as wife material. Even better."

"Did anything ever go anywhere?"

"No. Never beyond a first date and never anything physical — just a kiss or two. It felt like cheating to get emotionally involved with someone. It still does. Just the thought of loving someone or being serious with someone feels so incredibly wrong. And..." she hesitated.

"And?" He wouldn't let her get away with holding back and for some reason she liked that. She'd used every excuse not to think about her feelings, her guilt, that sharing them with someone who loved Jack so deeply, too, felt oddly cathartic.

"And, as if the shame weren't enough, each date really upset Carol. She would cry and ask me to sit and look at pictures of Jack with her after each one. It tore me apart." Tears sprang in her eyes and she saw him reach for her but she shook her head and he backed off, returning to the monotony of slicing the large sheet cake. She swallowed, "So I just stopped doing anything at all."

"But she let's that guy David hang around right? I mean she acted like he was family."

"David? Oh God, that's because he *is* like family. We would never think of each other that way. He was like a father to Jack after his own dad died. Carol likes to have him around for that reason."

"You're allowed to have fun, though, right?" Griffen asked.

"That's what the girls say. But even if last night *was* fun," she rolled her eyes at the cocky grin that appeared on his face. "That wasn't really the point."

"The point?"

"Ugh." *Dammit. What am I going to do?* "The girls dragged me out last night as a sort of desperate attempt to make me take some baby steps back into the dating pool. You know, for one night." Althea felt like her blush was blushing. *This is horrific.*

"One night...?"

"Argh," she looked away. "I was *supposed* to never see you again. There, are you happy now?"

"So you just used me for sex?" he asked with a grin. "Can't say that I blame you. I think you made an excellent choice."

"Your ego is unbelievable!"

"Among other things," he winked lasciviously. At her epic eye roll he cleared his throat and made a serious face. "Okay, I'll try to behave."

Griffen ran the knife through the cake again, creating more precise squares. Althea stared at his hands as he wiped the knife clean on a paper towel between each swipe to ensure the most perfect pieces.

"But the girls are right, I do need to have some kind of sex life before I go insane," she said softly.

"So, let me get this straight, are you planning on using anyone else's body in the future?"

"No! I mean, yes. *Maybe*," she said a little more loudly than she intended.

"And do you have an end game after a lot of meaningless sex?"

"Hey, it's not like that. It's just that sex without any relationship seems like a compromise — having some bit of a life of my own without the risk of someone expecting something I can't imagine I'll ever be able to give."

"What can't you give?"

"Jeez, getting personal enough?"

"Althea, we've been very personal with each other. I want to know more about you. Period."

She narrowed her eyes and when he wouldn't look away she huffed out, "Fine. Point is I can't ever love anyone again. Jack was my *one* true love. Anyone I would be with would need to understand that, so it's just been better to be alone. But now, the girls are pushing me to have a little fun, thinking maybe down the road I'll be ready for a nice guy who can settle for what little I can give."

"Well, after hearing all this, I have to say I'm pretty proud of myself about being your first baby step." He grinned at her exasperated expression. "You should take it easy with those eye rolls gorgeous, you'll give yourself a headache."

"Then take it easy with the ego, stud," she added with a raised eyebrow.

"I can't help it if I was born with a healthy dose of self confidence, gorgeous. But, seriously, I can't imagine how you've gone that long, I mean, you're really fucking beautiful."

"Language! This is a five year old kid's birthday you are crashing, after all."

She shout-whispered the admonition, but she couldn't help but smile at the compliment.

He put down the knife. "Hey, I'm not a party crasher, Carol asked my mom to bring me. Carol's always loved me," he said with a wink.

"I'll say! Your arrival had her worked up into a full blown tizzy."

"A tizzy you say? I like the sound of that. Do I work *you* into a tizzy?" When she responded with nothing but another eye roll, Griffen smiled and said with a wave to his handiwork, "I *have* made myself helpful by slicing this problematic cake for you and did a wonderful job of it, if I do say so myself."

"I'm relieved to see you're capable of such complex menial cake labor, professor."

"So you can't be too mad about me showing up, can you?"

"Of course I'm not mad — just shocked. Like I said, seeing you walk in..."

"And now that you're less shocked?"

"Well, um, I guess it wasn't wholly unpleasant to see you again."

"Oh boy, all this flattery is going to go to my head! What if I said I was sad to wake up and see you were gone and that I was *pleasantly* shocked to see you here?"

"Why don't you do me a favor and focus on plating those sugar bombs for me instead?"

"Of course." Althea stood and started to walk away, but paused when he said, "Althea." She turned and was hit again by a wall of lust when he focused his full attention on her. "I'd like to do a lot of favors for you."

She blanched for just a moment, working to recover her self-control, "Let's start with the cake for now, stud." With that, she walked away, feeling him follow her with his eyes as she left him to plate the pieces of cake in uneasy silence.

CHAPTER SIX

Griffen hugged his mother as she gathered her things to leave. "You can go on without me Mom. I'll get a cab."

He saw her eyes turn meaningfully to Althea, who looked stunning simply collecting plates from the kids' table. His mouth still went dry just from looking at her.

"Honey, what are you up to?" she asked warily.

"Johnny needs some throwing lessons. I figure I'll stay and show him some of my old tricks. Even tight ends know a thing or two, right?"

"Uh-huh. And are any of those old tricks one you would use on a certain lovely widow?"

"Mom, how could you suggest such a thing, it's like you don't even know me!" he said with no ability to hide the smile quirking at the corners of his lips.

"I know you perfectly, that's why I ask the question. Just be careful, okay? From everything Carol tells me about Tea, she's nothing like the other kinds of, er, 'ladies' you get involved with." She made rabbit ears around the word ladies and Griffen had to wince. "Plus, Carol says she's still grieving Jack. Doesn't that feel weird to you?"

Honestly, he didn't know how he felt about her being Jack's widow. The idea of touching Jack's woman should make him feel terrible and in a way it did. But it also made her seem that much more precious. Like he needed to take care of her. Make sure she was happy, because he *knew* Jack would want her happy.

He was also sure he hated the idea of her going out and having random sex with guys that won't appreciate her or may not treat her right. The irony wasn't lost on him that he was the first to benefit from her crazy baby steps plan. He wanted to intervene somehow and make sure she was able to experience the fun she so obviously craved and make it through this phase without getting hurt.

When suddenly it hit him — *maybe I can be some baby steps for her? I mean the last thing anyone as good as her needs is a relationship with me, but that's not what she wants. And I'm leaving, she can enjoy the time without worry.*

Griffen was no fool, he knew he had nothing emotionally to offer a woman as great as her — but sex and confidence-building fun? That he could do.

And there was another benefit to being around her. This woman was a window to all the years Jack was alive that Griffen was out doing his own thing, he missed his friend and he had made the mistake of just assuming Jack would always be there for him.

Could she give me a piece of my friend back, and with that, maybe some of my soul?

"Mom, that's all the more reason she could use a friend like me. And as for the kinds of 'ladies' I get involved with," he added. "I don't know, maybe I'm due for some changes. Maybe a real 'lady' could be good for me."

"Just be careful."

"I don't plan to hurt her, if that's what you're thinking."

"Her feelings aren't the only ones I am worried about. Oh well, let me gather my bag of cookies and head out. You know where to find me. I love you. I just hope you know what you're doing."

Me too, he thought.

"Love you too, Mom." She kissed his cheek and walked away. He immediately went back to looking at Althea, cooking up a very pleasant proposal in his brain.

Griffen shook his head and jogged over to Johnny who was on the ground wrestling with four of his buddies, a junior sized football lying desolately on the ground next to them.

"Hey guys! My name's Griffen. How would you like to learn some things you can do in your next football game?"

"Sure!" they all yelled.

"All right, huddle up here with me. I know Johnny is quarterback, let's go through everybody else's positions and have some fun!"

What Griffen hadn't anticipated was how much fun *he* would have. Johnny was the spitting image of Jack as a kid and had the same innate talent and clever mind. The other boys seemed to naturally idolize him, including Chris, his dark-haired, blue-eyed best friend. The sight of them together twisted Griffen's chest in a vice, but once that initial pain passed, it seemed to bring him the oddest sense of peace.

Griffen had just taught them a simple passing play, one of the first he'd ever learned, when Carol joined him. "How are you Griffen?"

"Getting used to calling me Griffen, huh?"

"Getting there. I can't say that I blame you. You know I understand as well as anyone how you wouldn't want to share a name with that son of a bitch father of yours. Pardon my French."

"No problem at all. Actually I think that is how his name is pronounced in French."

Carol laughed and hugged him. "You've always made me laugh. So, are you enjoying a little football?"

"The kids are so much fun, and they seem to really like playing on a team."

"I bet that brings back memories, huh?" she asked softly.

Griffen's throat tightened a little. "Yeah," he whispered. She cleared her throat as Griffen rubbed his eyes and looked away.

"Well, their coach can use all the help he can get, he's in over his head. Never actually played the game. And just got a new job. I bet two weeks of you pitching in would do wonders."

"Hmm, I like the way you think, Carol."

Johnny connected on a short pass with Josh, a scrappy little running back and Griffen cheered as Josh kept on running. "Way to go guys, that was perfect! Now let's huddle up again and talk about how we can build on that."

The boys ran up and Josh handed him the football. Griffen turned around, small football still in hand, and caught Althea watching him from the backdoor. She gave a small smile before she turned around and disappeared deeper into the kitchen. God, she was so gorgeous and so damn sweet. Just her smile made his head spin.

"Uncle Gwiff, are you gonna thwow it or what?"

Him calling him uncle made him so happy he almost dropped the ball. He'd fucked up royally with Jack, but maybe he could make the most of this time back home. He could build Althea's confidence, spend time with Jack's awesome son, and maybe, just maybe, not feel like hating himself every time the thought of Jack came up. He was no real good for anyone long term, but he didn't have to worry about that. He would be long gone in two weeks.

"While we're young, Gwiff," Johnny demanded. *I love this kid*, he laughed to himself.

"Coming right up, Johnny."

Althea took a deep breath and willed her heart to stop pounding for the fiftieth time that day. It was almost over. Unfortunately, Griffen was making it take even longer, hanging out and playing football with the kids. Althea couldn't exactly be a grouch and make him leave. He was a huge hit and she didn't want to mess up Johnny's great day, so instead she could only stare in frustration.

Why couldn't he have disappeared like he was supposed to? Why does he have to look so good crouching, running and passing a small football in my backyard?

Before she could realize she was staring, and possibly drooling over his muscular arms, rippling under the short sleeves of his tight, navy blue T-shirt, he caught her eye and winked.

"Hi Tea!"

She grimaced and turned around at the jarring sound of Curt's voice coming from behind her. The handsome doctor was everything most women wanted but she had more than enough on her plate today.

"Curt. Hi. Did you have fun? We were so glad you could make it."

"You don't mind me being here? Jenna said it would be okay."

"Of course! It's always great to see you." Althea felt eyes on her back and just knew they were Griffen's.

"Great."

"I have to head out soon, but what I asked about before, at lunch. What do you think?"

"I'm sorry, can you remind me?" His face fell and she felt a pang of guilt.

"About watching a movie together? Or we could go to dinner. Whatever you like."

"Mommy, Mommy!"

"Johnny what's wrong?"

"I don't feel good. I need help."

"It must be bad. You never ask for help."

"Maybe I can help Johnny. I mean I *am* a doctor," Curt interrupted.

Johnny glared at him with his chin thrust forward, "No. Not you. I want Mommy."

"What hurts Johnny? Your tummy maybe?" Vivian came up behind Althea and asked pointedly.

"Yeah. That's right Maw-Maw, it's my, uh, tummy."

"Aw, you heard the kid, Curt," Althea's mother said with a lilting tone. "You're an ear, nose, and throat doc right? Looks like this is a case that requires a prescription of some mommy TLC. Why don't you come with me and tell me about your recent piece on peritonsillar abscesses? Jenna says it was, um...descriptive."

"My pleasure, Viv," he said excitedly as they walked away. "You know, most people think abscesses are just..." Luckily his voice faded off before Althea had to hear more.

"Mr. Personality, huh?" Althea breathed deeply at the sensation of Griffen's warm breath at her ear. She turned and raised an eyebrow at him. "Excuse me," he added with a smirk, "*Doctor* Personality."

Althea looked down as Johnny whispered, "How'd I do Uncle Gwiff?"

Griffen winced but said, "Great buddy. Why don't you run some plays with the guys while I talk to your mom?"

Althea raised an eyebrow as Johnny ran off, "Enlisting my son to corner me. Isn't that pretty low?"

"He *was* injured. That ass of a doctor was making him nauseous."

"I'm going inside. You're unbelievable."

"Thanks."

"It wasn't a compliment, stud."

"Hmm. Sounded like one to me." He grinned and she could tell he was thrilled to see her eyes widen and lips part despite her attempts at self-control. *Dammit.*

"Besides, all's fair, right?" Griffen added.

"Is this love or war?" she asked.

"That's up to you. I just know I'm not giving up on getting you to stop avoiding me."

"Humph," was all she could manage and then flounced off to the kitchen. She never flounced. This was getting serious.

She wanted to be mad, that would make it easier, but then he ran back over to Johnny and bent down to correct Johnny's throwing technique so he could connect a perfect pass to Chris. The sheer joy on Johnny's face fed some deep emptiness and hurt inside her she didn't even know was there. She sighed.

"I guess a little bit longer won't hurt," she said to no one in particular.

As Althea turned and slowly walked into the kitchen she caught Jenna and Aubrey searching through images and articles on *Google* about Griffen with maddening speed. "Um, guys, could you please stop cyber-stalking the man long enough to help me get some food put away?"

They simply ignored her.

"That's where I know him from!" Jenna exclaimed. "I thought he looked familiar, but I figured it was because he had such an athletic build." Aubrey smirked at her. "Ease up, Brey — athletes' bodies are my job." Aubrey smirked again and made some kind of dirty gesture with her mouth and hand that Althea was sure she couldn't do without dislocating a thumb. "*Fixing* their bodies. Jesus, Brey."

"Calm down Jenna, I do believe you've gotten yourself quite worked up," Althea teased. "We know, you just doctor *on* them, you don't play doctor *with* them."

"Shut up you two. Point is, I didn't realize he was Nicky Tate. He was a star tight end at Pitt when we were in college. But he just dropped out and disappeared."

"Christ! He really is famous, Tea," Aubrey shrieked. "Look at all these red carpet shots. He's even on TMZ. Looks here like he only bangs models and movie stars."

"'Bangs'? Real classy Brey," Jenna laughed.

"Excuse me, 'makes looooove,'" Aubrey cooed sarcastically, rolling her eyes.

"Okay, coming from you, that sounds even worse," Jenna cringed.

"Whatever, Jenna. Point is, he only dates A-list hotties. And a lot of them. I don't see any relationships anywhere here. Not even any long hookups. Either way, *mamacita*, you are in some smoking hot company. Up top."

Althea grimaced when Aubrey held up her hand for a high five.

"Don't leave me hanging, Tea! You are right up there with some really famous honeys, like we didn't know that already."

"Stop it you guys," Althea begged.

"I agree. Althea is far more beautiful than any model or movie star. For the record." All three women turned around quickly at the sound of Griffen's masculine voice coming from seemingly out of nowhere.

"Jesus!" Althea had been surreptitiously sneaking a peak at the laptop screen when Griffen had walked in and the shock of his voice made her jump. She watched in defeat as a dozen leftover brownies slid off their tray and fell to the floor, a thin layer of saran wrap preventing their total destruction. "Dammit. Griffen, you need to stop sneaking up on me," she said looking dejectedly at the chocolate mess at her feet.

"But it's so much fun. Makes your eyes bright and your lovely cheeks flush." He stood very close and tilted her chin up to look down into her eyes. He glanced over at the laptop and turned back to Althea, his thumb stroking across her face. "Can't get enough of me, I see?"

Althea huffed, thrusting her chin away from him. She slapped the plastic tray for the brownies down on the kitchen table a little too hard, "I was not checking up on you. These two deviants were. *I* couldn't care less."

"Oh, come on, admit you were a little curious about me, I saw you peeking." He turned back and nodded toward Aubrey and Jenna, "Ladies, good to see you two again."

"Oh yeah, good to see you," Jenna offered quickly. "Aubrey, do you remember that thing we need to get in the living room?"

"Huh?" Aubrey asked and Althea rolled her eyes. She couldn't be sure, but she suspected Aubrey's current bout of deafness was caused by her focusing all her energy on undressing Griffen with her eyes.

"Aubrey!" Jenna shouted.

"Oh shit, oh yeah, that thing. Of course! Right behind you." And with that, Althea was left with only the company of Griffen and the army of butterflies in her stomach.

"Get back in here you, two. Right now!" Althea yelled helplessly after them.

"They seem to always run off whenever I appear," Griffen said with a knowing smile.

"Yeah, imagine that. Don't get too used to them, I'm trading them in for new friends who actually listen to me," Althea muttered, crouching down and trying to busy herself with picking up the brownies from the floor when she felt Griffen's warm breath on her hair as he crouched beside her.

"I had a really nice time today, and last night, Althea," he purred in her ear as he picked up a brownie for her. She turned her face to him trying to look fierce but realizing she probably only came across like an irritated child. "Why are you trying to act like you're mad at me?"

Breathe, breathe, she instructed herself. "You're unreal."

"Thank you," he smirked.

"I keep telling you, it's *not* a compliment!" She caught that she was almost yelling and turned it down a decibel or two, when she asked, "Can't you just let me deal with this alone, in peace, for maybe, I don't know, forever? Yeah, that sounds good."

"I don't think so, sorry. The more I saw you today, the more I think it was the best thing that could have happened. In fact, I think we should do a lot more of it. For two weeks to be exact."

"*What?*" There was no hope of discretion; she knew she was straight up close to shrieking now.

"I think we should enjoy each other while I'm here."

"And why would I want to do that?"

117

"Because we had fun together, and I think you deserve to have a little fun. And, well, I want to be around you more. I also want to get to know Johnny. And if you're really going to start with some baby steps I think they should be with me."

"Ex-*cuse* me?"

"You're considering more nights of fun, right? Well, let me be the noble one here and offer you my services. While I'm here, we have hot sex, fun, friendship. I help you with Johnny and anything else you need and then I'm gone. Built-in expiration date, so no guilt about moving on before you're ready, just some baby steps, like you call them."

"Your services? You know I was kidding when I told the girls you had a stud fee last night. I hope I wasn't actually right," she said.

"I don't charge baby," he answered with a laugh. "Though you know I'm skilled. I'm here for only two weeks and have no interest in love either. You know I'll look after you and treat you right. And I don't do relationships or emotions — just sex — so it seems like I'm your guy, right?"

"So we have fun, and then you go. No strings attached?"

"That's right, gorgeous. Then I leave and you can move on with a guy that fits into the limited whatever that you decide you're looking for. A nice guy — not some jerk who picks you up in a bar," he added with a wink.

"Let me think about it," she said, gnawing on her bottom lip with a determined focus.

"Meet me tonight at my hotel room at seven if you're game. And I really hope you are."

Althea barely had a chance to catch her breath and bring her libido in check before Aubrey, Jenna and her mother stampeded into the kitchen.

"I think it's a great idea, you should do it," Aubrey ordered.

"Well, I guess I don't need to ask if you guys were eavesdropping or not." They had the decency to pretend to look ashamed, well, except for Aubrey of course, who just kept grinning like an idiot.

"I agree," Vivian purred, adjusting her elaborate silk robe as she spoke. Since most of the guests had left, her mother had decided it was time to dress like she was on the set of a 1940s film noir. "You know he won't treat you like crap and there's an end date. He's only in town for a short time, so things won't get out of your comfort zone."

"Glad you're on board, Mom. This is not weird at all. It seems you've all had plenty of time to consider this in the two seconds it took you to ambush me," Althea grumbled.

"Oh stop being such a whiny baby. If you're worried, just blame us, say we forced you to do it. Never regret what you do..."

"Only what you don't do, I know, Mother. But what about Johnny and my job? I know you think it's wrong that those are all I ever focus on, but I can't exactly disappear for two weeks."

"No, but you just settled that big pharmaceutical liability case, you told me yourself work has been light since then," Jenna countered.

"Damn you for listening to me and my boring work talk," Althea said through a smile. "Besides, I've got other stuff going on. I don't really have time for distractions."

"Oh, sorry, I'm sure this 'distraction' would interfere with you making it through your instant queue on *Netflix*, I mean those *Psych* and *30 Rock* reruns aren't gonna just watch themselves, right?" Aubrey challenged. Althea petulantly swatted at her hands that were still doing rabbit ears for the word "distraction."

"Tina Fey's funny," Althea muttered.

"I'm on board, too," Jenna chimed in. "Not about Tina Fey, well, yeah, she's funny, but I mean about Griffen's idea. What more perfect person to ease back into a love life with than someone known for avoiding any commitment and intimately understanding your loss and how it's affected you? Plus, he's super hot," she added with a smirk.

"*Et tu,* Jenna?"

"I know, I can't believe it either," Jenna laughed. "Honestly, I'm not sure why you're even hesitating," Jenna scoffed. "This offer is tailor-made for you. Especially because Griffen wants to spend time with Johnny, too, while he's here. How great is that?"

"And when you two need some privacy for grown-up sexy times, well, Jenna and I can help," Aubrey added doing an elaborate dance with her eyebrows.

"Yep, and I can help tonight. If you need me more than that, I can try to come up again." Althea resisted the urge to roll her eyes. That is *so* much her mother — she couldn't visit regularly but promise of her daughter getting laid regularly for two weeks and she was on it. "That way Carol doesn't need to know about your little arrangement."

"Oh God, *Carol.* She can't know about this! She still views me as Jack's wife, this would kill her. Especially with Griffen of all people!"

"You know how I feel about Carol and her little comments about you. What she did today was outrageous. You need to stop obsessing about protecting that woman's feelings. It's not fair to you for her to treat you like you are biding your sexual time until you can meet Jack in heaven. You have your own grief to deal with." Vivian was getting worked up, like she often did when she got to talking about Carol's view of Althea as Jack's forever wife.

"Mom, don't start again about Carol. Please."

"You realize you are simply enabling that woman's never-ending denial that Jack's gone. At some point, she will accept that you have to move on..."

"Mother..."

"Fine. I'll drop it. *For now*," Vivian assured her. "As for Griffen, just don't tell her anything about it."

"Well, I guess we've thought of everything. I'll call him tomorrow."

"What? No way. He asked you to go by at seven."

"How nice of you to pay such careful attention to my conversation."

"You're welcome." Aubrey shuffled her out of the room. "And put on some slutty lingerie, that's assuming the moths haven't eaten all your old relics."

"Gross, okay, leave me to it guys. I guess I'm doing this." Althea took a deep breath and slowly walked to her bedroom to get ready.

Griffen had been waiting outside five minutes when he heard female voices calling his name. He turned to see Althea's two girlfriends rushing his way.

"Hey, wait up. Let us give you a ride. You're on our way," the blonde, Jenna, said.

"Oh thanks, but I already called a cab. I'm good," he said.

They laughed at him. "You *have* been gone from Pittsburgh for a while. This ain't New York, pretty boy. You could wait in Tea's yard all night for it to show up. Get in. You can cancel the cab from the car."

This from the willowy brunette. He knew he wouldn't get out of this peacefully, so he just sucked it up and walked toward what he could only assume was a repurposed clown car.

"Which one of you claim this, uh, special piece of machinery?"

"It's a Mini," the brunette chirped, "and I love it, so shut up and get in."

"Sorry," Jenna said in an appeasing tone. "Aubrey likes you, really, I promise. She can be a little gruff with strangers and she's very protective of her little baby. I agree, though, the car's ridiculous, I don't even know how she fits her giraffe legs in it."

"Jenna!" Aubrey huffed and blew her wayward bangs off her forehead.

"It's true. Now stop being so mean to him and let's go. Griffen, you can sit shotgun where there's more room."

"Much obliged, ma'am," Griffen said with a smile and a tip of an imaginary cowboy hat as he folded his muscular 6 foot 2 inch frame into Aubrey's portable tin can. He managed to buckle his seat belt moments before Aubrey peeled out of Althea's driveway with a squeal.

The city was opening up to them over the steep incline of Mt. Washington as Aubrey barreled toward downtown on P.J. McArdle Roadway — a curvy and narrow street with dizzyingly beautiful views of the city and river below.

Well, they would have been lovely if Griffen weren't so busy clutching his armrest and trying to avoid looking out at what he figured would be his fiery death off the side of the mountain.

Griffen was getting his heart rate back down below 100 beats per minute when Aubrey looked over at him. He silently begged for her to put her eyes back on the road as she said, "So, we heard you in there with Tea."

"Oh?" So that was the reason for their generous offer of a ride. He felt self-conscious all of a sudden. These two beautiful women were as intimidating as any Mexican drug lord.

"Yup, and we already told her to do it."

"What?" he asked, apparently only able to provide these women monosyllabic responses.

"We think it would be good for her, but we need to know — why did you make the offer? Are you just *that* hot for her?" Jenna said, popping her blond head between the two tiny front seats.

"Um, well."

"Gotta do better than that, pretty boy," Aubrey prodded and he regained his ability to speak.

"Of course I think she's hot, but it's way more than that. She wants someone to show her a good time and not demand a commitment, I can definitely do that. And I think she deserves to enjoy herself. I *know* I can help her with that." Aubrey rolled her eyes at him. "Look, I can't offer an awesome woman like her much, but I can give her a great couple weeks and keep her from getting hurt by someone else while she's in this...what are you guys calling it? Baby steps phase?"

"Good," Jenna answered. "That's what we were hoping you'd say. She really needs this. It's weird. Her whole life revolves around losing Jack but she does everything she can to avoid thinking or talking about him. At least not the good stuff, you know, the happy memories."

"Yeah," Aubrey added. "And she still feels guilty about how he died."

"Why would she feel guilty about that?" Griffen asked.

"Why does anybody feel anything?" Aubrey said flippantly.

"Point is she does. She thinks she has her reasons and so she's never moved on, at all, really."

"That's why we have *our* reasons for supporting this," Jenna said.

"But we know your reputation," Aubrey said.

"*Google* can be misleading," Griffen warned. "I'm not nearly as exciting as I seem on the Internet. I promise."

"I hope that's true, because believe me, you hurt her or use her and we pull the plug on this, no hesitation," Aubrey assured him.

Griffen felt almost like laughing. He twisted in his seat to look at them both. They were definitely not kidding. "Seriously? You guys act like you run her life. Last I checked she's an adult woman."

"Watch it buddy. We had your back with her before, but you're still on probation in our book." Aubrey was clearly trying for her tough girl act, so he let her go with it. "Yes, of course we know she's an adult, but Christ, she met Jack when she was nineteen. He died when she was twenty-four, and honestly, she really hadn't lived too much of a life before then. She's brilliant, yes. A genius. But she's younger than her years, believe me."

"It's true," Jenna added. "She's innocent. Her dad ran off when she was in high school to a new family with this really young woman, and you know, her mom's kind of into her own thing..."

"Viv's awesome!" Aubrey protested.

"Yeah Brey, she is, but you know Tea's the serious one there. By the time we met Tea at school, all she'd ever done was study hard. Then she met Jack and he was insanely protective of her. He looked after her, never let anything bad happen to her. And ever since he died, she's got this crazy idea she can't love again. That you only get one chance at happiness and she screwed hers up. She thinks if she were to get serious with someone emotionally, that's cheating," Jenna said seriously.

"So, she's never been really young. Never had fun. That's where you come in. She can spend a couple weeks with you, but you won't do anything stupid like fall in love with her because you're leaving soon and that's clearly not your thing. So she can tell herself you're safe," Aubrey said.

"Not sure I ever thought of myself as safe, but, you're right, definitely no love or relationship for me. Ever."

"Just what I thought," Aubrey responded. "I know your type."

"Oh really?"

"Yep. Arrogant, refuses any commitment. Only in love with himself."

"Well, shit, if you have so little faith why did you even support it?"

"Seriously, don't hold back Aubrey. Jeez," Jenna said. She looked to Griffen. "Sorry. We're a little worried about all this, but we know if we didn't get behind it one-hundred percent Tea would latch onto that as an excuse not to do it," Jenna said softly. "So don't let Brey get to you. I'm sure you're not really an asshole or anything."

"Wow, thanks. Look it's okay. You can think what you want. What I will say is, I know my limitations and Althea deserves to end up with a nice guy, someone like..." His voice caught.

"Jack?" Jenna said.

"Right. And I know I'm no Jack."

Jenna placed a hand on his shoulder. "Thing is, we know you were Jack's friend, and that gets you a lot of points in our book. But we don't know much else about you. We love Tea and we want to do whatever we can to help her move on but we're going to be here with her after you're gone. We need to be sure what you do for her is a positive, not a negative. Understand?" Griffen could see why this pretty blonde was such a successful surgeon. Her calm logical manner almost made him offer up his own shoulder for a quick slice and dice.

"Got it," he said with a smile, swallowing any further comments that may piss them off. It was crazy what he was suggesting to his dead friend's former wife. He figured he should probably question the merit of any friend who didn't warn him not to be a prick.

"Excellent," Aubrey said with a smile. "Now that we have this understanding, we can go through Althea's schedule, likes, dislikes, etc."

"Should I take notes?" he joked.

"Don't be a smart-ass. We want this done right. We want her to get the most out of it," Aubrey said sternly.

"She's right," Jenna said with her calm tones. "We want these two weeks to be perfect for her in, *and out*, of bed, so yeah, maybe you *should* take notes." And with that, Griffen's Althea education began.

CHAPTER SEVEN

Griffen looked out the back window of his suite, still not quite sure what had come over him when he proposed this crazy idea to Althea. He'd been overwhelmed by everything — the hot night with her, the desire to touch her again, the need to connect with Jack's son — making him terrified of letting this opportunity pass him by. So, he'd grabbed at whatever straws he could think of to see her again and that straw ended up being the offer of two weeks with him.

He heard a knock at the door and became so excited at the thought of seeing her again that he reminded himself to get it together or what he hoped would be the inauguration of their arrangement would be as embarrassing as his first time under the bleachers with Candace Johnson freshman year.

When he opened the door the sight of her blew all control out the window. He pulled her inside and placed his hands on each side of her face. He kissed her gently at first, just brushing her lips with his but when he heard her gasp he had to taste her. Swiping his tongue across her lips, he stroked her mouth and groaned when she met him with her own tongue. She nibbled his lower lip and he thought he would go insane. He leaned back and looked in her eyes, almost entirely green now and full of desire.

Griffen leaned his forehead against hers and whispered with a half smile, "Hi."

"Hi," she said on a soft breath.

"I'm so glad you came. Does that mean you're willing to do this with me?"

"Maybe you should have asked that before you attacked me," she teased.

"Hell no, if you came to turn me down, I had to make sure to get a kiss in first."

She smiled and then her face turned serious again. She backed up out of his arms and walked into the suite, stopping in front of the wall of windows that looked out onto the Monongahela River side of the city.

Althea turned to look at him. "So, let me make sure I have this right. Your plan is we spend time together having fun and lots of sex and then you go back to New York in two weeks and we're done?"

"Well, when you put it like that, it sounds kind of..."

"Perfect."

"Huh?"

"I'm in. But, if we do this no one can know. I mean the girls know of course, but no one else, especially not Carol."

"Why not Carol? She's one of my biggest fans." Griffen bristled.

"I know you think of yourself as very lovable, but whether she likes you or not is irrelevant. You aren't Jack. That's all that matters to her. She can't accept me being with anyone else and I'm not ready to push her on that."

"What about what you need? That doesn't exactly support this baby steps program you've set up for yourself."

"That doesn't matter right now. I just don't want to open Carol up to that when you're leaving so soon...it's better just not to upset her."

"But people will know we're hanging out. I don't plan on just being a back door man...unless you're into that kind of thing," he said with a wink.

She rolled her eyes. "Can you be serious for even a second?"

"Hmm, let me try." He schooled his face into a stern mask, holding it for two seconds, then grinning at her. "How was that?"

Althea couldn't hold in her laugh.

"Not bad. But you need to do more reps. Improve your stamina."

"You'll find I have great stamina and there are some things I'm incredibly serious about. Giving you pleasure and happiness over these two weeks is definitely one of them. In fact, I hope to make *you* a little less serious by the time I leave."

"That's a lofty goal."

"And in the interest of seriousness, I'm not sure how we can keep ourselves secret."

"We won't need to hide from each other or anything. Yes, people will know I'm spending time with you, but you were Jack's friend, that's expected." Griffen cringed at the mention of Jack. "They just won't know that we're spending *time* together."

"Is that what the kids are calling it these days? 'Time'? "

"Honestly," she said, "I have no idea what they call it. Not sure what they ever really called it. I'm not exactly...experienced." He raised an eyebrow and she looked away with an embarrassed wrinkle appearing between her eyebrows. "So now let's, uh, get to business."

"Are you sure about this? You seem kind of...nervous."

"What? Nervous? No." Griffen raised an eyebrow at her and examined the way she shifted her weight back from one foot to the other and looked everywhere in the suite *but* at him.

"Really?"

"Okay, yes, I'm a little nervous. But I do want to do this, I just have no idea how to start *this*."

"Just enjoy it. Let me make you feel good."

"I appreciate your confidence, but..."

"Just leave everything to me tonight. How about that? I would love nothing more than to help you get started, gorgeous." She let out a delicious squeak as Griffen placed a hand at the small of her back and pulled her quickly to him.

"You do know we've done this before, right?" Griffen continued.

"Yeah, I was there, thanks," she laughed.

"Good, I would hate to be totally forgettable." He stroked her cheek with his hand and kissed her slowly. "You were pretty bold last night."

"That's when I thought I'd never see you again. When I could pretend to be someone else. Now? It's just me."

"I think you're pretending if you act like you aren't a beautiful, confident, sexy woman. You're pretending if you act like you have no desires." Griffen backed away and fiddled with his laptop until the soft tones of David Gray started to fill the room. "Come on, room service won't be here for a while. Let's dance," he said, pulling her softly against him.

"Um, I'm pretty klutzy, I hope you aren't terribly attached to your toes."

"I'm tough. Besides, we can go old school." He placed her hands around his neck and hugged his arms around her waist, swaying them gently back and forth.

"So when you said old school, you meant middle school," she said with a laugh.

"Yep. You know how to sway, right?" he asked, dipping his head into the crook of her neck, reveling in how fresh and warm she smelled. It was something like jasmine and cherries, but very clean and all Althea. "We can pretend like I have a crush on you and finally got the nerve to ask you to dance."

"Oh boy, the jock asks the nerd to dance. That really was my eighth grade fantasy."

"I don't like you fantasizing about other jocks."

"Oh, don't worry, I was dreaming of you the whole time. Even though I hadn't met you, you were a glimmer in my eye. Is that better?"

"Much better," he smiled. "Now, if we want to be authentic to me in eighth grade, I would be trying to do this." Griffen gently crept his hands up, curling them under the swells of her beautiful breasts.

She playfully squirmed and nudged his hands down. "Do you want to get me put in detention?"

"I can punish you if that's what you're into, but I was more hoping to get to feel these a bit more," he answered, lifting his hands again, this time caressing her breasts.

"Well, if we were really true to my eighth grade experience — or most of high school for that matter — you'd still be searching for something to cop a feel of."

"Hmm?" he said leaning forward and pulling the V-neck of her jersey dress down until it revealed her breasts encased in a lacy pink bra. He licked her nipple through it and she gasped. "Were you a late bloomer, gorgeous?"

"The latest."

"Well, good things come to those who wait. You're amazing," he murmured as he licked over to her other breast, yanking down her bra and using the straps to hold her arms in place. He pulled her dress further down, kissing and licking her stomach. She expelled a frustrated moan, "Gri-iffen?"

"Need something, gorgeous?"

"More," was all he heard her squeeze out.

"Patience, baby. You ran out on me this morning, then I had to watch your cute ass scurrying away from me for hours. Made me wait all day to taste, tease and touch you. To make your body mine again. So, I want to take my time."

"Please!"

"We've already moved well into high school, gorgeous. Are you trying to graduate already?" His strong hands were kneading the cheeks of her ass while his lips kept moving further down her stomach.

"Yes. Please. More."

"My three favorite words." Griffen yanked down her dress the rest of the way, grabbing her panties with it. It may have ripped, but he didn't care. She was still detained by her bra, standing naked but for her heels and he reveled to see her embarrassment almost completely gone.

Griffen stared at her for a minute.

"Is everything okay?" she asked.

He swallowed. "Everything's wonderful. I just like looking at you like this. So pretty." With one movement he picked her up and laid her on the nearby bed. Griffen kissed her slowly, stroking down her neck to her perfect breasts. "I was thinking about your body all day. I woke up and you were gone. I was going to find you and bring you back here."

"I would have liked that," she sighed.

Her words surprised him. Griffen looked up from the valley between her breasts and kissed down her stomach.

"Were you thinking about me today, gorgeous? What we did together. What you want me to do to you?"

"Ye-es."

"What were you imagining I would do to you?" He licked down past her belly button and she moaned as he edged closer to her sex. She arched her back, pushing into him.

"I wanted you to kiss me," she panted, starting to writhe unabashedly against him.

"I *am* kissing you, gorgeous," he said as he deliberately diverted his mouth away from her center, moving down to her thighs and then laying sweet kisses on her knees. He kissed his way back up to the three birds tattooed on her hip. "Must say, this tattoo surprised me last night."

"Jenna, Aubrey and I got them Jenna's senior year before she graduated and left us," she gasped out.

"It's sexy as hell. Now, where was I? Oh yes, I was kissing you," he whispered as he gently kissed across her hipbone and nibbled the sensitive flesh.

"No, I want you to kiss me...somewhere else."

"Don't be shy, tell me," he wanted to hear her say it, needed to hear that sweet mouth turn dirty for him. He kissed up even closer to her mound now, licking her inner thighs and blowing against them until she shuddered.

Althea groaned in apparent frustration, grabbing him by the hair and thrusting his head up to look in her eyes. "I want you to put your tongue inside me, Griffen. Now!"

"I thought you'd never ask, gorgeous," he smiled, descending upon her glistening pussy and thrusting his tongue deep and hard in her from the beginning, rubbing her clit in tight circles with two fingers.

"Oh, Griffen, yes!"

He hummed against her, loved that she was losing some of her carefully maintained control for him, *only him*. She clutched his hair tightly and he pulled his hand out from under her ass, thrusting two fingers in her, swiping long licks up her sex and pressing into the soft special place inside her until she screamed.

"I want you inside me Griffen, please!"

Griffen grabbed the condom he'd left on the bed in hopes of this moment and suited up so he could thrust in her before her orgasm subsided. She kissed his mouth hard, moaning into him. He was thrilled to feel her wrap her legs around him and roll them both over so she was on top.

"Getting bold again, gorgeous," he whispered, looking in her eyes. "I like that."

She sat astride him, her breasts thrusting into his hands as she slid up and down his length. Griffen shifted the angle so she would moan even louder. He could feel her clenching around him again.

"Now gorgeous, come with me, now." He reached down and touched her clit setting her off like a rocket again. He thrust deeply up into her one more time as they flew into space together.

Althea and Griffen were resting lightly after coming down from their orgasms when a polite knock came across the suite door.

"That would be room service." Griffen slipped out of bed and pulled on a fluffy robe, handing one to Althea as well, with a soft kiss on the forehead. "You better cover up, no need to give the waiter too much of a thrill." He opened the door and wheeled in the tray.

"Griffen, look at all these yummy sweets! Chocolate meringue pie, strawberries, fresh whipped cream, hot chocolate. Wow, I love all these things! And champagne, too? This is too much."

Griffen felt warm and happy to see her relaxed and sexy from their lovemaking, clearly delighted at such a small gesture of thoughtfulness. He felt his heart tighten at the realization that it had probably been years since she'd let someone do something just for her pleasure. After handing her a glass of champagne, he took a fork and cut through the pie to fix her a perfect bite.

"Here, try it," he said slipping the bite between her white teeth and groaning a little as her little pink tongue licked her lips and she moaned softly. She had just drained him dry but his cock acted as if it hadn't had attention for months. This woman would be the most delicious death of him, but what a way to go.

She gradually opened her eyes. "Griffen, that is a total mouth-gasm. I didn't even know you could get good chocolate meringue pie north of the Mason Dixon line."

"I had the hotel's pastry chef make it especially for you. I owe him a box of autographed Cade Jackson books."

"For real? You must've been pretty confident I'd accept your offer."

"Hopeful is a better word."

"What if I refused? Never showed up?"

"I guess I would've drowned my disappointment in this pie." He looked down at the pie and made a face until Althea laughed out loud.

She smacked his chest and he grunted and laughed at her childish glee. "How'd you know? I mean these are all my favorite sweets. And I *really* like sweets."

Griffen felt a little guilty taking all the credit and said, "Full disclosure? Jenna and Aubrey may have given me a crash course on all things Althea."

"When they gave you a ride here after the party?"

"Uh, yeah, and I would say the emphasis was on the *crash* part of the course," he grimaced.

She rolled her eyes. "Aubrey's driving can be a little terrifying."

"Definitely. But it was really helpful information, though it does sound like you have a sweet tooth, half the tips were sugar and chocolate related," he smiled, moving the pie to the bedside table so he could pull her against his body. "Amongst other things," he said as he smirked and then kissed her deeply. "Yup, definitely sweet."

"Oh brother," she rolled her eyes. "I don't want to know what else they told you. Oh God," her eyes widened, "nothing sexual I hope!"

"A gentleman never tells."

"Ugh, they did say sex stuff, didn't they? They can't seem to keep their noses out of things, can they?"

"Definitely not, but I'm grateful for the help. You know, beyond Aubrey's driving those two can be kind of scary. You better put a good word in for me with them or I expect to find a horse head in my bed," he said with a smile.

"Oh, I know. Trust me. They're intense, but they mean well."

"They do. They love you. You're lucky to have friends like that." His throat caught unexpectedly. He hasn't had any true friends since Jack.

"Seriously, you didn't need to do all this. I'm not really used to it."

"All the more reason that I have to do it." He kissed her slowly, gently. "You're taking a chance on me, let me spoil you, please."

"All right, let me think about it...okay!" she said with a laugh.

"Good." He kissed her again. "Hmm, so sweet. I need to try some of this chocolate for myself," he whispered, reaching over and scooping up chocolate from the pie then rubbing it in circles over her taut nipples. He licked gently and sucked harder. "Mmm, you're right, this is delicious." He scooped up some meringue and dotted a trail of it down her flat stomach and sucked and nibbled at her soft flesh all the way down to her pussy.

"Griffen, what are you doing?" she panted. "Is this that stamina you were bragging about?"

He chuckled against her inner thighs as he started to lose himself in her scent again.

"Apparently so. I don't think I can ever stop with you, Althea."

CHAPTER EIGHT

Griffen looked down at the lockbox he'd dug out from underneath his mom's old deck. His classes didn't start until the next day and Althea had to go to work, such that he was left with no more excuses.

Griffen knew he couldn't keep hiding from his childhood home and the torturous memories that permeated each square inch of it. He had to come to this spot, the place where he and Jack had spent so much of their time together growing up.

His mother still lived in the same 1920s era row house he'd grown up in. He'd tried to persuade her to let him buy her a beautiful mansion in Sewickley Heights out of town but she wouldn't hear of it. He'd even tried to persuade her to move to one of the homes on the other side of Mt. Washington where Jack's mom and Althea lived. She could drink a glass of wine and look out over world famous views of the city, without having to step on floorboards that had once supported his father's angry steps. No longer clean a kitchen where she'd gotten icepacks for another black eye received at the hands of the cruelest, most bitter person they'd ever known.

But she wouldn't hear of it. This was her parents' home

and the place where she'd raised Griffen. He could never persuade her to leave.

She'd finally caved on letting him pay to have it updated and remodeled, with top of the line security installed. Even though she let him get their old deck refurbished, it still looked the same as when he and Jack would sit underneath it for hours on end, hiding from his father, laughing, talking about girls.

How many times had they pulled away the lattice until they could squeeze through so they could play here after school? They'd both grown up on Mt. Washington, except Jack had been on the good side, not the poor side where Griffen lived. Jack looked out at a city with everything to offer, while Griffen and his mother simply saw patchy pieces of brown grass and his father's empty beer cans. Life for them had been bleak and poor.

So much had changed, so much had been lost.

Jack was gone.

Griffen's bastard of a father was gone.

But this box and all it represented of his friendship with Jack still remained.

Griffen reached into his pocket and pulled out his keychain. It was still on there, the tiny padlock key. He and Jack had both had one. His hand was shaking and his eyes were blurry with tears as he pushed it into the lock, praying it would still work, yet praying that maybe it wouldn't. Before he could second-guess his courage, he heard a soft click and the lock popped. He removed it and flipped open the lid.

Through tears, he felt a smile form at the contents. When they were little, he and Jack would hide candy here, baseball cards, little pieces of buried treasure they would find when they played pirates. As they got older, they would hide beer and other contraband in this locked steel chest. In it he found *Playboys*, pictures of the two of them together, some of the old candy and baseball cards they'd been too sentimental to remove.

Griffen's breath caught when he came upon his own handwritten scrawl in several spiral bound notebooks. These were the stories they wrote together for over 10 years. Griffen flipped through the notebooks. They were exciting stories, developing in sophistication as each scribbled year on the top right corners reflected how they were getting older. The stories were exciting, but they were also thoughtful and emotional, so different from what he'd made his millions writing.

They'd had to hide them, knowing Griffen's dad would make sure to beat the shit out of him whenever he found out he was wasting his time writing when he should be practicing football.

Dear ole Dad had been a star in high school. A quarterback phenom, but everything stopped short for him his senior year when he knocked up Griffen's mom and blew out his knee. He'd lost his chance at a football scholarship, settling instead for whatever factory jobs still remained after the steel industry had already deserted Pittsburgh.

Maybe he'd been something once, maybe he'd been charming, but all Griffen knew was an angry, frustrated monster.

The smell of the wood, the dirt, the way the sun shone against the house all took Griffen back to a place he hated. He twisted a notebook in his hands, the memories beating him like so many punches and belt whippings from his dad. The pain still felt real, so fresh. All he had to do was look at the dip of the backyard into the hill and he felt his father's hot drunk breath against his hair.

"Come here Nick, you little pussy." Griffen could still hear his hot slurs. *"Want to keep writing your stories like a little girl?"* Then the smack, so hard the pencil and paper flew out of his hand.

"No, dad, I don't need it. It's homework. Please stop."

"Fuck you, you pussy, our only way out of here is football. Get the ball and get back to practicing. And get my drink while you're at it you little shit."

Griffen shook his head. How could he stop the painful memories?

Griffen felt the bile rise in his throat when he saw a story with dark splatter marks all over it — the paper crinkled where the liquid that made that imprint had dried. He swallowed, remembering it was blood. He'd managed to keep his dad's brutality a secret for so long, hide the bruises, make the excuses.

He and his mother were pros at it, especially when hiding the wounds from each other. Griffen wanted to protect her, but he couldn't beat the bastard. So all he could do was hide from her what his dad was doing to him and let her hide her wounds right back.

But Jack knew. He handled it for so long by having Griffen stay at his house. But it all came to a head one fateful night during their junior year. They had just won the state championships. They had the world in their hands. Jack was varsity quarterback, throwing to his best friend. They were going to meet up with Teri and Susan to go to a party celebrating their big win. Jack had snagged a bottle of bourbon from the restaurant and it was going to be a great night. They just needed to stop by Griffen's house for a minute so he could grab a clean shirt.

"There you are you piece of shit." His dad was staggering already and stank. *"I watched the game. Watched you fuck up, you little shit. You jumped your route. Almost blew the whole championship."*

"Mr. Tate, you're tired," Jack said calmly.

"Fuck you. My son should've been the quarterback. That's where the money is. You spoiled little shit — you have to have everything. You're not even going to play in college, you brainy little asshole."

"Mr. Tate, please, Nick's a great tight end."

"Bullshit. He's a pussy." Griffen's dad was swaying on his feet now. *"Just like his mom, worthless."*

Griffen could still feel the heat, the anger, boiling through his body.

"Don't you fucking talk about my mother, don't touch her." He ran to him and tackled him with all the force of his shoulders and hatred. *"I'll kill you, you son of a bitch."*

"Oh, the little shit grew some balls." It was like he enjoyed it. His dad pushed him off and kicked him in the stomach until he felt like he could taste his liver. His dad punched him so hard, cursing him and spraying hot, drunk spit in his ear. Griffen heard something out of the edge of his brain. He knew they were words but it was so hard to hear through the pummeling fists and kicks.

"Mr. Tate, stop it. You'll kill him."

But Griffen didn't feel pain now, just warm blood across his teeth. *This is how it ends he'd thought. He felt more shame than pain.*

"Griffen, get up, stop him!"

But Griffen was so warm, he'd been here before and he knew the best thing was to curl in a ball and wait for the end.

Then he heard it, *"Mr. Tate, I said you need to fucking stop."* Suddenly, the kicking stopped. Griffen rolled on his side and enjoyed the moments of relief. Then he started coughing till blood came out. The sight drove Jack wild. *"You fucking bastard."* Jack plowed toward Griffen's father, pushing him straight off the deck. His father fell on his back and *huffed but Jack was on him, punching his face, his body, everywhere. "You touch him or his mom again, I'll fucking kill you." Griffen's mother came home and saw them at that moment. The blood drained from her face, from her body.*

"Mom. Police. Please," Griffen had gasped out.

Griffen fell into blissful unconsciousness and never saw his father alive again.

Griffen raised his left hand to run his fingers across the jagged scar by his left eyebrow — the only physical reminder of that awful night. He only missed a week of school but he wondered if he or his mother ever recovered emotionally.

There was protection from abuse orders, ordered probation, but eventually his dad died a quiet and ugly death, drunk and shivering by the banks of the Ohio River, almost two years later. The important thing was Griffen knew that Jack had saved his life and he'd done nothing for him in return. And now he was fucking dead.

What a world. Jack was the greatest person he'd ever known, while Griffen's dad was a fucking monster. Yet they were both the same thing — dead.

Griffen's heart twisted and split in his chest. This box was all he had left of Jack. Jack was everyone's golden boy, the hero, and he lived up to that image when he saved Griffen's life that night.

Yet Griffen had abandoned Jack when he'd needed him most. He ran away from the painful memories of his dad, only to create new terrible ones of his own by deserting the only true friend he'd ever had – his brother, even if not by blood.

You don't deserve happiness or love, Griffen thought to himself.

Dad was right, you're not good for anything, and you proved that when you failed Jack — ignored him and left him to die, because your crappy book and money were more important to you.

All Griffen had left were these trinkets, these stories he and Jack wrote together, and an unending supply of guilt to remember Jack and all he'd done for him.

You fucking failure, he thought. *It should be Jack here crying over this junk, not you. He's the one that should be alive making Althea happy and laughing with Johnny. All you are is an intruder, that's good for nothing besides fucking and misery. You break everything you touch. Just like your old man did. Jack is just one more in a long line of lives destroyed by us Tate men.*

Griffen opened his mouth on a roar and upended the lockbox with a furious thrust of his arms. The contents flew everywhere and immediately Griffen regretted it. He took a breath and started to fill the box back up.

Get your shit together. This is all you have left of him, don't fucking ruin it.

As he grabbed the last few baseball cards, something plastic and metallic caught his eye. *What the hell is a flash drive doing in here?*

Jack must have placed it there recently since the technology didn't exist when they were in high school. Griffen pocketed the flash drive and wiped a shaking hand across his face. Whatever was on it was Jack's before he died and he would never have put it in here if it wasn't important.

He breathed in, locked the box, replaced it in its hole and left.

Griffen groaned in frustration. He'd spent most of the last hour trying to explore the contents of the flash drive, with little to no luck. It was heavily encrypted, with multiple forms and layers of security that were way beyond him. Luckily he knew someone who could help.

"Hey Trey, what's up?"

"Griffen? What's up, man? Aren't you in Pittsburgh or something?"

"Yeah. I'm here for a couple weeks. I have an exciting challenge for you."

"Hmm, your challenges usually involve avoiding the business end of a gun at some point. Is this Mexico all over again?" Trey asked with a laugh.

"Hopefully not," Griffen chuckled out. Trey had helped him on his second book, as well as secret consults he did to support other investigative journalists behind the scenes. Some situations had ended up a bit hairy, but Trey liked danger, so he wasn't worried. "I've got this flash drive. I can read some of it but the rest is so heavily encrypted I can't make a dent."

Trey was the best analyst he'd ever met. A hacker when he was younger — he'd been picked up for it as early as 14, a prank that led to one of the most major overhauls of a leading operating system in history. He'd cleaned up his act and gone legit but still had the spirit of a rebel. Not unlike Griffen.

He was the perfect person to get to the bottom of this mess. Third in line of some seriously respected geniuses — great minds behind some of the first computers, Griffen suspected he was loaded with family money. Yet Trey preferred to hole up in Brooklyn, generally operating on the right side of the law.

"Where'd you get it?"

"It belonged to a friend of mine that died."

"That sucks."

"Yeah. He hid it in a lockbox only we knew about."

"Why?"

145

"I think he knew it would be safe there."

"Was he another writer?"

"No. He was an associate professor in the *CMU Robotics Institute*."

Trey whistled, "Impressive. Sounds cool. Send it on up, man. I just wrapped up reverse engineering some virus software, I'm definitely ready for something a lot more fun."

"Cool, I've made arrangements to send it up with a courier. Mail makes me nervous. You'll get it tonight."

"I gotta ask — anything illegal, dude?"

"No. Not illegal. At least I hope not...but definitely confidential."

"I feel you. Let's do this." Griffen could almost hear his smirk over the line.

"Yeah," he answered seriously. "Let's do this."

Griffen looked at the time. Eleven a.m.

He moved back from his laptop and rested his elbows on his knees, trying to get his head right. The only thing that made sense right now was Althea's face. He pictured her smooth skin and soft curves and had to see her.

CHAPTER NINE

As Althea watched her mother walk toward the cab in her front driveway her heart sank. It doesn't matter how old you are or what you do with your life, sometimes you just miss your mom.

As if sensing her mood, Vivian turned around and smiled. "Come here, baby." She pulled Althea into her arms, her mother's *Annick Goutal* perfume wrapping around Althea as her huge purse knocked her on the butt. "I love you honey. So much. But I worry about you, too, you know."

"I'm okay, Mom."

Vivian pulled back and held her at arms length, answering, "Are you, honey? I'm not so sure. I know you never really come back from what you went through, especially with such a demanding job and a baby, but you need to try."

"Mom, please, I don't want to talk about this right now."

"I know," she sighed. "You never want to talk about it. We've tried to be patient, just waiting for you to come around, but you still seem to be deeply in pain. Sort of stuck. You were always so responsible, so in your own head. I loved Jack, like a real son, not a son-in-law. He brought you out of your shell, but then you went right back into it after he died."

Althea felt tears prick at her eyes. "I'm sorry."

"Don't apologize. Don't be silly. I want you to have some fun and just let go for a bit."

"How?"

"Start by letting yourself enjoy this time with Griffen, okay? You know I think sex is pretty much the main reason for everything, but that's not all this is about. It's about doing something for yourself for once. Letting yourself enjoy something without feeling guilty or like you are betraying someone."

Althea smiled weakly. "Okay. I promise. And I love you, too."

"Good!" Her mother sealed the deal with a smack on Althea's rump. "Now go get you some!"

"Eww, Mo-om!" Some things never changed. Althea waved goodbye as her mother loaded into the cab and it pulled away.

Althea stared at the cursor blinking dumbly at her from her computer screen. It felt odd to be back in the office after another evening of spending several hot hours in Griffen's hotel room, only a few blocks from the stuffy desk at which she sat. There was just something about writing a motion in a contract dispute that was so much less stimulating than being alone with Griffen. Althea's mind began to wander to how he'd greeted her at his hotel door and her office started to get unbearably warm when she was rescued by the phone's loud ring.

"Hey gorgeous."

"Hey stud, I was just thinking about you."

"Hopefully they were not safe for work thoughts."

"Of course. With you, that's pretty much a given, right?"

"Well, if thinking of me is not safe for work, how about I steal you from there for lunch today."

"I like the sound of that. Give me an hour to get my filing out and then I'll definitely play hooky with you." *Or any other games that might strike my fancy*, she thought, shocked by her own mischievous glee.

"Perfect. I'll meet you outside your office at twelve-thirty. And gorgeous..."

"Yes?"

"I'll be counting the seconds."

"Oh please, you smooth talker. Bye." She smirked but knew she was beyond eager to see him again.

Griffen was nothing if not good for Althea's productivity. As soon as she knew she had a midday escape with him to look forward to, she wrapped up her motion and filed it in no time. Looking at the time on her computer, she put it to sleep, checked herself out in her compact mirror, grabbed her purse and darted out the door.

"Tracey, I'm going to lunch. I'll be gone at least an hour. Maybe two," she breezily said to her secretary on her way down the hall.

"Client meeting?"

"Uh, no. A personal lunch." Althea bit her lip. She adored her secretary, but Tracey had the biggest mouth in the firm.

"*What?* Yinz is leaving the building for lunch? Get 'aht of here!" she exclaimed. "Who with? I'm dyin' to know!"

Tracey also had the thickest Pittsburgh accent Althea had ever heard and used so many colloquialisms from Pittsburgh's distinctive dialect that at times Althea struggled to understand her at all.

"Oh, just a friend that's visiting town."

"Whoever it is, I'm thrilled, hon. It's about time you did something besides work and PTA meetings."

She was right. Althea never went out for lunch, never did much of anything other than work and rush home to Johnny.

"And if yinz feel like any more personal lunches, let me know. My nephew is a real cutie, you and he'd get along like a house afire."

And there it was — another try at a fix up. But this time it didn't make Althea want to grind her teeth. Maybe these baby steps were working. "You never know, Tracey. Thanks."

"I'll cover your phone and keep an eye on your email. Go have fun," Tracey said with a wink.

"Sounds like a plan. See you soon!"

Griffen was waiting outside the door of her building, as promised, and damned if he didn't look hot, as usual. She smiled and took a moment to enjoy his low-slung jeans and navy blue Henley shirt with sunglasses tucked into the unbuttoned neck. "Wow, I feel over dressed," she teased.

"No problem. I love you dressed for work." And from the looks of the way he was eyeing the knee-length pencil skirt and fitted top she was wearing, he certainly did.

"Where do you want to go for lunch?" Althea asked.

Griffen smirked and pulled out a picnic basket from behind his back.

"A picnic? How great! That should also leave plenty of time for you to have your wild way with me. Isn't that what nooners are?"

"I didn't know anyone still said that, but I'm certainly game for one if you are, but first, I want to feed you. In public."

She laughed. "In that case, follow me. Let's eat it at the fountain."

"Perfect. How much time do you have, I don't want to miss out on that nooner."

"I got my filing out and no meetings this afternoon — so a couple hours."

"The fountain it is then," Griffen said as he led the way.

They walked side-by-side straight to Point State Park at the edge of downtown, where the Allegheny and Monongahela Rivers met to begin the dramatic Ohio River. The confluence of the rivers formed a natural triangle featuring a giant fountain that drew onlookers all day to marvel at its high plume and series of water shows.

Downtown was at their backs, sprouting with huge skyscrapers but all they saw was the mighty rivers meeting before them, crisscrossed with more bright yellow bridges than you could count. And all this was cradled on both sides by hills and cliffs. Griffen felt lucky to be in this spot with this lovely woman next to him. He'd run from this place and all it represented but now he felt the pang of realization that part of him had missed it.

"Beautiful," Althea whispered.

Griffen pulled her onto his lap and looked in her eyes. "Yes, so beautiful."

He silently thanked the *Fairmont Hotel* for being so close to her office. It had been his idea to take her to eat in public, but the sight of her had him already eager to steal her away for a quickie as soon as possible, even though they'd only been apart for a few hours.

Griffen took out the basket of goodies the hotel had put together for him. They took a seat on the concrete benches ringing the fountain, choosing to sit closest to the point where the three rivers met.

This feels like we're a real couple. It shocked him how nice that thought felt to him. He looked over and kissed her softly at first. She tasted too good, he began to deepen the kiss and stroke her tongue with his. She backed away and looked around nervously. When she must have registered that no one she knew was nearby she kissed him again. She was always so delicious and receptive that he had no idea how much time passed when he finally broke the kiss and looked in her eyes.

"I should probably feed you instead of feasting on you all afternoon, huh?"

"You did invite me to lunch, I would hate to feel like I was getting ripped off," she said with a wink and squeezed around his waist with her arms for good measure.

"I'm nothing, if not a man of my word." Griffen adjusted her in his lap and began to feed little bites of salami and parmesan atop freshly baked bread into her mouth.

"Mmm, that tastes good, and you are much sexier than a fork. I could get used to this."

"Good," he said and licked a breadcrumb from the corner of her luscious mouth.

Griffen watched her beautiful eyes as they looked up to take in the view. It was objectively spectacular. As any good Pittsburgh boy, he'd seen it countless times, but sitting here with this perfect woman in his arms, it was as though he were seeing it all for the first time. Mt. Washington rose up above them to the left. Covered with trees, their leaves not yet changing into the bright fireworks of colors that autumn would soon bring, leading to the top ridge and its luxurious apartment buildings, spectacular churches and sightseers looking down at the city below. On their right the sports stadiums and boats dotted the landscape, but it felt to him like they were completely alone.

"I love this spot so much," she whispered, breaking his own reverie for a moment. "Jack brought me here when he wanted to persuade me to move to Pittsburgh with him after I graduated."

"I believe it. We used to come down along the river and hang out. But we would go to a much less public place and..."

"I'm guessing there was beer and girls involved?" she asked with a laugh.

"It's my turn to take the Fifth," he said with a squeeze. "So, what did you think when he brought you here?"

"I knew nothing about the city, just the old cliché that it was a polluted steel town. As soon as I saw the city for myself I knew that was wrong. When we came, he took me on the incline up Mt. Washington. I looked at this point, where the rivers meet and this beautiful fountain and I thought it was so pretty...but now, it's more."

Griffen held her tighter, sensing her new tension. "How so?"

She sighed. "I don't know, it's depressing. Maybe we should talk about something else." She looked back at the rivers.

"Althea, I am here to make your life happy for a couple weeks, right? If part of that is talking about things that aren't really pleasant, then that's what I want to hear."

"Are you too good to be true, Griffen?" she asked, looking back into his eyes.

"I'm not that good a guy, but I'm trying to be for you, if only for a few days. Does it help to talk about it?" he answered, kissing her lightly.

"It feels good, yes," Althea said softly.

"Then go on, gorgeous."

"Okay." She took a breath. "This is where I would come after Jack died when I started to feel really lost and alone. I would watch the rivers meet each other and flow right on forward for hours."

"What would you think about?"

"Anything and everything. Memories sometimes, other days I would just think about how scared I was to do all this by myself. Losing someone you loved so much, so young...I was totally isolated. It wasn't like I was Great-Aunt Gertrude in the retirement community in Boca with twenty other widows. No, I was completely alone, with a baby growing in my belly." He could see tears falling down her cheeks and he gently collected them with his hand, cupping her cheek. The touch of his hand made her stop.

"And..."

"Thing is, even through this grief. This missing him. I do whatever I can so as not to think about him. It just hurts too much. How messed up is that? But coming here and seeing these rivers move along, this is where I would let myself think about him and that would make me feel calm again. These rivers took him from me, but they also give me peace."

Griffen hugged her closer and marveled at how much she'd suffered through alone. He quietly hoped that his short time with her could help her deal with the sadness some.

"Why do you think it helped?" he asked softly into her neck, trying to make her get all of this out. "Please go on, it's okay."

"Here is where I would think about death. Death means nothing to these rivers. It's just death, it doesn't affect the currents. The rivers just keep on moving. The pain and aftermath of the loss of one little life doesn't change that."

Griffen looked forward at the rivers, as if he were seeing them for the first time. This time through her eyes.

"Death be not proud," Griffen said against her neck.

Althea spun around and looked at him, eyebrow raised. "That's a lofty quote, quite impressive."

Griffen shrugged and gave her a half-smile. "Hey, I mean I *am* a writer. Give me some credit."

"I didn't know John Donne wrote a lot of explosion scenes in Afghan caves."

"Yup, it was in his later lesser-known sonnets," he said with a wink and a squeeze of her waist. "Besides, that's not all that my books are about, college girl."

"Yeah, from the book jacket, there's a lot of sex, too," she said nudging him.

"Write what you know, right?" Griffen winked, thrilled he could lighten her dark mood. "Hey gorgeous," his voice came out surprisingly scratchy. "How about I feed you dessert in bed?"

"That sounds perfect," she said with a soft smile.

They were lucky enough to get an empty elevator. Althea felt a thrill when Griffen placed his hand at the small of her back and gently led her in. The doors shut quietly behind them and he slipped his hand down across the curve of Althea's bottom burying his face in her neck as he scanned his key card for his floor. Althea arched into his crotch and gasped at how hard he was against her and hot to the touch even through her tight skirt. Everything became unbearably silent except for her panting breaths as he squeezed the globes of her ass with one hand and started to stroke her over her blouse with the other.

"You aren't still nervous around me are you, Althea?" he murmured against the point where her skin peeked through the gray silk of her half unbuttoned top. His tongue flicked against her and she thought she would go insane.

How can he do this to me? Every time he touches me, no matter where we are, he drives me completely out of control.

"No. I'm just wondering when the nooner can start," she answered, her voice was husky sounding even to her own ears. She reached behind him and started to pull his shirt out of his jeans, sneaking a hand under the waistband.

He ran his tongue back down between her breasts and looked up at her with hooded eyes. The way his dark hair was falling across his bright blue eyes was such a contrast she couldn't look away, even if she wanted to. "We make the rules here, gorgeous. I will start whenever you want. Wherever you want."

"We haven't started yet?" she said on a gasp as he slowly pulled her skirt up inch by inch with his hand until the point where the top of her stockings met her garters was revealed. He groaned and smiled against her skin.

"Hardly."

Just when she started to think she could do something crazy in an elevator she heard - *ding!*

Griffen's face was at her waist now. He smiled and smoothed her skirt down, stepping aside to let her out. Althea was wobbly on her feet, trying to walk normally when all she could do was pay attention to the heat between her legs. She stepped in the hall and began walking toward his room, making sure to let her hips sway lasciviously, knowing he was staring at her from behind.

"To hell with this," she heard him mutter, right before he grabbed her waist, spun her on her toes and threw her over his shoulder, like he was rescuing her from a burning building.

"Griffen, stop that," she yelled, pounding on his back as she bounced up and down on his shoulder with each of his quick trotting steps.

"Sorry, gorgeous. You're killing me. I can't wait anymore."

"If you tell me you're doing this because there's a fire in your pants, I'm leaving," she spluttered out through giggles and the pressure of his shoulder against her belly.

"Good one. Wish I'd thought of it. But, nope, I'm on the clock here. I don't have you much longer, so there's no time to waste." She wriggled against him as he slowed to a halt in front of the door and fussed with the key. He swatted her butt. Hard.

"Ow! Hey!"

"Stop squirming."

"You can put me down now, we're here," she said beating against his back. The door opened and she felt his rough hand slide under her skirt, between her legs. She was squirming now for a different reason.

"With pleasure." He stalked across the room, still stroking her thigh and between her legs with his free hand. Once he reached the bed he threw her on it so that she bounced up and down a couple times comically. He stopped and stood at the foot of the bed looking at her from head to toe.

She knew she must have been a sight. Legs bent at the knees, skirt pulled up around her thighs revealing the garters she'd worn to make the most of how sexy he made her feel. Her gray silk blouse unbuttoned so low the edges of her push up bra were revealed, as well as the cleavage it had created.

He was breathing heavily and she was thrilled to see the large bulge in the crotch of his jeans.

"Take down your hair," he said.

She licked her lips and he groaned as she reached up and undid the barrette that held up her massive amount of hair. It fell heavily against her shoulders. Althea unbuttoned her top and took it off, her eyes never leaving his. She then got up on her knees in front of him. Reaching behind her, making sure her breasts pushed forward on the movement, she slowly unzipped the back of her skirt and slid it down, revealing the stunning sheer lace and cream silk panties that completed the bra, panty, and garter set she'd bought three years ago in New York on a depressed whim during a lonely business trip, yet had never worn.

His eyes flamed with desire and she knew it was because of each of her calculated moves. She really knew nothing of seduction, but she sensed she drove him just as crazy as he did her and damned if she wasn't going to enjoy that. There she was, on her knees in the most provocative underwear she owned, feeling sexy and powerful in front of the most stunning man she could imagine.

Althea arched her back to let the curve of her ass press against the flimsy silk and draw his eye. He ran his hand down her arm, over her back until it rested on that piece of round flesh she'd teased him with just moments before. Griffen squeezed her ass and she moaned, closing her eyes at the pressure of his hand, his long fingers reaching under the silk band to stroke her bare bottom, then moving lower, touching her wet slit and pressing into her ever so slightly.

Althea looked into his eyes and shook her hair so it fell more perfectly in waves down her back. She'd never felt so on display and she loved it. Without a sound she moved her hands slowly up the edge of his jeans and reached up, gathering the material of his shirt into each palm until it was free of his pants. She pulled up the soft cotton shirt slowly, loving the flesh and smattering of dark hair that appeared like a prize with each motion of her hands. Rubbing her fingers against the ripples of his muscular flesh she ran her tongue along each warm, hard spot her hands had just enjoyed.

His hands were still touching her, exploring her body inside and out until she thought she couldn't take it anymore. Quickly, she unbuttoned his jeans and lowered the zipper. It was the first sound in the room other than their breathing and it seemed like a sensual shout against the silence. He was so hard, the head of his penis was peeking out of his boxer briefs and she had to taste it. He groaned loudly and squeezed her ass with both hands, clearly using all of his self-control not to disturb the control she was so enjoying over his body.

When she took him into her mouth, his answering moan made her feel heady with power. The salty drop on her tongue let her know he enjoyed being with her — Althea. Touching her body. No one else's. In this moment, he belonged to her.

She took him more fully in her mouth and with each swipe of her tongue across his head and down his length she felt so close to peace and so far from loneliness, that she had to force herself not to think about what that could mean.

She pulled his jeans down and ran her nails against his thighs, over his muscular ass, until suddenly, her mouth was empty and he'd pulled her away. The sense of loss was so great that tears threatened, making her feel stupid and embarrassed. Althea had to look away, but he grabbed her chin and pulled her face to look at him. "Stop."

"What?" she whispered, averting her eyes from his, but he pulled her right back and leaned forward, his lips only inches from hers.

"Thinking something awful. That was incredible. Fucking amazing, but you're driving me nuts. This outfit, your face, your hair, your fucking tongue," he groaned and closed his eyes a moment before opening them and staring at her, his sapphire eyes full of fire.

The panties tied with ribbons on both sides. Griffen fingered the bows and whispered, "I like this design, very convenient," as he slowly undid each tie until the silk fell quietly off her body onto the bed. "I have to be inside you Althea. Now."

She smiled, feeling so wonderful just from his words and the effect she had on him. She straightened her back and with all the confidence she had in that moment asked, "Then what are you waiting for stud?"

He grunted out what may have been a tortured laugh. She couldn't determine what because in a moment he'd picked her up off her knees and threw her down on her back on the bed. In an instant, he had a condom on and was inside her, his boxer briefs pulled down just to his thighs. His desperation caused her to feel beyond aroused. The stroking of his flesh inside hers was smooth and deep, yet harsh all at once. His mouth was everywhere. If she'd been seducing, he was simply taking. Possessing her body with every inch of his.

His hands moved up her body until they rested on her throat, his thumbs pressing up on her chin. "Look at me, Althea."

She opened her eyes and their gaze locked as he pressed so deeply in her she didn't know where he ended and she began. He moved one hand down her throat, over her breasts, until it found its way under her ass and he tilted her in such a way that he was even deeper and stroked fire with each thrust.

Althea heard screaming and it took a moment to realize it was her own voice, shouting Griffen's name. The pleasure was so intense it was almost painful but she never wanted it to end.

They were still looking in each other's eyes, but he was as crazed as she was. He thrust again and stars shot across her vision. In the distance she heard his own shout of completion, but she could focus on nothing but the pulsing of her body around his, the warmth of joy and sensuality through her veins.

He pulled back, kissing every inch of her face, her shoulders, her breasts, muttering sweet words against her skin about how beautiful she was, how much he wanted her and she couldn't help but smile. He finally rested his head in her neck and she was sure he could feel her heart racing against him. Then she heard chuckling, the vibrations jostling her belly.

"What is it?" she asked confused.

"I should probably continue getting undressed." She looked up and laughed. Other than his half-lifted shirt and his jeans and boxers pulled down around his thighs, he was completely clothed. He stood, disposed of the condom, and gave her the best strip tease any woman could hope for simply by removing his shirt, jeans and boxers. "What?" he asked as she stared at him from the bed, unknowingly licking her lips.

"You really are a stud. I like watching you strip."

"I'll keep that in mind. Any time you like, gorgeous, you just have to ask. Though you do make me pretty wild. Maybe I should just never wear clothes again so we don't slow down you having your way with me."

"Hmm, I like that idea. You okay with being my kept man?"

He climbed on the bed to lie beside her. "Hell no, I don't mind. Is there an application or do you feel pretty sure I'll get the position?"

She laughed and straddled him so that her warm pussy was rubbing against him as she slowly moved back and forth. "I'm pretty sure I'll get you in every position."

He laughed and flipped her over so he was fully on top of her. He suddenly got serious, and she couldn't place the emotion she saw in his eyes. It quickly flashed away and back was the cocky man she was so used to seeing.

He cleared his throat, "Now, I believe I promised you dessert."

She squeezed his butt playfully, "I thought you just gave me my dessert."

He laughed and stood, walking in his naked beauty across the room to a lovely little kitchenette and returned with a saran wrapped covered plate full of chocolate mousse and fresh berries. He flopped down and without a word began to spoon a morsel for her. "Open your mouth."

She obliged, tasting it and closing her eyes on a groan. "You spoil me, Griffen Tate."

"I thought that was the idea," he said.

"I like the sound of that, though I suspect you're trying to fatten me up before you leave." She said it teasingly but her heart jumped when she saw sadness cross his eyes so quickly she thought she imagined it. "Griffen...?"

Before she could say anything more he kissed her until there was no room in her mind for questions — only thoughts of how good he made her feel.

Althea had left and Griffen groaned at the thought that he wouldn't see her again for several hours.

They'd made love again, it wasn't as frenzied as before, but still more rushed than he would've liked. She was so perfect in every way that he wanted to take his time tasting her and enjoying her body, but she'd had to get back to work.

162

It surprised him how thrilled he was to have her ask him to her house for dinner and to stay the night after Johnny went to sleep.

He suspected she didn't want to risk going out with him in public because of her crazy obsession with keeping their time together secret, but he was getting to spend time with her and would simply have to take what she would give him. Maybe it was better this way anyway. She was already getting deeper under his skin than anyone had before.

He pulled himself out of bed and took a shower. He'd been half-tempted to simply let the smell of her body and their lovemaking stay on his skin all day, but he knew it was better to appear half human when he showed up at her house.

As he walked out of the shower drying his hair roughly with a towel, his laptop caught his eye. He sat down and pulled up Jack's flash drive file. Nope, the security was still beyond him. He'd packed up the flash drive for the courier to pick up, but he was quickly restless again and couldn't figure out what to do with himself.

As he was about to put the computer to sleep, his finger instead hovered over the Word icon. He opened a blank document and for the hell of it typed out "Chapter One." Then he wrote a couple lines about the day he met Jack, back when he was five, so shy and scared of the world, living in a world of terror and Jack was there with a football and asked if he wanted to play.

Then the strangest thing happened. Griffen kept on writing and couldn't stop. He released everything inside him onto the keyboard, from his guilt over Jack's death, to his passion for Althea to the mysterious contents of the flash drive. It wasn't until he looked at the clock on the bottom right of the screen to see it was almost time to meet Althea after work that he realized a new book had begun.

CHAPTER TEN

It was Wednesday and Griffen called Trey on the way to campus to teach his Investigative Journalism class. He knew he needed to focus on a lesson plan but his mind kept wandering back to thoughts of Jack.

Griffen had spent the last two evenings with Althea and Johnny and it shocked him just how enjoyable that time had been. When he'd arrived for his first dinner there Althea had been pretty shy, understandably. It was very important to her that Johnny not have any idea that she and Griffen were — well, whatever they were.

Yet from the first moment Griffen arrived, Johnny had been eager to spend time with him, playing football and learning more about his dad. Each moment filled Griffen with happiness in a way he'd never anticipated.

The time with Althea also became better by the second and they even found the boldness to sneak a kiss or an embrace every time Johnny was outside or in his room, well before Johnny went to sleep, when Althea and Griffen would go to her room and enjoy their heated nights together.

Even though Griffen had to leave both mornings long before Johnny awoke, he couldn't deny the bizarre sensation of joy he felt at being a part of this unit. The pleasure of being with Althea and Johnny was so foreign from everything he'd ever known before. Each moment with them filled him with an emotion he couldn't quite name, but didn't want to lose, if even for this brief time.

That happiness quickly turned into a desperate fixation on a need to resolve why Jack — the actual touchstone of this family — had reached out to him so many years ago.

Griffen had always known that he would never be free of guilt as long as the mystery of why Jack reached out to him before he died still hung out there. It was still a blinking spotlight on Griffen's greatest shame, but now it was more than just the matter of resolving his own regrets. It now represented Griffen's opportunity to leave Althea and Johnny with some of the peace that Jack's unexplained death had stolen from them.

Now he felt an overwhelming desire to resolve this issue for Johnny and Althea's sake. He knew he needed to leave them soon, that he would never be more than a passing visitor in their lives, but maybe he could use his skills to give them some peace by getting to the bottom of what Jack had been working on when he'd asked for Griffen's help.

"Hi Trey."

"Dude. I was just about to call you. I got your flash drive late Monday night. So are you finally writing another book or is this just for you?"

"Both. I'm including the investigation in the book like I always do, but it's also for my own peace of mind. So, what do you think? All I was able to open were a couple of requests for proposals from the military. Did you have any more luck?"

"Of course I did, that's why you called me, right?"

"Yes, you arrogant ass. What have you found?"

"Hey, play nice, man. I just speak the truth is all. But I'll tell you this is some serious technical security on here. Your friend knew what he was doing."

"I believe that. Can you crack it?"

"Well, it's not that simple. Basically, he loaded data on this flash drive over a period of several weeks. The first materials were pretty simple to break into. There were military contracts following up on those requests for proposals you mentioned and drawings of some components for robotics equipment for the military. With each file he loaded, his security features became more extreme. I'm peeling through them as I go, but I won't be able to resolve everything all at once. Do you know what he was working on? That may help."

Guilt rose like acid from his throat. "No. He, uh, reached out to me asking for my help with something before he died."

"And what did he say when you talked to him? Anything could be helpful."

"Nothing."

"He called you and wouldn't tell you anything. That's weird."

"I never called him back, all right!" Griffen shouted into the Bluetooth speaker, his fingers white from clenching around his steering wheel.

"Oh, shit man... Well, I guess I don't want to go there. Doesn't matter now. That's all done, right?"

"Right," Griffen blurted out sarcastically.

"You did know him, though, and he knew you. If you really want to figure this out, you have to think, why would he have wanted your help? You don't know robotics or computers."

"No clue. I was hoping his flash drive would tell me."

"Well, he didn't need you for technical shit. He certainly had that covered. Only other thing you're good at is digging up shit other people did and maybe kicking somebody's ass."

"Trey — you're right! Maybe something was going on and he was trying to figure it out."

"Or..."

"Or what?" he growled out.

"Or maybe he was involved in something bad and needed your help to get out of it. You do know some tough dudes and you've disappeared for long periods before."

"No way. Jack was a golden boy, no way. Got it," Griffen said adamantly but he hated that the same thought had invaded his brain.

"Right, sure. Thing is...I was able to open up one pretty interesting file, it was an email that had markers of what I'm pretty sure are the *CMU* server, but sender and recipient are hidden. It's referencing military projects I saw in the contracts I found, but they're broken out and tagged with notations regarding which ones 'the Chinese want.'"

Griffen suddenly felt sick.

"Point is Griff, I think I should go beyond the flash drive, maybe look into..."

"Jack. You want to look into Jack."

"I think we have to. Either way I'm going to keep plugging away and you see what you can figure out over there. Okay?"

"Okay. Do what you gotta do."

"I always do, man."

Althea was watching as the clock on her computer slowly ticked forward. All she could think about was getting down to Oakland to see Griffen. Just the thought of his hands on her again made her feel hot all over. She was starting to wonder if maybe she should just leave when her office phone rang.

After reading the caller ID she answered and said, "Hey David. What's up? I thought you were teaching class today?"

"It's done, I just wanted to check in with you. How are you?"

"Good. You have a doctor's appointment later, don't you?"

"Yeah. Just a lot of the same, I'm sure. More bad news about what the accident did to my body...want to cheer me up after? Maybe have dinner tonight at your place?"

"Oh, that would be nice, but I'm having dinner with Jack's old friend Griffen." *Why do I feel so shy about this?*

"The guy from Johnny's party?"

"Yeah, that's right."

"Why are you having dinner with him? Are you sure he's an okay guy?"

"Calm down, David."

"You know I worry about you is all."

It still touched Althea that David did so much to help her. Even thought it could be cloying at times, he'd always been there for her after Jack died and she couldn't just stonewall him now.

"Griffen's in town for two weeks and he wants to take the time to reconnect with Jack's life."

Dammit, now she was thinking about connecting with Griffen and it was getting her all hot and bothered again.

"Does that mean you'll be spending a lot of time with him?"

"I don't know, maybe, why?"

"Well, what do you really know about him?"

"I know he was a dear friend of Jack's, and that's enough reason for me to get to know him."

"Sorry, it's just Jack was important to me. You and Johnny are important to me, I don't want anyone to take advantage of you."

"Oh, David, you are always so good to me. You know I appreciate it. I promise we'll have coffee soon."

"And dinner, but only once you stop entertaining this interloper, I suppose."

"Oh David, stop. You know you're like family to me, nothing will change that."

"Right, *family*." His tone sounded so much like jealousy that Althea paused.

"David, what's going on?"

"Nothing," he said with a false brightness that didn't fool her, even through the phone. "Have a great day. I'm fine. I'm not going anywhere. Trust me."

She smiled. "Thanks David. Take care!"

"See you soon, bye."

Althea craned her neck up and stared at the *University of Pittsburgh's* Cathedral of Learning, a fierce spire of a building, imposingly reaching to the heavens, piercing the steel gray sky. It was an urban campus right in the heart of the city, barely three miles from her office downtown, but she did everything she could to avoid this whole area.

Fact was being back on Pitt's campus was yet another thing that brought back a flood of memories and feelings of panic for Althea. She walked away from her car and by the grand Carnegie library, catching sight of the eager students spilling out of it, so full of promise with the start of the new school year. They were all blissfully unaware of how precarious — and brutally fragile — life truly was.

Althea's mind went back to that painful last semester after Jack died. She'd buried herself in her studies and law review, all while her belly swelled with baby Johnny. The law school had been kind and sympathetic. Offering to let her take a sabbatical until the next semester, but she'd declined. Even then she suspected that time wouldn't make anything easier or the ache in her body and heart subside.

No, all she felt truly sure of was that work and achievement were the only things that hadn't deserted her. Being driven and wanting to do their very best at everything was one of the aspects of their personalities that she and Jack had shared. Somehow it felt to her like graduating on time, and well, would make him happy — proud of her. So that was what she did. She went back with everyone else after the holidays, managing to avoid the whispers and looks of pity from the other young students with no understanding of what she was going through.

Her heart was still racing, hurting, as she walked onward. *Breathe in, breathe out, breathe in, breathe out,* Althea recited to herself as she walked toward Griffen's office, until she finally pulled herself together.

Before she knew it she was standing in front of a door designated as Professor Stevens' office. She breathed deeply and put on a smile before she knocked. When she opened the door Griffen turned and smiled at her, both dimples showing, and she forgot all about feeling melancholy.

How did he always make her feel lighter? Instead of fixating on the turmoil of her final months at this place, all she could think of was how quickly she could peel the hot, nerdy tweed blazer right off his body.

"Why, Professor Tate, hello."

"Hello to you, Ms. Taylor. Made it for my office hours I see."

"I think I definitely need some individual assistance, I've had this problem all day I just couldn't handle by myself."

Griffen groaned and pulled her into his office. "You're going to get me in trouble Ms. Taylor."

"Hmm, I've never gotten anyone in trouble before. You know, I really am such a good girl," she said emphasizing her big eyes and pouting her lips for full innocent appeal.

"So you say. Well, your recent actions make me question how good your behavior really is."

He pulled her in closely and kissed her until every last negative thought of the day was gone. They were breathing as one and he was sucking on her bottom lip so delightfully that she felt almost dizzy, until she couldn't help but grab his arms and pull away to catch her breath.

She stroked his arms. "Mmm, it's so good to see you. Wait, oh God, are those patches on your elbows?"

"You like them? I thought I'd go all out. You know, do the whole academic look," he said, dramatically stretching his arms and flexing his biceps to show off the jacket to its fullest.

"I like it all very much. I, uh, think you're frying my brain."

"That's the idea, gorgeous." He placed his hands on her hips, spreading his fingertips so they skimmed her ass. Then pulling her into him even more closely, parting her thighs just enough so that his erection rubbed deliciously against her core.

"I have a confession to make," Althea whispered thickly.

"What's that, gorgeous?"

"I've always had a fantasy about, you know, having sex with one of my handsome professors in his office. What do you think that means?"

"Um, well, I'm having a hard time analyzing anything right now after you said that, seeing as all the blood has left my brain." She giggled and loved that his eyes couldn't leave her mouth, until they moved down to stare at the rising and falling of her breasts. "Perhaps you have a thing about giving into authority."

"Hmm, maybe."

"I think it's very healthy to act on these kinds of urges, you know, for your personal growth."

"I feel your personal growth right now. What does that mean?" she asked, rubbing herself teasingly against him.

He smiled and shook his head, appearing to make a decision about something. Quickly, he schooled his face into a serious scowl. He stepped away from her and walked across the office to a small chalkboard, grabbing a long wooden pointer from the metal tray at the bottom.

Flexing the wood slightly in his hands as he turned to look at her, Griffen said, "Ms. Taylor. I was extremely disappointed in your recent exam. It seems to me that you're not focused on applying all of your talents to me — or my class. I have no choice but to fail you."

"Oh no Professor Tate! I can't fail your class. I'll lose my scholarship. I need that scholarship. I'll do *anything* to keep it." He turned to her as she placed a hand dramatically on her chest.

"Well, I never offer extra credit, but..."

"Oh please..."

He slammed the desk with the pointer and she jumped. "Do *not* interrupt me Ms. Taylor. You're already treading on thin ice as it is."

She looked down, to stay with the moment, but also to hide the delicious grin that was spreading across her face.

"Of course. I'm so very sorry, Professor Tate."

He approached her and looked down into her eyes, making the most of his impressive height.

"What I was trying to say, before you so rudely interrupted me, Ms. Taylor, was that I never give extra credit, but I feel that I may be willing to make a special exception in your circumstance. Since you are so desperate and you do have so many skills you've not had a chance to bring to bear in my class." He placed a long finger into the V-neck of her shirt and pulled down ever so slightly until Althea's heart quickened. "It seems only fair that I give you the opportunity to show me what you can really do."

"Oh yes, Professor Tate. Whatever you think is best."

"Excellent. We'll begin the extra credit now."

"Now? Here, Professor Tate?"

"Oh yes, Ms. Taylor." He stepped back. "Lock my office door." She blinked at him deliberately. "*Now*, Ms. Taylor."

She scurried over and locked the door, stepping back in front of him.

"Good. Now turn and grab the edge of my desk." She swallowed and did as he said. "Well done. Now pull up your skirt for me," he commanded, running the pointer slowly up one leg and underneath her skirt, lifting it up, until she trembled in response.

Althea was so turned on she started to yank her skirt up. "Eh, eh, slowly," he growled, correcting her with a light swat of the pointer against her clothed bottom sending tingling sensations throughout her body. She slowed her movements and wiggled her hips with each swipe of the fabric up her skin. "Much better. I'm glad that you can finally take some instruction, Ms. Taylor. Now lean forward. Deeper. Do as I say or I will force you to bend deeper myself. There you go, that's better. Perfect."

Althea couldn't see him but she felt the pointer rubbing across one cheek, then the other, until it moved between her legs.

"Spread your legs, Ms. Taylor. Excellent. Now, touch yourself where you want me to touch you." Althea's hands trembled. She'd never touched herself in front of someone else, not even Jack. The pointer slammed on the desk hard. "What did I tell you to do, Ms. Taylor? Answer me or this extra credit opportunity will stop right now."

"Y-you told me to touch myself where I want you to touch me."

"And why am I still waiting, Ms. Taylor?" he whispered in her ear hotly, his voice taut with tension and his whole body bent over her back from behind.

Despite his complete control over her in this moment, she could feel his erection pressing into her and his breath quickening. It drove her even crazier to know that this most private fantasy of hers was turning him on, too.

He stood and she immediately missed his masculine warmth as he stepped away from her. Terrified that he would stop this delicious torture, Althea became bold, bending over more fully so that her ass was completely in the air as she touched her warm center, making sure that he could see every desperate stroke.

"Much better Ms. Taylor. I knew you could be a good student." Althea felt the cool tip of the pointer against her bottom again. "Spread your cheeks with your hands, so that I can see you better. Ah, perfect. Such a good girl. Now touch yourself faster. Are you wet for me, Ms. Taylor?"

"Y-yes," she stammered out, feeling her clitoris hot and swollen beneath her rapidly moving fingers. She heard him grunt out a curse from behind her.

"Very good. Are you going to come Ms. Taylor?" he rasped.

"I'm close, so close," she whimpered.

"Don't come yet. If you come there will be consequences," he warned as he rubbed the pointer up and down the side of her leg slowly.

She was so wet and close to release that she had to breathe steadily until she could calm down and keep from coming as he'd instructed.

"Better, Ms. Taylor, such a good student. I knew I was right to have faith in you." She started to turn to him to enjoy the praise until the pointer struck on the desk next to her again. "No, no, no. Just when you were doing so well. Look forward, Ms. Taylor. Now," he growled.

She did as he said but found herself so desperate to see his face and to feel him touch her that it was almost unbearable. Before she could stop it, a soft whimper escaped her throat. Suddenly his body was close to hers again, draped across her from behind.

"Do you need me to touch you Ms. Taylor?" he whispered gently in her ear, rubbing his nose against the lobe for a brief instant and the shock of tenderness made her heart turn over.

"Yes Professor Tate. I need it so badly, please."

He hummed in approval and licked slowly up her neck to her ear as he pressed his firm erection against her bottom. She could feel his heart beating quickly — almost pounding — in his chest making her even more desperate for his fervent touch, until he finally said, "Perfect, you are such a very good girl, after all. You've made me very pleased. Now, hands on the other end of the desk."

He grabbed her hands and scolded her, "Tsk, tsk, your fingers are so messy, Ms. Taylor. We can't have that." He brought her hand to his lips and torturously teased her as he licked her juices off of each of her now shaking fingers. A deep groan rumbled in his throat. "Much better."

Each pull of his warm mouth had caused her center to clinch in delicious agony. Griffen pulled her hands forward and wrapped her fingers around the far edge of the desk. Her hot cheek was pressed against a cool manila folder placed on top of it. He had her so crazed that she was writhing back against him, craving the relief only he could give her.

She gripped the wooden edge of the desk, blindly registering the friction he caused as he ran his body down her back until she felt his breath against her ass. Griffen grabbed her bottom and licked deliciously across one cheek, until he bit her through the silk of her panties and she yelped.

"These won't do, Ms. Taylor. If you were a truly good student you'd know not to wear panties during my office hours." She felt his hot, rapid breath against her as he tugged hard on her panties until they tore away, leaving her ass bare.

Griffen bit her other cheek, now that her skin was exposed, but this time she groaned. He licked further down until his tongue entered her and she spasmed warmly around it.

He pulled back. "Very responsive. I appreciate an attentive student." She felt his fingers stroke her where she had just touched herself and enter her while his tongue charted a path that was simply incredible — made all the more intense because she couldn't see what he was doing. He didn't let up until she was coming strongly against his mouth and hand. He stood and ordered, "Release your hands."

She did so and they felt numb after she'd gripped the wooden edge so tightly. Before she could flex her fingers, he'd spun her around so her ass was on the desk.

"Remove your shirt and bra Ms. Taylor." She obeyed and groaned as he took one breast in his mouth, then the other. He looked up at her, his hair falling across his forehead as he smiled wickedly around the nipple firmly pressed between his teeth. Althea closed her eyes in ecstasy and instinctively pushed her breast more fully against his face.

She felt Griffen replace his two fingers inside her, stroking her back into a frenzy. After a moment he slowly removed his fingers from inside her and she whimpered again. "Don't worry Ms. Taylor, it's time for your gold star. I am quite impressed with you. Look at me. Now."

She'd barely opened her eyes when she saw the condom wrapper flutter to the ground from his fingers and Griffen was fully inside of her in an instant.

He lifted her right leg so that her knee was grazing her chest, letting him press into her ever so deeply. Her skirt was crumpled around her waist and every part of her loved the rubbing of flesh and fabric against one another. He thrust hard and fast — just like she needed it — until she came so powerfully that she shook as she pulsated around him.

He grunted as he let go and rested his head in the crook of her neck to compose himself. He straightened and looked down at her. Still deep inside her as he softened. He kissed her softly then pulled on her bottom lip, whispering, "Now, thank me for your exemplary lesson."

Althea stroked the suede patches on his arms and said, "Thank you for the extra credit Professor Tate. Did I do okay?"

"You did very well," he said with a devious half grin, "now you are at a 'C' grade."

"A 'C,' Professor Tate?" she pouted.

"No need for concern," he said in a cocky voice as he ran a finger underneath one breast, then the other until Althea's heart started racing all over again. "I think I can come up with lots more extra credit to help you keep making up the difference."

"Absolutely," she answered, straightening her back and looking at him seriously," I won't stop until I have an 'A+.' I take my performance very seriously."

Griffen laughed and leaned down to wrap his arms tightly around her waist. "Althea, you're full of surprises. That was amazing. *You're* amazing."

"You're not so bad yourself, stud," she said with a grin.

Griffen was pulling himself back together — both mentally and sartorially — after Althea's smoking hot game, when she teased, "This is one fancy office, I must say." She then sarcastically ran a finger across the rough wooden desk beneath her bottom and held up a finger covered in dust.

"The best. After what we just did, I'm glad I hadn't gotten to putting too much stuff on my desk."

"Oh yeah, good thinking."

She began to smooth her sexily rumpled hair down, but Griffen took over, running his fingers through her hair repeatedly.

"Careful, Griffen, you may lose a hand in there," she said with a smirk.

"Fine by me. I love your hair. There's so much of it, too."

"You should try blow-drying it, stud."

"Is that another one of your fantasies?" he asked.

"No, it just seems like a good test of how strong these massive biceps of yours really are. Though you may get tennis elbow from all that exertion," she teased, trailing her nails down the ripples of his arms until he groaned and had to kiss her.

"Mmm," she moaned when they came up for air, "so, tell me, how was class today?"

"It was good. They mostly wanted to hear about my books and how they got to be movies, but I did try to teach them something actually helpful."

"I'm sure you were great." She put her bra back on and he felt a pang of sadness at no longer getting to stare at her perfect bare breasts.

He forced himself to look at her eyes, chiding himself that every time he was around Althea he acted like a horny teenager. "I could never do justice to Professor Stevens' classes. He is the best teacher I've ever met."

"Oh, I'm sure he appreciates the chance to rest more and that students got a great opportunity to meet a real writer," she said, wrapping her arms around his neck and kissing him soundly. "What is the university going to do about his classes after you leave?"

"Mmm, what?" he murmured. She then giggled and moved on to kissing him lightly on his neck. "I'm not sure. They'll have to think of something because I think by the end of two weeks I'll have had my fill of being back in this damn city."

Her eyes widened, "Wow, I didn't know you hated it here *that* much."

Griffen pulled her close again, "I have my reasons for hating this place. It's not the city so much as what it represents to me."

"Is it because of your dad?" Griffen's jaw clenched and

Althea swallowed nervously. "Uh, Carol said he was a bad guy and you said as much, too, and I recognize the look — mine wouldn't exactly win any father of the year awards, either. I'm babbling again, it's none of my business, sorry."

"No, don't be. I'm constantly dragging stuff out of you. I guess it's only fair I let you ask a question or two," he said with a smile. "Yeah, my dad is the reason for a lot of how fucked up I am about many things, including getting hives thinking about coming back here. And there are...other reasons." Griffen swallowed at the thought of how he'd let her husband down so terribly — that he may have contributed to her becoming a widow by being such a self-absorbed prick.

She looked at him worriedly, "Griffen, are you okay?"

He swallowed and replaced his signature cocky grin back on his face. "Absolutely, gorgeous, but you're making this time here way more bearable."

More than bearable, he thought.

In fact, more and more, his hatred of the idea of leaving her was overtaking his discomfort at being home.

"Bearable, huh? Don't pump my ego up too much, stud," she said teasingly.

"Trust me, our time together is awesome. Anyway, I think Stevens is planning to be better by then. Not that you can control that."

"No, you can't. That's true. Just like Javier Jimenez couldn't control Cade Jackson from bringing down his cartel single-handedly in *Bloody Tequila Sunrise*."

He pulled back from her intoxicating little feather kisses and asked, "You read one of my books? Not just the jacket?"

"Yep. I was curious."

"What did you think?"

"It was...thrilling," she smirked.

"That *is* what they tell me."

She leaned back and looked in his eyes. "When did you decide to become a writer?"

"I wrote for as long as I can remember. I was always an observer, my whole life. I don't know if it was a choice or a dream. I never said — '*this is what I want to do.*' It was simply what I had to do. I actually figured I could never do it publicly."

"Why not?"

"I had to hide my writing from my dad for years. He said it was weak, so as soon as he was dead and I was free, in college, I made my choice and that choice was running around the world instead of on a football field and I kept on writing."

"Did you always write stuff that was so...um..."

He laughed, "Not a fan of action-adventures?"

"No, it really was exciting, actually, just not very..."

"You can start breathing again Althea, you won't offend me. I know my books aren't too deep. Cade Jackson isn't exactly Holden Caulfield. I know that. When I was young, writing was my escape. Jack and I would make up these adventure stories out loud and then I'd write them down. We did it in my backyard but then..."

"What?"

"Then we stopped. Now, tell me, why'd you pick that one?" He swallowed and ran a finger down her arm. He took a step forward, leaned in and licked gently across her lips until she moaned.

"I. Uh, oh God. It was the most recent one I could find, but it was a few years old. I couldn't find anything newer."

"That's it. Just two books." He leaned over and nibbled right below her earlobe.

"Wait, how many years is that?"

He swallowed, "My second book came out five years ago. I'd stopped writing several months before that."

"So if you don't write, what have you done with yourself all these years? Maybe working on your perfect shaggy author hair?" she teased rubbing her fingers through his wavy soft hair that had fallen across his forehead.

"A lot of that, I guess," he laughed. "If you like the hair then it was worth it. Other than that, I have obligations to promote all that Cade Jackson crap. I've traveled around and consulted on some investigations for other journalists — but no writing of my own."

"What about people? Relationships, attachments?"

"Not much of those either. I don't think I'd be very good at them. I've never really had a relationship that lasted longer than a couple weeks. Must sound weird to you, huh?"

"I'll say! My life has *only* been work and attachments. That makes you and this arrangement perfect for me, though, right?"

"Right." He kissed her again but felt a pang in his chest that was becoming all too familiar whenever she reminded him of their expiration date.

"But you're so successful as a writer. Doesn't your publisher or fans want you to write more?"

He licked a trail from her cleavage all the way to her other earlobe. "Oh yeah, gorgeous, they definitely want me to write another book."

"So, are you? Writing another book, I mean."

He straightened and looked in her eyes seriously, "My agent and publisher are hungry for more installments but I've felt disconnected, uninspired for a while now." *That inspiration died with Jack it seemed. Gone was the friend who helped me escape by weaving elaborate stories where the hero was strong and always won.* "But

I've actually started writing a new book. I guess being home has stirred up all kinds of things in me, including inspiration," Griffen continued.

"That's wonderful! What's it about?"

Oh no, not going there. The last thing in the world she needs to know right now is what my book is about. If she learned what I found of Jack's, my darkest suspicions that Jack may have sold military secrets in his last days — it would break her heart. No telling her until I know the whole truth.

"Well, this one is actually deeper, more personal."

"Come on, now I *have* to know what it's about!"

"Uh, it's still a secret and besides I'm a little shy when I'm in the early stages of a book."

"You, shy? I find that hard to believe."

"Oh, I can be shy."

"Show me your best shy face." He turned his head down and looked up at her with big puppy dog eyes and slightly pouty lips, his hair flopping across his forehead. "Come on. That's not shy, that's just a sexy face."

"That works too," he said and grabbed her, pulling his pelvis to her center.

"Well, now I'm all distracted."

"Good, I like you distracted. You need to turn off that big brain of yours once in a while," he said and kissed her hard. He pulled back, letting his hands linger on her waist as he stood between her legs. She sighed and he asked, "So, did you do anything exciting today, baby? I mean other than me?"

Althea slapped his shoulder but couldn't help laughing. "Not really. I talked to David. He wanted to have dinner but I said no."

"Because you want to have dinner with me, gorgeous?"

"Well, uh."

"Hey," he said pulling her back close to him. "Of course I want to have dinner with you and spend the evening with you. That's why I asked you to meet me here."

"Are you sure? I didn't know if you wanted this to be all, you know..."

"Sex?"

"Right."

"Althea, we had dinner the last two nights."

"Yeah, but I asked you, those times. I just assumed because you asked me, and, argh," she hid her face behind her hands.

Griffen pulled them away, kissing each palm, before saying, "I want to spend as much time with you while I'm here as you'll let me. Yes, sex with you is great, but I do enjoy just being with you."

"Good, well now I'm really glad I said no to David," she smiled and kissed his nose. "I think David was hurt I said no, though. I haven't been giving him much attention lately."

Griffen felt a knot of jealousy rush through him at the memory of how David looked at Althea at Johnny's birthday party, but quickly shoved it down. He was in no place to get possessive, even though he felt the urge coursing through his veins. Besides, David was a good ten years older than Althea and she clearly did not return his affections. "Oh yeah? Well, since you had to let down a friend, I'd better take you somewhere great. Is Johnny all right if I take you out tonight?"

"Yes. He's with Carol tonight. She likes to have him spend the night at least one night a week. I try to let her be with him nights that she's not working at *Viola* so she won't get lonely or sad in that big house by herself."

"Okay, how about we go to Silver?"

"Oh wow, I read about that place in Bon Appétit! I've tried to go for months. But it takes forever to get in there and I can't go dressed like this," Althea said pointing to her clothes.

Griffen leaned over and kissed the corner of her mouth. "You look beautiful, as always, and come on, it's Pittsburgh, a fancy restaurant just means you need to pull out your dress Pittsburgh football jersey."

"Ha ha, that doesn't change that we won't be able to get in."

"I'm old friends with the owner from high school. Don't worry."

"For someone that left over ten years ago you sure know a lot of people."

"Pittsburgh's a small town dressed up like a big city. I'm starting to realize that when this is your hometown, you never really leave it."

"I get that. I'm so far from where I grew up, but I can't imagine leaving." Her smile dropped and Griffen squeezed in closer. He was starting to read her well enough to know when she was about to shut down, so he asked her something to keep her in the moment with him. "I was wondering about that actually. Why didn't you leave Pittsburgh after Jack died? You don't have family here. Are Jenna and Aubrey from here?"

"No, they aren't. They moved here for me."

"Wow."

"I know. I really shut down after Jack died. My life was work and Johnny. Work was the only thing I allowed myself to do separately from Johnny. His mother helped and David came around all the time, but I cut out anything that didn't directly relate to my memories of Jack. Even with all those sacrifices, I was so lonely and overwhelmed. The girls gave me some space for a while, but when opportunities came along that let them move here, they did."

"That's pretty awesome of them."

"Well, for Jenna it was no hardship. The sports medicine and orthopedic surgery groups here are some of the best in the world, and Aubrey can be a freelance photographer anywhere. She does a lot for the local magazines but she travels all around the world for shoots."

Althea glanced down for a minute and paused. When she looked up again and her eyes met his they were wet with tears. "I was lost when Jack died. Totally lost. And without them — Carol, Jenna, Aubrey, David — I don't know..." Althea breathed deeply and Griffen could hear the catch in her throat. "Point is — if it takes a village, they're the folks in my village." She paused and he watched her chest rise and fall as she regained her composure. "So, are you gonna go wine and dine me now or what?"

"You better believe it gorgeous," and he couldn't deny how warm it made him feel that he was the reason a huge smile spread across her face.

As she grabbed her purse and finished pulling down her skirt she asked with a pout, "Will it be a problem that I'm not wearing panties at dinner, Professor Tate?"

He groaned and smacked her waiting bottom soundly.

She inhaled deeply when he brushed her hair from her neck and whispered in her ear, "No problem at all Ms. Taylor. Maybe you can get some extra credit under the table while we're there."

With a nip he opened the door for her, but he was pleased to hear that now *she* was the one groaning.

CHAPTER ELEVEN

The remainder of the week together flew by and it was Saturday night before they knew it. Althea and Griffen had fallen into a nice almost routine. Griffen would come by after he was done with his classes and writing for the day. Then he would help Althea with dinner and practice football with Johnny and whichever of his friends that wanted to play with his cool "Uncle Gwiff" that day.

Griffen was even coaching Johnny's local youth football team. They would eat together, read to Johnny and tuck him in. Then she and Griffen would make love, talk, laugh, and enjoy each other's company. Althea was loving this time they had together and doing all she could not to think about how much it highlighted her own loneliness during the last several years.

Johnny was changing into his pajamas so Griffen took the opportunity to slide his hands around Althea's waist, pulling her in close so her back was flush with his chest. She sighed and curled her head back toward him so he could brush aside her hair and kiss along her neck until she shivered.

"Mmm," he groaned. "I should back off or I'm going to

have a raging hard-on I can't do anything about during dinner."

She turned and smirked. "Serves you right for getting me all worked up."

"Don't I always have that affect on you?" he asked, stroking her neck again and rubbing his thumb across her jawline. As his other hand gripped her hip, his fingers traced figure eights across the fabric of her pencil skirt. He loved her sexy librarian work clothes and she was more than happy to oblige — adding stockings, garters and sexy underwear underneath to drive him extra crazy.

"Cocky bastard."

"Only for you," he whispered and turned her face to his to kiss her. Pulling away he looked over her shoulder. "What's for dinner?"

"Mac and cheese and broccoli for Johnny. Moussaka for us."

"Mac and cheese huh? Where's the box? I need to know if you're a Kraft or Velveeta woman."

She scoffed and let her latent southern accent come through. "Damn Yankee. *Boxed mac and cheese? Blasphemy!* I'll have you know I'm a good North Carolina bred woman. No boxes for our macaroni and cheese. It's in the oven bubblin' with buttah and cheddah right now."

"Holy shit woman, that accent is sexy. Now I'm definitely going to need a cold shower before dinner." She laughed and slapped his hand as he reached over to finger a bite of the cooling Moussaka.

"Now, even this Yankee knows that's not southern," Griffen said confidently.

"No. I went to the farmers market at the courthouse after my hearing yesterday. They had eggplants and local lamb. I couldn't resist. I also got fresh berries for a cobbler. That's bubblin' in there real good, too, sugar," she said with a saucy wink and loved the deep groan that came from his throat in response. She was thrilled she'd treated herself to the stop before going back to work. Normally she would have simply hurried back to the office, rushing past the geriatric tour group taking a historic Segway ride around downtown, rather than relaxing to enjoy a moment at a farmer's market.

"Good. Afterward I'll make sure you don't resist me," his cheesy line broke through her thoughts.

She groaned happily, "Nice line stud."

"I'm so hurt. I honestly don't want you to resist me."

"Oh, I believe that. Like I ever could," she teased with batting eyelashes.

"Uncle Gwiff?"

She jumped a bit. They weren't touching but they were close and she quickly skittered away to check on the oven. Griffen's scowl wasn't lost on her as he said, "Hey big man. What's up?"

"Yo mommy…"

"Yo Johnny," Althea answered, averting Griffen's icy gaze on her.

"Uncle Gwiff wants to teach me and Chwis pway action passing."

"In your pajamas?"

"Yep." Johnny grinned at her.

"Put your sneakers on then."

"Okay mommy. So, we'll see ya later! Come on Gwiff." He ran outside and Althea looked back at Griffen.

"Thanks for playing football with him. I would probably break my neck," she said softly, feeling guilty about pushing him away just moments before.

"I love it," he said with a smile, though she could tell it was forced. "It's fun to get to show off all my mad skeelz," his words were light but his eyes still looked guarded.

Althea kissed his cheek and whispered, "All right all star. But I do appreciate it, I mean, the football, playing catch, teaching him how to fish this morning. Sometimes I wonder if Johnny is missing out being raised by a gaggle of women, so I really am grateful."

"I'm happy to do it."

She looked out the window and saw Johnny out back getting ready to knock over Chris and added, "Um, coach, I thought they weren't really supposed to tackle each other? Why don't you get out there before he knocks out his best friend. I'll finish dinner."

He pulled her tightly to him so she was pressed against him and said, "Sounds good, but since we're alone again..." He leaned forward and kissed her neck slowly when his phone buzzed. Althea turned to see him look at the screen and his face closed off suddenly, becoming fraught with tension.

"Griffen, what is it?"

"It's, uh, nothing, just something about my book." He turned to her, "I need to take this, then I'll be right out to help Johnny, okay?" he said on a swallow.

Althea watched as he walked away, suddenly feeling a sense of anxiety she couldn't place. This was just one of many times a call or a text to Griffen had interrupted them. Each time it would change his mood and he would either leave to deal with it or be closed off for the next several minutes. It was a constant reminder that she knew so little about this man.

Is he hiding something? Is that a girlfriend or something? No, Aubrey would have read about something like that — his whole life is on the internet. You're just paranoid after Jack's secrets. She knew he was *definitely a playboy when he wasn't with her, but she felt confident he was honest when he said he wasn't attached to anyone. The calls were upsetting to him, but she didn't know why.*

Althea tried to shake her unease, but to no avail.

All the more reason not to fall too deeply into this. Stick with the plan, she reminded herself.

"Trey, what's up? What have you found?" he whispered as he walked out of earshot of Althea.

"I unlocked a file of some handwritten notes that were saved about a week before Jack died."

"What? Like they were scanned? Why not just keep the hard copies?"

"Hard copies are dangerous, just more to be found or lost. Jack clearly wanted everything together."

"What do they say?"

"They're of more military contracts with those same kind of notations indicating that there were specific ones the Chinese wanted. But on these there's also amounts of money written down in Chinese Yuan, with different amounts for specs, versus full coding and robotics plans. Check your email and see if you can tell me if you recognize the handwriting."

"Sure, give me a minute. I'll check it out and call you back."

He hung up and quietly walked through the house. When he arrived to the study, he yanked open some drawers and looked in the closet. Finally, he landed on a shoebox of cards Jack had sent Althea. His heart twisted at the words of love and devotion. On a swallow he opened Trey's email on his phone, quickly looking at the downloaded attachment when his heart sank. The handwriting was clearly Jack's.

He replaced the card and closed the closet door, his heart rate racing into his throat.

"Griffen?"

He jumped, turning to see Althea.

"What are you doing in here? Are you done with your call?"

"I was just looking for a pen. I need to write down a note from my publisher." The lie burned his tongue.

"Okay, well, help yourself. Johnny's getting anxious, though."

"You got it," he answered on a swallow as he tried to avoid her suspicious gaze.

They were cleaning up the dishes after putting Johnny to bed and Althea couldn't resist asking, "Griffen, did your call before dinner go okay? It seems like you've gotten a lot of calls that made you upset. Is there something wrong with your publisher?"

"It's nothing you need to worry about."

"Griffen, are you hiding something from me? You know how much I hate secrets."

"Of course not. I told you. It's just annoying book stuff. The early stages can be intense." Despite his reassuring words, his muscles stiffened against her. This deflection was all too familiar to her and Althea felt overwhelming anxiety begin to course throughout her body.

She'd allowed herself to be so comfortable and at ease when she was with Griffen after barely a week together, but she needed to remind herself every day that this was temporary and that's the way she wanted it. The whole point was to enjoy herself while keeping her heart distant. Fixating on his every move wasn't going to accomplish that.

There was no denying how happy he'd made her but her instincts told her to keep everything in perspective, especially when so much of his life was closed off from her. For all she knew, he had multiple no-strings-attached arrangements waiting for him back in New York. She bit her lip in a surprisingly melancholy reflection at the thought.

Griffen put down his drying towel and wrapped his arms around her waist.

"Forget about my book. It's a long weekend. What should we do? Want to take Johnny to *Sandcastle Water Park* or something outside the city — a hayride, maybe? Or we could just relax."

Althea tried to get back to enjoying the moment. "Hmm, good ideas, but Carol hosts a Labor Day picnic on the Sunday before every year. It's pretty epic, you should come and bring your mom."

"Will you be there, gorgeous?"

"Of course."

"Then I will definitely go," he said with a kiss on her nose. "When should I pick you up?"

"Um, maybe you should come with your mom. Wouldn't that make her more comfortable?"

He gritted his teeth and let go of her waist. "Don't you mean make *you* more comfortable?"

"Griffen, please. You know I can't show up to *Carol's* party with you."

"No, you're right. This is the deal I agreed to." But his jaw twitched as he looked away.

She leaned over and kissed his neck. "That's right. You're leaving in a week, let's not spoil our fun, okay? Why don't we go to bed? That's the part of the deal we both like," she said with a smile and reached down to stroke him through his jeans.

"I know what you're doing, gorgeous," he warned, but smiled and kissed her deeply. "Lucky for you it's working."

They'd made love again and the moonlight was shining beautifully against Althea's skin until Griffen couldn't resist kissing every spot the moon had caressed before him.

"Mmm, that's nice. This week's been so much fun. You're making me wonder why I didn't do this sooner."

He nibbled a shoulder. "You were waiting for me, right? Come on, stroke my ego."

"Your ego is perfectly fine and I've stroked you quite a bit tonight as I recall."

"Indeed." He suckled a breast and looked up at her. "Althea?"

"Mmm hmm," she said sleepily.

"I've been wondering, why has it been so hard for you to move on?" He lay on his side and pulled her to him. Playing with her hair as she clearly thought of the words she wanted to use.

"I loved Jack very much and when he died I found out right away that I was pregnant and I was so young and scared. I think that delayed any meaningful grief."

"But what about later?" he asked. "Are you afraid of losing someone else?"

"Of course I fear loving and losing again. All widows feel that. I also feel so guilty about how he died, like I should have prevented it."

"How? It was a car accident you weren't even in the car."

"Yes, but you know how controlled Jack was, how steady he always was." She hesitated. "For a couple weeks before the crash he was incredibly agitated, acting distant, not like himself. I asked him what was going on, what was wrong, but he said he had it under control, that he had wrapped up the issue. He died that night."

"That can't be your fault Althea."

"Of course it was. I let him keep putting me off and just accepted his excuses. Maybe I was happier taking no for an answer. It was easier that way. I was so young, too focused on myself and my career that I let myself believe it when he said he was okay."

Griffen swallowed. He needed her to keep talking. He did care about helping her break free of these feelings but he also needed information. His entire investigation was pointing to Jack's guilt and it was time he asked her the tough questions.

"Was it something at work? What was he working on? Anything intense?"

"His robotics work you mean?"

"Yeah."

"Well, he was staying at his office really late. I thought it may be what he was working on, but he was doing pretty light stuff. I mean it was challenging, but it was technology for making 3D maps more accurate. It wasn't exactly high pressure."

"I thought *CMU* robotics got a big defense contract around that time?" The military contracts with *CMU* on Jack's hard drive were some serious shit — way more sensitive than 3D maps.

"Oh no, he and David weren't working on that. He was David's research assistant and pretty much worked on whatever was on his plate."

"David didn't get military assignments?"

"No. David's really talented, but he and Jack weren't on those. Jack probably could've moved on to more high profile stuff but he felt he owed David. He'd done so much for him after Jack's dad died."

"So if it wasn't what he was working on, what was it?"

She started to cry softly and he pulled her in close to his chest, stroking her hair. "I don't know. I chose not to push, thinking everything would pass. It just got worse."

"How so?"

"The night he died, the police said he was driving home late at night. He lost control and drove over the edge into the Allegheny River," she whispered.

"How could he drive into the river?"

"We lived right along the Allegheny River in this condo overlooking the bank. You could take a service road shortcut. It was late and the weather was awful. Someone saw the car lose control on the ice and drive into the river and called the police."

"Do you know who made the call?"

"No. It was anonymous. The police said it was from a pay phone nearby. That was back when pay phones still existed. They said it was common — people are partying by the river and want to help but don't want to get involved with the cops. The conditions were really bad that night, but more importantly..." She breathed in deeply. "The toxicology report found there was Vicodin in his system. A lot of it. I never knew him ever to mess with that stuff."

"That wasn't in the reports I read," Griffen grunted as his arms tightened around her. *Drugs will also make you desperate enough to do just about anything, even steal.* He breathed through his guilt and suspicions, bringing his heart rate down.

"No, it wasn't. Carol had a friend on the force. He helped to keep it quiet. I didn't find out until later, from Carol. He died and I didn't prevent it. It was my selfishness that killed him."

He moved her face to his and kissed her. "Stop that, now. It wasn't your fault."

"But I was his wife, his best friend. I was supposed to be his rock, was supposed to support him. That's what Carol thinks, too."

"*What?*"

"She blamed me for not recognizing he was on drugs or stopping it. She was right."

"No, she wasn't. It wasn't your fault!" Griffen swallowed hard and took her hand and made a gentle circle with his thumb in her palm. Griffen hated to push her, but he needed to know more. "Were you guys having any money problems?"

"Um, well, we had been. My scholarship got cut with budget shortfalls and I was having trouble getting a good loan in time — especially with our maxed out credit cards. But Jack said he had it under control. And he did. A week before he died he told me he got a big bonus, so it wasn't money he was worried about."

"Do you know how he got the money?"

"Griffen, this is getting a little personal. Why do you need to know that?"

"Uh, sorry, I just want to understand what you were going through." He tried to dial down the inquisition before she got too suspicious.

"Oh, well, okay. Point was he was dealing with *something*. I wish he would have trusted me with it. He was so protective of me, always making sure I ate, put on sunscreen, had a safe car, didn't drive fast. He was terrified of worrying me and I was so honest with him, but he wasn't honest with me when it counted the most."

"Are you angry at him?"

Althea blanched, "I can't be angry with him, he's gone."

"Just because he's gone, doesn't mean you can't resent that he wasn't open with you." Griffen swallowed, recognizing how much he was keeping from her himself.

"I guess. I just can't let myself go there. I feel like being angry or disappointed with him would hurt what we had."

"So you just blame yourself? That doesn't seem fair. Don't you think you should let those feelings go? You know the guilt, the regret."

"Without the guilt and loss, I don't know what I have left."

Griffen's heart seized in his chest and he held her so tightly he worried he may crack one of her ribs.

He breathed slowly until he calmed down a bit and was able to loosen his hold. Deciding it was best to change the subject, he ordered, "You know, the best thing we can do for Jack is to be happy, to remember when he was happy. Only fun memories. Shake on it."

Althea playfully shook his hand and his heart squeezed at the sight of her brave smile.

"Deal," she giggled out.

"You go first. Good Jack memory. Now."

She laughed, "Uh, okay. Jack was obsessed with lemon juice. Not fresh squeezed or anything, but the big bottles of reconstituted grossness, like you get at *Costco*."

"Ugh, yes! He would mix it with Captain Morgan. He acted like it was some kind of great cocktail. Tasted worse coming back up. Trust me."

"Yes! He tried to make me drink one of those once. No way! And he would make 'lemon chicken' with it. So awful."

"Come on, gorgeous, you were lucky. By the time he was with you I'm sure he'd fine-tuned the recipe. I was his guinea pig with that shit. He didn't inherit whatever cooking gene Baxter got."

"No definitely not."

"Hey, what's Baxter up to? He was just a little kid the last time I saw him."

"Oh, he's quite the player. When he's not chasing girls, he's training to be a chef and he got a business degree in undergrad so he can run *Viola*. That can't come soon enough." And with that they snuggled and talked of happier things late into the night.

CHAPTER TWELVE

Griffen arrived at Schenley Park for Carol's picnic with his mother. As he opened the door for her, she craned her neck behind her. "She's really quite lovely."

"What?" Griffen hadn't even realized he was already staring at Althea over his mother's shoulder. Apparently he had no control over any part of himself when she was nearby.

"You're spending a lot of time with her, aren't you?"

"Mom, stop."

"Look, honey, no one knows better than me what Jack did for you." Her voice lowered, "What he meant to you. Is that what this is about?"

"No. Dammit. I don't know. Yeah, it's about Jack. Or it was," Griffen rubbed his neck, walking away from her.

"I see the way you look at her. You've never looked at anyone like that before. What's happening with you two?"

"Mom, I have no idea."

"You don't always have to know what's going to happen. Sometimes you can just fall."

"Like you did with Dad?" Griffen cringed when he saw her face twist.

"Oh, Griffen, you know I wish I'd stopped him sooner."

"So do I," he groaned. "But neither of us was strong enough, were we? Jack saved us. Now I'm hung up on his wife, so everything's pretty messed up, I guess," Griffen grunted, kicking a tire.

"Stop it. You're just looking for a reason to mess this up. Maybe you two need each other, you asshole."

"Mom, you never curse."

"Yeah, well, I'm a little sick of watching you be unhappy. You've been completely lost since Jack died. Maybe you need each other because he died, but that doesn't change the fact that you may love each other."

Her words twisted his insides. "I can't stand being away from her. I know that."

"So stay. Be with her a while longer."

Griffen's heart fluttered at the thought, then it sank right back into his stomach.

"Doubt she'd go for it. She's been pretty clear she doesn't want me to stick around. I guess that's only fair, right? I finally want to try for something with a woman and she's already got my bags packed for me."

"You can be very persuasive, honey. Maybe you shouldn't give up so easily."

"Maybe. How about we stick with going to the picnic for now?"

"Sure, dear," she said slowly.

They walked toward the crowd and he felt his jaw tic when he saw David hovering over Althea possessively. David looked up and jealousy flared in his eyes when they landed on Griffen. David gave him a self-satisfied smirk as he placed a hand on Althea's lower back, steering her back over to the food.

Griffen felt his hands clench into fists, wishing he could grab this woman and kiss her firmly until the whole world knew she was his. Instead he simply tried to calm his breathing, his nostrils flaring.

Going full Neanderthal at her family picnic because she was being friendly to her dead husband's former boss wasn't going to help him gain any favor with her. Particularly since she clearly credited David with helping her through many hard years when Griffen hadn't even been in her life.

His mother walked up behind him, hefting a pastry carrier full of cookies when she followed his line of sight. "Humph. You're fine with just walking away, huh? *Right*."

"Mom," Griffen said in a warning tone.

"Here," she smiled, thrusting the cookies into his hand. "Get those over to the food table. Maybe Althea could use some help with something."

"You got it, Mom. I do aim to help."

"Good boy. Now get over there before someone else monopolizes her time that's not you." Griffen couldn't help but smile. He knew his mom could tell he was twisted in knots over this woman. He strode over to the table, decked out in every picnic treat and type of dessert imaginable. Althea turned and saw him and her answering smile immediately made him feel lighter.

"Hi Griffen," she said, clearly trying to seem casual, but he was thrilled to see the spark of desire and excitement that flashed across her beautiful eyes at seeing him. The sun was illuminating her hair to a warm, golden fire, matched by the golden flecks in her eyes.

He stepped forward, placing the cookies down on the table, making sure to break the connection between her and

David, brushing her waist gently as he walked by. He was sure he didn't imagine the small gasp that escaped her throat.

"My mom baked more cookies. Your little functions are keeping her on top of her game for sure. I also brought this." He handed her the bag of food he'd brought in his other hand and was thrilled to see her eyes widen with happiness when she peeked in to see pulled pork, potato rolls, and fried chicken.

"How did you get North Carolina barbecue?"

"Not just any North Carolina barbecue," he said with a glimmer of pride in his eye. "Look."

"Holy crap, Griffen! This is from my favorite place back home."

"Yup. I had it delivered overnight, just for you." Griffen put down the food and hugged her. She smelled so good he couldn't resist nuzzling into her neck with his face. When she physically stiffened and pulled back, he couldn't help the spark of frustration he felt.

He was seething when she moved back to him and whispered so only he could hear her.

"Come on, Griffen, you know the rules. There are *tons* of people here."

"Right, of course. Your fucking rules," he bristled, stepping back.

"Don't be mad, *please*. I just don't want Carol to see."

"Or anyone else, right? David over there looks pretty pissed. Maybe you're embarrassed to have the *Viola* staff see me touch you. Is your mailman here? Now *that* would be embarrassing."

"Griffen, please keep your voice down," she whispered.

Althea leaned back and forced a smile and laugh as she looked around. Her brazen pretense was tossing kerosene on Griffen's fiery emotions.

With each nervous dart of her eyes, Griffen's heart pounded with more anger. He leaned closer and whispered hotly in her ear, "Is that better? Am I making you uncomfortable? God forbid someone thinks you aren't perfect, that you're living an adult life," he growled. "Maybe I should ignore your rules and touch you anyway. I know you like it when I do."

"Stop it, *please.*" She breathed slowly, calming herself. "We can touch. Just not here."

"Fine. I get it." Griffen couldn't stop how angry he felt. The irony wasn't lost on him. Most women he'd been with begged him to be serious with them and tell the world they were together. That had never appealed to him, until now. Yet here was this beautiful, desirable woman that he wanted to express affection to and she couldn't bear to let anyone know they were together. He hadn't even realized how furious it made him until he found his heart was racing and he was feeling hot with anger.

Althea must've sensed it because she leaned over and whispered, "No. You don't get it, and you shouldn't have to. This is my thing. *My* issue." She looked around to see if anyone was staring at them and looked into his eyes. "I do want to touch you. I want you to touch me." She swallowed and lowered her voice even more. "Very much."

"Fine," he gritted out. When he looked down at her, with her eyes turned up so full of concern while her lips parted and she panted just a little from the desire that coursed through them every time they were near each other, his heart pounded for a different reason. "I *need* to touch you, too...everywhere."

"Yes, please," she whispered. He glanced to his right and saw Johnny was happily playing with friends under the watchful gaze of Aubrey and Jenna, who were also looking at the two of them with concern.

He looked to the left and saw his mother was working hard to keep Carol well distracted. Ensuring Carol's back was to them Valerie gave Griffen the slightest nod, so that he knew he could slink off with Althea's mother-in-law being none the wiser.

"Come on," he said on a swallow, "let's go for a walk."

"Okay," she turned and he walked near her, careful to resist the urge to touch her. Out of the corner of his eye he caught David glowering at them. Griffen glared back at him, in no mood to humor the guy. David was smart enough to stay in the same spot, staring at them as they walked away.

As soon as they got to the wooded walking path, Althea took his hand and entwined her fingers with his. She slowed and looked up at him in that sweet way that always made him feel warm and liquid-like inside, even now, as mad as he was, it still got to him. "Griffen, I'm sorry. That was rude and insensitive of me. I shouldn't have reacted to you like that."

Griffen tried to shove down his anger from before, but it just wouldn't go away. He'd been feeling closer to her by the minute, more eager to open up and show her how special she was...to him. But when she insisted on hiding whatever they were from everyone that mattered to her it made him feel like he was all alone in feeling whatever was developing inside of him.

There were tears in her eyes and Griffen felt terrible. He was being a prick but he just couldn't stop. He felt hostility and frustration down to his fingertips. "Look, I'm sorry I'm being an ass. I know your rules. But that doesn't mean I have to like them."

"I'm sorry," she whispered.

"I understand. You've got an image to maintain and God forbid you not always be a good girl. The perfect widow."

"Come on, please, don't be like that," she said. "That's not how it is at *all*."

He breathed hard and looked across her shoulder into the woods. He turned back to gaze in her eyes and said, "Then tell me how it really is, Althea."

"It's just that I can't be in public with you and then you leave."

"What if I didn't leave next week, what then?" he asked softly, but his heart sank to see how her eyes widened with fear and panic.

"Stop that, Griffen. You know I'm not ready for that...for more."

"Then what the fuck *are* you ready for Althea?" he bit out.

She jumped at his visible anger, but regained control and slowly wrapped her arms around his shoulders, looking deeply into his eyes. "This," she said. "What we are right now, for these few days. It makes sense. This I can do. I just need it to still be only for us, though. I'm sorry. You've been nothing but kind to me. I hate the idea that my weakness is hurting you."

"You aren't weak Althea," Griffen wrapped his arms around her waist, pulling her flush against him where she belonged. "You're the strongest person I've ever met."

"But I did hurt you, and I'm so sorry for that."

She placed a hand behind his head and pulled him down to her hungry mouth. He loved when she took the lead with him. It showed him that at least when it came to their intense attraction, he wasn't alone in that.

He pulled her off the ground against him.

She moaned in his mouth as her tongue parted his lips. She nibbled and sucked at his tongue, his lips, everywhere, as she rubbed her perfect, tight body deliciously against him. Her eagerness was driving him crazy. Griffen pulled back and looked around them. Even though it was a public park they were in a pretty deserted area. It would have to do because he was bursting to be inside her. He leaned down to kiss her again. All his anger and frustration from before was pouring into his almost violent kisses and every scorching touch of his fingers against her smooth skin.

"Griffen, I want you...now...here."

"Fuck, gorgeous, that's all I needed to hear." He spun her around and she pressed her hands against a large tree. Sliding his hand up her leg he whispered in her ear, "I'm so glad you wore a dress. Did you want me to do this? Fuck you up against a tree here in the woods?"

"Yes," she was already breathless and he loved it.

He pulled the hem of her sundress up and breathed in sharply when he felt her warm pussy in his hands. "Jesus, no panties, gorgeous? Are you trying to kill me?"

"I was hoping we could sneak away and I didn't want to slow you down. Oh!" He slipped two fingers inside her and groaned.

"So wet. My good girl is a little dirty, huh?"

"Only for you. You make me crazy, Griffen."

"Did you think about me when you put this dress on, leaving yourself uncovered for me?"

"Yes. I couldn't wait. I touched myself just thinking about you pulling my dress up here." She reached down and rubbed her fingers across her clit, touching him lightly with each stroke as he pushed his fingers in and out of her. Griffen unzipped quickly and his cock fell out hard and heavy into his hand. He took a condom from his pocket, tore the wrapper with his teeth and slid it on. They were both panting and desperate, all pretense of sweetness gone. She looked back at him over her shoulder and he saw the same need and frustration he felt. In that moment he knew she felt the same way he did, overwhelmed by their attraction to each other. Still reeling from their argument.

He turned her around so she could wrap her legs around him and he thrust into her, hard. He stroked in and out, pulling her soft legs tightly around him, but he needed more. Her sundress had little buttons at the top and he fumbled with them until her breasts fell out. She was wearing the thinnest lace bra and with his next thrust he ran his tongue hotly across the tops of her beautiful breasts. She squeezed her legs around his waist so that he could go deeper and as she arched her back he was able to enfold her breasts in his hands and lick each nipple with abandon.

"Harder, Griffen, please. I need you to fuck me harder." The words drove him over the edge of sanity so fast that he began pounding into her, pressing her back roughly against the hard bark of the tree. He sensed her release coming and knew she would need to scream. Griffen kissed her roughly, rubbing his tongue over hers in and out, mirroring the thrusts of his hard cock in her body. She tightened around him and he swallowed her cries of pleasure. He grunted long and hard as he fell over the edge with her.

He leaned his face into her neck, breathing heavily into her hair as she slowly lowered her legs.

"Wow."

Griffen chuckled and rested his forehead on hers. "Yeah. Wow." He removed the condom, tied it off and put it in his jean pocket with a grimace.

He wrapped his arms around her again and they stood like that for a while, holding each other tightly as they regained some semblance of composure.

Griffen still hated that he would have to leave this beautiful moment and go back to acting like they were the vaguest of acquaintances, brought together by six degrees of grief.

Yes, he understood where she was coming from, but he also knew he needed time with her away from all of this sense of duty and embarrassment that wracked her every move — a chance to let him show her how good being open with him could be.

The sun was starting to get lower in the sky and he kissed her deeply and pulled back. "I hate to say it but we should probably head back before they form a search party."

Althea laughed, nodding in agreement. As they started to approach their group Althea looked at him with what he could only read as sadness in her eyes and dropped his hand.

"It's okay. I get it. For now." But even then the germ of an idea began working in his mind. He needed to get her out of town and he knew just where he wanted to take her as he led her back to the picnicking crowd.

Griffen sat up in Althea's bed and watched her as the sun was gradually peeking through her bedroom window and across her lovely face. He wasn't ashamed to admit he spent most of the time they were together just staring at her, whether she was awake or not. It was still pretty early, but Griffen knew he had to leave soon before Johnny woke up. That was another of her rules — Johnny couldn't know they were together, either.

His heart raced a bit as he saw Althea stirring. It still excited him to wait for the moment those beautiful eyes opened and looked up at him, wide and a little hazy from sleep, but still so hypnotic to him.

"Morning, gorgeous. How'd you sleep?" he asked.

"Mmm, good," she said on a stretch. "It helped that I was dreaming of all the deviant things I want to do to you," she said reaching up to stroke his cheek and kiss him softly on the lips.

The sheet fell down revealing more of her full breasts. Griffen didn't wait and cupped one with his hand, stroking the sides while his thumb brushed over her nipple. She groaned and he leaned in, whispering into her lips, "I like the sound of that. Glad you brought it up actually because I have to leave tonight for a meeting with my publisher in New York. It's just for a couple nights but I'll need to cancel my classes tomorrow..."

"Oh," she said suddenly stiffening as she leaned away. She pulled the sheet up against her and started to look anywhere but at him. "Well, I guess I can't expect to monopolize all your time. Um, I hope you have fun."

"Althea..."

"No, it's okay, I get it," she muttered, starting to sit up.

Griffen grabbed her, yanked down the sheet and rolled on top of her, penning her beneath him. She gasped at the force of his movement and her eyes widened when she looked into what he was sure was fierceness in his. "No, Althea, I don't think you *do* get it." Her breath caught and he brushed a hand against her cheek, running it down her throat and back over her breast. "I was going to say that I would like you to come with me," he said with a smile.

"Oh? Really?"

"Yes. We can stay in my apartment. We'll be back in time for my Wednesday classes and you to go to work."

"Um," she said, biting her lower lip and making him even more desperate to get her out of town with him.

"Pleeeease," he said with a fake pout, dipping his hand between her breasts, sliding down until he palmed her mound, testing her and gladly finding she was already getting wet. "I can spoil you and do dirty things with you," he promised as he slipped two rough fingers inside her, making her moan with pleasure and arch her breasts closer to his mouth. He leaned down and took a nipple between his teeth, nibbling gently.

"Don't you spoil me and do dirty things with me here?" she panted her breath quickening as she started to writhe and jerk beneath him.

"Yes, but there I will have you all to myself as much as I want, as dirty as it can get in the city that never sleeps."

"Hmm, that does sound promising, and things are pretty dead at the office Labor Day week," she thought out loud. Griffen looked into her eyes as he added a third finger and twisted gently. She moaned and said, "Throw in a Gray's Papaya dog and you got a deal."

"Done and done. Now for some dirty things to tide me over..." Griffen slid down her body until his face was between her legs and licked and fingered her until she climaxed.

Oh yeah, New York is a great idea, he thought.

"I'm sorry, who's this?" Aubrey's voice said over the phone saucily.

"Aubrey, you know it's me, Tea. Stop being a dumbass."

"*Who is it?*" she heard Jenna ask in the background.

"*Someone named Tea,*" Aubrey responded to her.

"*Tea who?*"

"*That's what I asked.*"

Aubrey returned to the phone. "Hmm. I knew a Tea once. Sweet girl, but then she fell under this hot bad boy's sex spell. Never saw her again. Such a shame."

"Ha, ha. Okay, point made. You do remember you guys masterminded all this mess, right?"

"I do," Aubrey stated coolly. "And I take all credit for everything good that comes of it. And for that I reserve the right to torment you for disappearing like you're sixteen and just learned that a boy can make you feel funny. You know, *down there,*" she said with a stage whisper.

"I knew I should have called Jenna," Althea grumbled.

"Probably right. Rookie mistake. Must be a side effect of the sex brain. That's potent stuff. But you called me — so time to spill about positions, girth, and what-not."

"Keep your what-not questions to yourself, you perv. I'm too sober to discuss this right now. Besides, I need a favor."

"Say no more. Jenna's off today, too. How about you meet us for some Labor Day cocktails? Favor will only be granted after drinks and much spilling about what-not."

"Fine. Meet me at *Viola* in twenty minutes, but you better behave yourselves and keep your voices down there. Carol wants to spend the afternoon with Johnny, so she can pick him up first. *And* you're buying a round of dirty martinis."

"Of course. What do you take me for, a heathen? Dirty martinis for our finally dirty girl, it is!"

Althea waved to the girls as she walked into *Viola* while holding Johnny's hand.

Frank Sinatra wafted through the dining room as she caught sight of them already slurping dirty martinis at their usual booth with one chilled and waiting invitingly for Althea.

Viola hadn't changed much over the years, and it was still a classic choice for wedding receptions and graduation parties, even if it wasn't part of the ever-expanding, sophisticated cosmopolitan restaurant scene that was taking over the city below.

The decor was old world Italian with a discreet bar and hidden kitchen, but the real draw was the wall of floor ceiling windows providing patrons an unrivaled view of Pittsburgh from the dramatic cliffs of Mt. Washington.

Johnny pulled at her hand as Carol emerged from the kitchen and walked toward them.

"Gwandma!" Johnny exclaimed, running into her outstretched arms.

"Hi handsome! Oof, you are so heavy," Carol said.

"I've been playing football with Uncle Gwiff. I'm getting huge!" Johnny assured her.

Althea schooled her face at the mention of Griffen.

"Is that right? That's very nice of him." Carol looked up to Althea. "Isn't it Tea?"

"Yes, he's been making the most of his time in town. I think Johnny has really enjoyed being with him." Althea's palms started sweating as she prayed her voice was still neutral.

"Good. It's important to include Jack in Johnny's life however possible."

"Of course," Althea whispered, then squatted down to look in Johnny's eyes, "hey honey, why don't you go over and say hi to Aunt Brey and Aunt Jenna while Grandma and I talk real quick?"

"Okay, Mommy." He immediately sprinted off to high five the girls.

"When will you be picking Johnny up tonight?" Carol asked. "I feel like I haven't seen you for ages. I thought I could take the night off and we could pull out Jack's old football videos to watch with Johnny, since he's really getting into it these days."

"Oh, Carol, that sounds, uh, really nice, but I have to leave town today for a business trip. Last minute thing." The lie fell awkwardly off her tongue. That combined with the mention of Jack, made Althea feel like she was drowning in shame.

"Oh, that's too bad. Do you need me to watch Johnny?"

"I think the girls will watch him, since the restaurant will probably be busy this week. I don't want to put you out."

"I guess you're right. I've just been pretty overworked and lonely these days, but I know your work is important. Maybe Johnny and I will watch those videos just us two this afternoon then." She turned and said loudly, "Johnny, come on over honey, let's get going."

Johnny leapt up from Aubrey's lap and shouted, "Sure Gwandma," then ran to her, displaying his limitless energy.

Carol took Johnny's hand and said, "You're such a good boy. I don't know what I'd do without you. Well, Tea, I hope you and the girls have a nice lunch. Johnny and I are going to head out."

"Okay, thanks." Althea reached down and kissed Johnny. "I'm going to see you in two sleeps, okay honey?"

"Sure Mommy. Love you."

"Love you, too."

Johnny followed Carol as she grabbed her purse and headed out. Althea breathed a sigh of relief as she walked over to Aubrey and Jenna.

"Everything okay, Tea?" Jenna asked.

"Fine," Althea sighed. "I've honestly been kind of avoiding Carol since this whole Griffen thing started and now I know I made the right call. I feel so bad keeping this from her, but I know she'd never understand. I'm not sure if I do." Althea sighed again and took a sip of her sweating martini.

"Tea, aren't you being a bit dramatic?"

"No, Jenna, I don't think so."

"Chill out you two. You aren't avoiding us too, are you Tea?" Aubrey asked with a grin.

"Oh come on, you know I'm not. I've just been...busy."

"Getting busy," Aubrey said with a chuckle.

"Real clever, Aubrey. I don't know what the big deal is. You guys just saw me yesterday."

"Saw being the operative word. If you remember correctly, you almost immediately ran off with your sexy boy toy."

Althea rolled her eyes and bit into a blue cheese stuffed olive. "Did Carol notice?"

"Nah. Don't worry, Griffen's mom covered for you with her," Aubrey assured her.

"*Griffen's mom?* Does she know about us? Would she tell Carol?"

"I don't know," Aubrey said suddenly sounding slightly annoyed. "And so what if she does? You're so fixated on keeping all this a secret when you're doing nothing wrong."

"Come on, Brey. You know how Carol is. She'd go into a total tailspin if I fell for someone else."

"Are you falling for Griffen?" Jenna asked eyes wide.

"No, he's leaving in a week and that's final. What did Val tell Carol?"

"I don't know. I think she said you two went off to reminisce about Jack, you know, you're getting to know each other, blah, blah, blah," Aubrey said with a wave of her hand.

"Thanks for thoughtful summary," Althea said sarcastically.

"Was there anything *else* you two were doing?" Aubrey said, waggling her eyebrows.

"There may have been a hot and sweaty part, too..."

"I knew you two got busy in the park. You're a *bad* girl Tea!" Aubrey looked beside herself with excitement, splashing some of her martini onto the table in her glee. "So, was it good?"

"Ahh. Yeah, it was good. Everything he does is good. So good."

"That a girl!" Aubrey chimed out. "Now we're talking."

"By the way, Griffen looked pretty pissed there for a bit," Jenna piped in finally.

"Way to be a buzzkill Jenna. I was hoping for at least some details on positions. I guess we've moved onto the serious part of the discussion. Tea, Jenna's right. We talked to him after you came back from your, uh, walk, and he was pretty worked up, for sure."

"Yeah, I know. He's getting a little sick of the secrecy, but that's just the way it has to be," Althea said.

"I had your back, even though I still think all this cloak-and-dagger shit is silly. I told him to stop being such a typical male," Aubrey declared. "You know, thinking he can swoop in for two weeks and act like he owns the place. Then get all caveman just because you set some rules."

"And I told Aubrey to stop being so hard on him," Jenna said. Then her voice dropped and her eyes fell. "No one wants to feel like the person they're with is ashamed of them."

"Jenna, I'm not ashamed of him, you know that."

Jenna straightened up and became her usual steady self again. "Point is, you know you can't hide your life from Carol forever, right?" Jenna asked. "If this really is even about Carol."

"What do you mean?" Althea bristled.

216

"Maybe you think keeping it secret will make it hurt less when he leaves," Jenna responded.

Althea took another big gulp. "I really don't want to talk about that. He's leaving and that's final, so being public with him for a few days doesn't make any sense."

"Fine. So, what's the favor then?" Aubrey asked.

"Griffen wants to take me to New York for a couple of nights when he goes to meet with his publisher tomorrow and..." She looked up and couldn't miss their meaningful glances at each other.

"A trip together. That's a big deal," Jenna said.

"No, it's not. We don't have many days together so this makes sense. Will you watch Johnny while we're in New York, or not?"

"Of course, jeez, calm down," Aubrey said.

"Thanks. You can pick him up from Carol's later. If anyone asks, I'm on a business trip. That's what I just told Carol."

"Mmm, the gettin' busy kind of business," Jenna teased. Althea smirked and took another sip of her martini as she allowed herself to get excited about a getaway with Griffen.

CHAPTER THIRTEEN

Althea walked through the door to Griffen's two-story penthouse apartment and gasped. It was stunning and spacious, with pre-war era details and high ceilings. What was almost as surprising as the fact that Griffen didn't live in some ultra-modern bachelor pad, was that it was in the lower Fifth Avenue part of Greenwich Village.

She turned to him as he was returning from dropping their luggage in the bedroom and asked, "I thought you cocky multi-millionaires all lived in the Upper West Side."

"Hmm, we do now, do we? You know, if you're going to make me a cliché I'd prefer you go with Bond villain," he joked as he stalked over to her, grabbing her hand as he pulled her to the bedroom.

"Ooh, good idea," she said as she let him drag her along the parquet floor, illuminated by the light coming through massive windows overlooking the bustle of the vibrant city below. "Though you'll need to redecorate. I suggest a shark tank over there," she pointed by the open fully equipped kitchen she doubted he ever used, "and a hidden command center over there by your fancy sofas and such, so you can video chat with the other mega villains around the world. Though you need a very fluffy white cat with a pissed off expression. Do you know where you can get one of those?"

"Oh, I know a guy," he smirked as he led her to the bed and began taking her clothes off. She smiled and quickly made work of removing his shirt. "Despite my secret Bond villain identity, you forget that I also happen to be a down-to-earth multi-millionaire, and an artistic one at that. This area is definitely more my speed."

"That's true. You *are* a writer, after all. You need to have the full experience, right? I'm glad you live here. I love this part of Manhattan. Not sure if I would have liked it as much up there with all those other muckety-mucks." She slipped his shirt off and ran her fingers down his chest. She tried to take in how perfect his bedroom was, right down to what looked like the biggest bathroom she'd ever seen, but he'd stripped her down to the new bra, panties and garters she'd snuck away to buy for this trip and he was touching her so slowly that it was hard to focus on anything other than getting him naked and on top of her. Althea put her fingers to work and took off his pants and boxer briefs so fast she heard the fabric ripping.

"Griffen, I love looking at you so much." He was hard everywhere and clearly beyond aroused. He'd touched her surreptitiously during the entire flight, but the journey between Pittsburgh and New York was very short, leaving little time to do anything but get insanely turned on.

"The feeling is mutual, gorgeous," he whispered into her cleavage, licking across her breasts until the wetness and warmth felt so good she thought she might explode right there.

She stroked his length up and down, loving how velvety soft and hot it was under her hand. "Come here," she said and smiled at him wickedly. "I want to make the most of all this hard goodness." She lay down on the bed and pulled on his hand and positioned him to straddle her chest. She placed his hard cock between her breasts and squeezed the soft flesh around him.

He smiled and groaned, quickly taking over and thrusting through her breasts. She sucked and licked at his full, hard head every time it peeked up through the channel between her breasts. The action looked so erotic, she could barely stand it.

Griffen quickened his pace across her silky soft chest and Althea rocked with the movement, squeezing herself around him, loving how aroused he looked — his eyes hooded as he bit his lower lip. She sucked his tip longer with each thrust, twirling her tongue around it in circles that had him shaking above her. He pulled back and thrust forward quickly and repeatedly, until he came in warm, silky streams across her breasts.

"Holy shit, I loved that," he said slowly, his voice breaking, as he rolled over to lay alongside of her.

"I'm so glad. I loved it too." She smiled again and rubbed his come over her nipples and licked her finger, "Mmm," she moaned looking in his eyes.

"Jesus woman, you keep doing that and I'm going to need to go again."

"I'm okay with that. Though I am a little dirty."

"Yes, my good girl has definitely gotten herself all dirty and I like that very much, but I promised you a fancy night on the town and I intend to deliver." He looked into her eyes as he began reaching down to stroke her slit, which was incredibly wet from the erotic pleasure she'd received from making him go so crazy. "But I can tell you *really* enjoyed what you just did for me. So, come on, let's take a shower. I want to take care of you, too, *then* I'll clean you up, dirty girl." He stood and held out his hand to her.

Griffen was certainly making the most of his newfound ability to touch Althea in public. He hadn't released her hand once since they'd left his apartment, unless it was to stroke her back, touch her hair, or whisper naughty things in her ear.

"So, where are you taking me for dinner, stud?"

"To school, my sweet bookworm."

"Huh?"

They walked up to the restaurant and Althea's jaw dropped. "It *is* a school!"

"Yup."

They entered the stately building, passing a proud plaque naming it a New York City Public School.

"They turned this defunct school into a restaurant. Its got everything a studious good girl like you would love, right down to the individually wrapped school soap in the bathroom. Oh, and the food rocks, too," he said with a proud grin. He then looked to her with a little worry in his eyes. "Like it?" He looked so nervous and eager for her approval that she couldn't help but feel worrisome butterflies take flight in her stomach.

"I love it! It's nerd heaven! You've done good, Griffen."

He smiled so brightly she thought she would need sunglasses. She leaned forward and kissed him passionately. "Thank you."

"Seriously. It's my pleasure."

After a fabulous dinner with menus printed on old card catalog inserts, Griffen held her hand and they walked along the streets of the West Village, ending up curled in each other arms on a bench in Washington Square Park. As they watched rowdy NYU students and hippies wander under the beautiful replica of the Arc de Triomphe Griffen stroked her back lazily with one hand as she sat on his lap. He looked in her eyes and asked, "Where to now? Your wish is my command."

"Anything I want?"

"Anything. Drinks, dancing, we can even do one of those touristy carriage rides."

"Wow, won't that destroy your tough guy writer cred?"

"For you, my dear, I'll embarrass myself for a night — and a day — if you like."

"Hmm, intriguing offer," she said as she snuggled deeper into his arms. "But I'm happy here, just being with you."

"Happy, huh?"

"Yes, so happy."

"That's wonderful, gorgeous."

Yeah, it kind of is, she thought to herself.

Griffen awoke to the sound of running water and smiled into his pillow. He had showered with Althea before in his hotel suite, but the idea of joining her there in his own apartment sounded so domestic and wonderful that he couldn't help but jump out of bed and rush to meet her.

The bathroom was foggy but he could make out the outline of her beautiful wet body under the multiple jets, glowing against the white and gray marble. He opened the glass doors, stepped in and wrapped his arms around her from behind.

She jumped a little and spun her head around so quickly that she slapped him in the face with a massive head of soapy wet hair.

"Ow!" he said through laughter.

"Oops, sorry! You surprised me," she said, whacking him again when she turned to apologize.

"Sorry gorgeous," he chuckled, wiping the soap from his eyes, "but I can't watch you in here covered in soap, water pouring down these beautiful breasts without getting a taste of you."

He leaned forward and kissed her, welcoming her tongue into his mouth and reveling in the feel of her wet curves against his body. She turned again, her back to him as she began to rinse out her long hair. With each rivulet of water pouring down her stunning curves he began to feel more panic rising in his throat.

All he could think of was returning here in a week, to being alone in this huge shower in his lonely apartment, completely isolated again — with only the memory of this passing joy left of their time together this morning. The sense of impending loss hit him like a sledgehammer.

Althea was humming happily as she began running conditioner through her honey colored locks, completely oblivious to the quiet torture wreaking havoc on Griffen's entire body behind her.

Frustrated at his lack of control over the situation, Griffen grabbed the soap to scrub down her back — desperate to distract himself from the confusing feelings he couldn't quite shake. Griffen leaned forward and rubbed the soap across her shoulders.

"Mmm, Griffen, that's nice, thank you," she said softly.

His throat caught at the sound of her voice and he croaked out, "Are you enjoying your trip so far? Glad that you came here?"

"Of course, I'm having a wonderful time here with you."

The words emboldened him. "You like what I do for you, don't you gorgeous? Do I make you feel good?"

"Yes, so good." Althea took his hand and ran it across her breasts and down to her warm wet pussy. "I especially like how you make me feel here."

Griffen groaned against her neck. He was aching to be inside of her, but his emotions were too out of control, his throat burning and painful. Yet when she rubbed her round buttocks against his thickening cock he became even more overcome with a desire for something he didn't understand. All he did know was that he could make her body feel good, so he began to stroke her eager center and she moaned deeply.

"See how I make you feel gorgeous? Don't I take good care of you?"

"Such good care of me. You make me feel so a-amazing." Althea shook against his hand as he stroked her faster, still slowly rubbing the soap in his other hand across her breasts until she came for him, trembling in his arms as he nibbled and licked the delicate skin of her neck. "Oh Griffen, you always make me come so hard."

Griffen felt like he was going insane. He'd never wanted more than these fleeting physical moments, yet now all he could think about was keeping this woman in his arms until she was crazy just like him.

Before he could bite back the words Griffen said, "You are so soft Althea...all over. God, you're perfect for me," he mumbled against her neck.

She was still quivering in his arms, leaning her head back against him and she asked, "What did you say? Sorry, I was in outer space there for a second," she giggled.

Griffen's heart squeezed again. "Nothing, I just said that I can't get enough of your amazing body."

"Mmm, I like the sound of that," she whispered.

Every ounce of him wanted to keep her with him, to

persuade her to consider opening up to him for real. Frustrated by her response and afraid such words would scare her off for good, he swallowed the sentiment and buried his face into her wet neck, water spraying against his back as he breathed deeply with emotion. "I hate leaving you today," he said huskily.

She turned around in his arms and wrapped hers around his neck, reaching up to give him a deep kiss. He gripped her hair in his hands, trying to express his emotion with his lips and tongue, nibbling her lower lip until she groaned against him.

"I'll miss you today, Griffen, but don't worry, I love this area. I think I'll make the most of my day off and treat myself to a shopping spree."

"Oh really?" Griffen cleared his throat and tried to school his face so he didn't upset her with his emotional turmoil. "And what are you going to buy while I'm out having to suffer through a meeting with my asshole publisher?"

"I'm not telling, but I promise you'll like it."

"That sounds sexy...I'll cancel my meeting. I need to come with you."

"Oh no, it's a surprise. Go have your meeting. I'll see you back here later stud. With surprises."

"Okay," he answered.

Althea rubbed her wet body against his erection, smiling as she looked up into his eyes. "Maybe we can go back to bed and I'll take care of this for you? Come on."

Griffen turned off the water and stepped out of the shower. He couldn't understand why nothing seemed to be enough for him with this woman. For now, he would settle for simply burying himself inside of her again.

Griffen's first stop was a meeting with his publisher and his agent. He strode in and took in the conference room and its two suit wearing occupants. These guys gave him hives, but it was worth it to get to share the news that inspiration had finally struck again.

"Griffen! Come in," Stuart Anderson, his longtime agent and sometime friend said boisterously. "We were just talking about how excited the world will be about a new Cade Jackson novel."

He walked in and took a seat. "Nope. This one's not Cade Jackson. It's a whole new character." Their well-fed faces fell morosely as though someone had stolen their brand new puppy.

"Not Cade Jackson? Now, Griffen..." James Masters, his publisher, grumbled out as his agent became visibly agitated.

"Calm yourselves. Wouldn't want either of you guys to have a heart attack. I've got another Cade novel in mind and it will be a good one. But this one, the book I'm writing now...this one's going to actually be great. It's still an action-adventure, but it has a lot more heart." He laid out the whole story — the hero's childhood friend, his death and the mystery surrounding it, including the possibility that the apparent perfect half of this duo may have committed an act of treason by stealing military technology.

They looked at him silently with dollar signs and critical acclaim flashing in their eyes, until James finally blurted. "Who's the villain? Who stole the military secrets?"

"Don't know. I guess you'll have to read it to find out."

"Is this based on true events like your Cade books?" James asked.

Griffen hesitated.

"Of course it is! All his books are," Stuart exclaimed as Griffen kept his face neutral.

"Is there a woman?"

"I hope so," he answered softly. He imagined Althea naked before him and his heart sped up at the thought of extending their story together.

The men gave him confused looks but perked up when he added, "I'm still in the early stages, but I've written a few chapters. You'll find the plot summary, outline and what I've written so far in your inboxes. See you later gentlemen."

He walked out hearing their frenzied excitement.

"Talk about crossover appeal. Women will finally buy one of his books."

"We can make this a hit."

"It's like Cade Jackson, but with a heart!"

Heart, huh? How about that? Griffen thought.

Trey greeted Griffen at the door of his Brooklyn brownstone, barefoot in nothing but a pair of jeans. He was jacked, with tattoos across his chest and arms,

"Hey Griffen. Come in, man."

"Cover up, dude. Jesus, you know I don't want to look at all that shit in your chest," Griffen said with a wince, referring to Trey's pierced nipples that were on display. "Couldn't you be bothered to put on a shirt before I got here?"

"Sorry man, I was, uh, pretty occupied this morning," he said, rubbing the back of his neck and smirking. He snatched a T-shirt off the couch and pulled it over his head.

As they walked into Trey's main room, a stunning blonde walked out of a back room in a sophisticated black sheath dress and just-fucked hair. She crossed the room to Trey, kissing him with copious tongue and slipping a piece of paper into his back pocket.

"Call me," she said with a husky voice. Trey smacked her ass and she giggled as she scurried out.

Trey sat down in front of a huge desk with multiple computer monitors and equipment Griffen didn't even recognize, when a hot redhead emerged from the same back room. She kissed Trey, stopping to tweak his nipple rings through his T-shirt and slipped a piece of paper in front of him with a smile before whispering something in his ear that caused him to kiss her again and squeeze her ass.

"Not right now, I have to take care of some business, but thanks for a great night, Monique."

She looked royally pissed before grabbing the paper back up and saying loudly, "It's Monica, *asshole*." And with that she stormed out.

"Got any more back there? A brunette perhaps?" Griffen said with a raised eyebrow, hoping the show was over.

"What can I say man? Chicks dig a nerd with muscles."

"A *rich* nerd with muscles," Griffen added.

"Yeah, that helps, too," he said with a lascivious smile. "And good thing, because I like variety."

"Yeah, that was some variety that headed out of here."

"You know me, I take all comers. The blonde was a stockbroker from Wall Street. She wanted to enjoy a taste of the wild side and I wanted to expand my portfolio. I got some stock tips out of her, too," he added with a wink.

"And the redhead?"

"Monique?"

"*Monica*," Griffen corrected and Trey simply smirked at him.

"Yeah, right. She was just smokin' hot and they didn't

make me choose," he grinned.

"Good for you, man. I hope you found some time between all your diverse pussy to work on my project for a minute."

"Hell yeah."

"So, where are we at now?"

"I've been decrypting piece by piece. There's only a couple folders left for me to get into. The most heavily encrypted are the ones before the day he, uh..."

"Died," Griffen said over a scratchy throat.

"Yeah, died, right, sorry bro." Griffen just grunted and nodded toward the computer screen. "I'm actually having some luck with the next set of documents. I just cracked into them last night. I was going to email them to you."

"What are they? Why the delay?"

"I wanted to look at them a little more, uh..."

"Bullshit, why are you stalling? Just spill it, Trey. Christ."

"Shit, all right man, I just wanted to be sure before I dropped this bomb on you dude. First one is a spreadsheet."

"And..."

"Jack prepared it, a few days before he died. It lists amounts of money and bank account numbers."

"Like he was tracking payments?"

"Or recording receipt of payments."

"Fuck. Can you try to trace these account numbers?"

"Are you asking me to use my computer to infiltrate bank records? For shame."

Griffen raised an eyebrow at him.

"I'll see what I can do." Trey turned back to his monitors. "Then there's this one here, designs for something seriously badass. Look." Trey pulled the image onto a huge screen in front of them.

"Holy shit, that's specs for some kind of iron man suit."

"Right. This would fall in the serious military shit category. Whatever this is, it's intense. I'm not into robotics, but I'm enough of an engineer to know that. There's a lot of these for different designs. Looks like a breakdown of how they're made, too. Was Jack working on this project?"

"Not that I can figure. According to his widow, he didn't do the military stuff."

Drew whistled slowly. "His widow, huh? She hot?"

Griffen's muscles twitched. "We are not going to talk about Althea, all right?"

"Oh, yeah. Sounds like she's definitely hot. Interesting. Well, what *did* he work on then?"

"He was working on 3D mapping when he died."

"That is definitely not this. Can you talk to anyone in his department to confirm Althea is right? Maybe find out more about him?"

"Yeah. I can do that soon."

"Good, because if he wasn't doing this serious military shit then that means he was accessing this info for another reason."

"Right. Look, I've got to go pick something up. Let me know what else you find out and about those bank accounts."

Griffen chewed on this new unpleasant information as he sat in the back of the cab. Just the mere idea that Jack could've been stealing this information for personal gain made him sick. It was so unlike him. No one was more clean-cut and honest than Jack.

Griffen took a deep breath. He had one more stop to make before he could get back to Althea, where his day would hopefully look up again.

Althea readjusted herself on Griffen's sofa. One arm was behind her head and her stocking-covered legs were stretched out before her.

She'd spent the day exploring lingerie shops and sex toy stores (from tasteful to ridiculous), stopping occasionally to treat herself to a bite to eat or a cocktail, and she had the pink and black shopping bags to prove it. The outfit she'd chosen to wear to greet Griffen was an elaborate lace and feather getup from *Agent Provocateur* that had cost her a pretty penny. It featured smooth elastic straps that wrapped around her curves in a way that evoked silk ropes and was so involved she'd had to ask the salesgirl to draw her a diagram of how to tie herself into it when she returned to his apartment. The whole experience had felt completely decadent and she'd loved it.

He was supposed to be home any minute, so she planned to be waiting for him, complete with overdone sexy hair and makeup. They didn't have many more nights together and none where they would have as much total privacy as this one. There was no way she wasn't going to make the most of it. Fortunately, right when she was starting to feel awkward, Althea heard a key turning in the lock.

"Althea, I'm back, I thought we could go out and get that Gray's Papaya's hot dog you..." He turned, saw her and dropped his keys along with his jaw. Just the response she was going for.

"Oh, I don't know, I think I'm okay with staying in for now. What do you think?"

He sat next to her, running his hand through her hair and down the length of her body. "I think staying in sounds wonderful. Is this my surprise?"

"One of them. Do you like it?"

"One of them? Damn woman, I love it, though I can't even begin to dream of what the others are if this one is any indication."

"Oh, they're good. Trust me."

"Well, I should give you the surprise I have for you first then."

"You got me something?"

"I did." Griffen reached in his jacket and pulled out a light blue box.

"I do love that color. Is it…?"

"Tiffany's? Yes."

"Griffen, this is so thoughtful of you, but it's too much. You already brought me here, took me to a lovely dinner."

"It's not nearly enough Althea. I've had such an amazing time with you and couldn't wait to give this to you."

"Well, in that case, I guess I can't refuse." Althea pulled the white ribbon, grinning from ear to ear. She hadn't received jewelry since her engagement and wedding rings. Jack had been loving and generous, but money had been tight with him working at a university and her in school. She wouldn't let him waste money on extravagances like that, but honestly, what woman could deny loving a little blue box?

She opened the box and gasped at the sight. It was a gold chain with a large pendant of tree branches, each with a perfect creamy white pearl at the end.

"Griffen, it's so stunning, I love it." She looked at him and curled her lips into a suggestive grin. "Though, after what we did last night, I'm not sure what to think of you buying me a 'pearl necklace.'"

He barked a laugh and kissed her. "Damn, so my good girl is turning bad. What a dirty mouth I've given you."

"I like everything you do to my mouth, dirty or otherwise."

He groaned and kissed her again. "I ordered it before we got here, I swear. I saw it online, but it didn't have the pearls. I requested they be added on a rush, because it's your birthstone. That it turned out to be a reminder of how good you made me feel last night is just a bonus," he added with a dirty smirk. "Here, let me put it on you." She pulled her hair away and he fastened it around her neck, slowly caressing her skin as he pulled his hands away. He kissed her and licked the skin around the spot where the pendant hung deeply in her cleavage.

"I didn't know Tiffany's would do things like that!"

"For enough money you can get people to do just about anything."

She blushed, "Griffen, you don't have to spend all this money on me."

"I've missed a lot of your birthdays. And I've made a lot of money over the years. I never wanted to spend it on anyone except for my mom before you, so humor me, please."

"Well, then, I can't say no. Besides, it will remind me of our fun time together when you're back up here being all Bond villain again," she said with a kiss but fell back against the cushions when she saw the sadness and frustration on Griffen's face, quickly replaced by resolve.

"About that. I was thinking — considering how much you like the neighborhood here, maybe you could come up here and visit me sometimes? You know, help me scope out fluffy white cats for my secret lair and all..."

She looked away and choked out, "Griffen, it's hard for me to get away from Pittsburgh."

"Then I can visit you."

"I think Johnny would like that," she answered, wincing at the words.

"Johnny? What about you? What are you really saying?"

"I just don't think it's a good idea to extend this."

"Come on, you're being kind of ridiculous here."

"Excuse me if I'm *ridiculous*," she huffed out. "That's how I feel."

Her heart raced and she suddenly felt panicked. So much of her wanted to say yes, but guilt and fear met each hopeful thought, quelling her desires. As much as a selfish part of her wanted to see him again — felt ill at the thought of him leaving for good — it was too quiet a voice next to the screams of loss and regret that had occupied her life for years.

She looked him in the eye and tried to feign courage when she said, "Point is I think it will be really hard to keep our boundaries if we do that. Besides, I know you live like a playboy when you're up here — I don't exactly fit into that."

"What are you talking about? A playboy? Do people even still use that word?"

"If the smoking jacket fits...I was greeted by a lovely note under your door from 'Vicky' when I got back today. She said she watered your plants and would be around for you to thank her in your 'special way.'"

"What? I haven't spoken to Vicky in weeks. I had no idea she'd do that."

"It doesn't matter. When all this started you told me you didn't have relationships. That you just do sex. That's your lifestyle."

"My lifestyle? Seriously, Althea..." he said through clenched teeth.

She softened, "Look, I know you think I'm being crazy, but please, don't be mad. I wasn't even going to mention the note, but it did make me even more sure that sticking to the plan makes sense. It's just too much for me to think about to be more than that. I'm really sorry, but going back to our own lives is going to be for the best." Tears started to sprout in her eyes and she could see his anger fade.

He hugged her close and whispered in her hair. "Please don't cry, gorgeous. I didn't want to upset you."

"Thank you so much, Griffen. For the necklace, for everything." Her voice broke on the words. "It all makes me feel very special."

She could see he wanted to say something, but he cleared away a frown and said, "You *are* very special. I want you to remember that every day." He touched the pendant gently, then lowered his head to inhale her neck deeply. "Mmm. I had to buy you something, I couldn't help myself. I thought it looked like tributaries on a stream, it reminded me of how much you like watching the rivers."

"What a poetic gift from my favorite writer," she said with a smile. "I love it. It really is beautiful, it's perfect for me."

He cleared his throat and she could see he was forcing a smile.

"Now, I think it's time for you to surprise me, right?" he said kissing his way up her neck, rubbing his fingers into her hair. She could tell he wanted to lighten the mood and she let him.

"Oh yeah," she said, as he began running his hands over her breasts until she felt the familiar tightening and twitching in her core.

"Let me show you what I got before you make me too stupid to think again."

"I like making you stupid," he groaned, sliding his hand down her body then pressing the heel of his palm against her mound and licking little circles against her neck.

Althea giggled, "I like you making me stupid, too. That's

why I bought what I did." His head jerked up, and she felt his dick follow suit against her leg. "Now I have your attention, stud. Give me a minute."

"You got it," he said, eagerly dropping his hands.

"And Griffen."

"Yeah?"

"I think we should order dinner in."

He smacked her ass, making her squeal. "Hot damn, gorgeous, you'd better get in there and get my presents before I burst with excitement...*literally*," he added with a wink, looking down at the significant bulge in his pants.

Althea giggled and ran into the spare bedroom where she'd hidden her purchases. *This is going to be fun*, she thought with a grin.

She smiled as she laid out the vibrator, silk scarves and lace blindfold. She called Griffen in and laughed as he stroked each of them lightly and smiled. "Holy shit, Althea, are you trying to kill me?"

"You like?"

"I *love*."

"And I know boys love toys, so I got one of these, too." She held up a ring with a vibrating bullet on the top and bottom of it.

"Well, that's certainly new to me. How does a sweet little thing like you even know about this stuff?"

"Well, I may be a good girl that has only had sex with four guys in her whole life..."

Griffen grimaced, "Can we not talk about your prior sex? Please."

"Oh, right. Okay, well my point is I have had to, er, entertain myself for the last almost six years, I've learned a lot about this kind of, you know, stuff."

"I'm looking forward to enjoying this with you, that's for sure. Where'd you get it?"

"A few different places near here, Lower East Side, Soho. Did I mention I love the location of your apartment?"

"You did once or twice, and I'm starting to love it even more. You'll be happy to know, I didn't even know this was around here."

"Sure you didn't," she teased.

"You better get into that bedroom and teach me what I've been missing all this time."

He swatted her bottom till she grabbed her goodies and ran into his bedroom. After their intense discussion, she was eager to get back to enjoying each other and teaching this sexy man a thing or two.

CHAPTER FOURTEEN

Althea laughed and it warmed Griffen's entire body. They'd taken an early flight back to Pittsburgh that morning and were grabbing a coffee and pastry downtown before Althea needed to go to work. He noticed a crumb at the corner of her mouth and reached across to move it gently between her lips. They curled into a smile while she trapped his eyes with her powerful gaze.

"Why thank you, sir," she teased, the word reminding him of all the naughty games they'd played the night before in his apartment. God, just the thought of seeing how sexy she was when he'd walked in the night before was enough to make him hard, but add in the toys and her complete openness to him and he felt completely undone. He'd used the vibrator on her in the bedroom. The ring on himself in the shower. Then they'd both had a round of the blindfold and ties in his study.

It was a miracle he could walk today, much less make the flight. But it wasn't just the erotic fun they shared that stuck with him, it was the warmth of her in his arms in his bed, the way her smile made his apartment finally feel like a home, instead of a cold place he simply used as an outpost.

Griffen couldn't stop smiling and suddenly felt something so powerful working its way through his limbs, his throat, his heart, and his head. It was as though an electric shock had started in his center and moved out to his fingertips and toes, up into his mouth — forcing him to tell her how deeply he cared for her. He fought it down, fixating on the bitter memory of how soundly she'd rejected even the simple proposal of them visiting each other. She didn't want more from him and he needed to accept that.

She would never let herself love him and that made Griffen want to punch a wall.

Althea's phone buzzed and she looked at it with a scowl.

"What is it?"

"A text from Curt."

"Curt? The doctor from Johnny's party?" Griffen's hands clenched around his coffee.

"Yeah, he's asking me to go to dinner with him tonight. It's so awkward since he's friends with Jenna."

The thought of her with anyone else made his chest hurt and his blood boil. She'd made it clear she wanted him to stick to the plan, the whole point of which was to help her be able to move on...probably with a guy like Curt. He wanted to do the right thing even if it felt like chewing on glass.

"Maybe you should go."

"What? I thought we would spend tonight...I mean..."

"Your plan was that I leave soon, right? And you get back out there, ready to take a risk without guilt, right?" Griffen said through clenched teeth, hoping she wouldn't see the fists at his side and the grimace on his face, "now's as good a time as any, right?" He swallowed through bile and what felt like sawdust in his throat.

Maybe I'm getting the flu, he idly thought in a lame attempt to fool himself. *Yeah, you've come down with a case of acute dumbass. You fell for her and she doesn't want you.*

"Baby steps, right?" Griffen added as lightly as he could through the acid rising in his throat.

"You think I should say yes to dinner *tonight*?"

"Is there a reason to wait?"

Please say there is. Please.

"Uh, I guess not," she said softly.

Fuck.

"So, okay, that's great then."

Why can't I just shut up?

"Yeah, great," she said, and her downturned eyes and quiet voice stabbed straight into his heart. He wanted to kill anyone who put that look on her face, but he was the one doing it. "I guess I better call him and see if he can still do it. I, uh," she looked up and Griffen thought he saw her eyes water but she quickly blinked them away. When she looked back at him she was beaming with a huge smile that didn't reach her eyes. "Thanks for breakfast and the advice. I think it is a great idea!" She stood up, grabbed her bag and rushed out of the café, almost knocking over a chair in her haste.

Griffen followed her with his eyes and saw his reflection in the glass — miserable, angry and definitely alone. He slammed his fist down on the table, gathering the attention of multiple other patrons. "Sorry, I just can't get over last night's *Pirates* game. I really thought we had that one." His lame statement was grudgingly accepted and a couple folks muttered their agreement. Griffen gathered his trash and started to leave thinking that the most disappointing loss was the one to which he'd just surrendered.

He didn't deserve Althea. He'd hoped that maybe he could, but every time he tried for more with her, she pushed him away or simply shot him down.

That damn note from Vicky certainly didn't help matters. Althea was already skittish and then she gets written evidence of what a man-whore I've been.

She was right to keep their time together limited. He just needed to forget that his heart felt like it had gone through a wood chipper.

Griffen threw down his briefcase as he slammed shut the door to his suite after returning from class. Tugging off his jacket, he threw it on his overnight bag, still packed from their trip to New York.

Fuck. He looked away, ripping off his V-neck T-shirt, trying to force away the thoughts of so many hot private moments with Althea running through his brain. Then he remembered how opposed she was to extending their arrangement to even another goddamned visit.

She was so ready to let these last few days fade away while he was slowly losing his mind. Griffen felt like he wanted to hit something, anything, a lot. Every time he closed his eyes he saw her — was going crazy about her — but she was content to let him go.

He turned on the TV, but couldn't sit still. Flipping it off, he stood and walked across the room, opening his laptop and glancing at emails. His jittery fingers closed the lid and he crossed the room to stand by the floor to ceiling windows.

Griffen felt hot all over and placed his hands against the cool glass, but that was no help. He could almost picture the steamy imprint of her perfect body against the glass from the first time he touched her and pressed into her so her bare ass and back were pressed fully against that glass.

Every inch of her body and each word from her lips drove him insane even then. Before he knew who she was and the grief that prevented her from letting him truly near her. Before he knew she would rather push him away then take a risk on him — and damned if he could blame her.

What could he truly offer a great woman like that? His father had been right — he *was* a piece of shit. He'd spent his whole life avoiding any attachments, sleeping with lots of women, running from every responsibility, and the worst sin — deserting Jack when he needed him most. His best friend, who — if Griffen was honest with himself — had apparently been desperate enough to betray his own country.

Griffen didn't deserve Althea. No matter how much he tried to fool himself that he could.

He slammed his hand so firmly against the glass that it reverberated around the impact.

He breathed deeply and rested his hot forehead against the window, looking down at the streams of people below, unaware of the desperate man above.

Is she getting dressed now for her date? Is she going to wear something red? She looks fucking hot in red. What is she going to eat? Will she like him? Will she end things with me early? I want more time but, fuck, if I lose the precious few she'll actually give me, I'll go nuts.

Every inch of this room was coated with memories of her — pulsated with them. He needed to get out of the room, the hotel. To go anywhere but here. He put on running clothes and grabbed his ear-buds, wallet, and iPhone as he stalked out of his room.

He walked briskly through the lobby, waved to the doorman, and then he ran for miles and miles. Threatening gray clouds pressed down from above, while below, each of his steps pounded the frustration through his body and down into the sidewalk and back into him, as though they were trying to beat each other into submission.

The streets, buildings, and people passed by him in a blur, all he could think of was the next pounding step, because beyond that there was nothing but loneliness, a return to his life before Althea.

It wasn't until his last step took him to the gates of the historic Allegheny Cemetery in Lawrenceville that he realized he'd run straight to Jack.

He grabbed the wrought iron gates for a moment, as the impact of where he was passed through his heaving lungs like oxygen. It had started drizzling and when he licked his lips they were tinged with a hint of the metallic rust from the gates he clutched.

Stepping back he looked in front of him to the acres of perfect trees arching over the rows of the dead. Some were famous, some were rich, some were poor, some had been here for centuries, some had been young, some had been old — but what they had in common was that they all were dead. And Jack was with them.

Griffen finally let his feet move forward, so slowly it felt like he was pushing through wet cement as he moved closer to his greatest shame. He bought white daisies from the guy at the gate, more to have something to hold onto instead of simply clenching his hands into fists.

His fear and regret had kept him from Jack's funeral. Instead, he'd stayed holed up in his New York apartment, sitting on the floor in the dark, drinking himself into oblivion and counting all the things he hadn't done.

Because often when you do nothing it's worse than doing the wrong thing.

And Griffen had done *nothing* for Jack.

Griffen followed the route to Jack's grave, having studied the map of the cemetery, and Jack's location in it, more times than he could count. It was a testament to the deep connections Jack's family had in this town that he was given a place of rest here.

His grave was marked by a simple, masculine tombstone in a patch of ground that looked like it would be bathed in sunlight on nice days:

Jack Taylor - Beloved husband, son and friend.

There was a framed picture of Johnny as a baby, apparently added later. It was engraved to say, "*To my Father with Love.*" The sight twisted Griffen's heart in a fist.

"Hi Jack. It's me, Nicky." Griffen's childhood name came out of his mouth on a twisted cry and he sat down in front of the tombstone to keep from falling down. The sweat from his run and the gentle rain were chilling on his skin, accompanied by warm fresh tears that fell silently from his eyes. His shoulders shook from the force of the emotion but he stayed silent as his body expelled the years of loss and pain.

"I'm so sorry, Jack. So sorry. I don't know why I didn't respond to you. I planned to, but I was too late. I let you down."

Griffen was finally able to catch his breath and stared straight ahead, his heart beating through the emptiness inside him.

"I've been hanging out with your son, Johnny. He looks so much like you. And he's awesome — so funny and smart. But someone really should work with him on his 'R's.' Plus he drops back to pass too slowly, just like you," Griffen added with a light laugh.

"I'm working on his passing with him. I've been coaching him. I forgot how much I actually liked about the game. I tell him about you. What we did together. I read him one of our stories the other day. He loved it. He always wants to hear all about you.

"I hope that you can see him from where you are. I don't believe in much, but I want to believe that's true. And I hope you forgive me for letting you down. For putting myself first. I've missed you so much, man. *So much.*

"I found your flash drive. I'm trying to figure out what happened to you. I know I let you down when you needed me, but I want to do everything I can to make it right. It's just…everything looks like you were into something really messed up, man. Like you did something bad." Griffen picked up a piece of wet grass and balled it between his fingers.

He looked straight ahead and finally said, "While I'm here, I should probably tell you that I think I'm in love with your wife. I know, its all kinds of screwed up and you probably want to beat the shit out of me. I guess you know how great she is, man. She makes me so happy. I don't feel angry or sad when I'm with her. And I think I make her feel better — because she's sad, man."

"She still loves you and won't move on. But I just want her to be happy. I'm not good enough for Althea but I want to try to be."

Standing up he rubbed his face hard with the palm of his hand and he knew he had to see her.

"Goodbye Jack." Griffen slowly turned away and pulled his phone from his pocket.

"Hi Jenna."

"Griffen?"

"I'm sorry to bother you, but do you know where Althea is? I need to talk to her."

"She's still out with Curt. Hold on...*Johnny, let me go get something from the kitchen. Watch SpongeBob, I'll be right back.* Griffen, what's going on? When Tea called me to babysit for a date with Curt I was pretty surprised."

"I thought I was doing the right thing."

"What did you do?"

She sounded stern and he felt like an errant child.

"I've asked her for more. First I said I didn't have to leave right away, but she shot that down."

"Not surprising from her," Jenna said gruffly.

"Then I offered to visit her after I leave. I don't know, I guess I wanted to test the waters...but she's pretty stuck on just two weeks with me, so I thought maybe this guy could make her happy. I just want her to be happy."

"So you told her to go on a date with Curt?"

"Yeah."

"And you're turning yourself inside out thinking about her with someone else?"

"That about covers it, yeah."

She sighed and said, "Look, Curt's fine. I pushed her on him myself. He's kind of annoying but he's solid and steady — two things I look for in a guy myself, but he won't make her happy. You do."

"She doesn't want me." *Shit*, he sounded pathetic even to his own ears.

"She wants you all right. I've never seen her like this, not since she met Jack. That's why she's pushing you away. Letting someone into her heart again terrifies her. She wants you to

246

leave *because* she's so crazy about you." Jenna paused and took a deep breath. "Look, they're still at dinner. She texted to ask about Johnny and told me she should be home in about an hour. If you get there in a half hour you should be able to catch her before anything, you know."

The image made Griffen see red and he growled, "He'd better fucking keep his hands off her."

"Ease off, Griffen. You want to find them, not kill the guy."

"I don't know, that option is sounding pretty attractive right now."

"I'm sure it does, but try to stay out of jail, okay? I'll text you the restaurant info."

"Hey, Jenna?"

"Yeah?"

"Thanks."

"Of course. I just want her to be happy, too."

He started jogging back to the main road, calling a cab on the way. The taxi gods were with him because one pulled up to him five minutes later. Griffen recognized the fancy steakhouse Curt had taken her to, as it was close to his hotel downtown.

Was she thinking of me when he brought her here? Only steps from where we've made love so many times.

He tipped the valets outside the restaurant heavily to let him wait outside the restaurant without hassling him.

She should be out any minute now.

CHAPTER FIFTEEN

Althea stared across the table at Curt and took a deep breath.

He was an okay guy. Steady, dependable, successful, and interested enough in her to pursue her for over a year now. He seemed to like Johnny and could be a potential father to him. She knew she'd never love him, never risk opening her heart to him, meaning he fit what she was looking for perfectly.

Isn't this what I wanted? Then why does being with Curt make me feel like a part of me is missing? Why am I so miserable?

Her phone vibrated and she saw a text from David: *Be careful on your date. I still think it's a bad idea.*

She rolled her eyes. She knew she needed to get back to David. He'd been repeatedly trying to get in contact with her since they last spoke but her life had been so crazy since Griffen stepped into it that she hadn't been able to give David her usual amount of attention, beyond little updates, like telling him she was on this date.

She reminded herself that it was for the best that Griffen simply move on. The best thing she could do was try to make the most of this date and get back into her routine with her friends, David included. Even so, right now all the attention people put on one date mostly just annoyed her.

"A date?" Carol had shrieked when Althea told her. She'd seemed beside herself.

Althea had debated keeping it from Carol, but then decided telling her about a guy she cared nothing about was a good baby step for the day. *"I've been on dates before, Carol."*

"I know, but that was years ago. I thought it was a phase. Are you sure you want to do this?"

No, she had thought, but not for the reasons Carol assumed.

"I mean, you're Jack's wife. It's just doesn't seem right, don't you think? You didn't see me dating after his father died," Carol had added vehemently. *"Besides, having strange men around Johnny is pretty irresponsible. Does David know? He would agree,"* Carol insisted. *"He thinks you dating is a bad idea, too."*

"It's not David's business, but yes, he agrees with you," Althea had said softly.

"He took Jack under his wing and has looked out for you and me like family. I'd say it's his business!"

"Well, you and David can pull back on the family protectiveness. I don't even like this guy, Carol. It's more of a favor to Jenna. He's her friend." That had seemed to appease Carol, but the excuses Althea gave made her baby steps seem pretty meaningless.

Now that she knew Carol's negative reaction to a date with someone that meant nothing to her she felt more sure keeping Griffen a secret and letting him go were wise choices.

So why do I feel so sad about him leaving?

She ordered herself to stop thinking about Griffen and refocused her ears on Curt.

"...I mean how are you even going to get something like that out of a shirt, right? Tea?"

"Hmm?" She cringed when she realized she'd been ignoring Curt for a solid few minutes. "I'm so sorry, I had a text. What did you ask?"

And at that, Curt started to drone on again and Althea used all her energy to try and pay attention.

Griffen suddenly understood what people meant when they said a person took their breath away, because when he finally saw Althea walk out of the restaurant he was pretty sure he would pass out from oxygen deprivation.

But then he caught sight of Curt's hand at the small of her back. The two were huddled under his umbrella and the closeness of their bodies shot an overwhelming wave of adrenaline through Griffen — making his fists clench and his heart race.

"Griffen?" Althea's mouth dropped open when she spotted him standing near the door. Her eyes were wide and Griffen realized he must've looked crazed.

The drizzling shower from before had turned into a steady late summer rain, the rumbling thunder in the distance threatening that the worst was yet to come. He'd been pacing outside for ten minutes, so he was thoroughly soaked — and that was on top of what he figured were wild eyes and a worn out body from the multiple miles he'd run not too long before. The fact that he was still in sweaty running clothes didn't help matters much either.

Althea walked toward him and water started to pepper her face and body as she left the protection of Curt's umbrella. She looked up at him, her face streaked with worry, and his throat tightened.

"Griffen, are you all right?" she asked.

"No. I'm not all right," he said gruffly, closing the last bit of space between them so that she had to crane her neck back to look into his eyes. "I had to see you," he whispered.

She'd done something with her eyes to make them look almost completely green with flecks of gold, all nestled in that black ring around them. Her hair was shiny and fell in soft waves past her shoulders. The rain was falling harder and it only made her look more luminous.

Griffen felt anger build inside him thinking that she'd gone to that much effort for someone else, but he still couldn't look away from those beautiful eyes. He thought he could spend every day of his life with her just to see how different her eyes looked from each moment to the next.

"Hey, Griffen Tate, right?" Curt held out his hand to Griffen, breaking the connection between him and Althea. "We met at Johnny's party, remember?"

"That's right."

"Griffen, I don't understand..." Althea whispered so only he could hear, a look of confusion on her face.

"Well, uh, it's nice to see you again, but Tea and I need to get going. Come on, Tea," Curt said.

"No, sorry. There's been a change of plans. I need to take Althea home. Now," Griffen said, not looking away from Althea or her slightly parted lips. He felt some relief that she hadn't stopped staring into his eyes either.

"Excuse me? Not sure what's going on with you, man, but Tea and I are on a date and now we're *leaving. Together.*" Althea finally looked away from Griffen, nervously eyeing the two men back and forth.

"Date's over," Griffen growled.

"Griffen!" Althea exclaimed, looking toward Curt apologetically. Griffen grasped her chin with his fingers and turned her eyes back to his. She fumed but took a deep breath and didn't pull away, making Griffen's heart slow slightly. "Griffen..."

"What the hell, man? Tea, what's going on here?" Curt asked.

Griffen finally stepped away from Althea and stood right in front of Curt, noticing the shorter man's breath quicken as he stared him down. "I told you *man*, the *date's over*."

Althea turned and said softly, "It's okay, Curt. Go home. Let me take care of this."

"Tea, I was really hoping to take you home." Curt sounded whiny and when he went to kiss Althea's cheek Griffen was thrilled to see her instinctively flinch away from him just a fraction. When Curt didn't give up, Griffen pressed a hand on his chest so firmly he had to take a step back to regain his balance.

"Please, Curt, let me handle this. I'll call you, okay?" Althea pleaded.

"Time to go, Curt," Griffen said, moving his firm hand to Curt's shoulder and steering him away from Althea.

Griffen noticed the valets were starting to get uncomfortable. He'd given them a lot of money, but they probably had a limit to what they would ignore. Griffen didn't care. He may have spent his whole life trying not to be a violent prick like his dad, but he was more than ready to beat the shit out of this guy if he didn't leave. In fact, it would feel pretty good, but then he reminded himself that it would get him nowhere with Althea.

Griffen took a breath and released Curt's shirt. "Head on home Curt. I mean it."

"What the fuck?" Curt shook off Griffen's hand and smoothed his shirt down. Griffen stared at him until his eyes widened. "Fine. Goodnight Tea," Curt said sullenly, finally turning and walking away quickly.

"Goodnight, Curt," she said to his retreating back.

Althea looked back at Griffen and he could see she was furious, but she hadn't moved, so Griffen took that as a good sign.

"Well, that was polite," she huffed at him, straightening her shoulders. "You said you had to see me. Well, you're seeing me," she said, raising her chin obstinately. "What do you want Griffen?"

Griffen turned to Althea and walked her slowly backward until her back was pressed against the craggy stone covered wall.

"You," he answered.

She started to pull away but he grabbed her hands in his, holding her in place and kissed her fiercely. This was not a sweet or romantic joining of lips. It was a fierce claiming of her with his tongue, lips and teeth, as he deposited all the desire and frustration of the day into her warm, perfect mouth. The rain was falling harder now, sliding down their cheeks and mingling in their mouths with their heated kiss.

When he released her mouth he ran his hands up her arms until they rested around her neck, his thumbs lifting her chin so he could stare into her eyes — almost totally darkened with desire.

When she instinctively looked around, he pressed against her harder growling, "I don't give a fuck who sees. I hope everyone in the world sees." Then he kissed her again.

"I don't get it. I'm feeling a bit of whiplash here, Griffen," she whispered, still leaning forward into his body. "You pushed me to go out with Curt. I was surprised at first, but after I thought about it, I decided you were right. I mean, we only have a few days left..."

He winced at the mention of her fixation on their end date, then he grabbed her roughly at the top of the arms. "I wasn't right, dammit."

Griffen breathed deeply and rested his forehead on hers.

"But at breakfast you said..."

"Fuck what I said, I was being an idiot. I thought it was what *you* wanted." He let her arms go and tugged his fingers through her wet hair. "But, fuck Althea! I don't want you with anyone else. No doctors, no lawyers, no accountants, no firemen. Just *me*."

"What are you saying?" she asked nervously.

"I'm so fucked up, Althea. I don't know what I have to give you, I know I don't deserve you, but I want to be with you. So much. I know you say you aren't ready for more, but please let me be with you tonight. Give me a chance to figure it out."

"Griffen..."

"We'll talk about it tomorrow. Don't turn me away. I can't think straight right now and I'm bound to mess things up with you even more. Just let me get a cab and take you home and we'll take it from there? Please?"

Althea looked in his eyes, raindrops glistening on each of her curled eyelashes. She searched his face and he knew she must see only tortured darkness. Griffen had never felt so crazed or possessive in his life. His hands kept touching her face, her neck, her shoulders, her waist. Like he was trying to convince himself that she was really there in front of him.

"I should tell you no," she whispered looking in his eyes. "I should let you go."

"Althea, please..."

"But I want you to come home with me."

"Thank you, Althea," he said, kissing her until he was lost in her again, the same way he felt every time they were together.

After the cab parked in front of her house, Griffen quickly led Althea inside by the hand to get her out of the now pounding rain.

Jenna met them at the door and her eyes widened at Griffen's appearance.

"Hi guys. Well, um, let me get out of your hair. Johnny's been asleep about an hour. He was pretty exhausted, so you've got the place to yourselves. Good luck you two, and good night," she said with an awkward smile as she scurried out.

As the door clicked shut, Griffen grabbed Althea around the waist and lifted her feet just off the ground so he could kiss her as he walked her to her room.

"You ever notice that you're always picking me up?" she breathed out as she nibbled his earlobe.

"That's because you're always making me impatient," he growled.

"I think you're just a caveman under all this sophisticated sexiness," she whispered, licking his neck. "Mmm, salty. My caveman tastes so good. It turns me on," Althea purred against his skin.

"Only with you. All of this is only with you," he whispered back to her, his heart soaring at her saying he was hers. No matter what happened next, he would let himself enjoy this moment.

When he placed her feet on the floor he looked down into her eyes, still so desperate for her. He closed the door to her bedroom and slowly began undressing her. He ran his fingers through her hair, letting the mass of soft, damp waves fall over his hands and down her back. He then peeled off her wet dress that was clinging to her enticing body and gently unhooked her bra.

He had to see her, had to feel her, but more than that, he had to know how willing she'd been to move on with someone else.

"Did he touch you?" he asked quietly.

"What?" Her eyes were unfocused and dilated, drunk on the pleasurable touches he was giving her.

Griffen pressed more firmly into her skin, "Did. He. Touch. You?"

"Griffen..."

He relaxed and stroked her shoulder. "Did he touch you here?"

"He took off my jacket," she answered.

Griffen growled a little. "So, he touched you here." Griffen ran his fingertips across her shoulder and collarbones. Following them with his tongue and teeth. Nibbling and marking everywhere the other man's hand had been until she was panting from his attention. "Where else did he touch you, Althea?" he whispered after licking up her neck to bite on her earlobe.

"He led me out of the restaurant," she breathed.

"I saw that. I didn't like it," he growled again. "So, he touched you here," Griffen said as his fingertips moved, barely touching the small of her back. Griffen knelt behind her stroking the cheeks of her bottom and massaging as he licked the small of her back.

He slowly pulled her panties down her legs, supporting her as she stepped out of them. Then he ran his tongue up her thigh and over to the seam of her ass — licking and grazing her flesh with his teeth.

"He didn't touch me there. Nowhere else. I wouldn't have let him," Althea said.

"Why, gorgeous? Why wouldn't you have let him?"

"Because I wanted it to be you touching me. So much. Not him."

"Good. So then I'll touch everywhere he didn't, too."

She spun around and knelt down in front of him, joining him on the floor. Placing her hands on his face she said, "Yes, please. But I need you inside me first. Now."

Griffen wrapped his arms around her back roughly and leaned her backward to suck on one breast, then the other. Each moan she released drove him crazier. His need to mark her becoming more intense by the moment.

"Please, Griffen. Now."

He couldn't wait either. He walked over to the bedside table and pulled out a condom from the stash he'd left there earlier in the week. When he returned to her on the floor she quickly pulled down his running shorts and boxer briefs, revealing his throbbing length. He was rock hard and his mind was still racing and feverish from his shit of a day. He kissed her deeply, running his hands down her sides and pulling her close. He was incapable of feeling anything but being completely lost over this woman, over his life, over everything.

But when he lay her back and thrust inside her in one stroke, peace finally found him.

He stilled for a moment, enjoying the completeness he knew he couldn't give up. She was just as crazy as him, rolling them over so she could straddle his lap and ride him — hard.

He leaned back on his hands, his muscles rippling from the effort, his legs straightened for even more traction. He had to take control. Needed it. Reaching one arm back around her he guided her up and down, deeper than he'd ever been before. She let go for him, throwing her head back and moaning, tightening and clenching around him.

On a final thrust she tightened hard around him and he pulled her firmly back against him, stroking his tongue in her mouth.

He swallowed her moans and vibrating screams, only matched by the intensity of his own. Griffen came powerfully inside her, leaving nothing for himself — all was given to her. They panted and held each other, silently caressing and reminding themselves they were back in each other's arms.

No matter what happens next, we are together now, he assured himself.

Althea finally broke the silence with a little giggle.

"Gorgeous you're lucky I have a healthy ego or I might be worried about you laughing right now."

"Oh no. Nothing to worry about, stud. I just think it's safe to say you've successfully made me forget all about Curt."

"Good," he said, squeezing her tightly. "Now let me get you off this floor and into the shower with me. I want to touch you all over properly like I promised and don't want to wait until after I wash this day off me. I've got a lot of sexy ground to cover."

"Are you up to the task?"

"It's a tough job but I'm more than happy to do it."

After leading her to the *en suite* bath and pulling her under the warm water with him he proceeded to kiss, touch, and tease her until the day fell away and there was nothing but the feel of each other in their arms.

CHAPTER SIXTEEN

Griffen reached across the bed but when his hand found cool, smooth sheets instead of a warm, sexy woman, he reluctantly opened his eyes.

He looked across the room and caught sight of Althea, wrapped in a light robe, her arms gripping her waist as she stared out the window, her eyes dark and distant. The room was dark but the contours of her forlorn face were occasionally illuminated by flashes of faraway lightning.

The rain was still coming down in violent sheets outside, sliding down the window in front of her as it beat onto the rivers nestled beneath the rock face on which her home perched. It was as though the sky was listening to the sadness in her heart, crying for her and he couldn't help but feel like he was intruding on their intimate conversation.

He walked over to her, running his fingers through his hair. She looked back at him with glassy eyes.

"Gorgeous? What's wrong?"

"I just couldn't sleep. Sorry I woke you."

She looked back out the window. He stood beside her, waiting for her to share whatever was going on in her head with him. It felt like years before she opened her mouth again.

"I love that I can see all three rivers from here. Jack and I had the coolest condo in Lawrenceville. Loads of bars, restaurants, artists — it was so cool — but I could only see the Allegheny River from there. This is better."

"Why'd you move?" Griffen asked cautiously. He could sense her mood was dark and he wanted to be careful, like he was approaching a spooked horse that may rear back and run off at any moment.

She turned to him slowly. "Carol wanted me to move here — closer to her — as soon as we found out about the baby. I fought it for a while. I couldn't leave the house at all for weeks, selling it seemed even crazier. Then it was robbed one night while I was at school. The whole place was ruined, ransacked. Not much was taken, thank God, but after that, well, I didn't fight Carol anymore. I just gave in — gave up — and moved. But I like it here. I like this view."

"Is that what you were thinking about just now? Is that why you woke up?"

"No." She looked away again, "I, uh, had a bad dream."

Griffen touched her cheek and found his fingers came back wet. "Why are you crying? What was your nightmare about?"

"Same basic one I've had since Jack died."

"Do you want to tell me about it?" he asked softly.

Her eyes moved over his face slowly, as if she was trying to make a decision about something. She finally looked deeply into his eyes for a moment and then turned back to stare at the rivers again before she answered.

"I dream that Jack is alive. Sometimes I'm big and pregnant and he's so proud and happy. He touches my belly and we talk about baby names. Sometimes I'm telling him I'm pregnant. We cheer as we look at the test strip. Sometimes I'm holding baby Johnny. Sometimes Jack's walking Johnny and me home from a youth football game. We both hold one of Johnny's hands and swing him back and forth between us as we all laugh. We are so happy.

"But when I let go of Johnny and reach out to touch Jack's hand it falls apart in mine and turns to dust. He just...disintegrates right there. Sometimes it's more gruesome. He's waterlogged from the river, with drug hazed eyes, reaching for me. He starts to bleed, out of his eyes, his mouth, everywhere. I try to grab for him but only come back with blood and bone. Then his flesh falls away.

"The dream may be different, but the end is always the same. In the end, everything is gone. Jack is gone. Our home is gone. Our baby is gone. It's just me, in the dark, with an aching heart and empty hands. I wake up clutching the sheet, panting, looking around. It's ridiculous. Like I'm in an eighties TV show, or something."

Griffen swallowed around the tightness in his throat. Her voice was eerily smooth but tears streamed down her lovely face like the rivers from which she couldn't seem to look away.

"Do they happen often?" he managed to choke out.

"Used to be I had them all the time, every few days." She looked at him and smiled faintly. "There is a bright side. It makes me productive. I get a lot of client work done at two-thirty in the morning."

"You said used to. Have they slowed down?"

"This is the first one I've had in almost two weeks."

"Oh," Griffen said, pausing to let the significance of that to sink in. "I'm so sorry baby," he whispered as he kissed the tears across her cheeks.

Althea sighed and touched his cheek gently. "Don't be

sorry, Griffen, it's not your fault. I don't want to think about whose fault it is. It just *is*."

But Griffen did feel like it was his fault that Jack was gone, leaving her here alone, and all he wanted to do was make her pain go away — if she would only let him try.

Griffen stroked her cheek and Althea thought how truly sorry she was to have woken him, especially because what she didn't tell him was that tonight it wasn't Jack's face that turned to dust and disappeared. It was *his*.

"Althea..." Griffen whispered.

"Shh. No," she said softly as she reached up and caressed his face gently in return. "Will you just...will you please make love to me, Griffen?"

"Anytime, gorgeous."

But it won't be anytime anymore, Althea thought. *He will turn to dust and I will be all alone. Again.*

And she knew it had to be that way, because this emptiness in her heart was the penance she would always have to pay for failing Jack.

Griffen led her to the bed and they made love. It was the most tender and gentle experience of their time together. Griffen touched her everywhere, stroked her hair, kissed her face and soothed away each tear. He ran his lips down her chest and she gasped as he sucked her nipple into his mouth reverently. He somehow managed to put on a condom despite touching every part of her constantly and slid gently inside of her. She was grateful because she didn't want any lead-in this time. She just needed him inside her, while her hands were full of his hair and his warm, giving flesh. She moaned and lifted his head from her breast to look at him.

"Baby," he said, kissing her eyelids and finally claiming her mouth. She wrapped her legs around his, even curling her feet around his calves, desperately trying to make every inch of her body touch his.

She was so preoccupied with how full and complete she felt that her climax surprised her. This had not been about an orgasm, it was about closeness and human contact. Running off the demons of loss and fear, if only for a moment.

But Griffen didn't know how to leave her unsatisfied. He couldn't touch her without making her body go off like a sparkler in the backyard on the fourth of July, and even now, with his gentle lovemaking, it was no different. He groaned in her ear and came right along with her, spurring more spasms and electric shocks through her body.

"Oh Griffen, yes, Griffen," she responded.

He leaned up and looked into her eyes, brushing her hair back from her face. His face looked so tormented.

"Oh Althea," he said sadly over and over again, almost like a prayer, until he rolled over and held her until she finally fell into a blessedly dreamless sleep.

Althea was sleeping deeply but Griffen felt totally wired. He stared up at her antique tin ceiling, trying to calm himself as every raw emotion of the day and night coursed through him with electric pulsing energy. He counted each square border, his mind repeatedly returning to the recognition that he needed Althea in his life.

He wanted to be the one to comfort her and hold her, but every time he made a move she shot him down, whether it was keeping them secret or refusing to let them go beyond this arbitrary two-week mark. He'd simply accepted it so far, but now, after having seen her haunted eyes after her dream, he felt even more desperate for something more.

There was no chance of getting back to sleep, so he simply rolled over and watched the gentle rise and fall of Althea's chest for hours, holding her against him in the nook of his arm. Her soft hair fell along her face grazing him enough to feel her presence with every gentle breath. He looked down at her face, marveling at how the colors of the night brightened into morning across her golden skin and honey hair.

Griffen felt like he'd been careening down a mountain since he'd met her. She had complete control and he felt no desire to take it back. This time with her was the best he could remember in his life, he would be a fool to let that go, especially when she so clearly needed someone — could he hope that someone could be *him*?

What an asshole he'd been all these years. Fixating on his own grief and guilt, knocking around the world, spending money and having meaningless affairs to hide his pain while this beautiful woman struggled to make a life by herself — with a kid. A great kid that Griffen wanted to be around as much as with her.

He couldn't take her to New York, but nothing was preventing him from staying in Pittsburgh. It's not like there was anything waiting for him there except for an empty apartment, he didn't even have a dog or cat. What was he going back to? Not his writing. His inspiration was here. All he had in New York was loneliness and empty sex — and he couldn't even think of touching another woman right now.

How had I thought I could swoop in and make this woman happy then disappear? How could I have thought I wouldn't completely fall for her?

Sick cold dread passed through him at the thought of leaving and all he kept reminding himself was that he didn't have to, that he could offer up whatever he could give to this perfect woman.

She could throw his offer back in his face and tell him again how she wasn't ready, but maybe he could make her see that there was no shame in letting them be something real. Maybe she would take another chance on him and let this be the start of something amazing.

Griffen picked up his phone and started to write an email to Professor Stevens.

Althea opened her eyes to see Griffen staring at her. She smiled up at him, enjoying the feeling of waking up in his arms. Even though she'd woken this way every morning since they made their arrangement, it still left her reeling with pleasure at the sensation.

"Good morning," he said tightly.

"Good morning, stud," she said and curled into him closer, only to still when she saw how tortured his face looked. "Hey, you okay?" She suddenly felt awkward, remembering her nightmare. She hoped it wasn't still lurking like a shadow over their last uncertain days together, but the way he was looking at her so intently made that appear unlikely. She sighed and looked more deeply into his eyes as she stroked his cheek. "Spill it, Griffen. What's going on?"

"I want to stay."

"Today? I have a client meeting this afternoon, I could maybe get coffee, but that's it. I'm sorry."

"That's not what I mean. I contacted Professor Stevens. He still needs someone to fill in, maybe for the whole rest of the semester. I can keep teaching and spending time with you and Johnny."

"I don't understand."

"I want to stay here in Pittsburgh...and be with you."

"What? Griffen, what brought this on? We talked about not making this more than it is."

He gripped her tightly. "No, *you* talked about that. I just didn't tell you how wrong I think you are."

Her heart sped up and she suddenly felt her lungs clench, like a caged animal she started looking for an escape from the bed. Griffen turned her head to make her face him. She tilted up her chin with more confidence than she felt. "Is this because of last night and my dream? If that's what's going on you can stop it. I don't want you feeling sorry for me."

"No, I could never feel sorry for you. But I'd be lying if I said it didn't kick my ass to see you in pain."

She clutched at the sheet, feeling so exposed all of a sudden. "You don't need to come here and swoop in to rescue the poor lonely widow."

"Come on, stop that bullshit right now." Her eyes widened at his hard words, but he kissed her forehead to soften the blow. "You give me too much credit, gorgeous. I actually happen to like you, a lot. Whether it's in bed, out of bed, dreaming or awake. And during each of those times I could never pity you."

"So it's not about last night?" she asked skeptically.

"All right. Yes, you worried me and I wanted to help you but I would never stay just for that. I'm way too self-absorbed for that," he said with a wicked half smile.

"So you're absorbed in me then, huh?"

"Well, right now I'm not absorbed in you the way I'd like to be," he said stroking her thigh.

"There you go, not being serious again."

"Oh, I'm serious as a heart attack, gorgeous. In fact, I feel like I'm turning inside out right now waiting for your answer."

"What are you suggesting, really?"

"I want to stay here in Pittsburgh with you. I want you give us a shot."

"You know I can't let you do that."

"I know you think you aren't ready. But I think you're capable of so much more than you give yourself credit for. I want to be here for you...to be *with* you." He swallowed and stared at a spot over her head as he breathed slowly. A moment later he was calmly looking back in her eyes, searching for something from her. "Honestly, I've been thinking about us trying to be something real for a while, even before last night when I came over to the restaurant..."

"And acted like a crazy person?" she teased and was relieved to hear him chuckle.

"Yeah, like a crazy person." He smiled and started to cup one breast, rubbing a rough thumb over her nipple. She let out an embarrassing moan as a now familiar wave of desire swept through her and her nipple puckered in response.

"No fair," she said though she couldn't help but push into his touch. He always seemed able to make her act like a cat in heat and it really interfered with her decision-making skills.

"Seems fair to me," he said nipping her earlobe with his teeth and whispering, "I'm totally lucid right now and I think this is a great idea."

Althea started to feel that tightness in her chest again.

He wants a real future together?

The thought of how deeply her feelings could grow for him terrified her.

"I'm already too attached to you as it is. Johnny, too. It wasn't supposed to be like that. I should've held back more."

"What's wrong with being attached to me?"

"Nothing's changed for me."

"Only because you won't let it. Look. I know I'm not good enough for you right now but I'm asking for a chance to try to be."

"Don't keep saying crap like that, Griffen. I think you're great. It's just...it's just been me and Johnny and this grief for so long...I don't know any other way. Caring about someone again? It still feels so wrong."

"What if we compromise? What if you give me a couple more months? Till the end of the semester? I can write anywhere."

"I thought you said you hated it here."

"I know, but I've spent so long hating this place and all...all the bad memories it represents for me, but seeing it with you again — being a part of something with you and Johnny here — it has already made so many new great memories for me. It makes me think I can move on, too."

"I'm just not sure. I mean the whole point of this was that it wouldn't push me too much."

"I don't want to push you, but I refuse to let you just push me away."

"Griffen," she whispered, "wasn't it supposed to be just, um, physical?"

"I think we both know we've shared more than just that by now." He stroked her shoulder and it felt so good to her, but the panic wouldn't subside.

"You're asking me to take a lot of leaps and risks that I just don't think I'm ready for. I mean what about all your other women? Like that Vicky person? You said no strings when this all started, and you clearly have entertainment waiting for you when you get back. I mean, you probably have a few other 'plant waterers' scattered here and there."

"Of course I wouldn't mess with other women if we were

together. Yes, that was how I lived my life *before*. Before I met you I never wanted anything real with anyone. You changed that and you know it. I think you're just looking for excuses to say no."

"No, I'm making sense and your lifestyle just makes me that much more uncomfortable with what you're asking of me."

"All I'm asking for is a chance. I've lived this way because I never had any reason not to. You are all that I want. Trust me. Please."

She looked away. "Honestly? I'm scared Griffen," she said so quietly, she didn't know how he could hear her. "I know I've pushed people away, but I don't know any other way anymore."

"Look," he said, turning her face back to his, "If you knew back when you were nineteen and met Jack that it would end the way it did, that he would die, that you would be heartbroken, would you change anything? Would you transfer out of the nineteenth century lit class you had with him?"

"No."

"Why not?"

"Because I wouldn't give up those memories, the joy, the growth, the love. It's all part of what defines me."

"So why won't you take a chance on us? On me? That maybe I can give you some more good memories, keep on giving you joy."

"I just don't know."

"If not for me, what about Johnny? I'm crazy about him. I want to be in his life — to share in that piece of Jack. I lost Jack, too."

"You may have lost a friend, but I lost *everything!*"

They'd been whispering to keep from waking Johnny, but she could feel herself getting out of control. She breathed in and out slowly.

Griffen reached across and pulled her to him. He tilted her chin up and looked straight in her eyes. "You didn't die that night, Althea."

"Didn't I? A piece of me did. The piece that didn't live every day with guilt. The piece that could take chances. The piece that wasn't terrified of fucking everything up all over again." She looked away but she could tell he wouldn't let her break their physical connection. He stroked her hair and rested her cheek on his chest. "You can't understand, Griffen," she whispered softly against his broad chest, his warmth and strength bringing her comfort even then.

"Yes, I can."

"How can you know about my guilt, my loss? How can you even try to understand? You've never lost everything, have you?"

He gripped her body so tightly she was sure he would leave her with bruises. "I know, dammit," he grunted out. She gasped at his passion and he breathed slowly, clearly trying to regain his own control. He rested his forehead against hers and they both stayed that way for so long she was worried Johnny would wake up soon.

"How?" she looked up at him, honestly curious. "How do you know?"

He softly said, "Althea, I know about guilt, just trust me, I do. And I know how your heart broke. That's because I feel that way, too. I lost a lot when Jack died, too. I know how you felt even more now because if something happened to you, I'd be lost."

"Really?" she whispered.

He looked down at her again and she felt the emotion as he choked out, "Totally lost, Althea. Christ, I can't even think about going up to New York in a couple of days without my whole heart turning over. I'm not ready for this to end between us. I'm not sure if I ever will be."

That reality tore through Althea, making her chest actually hurt. "I don't know, Griffen."

"Give me another baby step. Please," he said and held her tight.

"That's a lot of baby steps, Griffen. More than I think I can handle. I'm so sorry."

"Are you saying no?"

She looked up and stroked his cheek. "Not no, just I need some time. Let me think about it, okay?"

"Okay," he gritted his teeth and she reached up and replaced her hand with her lips on his cheek.

"I'll see you at Johnny's game later and then I promise I'll have an answer tonight."

Griffen clutched her even more tightly, until every part of her was touching some part of him. He kissed her eyelids, then peppered tiny kisses down her cheeks, licking across the seam of her lips. When she gasped he claimed her mouth with his, nibbling on her lower lip and then tangling his tongue with hers.

"Althea, please say yes. Please."

"You're persuasive, but just give me the hours, okay?"

"Okay, I promise to be patient today, but I don't have to like it."

"Thank you. I have to get dressed. I'll see you tonight?"

"Okay," he whispered and she walked out of the room — fear and hope fighting with each other at every step.

CHAPTER SEVENTEEN

Griffen was crawling out of his skin after leaving Althea's place. This was the first time in his life he'd asked a woman to commit to him and it hadn't gone exactly well. Instead of going crazy for her answer, he drove his car to *CMU*. He knew if he wanted to have something real with Althea he had to have this investigation resolved. It was bad enough he'd kept it from her this long. So he unclenched his teeth and refocused on figuring out what had happened to Jack, or — God forbid — find out what Jack had done.

He stepped out of his car and walked across the manicured grass of *CMU's* campus. Just a quick shot up a hill from Pitt, it felt like another world. Pitt was every bit a school in a city, with crowds and noise and urban skyscrapers, while *CMU* was a quiet refuge dotted with open spaces, traditional architecture, and quiet understated beauty. It was a sunny, pleasant day, attracting numerous students to picnic, read, and play Frisbee throughout the entire quad.

The school was especially known for its programs in high-tech business, robotics and theater — and it was easy to peg the students running past him to their respective departments.

He ignored the few beautiful people trying to be the next Matt Bomer or Joe Manganiello and instead grabbed a skinny, geeky looking guy with a homemade Yoda T-shirt on that said, *"Longer Last Taking a Picture of Me Will."*

Oh yeah, this power-nerd knows where to find the robotics department.

"Hey man, I'm here to meet someone in the robotics graduate department. Can you tell me where that is?"

"Uh sure," he looked up at Griffen and seemed more than a little intimidated. He gave him directions and hurried off, his backpack smacking his slight form with each step.

Griffen headed to his meeting with an associate professor from Jack's days in the department. He figured talking to David made more sense, but the guy bothered him, it was probably just because he clearly had feelings for Althea. That also made him more likely to spill the beans to Althea about Griffen's poking around. Either way, he needed to find another way to get information.

Jack had always had a lot of friends and here at *CMU* was no different. He'd delicately asked Carol about who he'd hung around with and she'd been accommodating, believing he was simply working out his grief.

He knocked on the door that said Alvin Pendergraft. *Seriously? This guy never had a chance of being cool.* The door opened to reveal a chubby ginger haired guy who would've barely seemed old enough to be a student if Griffen didn't know he was in his thirties. "Hi, I'm Griffen. We spoke on the phone."

"Yeah, Jack's friend, right?"

"Yep. I grew up here with Jack, but I left a long time ago and never made it back before, or after, he died. I'm here for a while and I just wanted to take the opportunity to reconnect with his memory, you know?" Griffen tried to make himself sound as nonthreatening as possible. No need to spook the guy.

"Sure, come in. It was so awful when Jack died, I totally understand you wanting to know more. Not sure what I can tell you, though."

"It will just be nice to talk to someone that knew a different side of him. His death was pretty sudden, huh?"

"I'll say! One day he's here, then the next he's gone, just like that."

"I would like to collect mementos from around his death. Did you guys have any memorial activities for him?"

"No, I hate to say it but it was crazy around here. We had a, um, a lot going on around here around the time of his death so he didn't get the attention he deserved. It was a real shame."

"A lot going on?" Griffen chose to play dumb on this one. "I thought you guys just built cool robots and taught class and stuff?" The engineer was viewing him with obvious condescension. Arrogant *and* a big mouth. Perfect.

"Well, that may have been true for Jack and David. Have you talked to David yet? He and Jack were really close, he knew everything Jack did."

"I'll be sure to catch up with him. What did Jack work on?"

"I forget his project, I think it was that map one that we did. That's right, because David finished it on his own. And Jack was also the go-to guy to fix our servers and any other glitches that came up. We're all computer guys, of course, and the school has people — but man, he could fix anything, so everybody just always called him when there was an issue."

"What other stuff was going on here that he was working on?"

"Oh yeah, well we definitely work on some crazy sensitive stuff here. *Cade Jackson* type shit," he winked.

"A fan? How great."

Yeah, seriously, how great, he thought sarcastically.

"I'm definitely a big fan. Could you..."

"I'll mail you a couple signed copies after I get back to New York."

"Great!"

"So what was the crazy sensitive shit?"

"We'd scored some government grants to do work for the military. It was a huge deal. David and Jack didn't work on it, but a bunch of us were all wrapped up in it. Couldn't focus on anything else."

"Did you need security clearances?"

"We did." He looked nervous for a second. "This wasn't public but there was actually a scare there was a breach right around when Jack died," he lowered his voice to a whisper. "But nothing came of it, so it just blew over."

"And you've wrapped up that project?"

"Yeah, got a couple new ones. You should set a book here!"

Griffen stood and reached out his hand. "I just may do that. Thanks man."

Griffen left Alvin's office and stalked across the quad, his heart heavy with the added weight of evidence against Jack. He grabbed his phone to call Trey.

"Hey, Griffen, what's up?"

"I'm at *CMU*. I confirmed Jack didn't work on the military robotics projects, but he did help out with working on their tech issues and servers. Could that have given him access to information on another project?"

"Hard to know without looking at the servers, but yeah, it should have. It's not the only way to get the materials, but it would work."

"Shit. And Althea said he was working in the office after hours."

"Yeah that matches up with the timing of when he saved the documents — when no one would have been around. I'm sorry but it doesn't look good, man."

"Any word on the rest of the files or your other searches?"

"I should have the files, bank account information, and phone records sorted out soon."

"Thanks, Trey."

"No problem."

Griffen hung up and tried to ignore the tight fist squeezing around his heart.

CHAPTER EIGHTEEN

"What do you think Tea?"

Dammit. She'd been preoccupied all day, not with preparations for the upcoming Crenshaw Mining case depositions. Nope. Griffen had occupied her brain all day, ever since he'd dropped his bomb of an offer.

After lamely participating for twenty more minutes, Althea finally hung up on her conference call and tried to focus. She stood and walked to her office window and its view of the Monongahela River.

She watched the river rush beneath a bridge and caught sight of a log snagged on a red buoy. The river was swollen and the current quick from last night's storm and the powerful water rushed around the log, paying it no heed. Its plight reminded Althea of her life after Jack's death.

The river was so high and dark today — but for this one buoy, time had simply stopped. For so many years she too had remained still while these damn rivers kept flowing, the only movement in a life halted by the swift hand of loss and death.

After Jack died, barges continued to trudge along delivering goods like they had for hundreds of years in this murky water highway. People had met, fallen in love, worked, gone to school. All unaware of the snagged log of a woman holding still while the world rolled, buffeted, and moved right alongside of her. Nothing changing for her but the date and the growth of her beautiful son, the only connection to a love long ago lost. She clutched onto Johnny and her memories with all the strength she had as the currents of life rushed powerfully past her.

Althea was honest enough with herself to recognize what she had wasn't really a "life." It was more like an "existence." It was getting by. It was one breath...then another.

She wondered if she hadn't had Johnny if she would've chosen no breaths. She knew it sounded crazy, but often she wondered if Jack was trying to protect her even after death, sending Johnny to her so that she could make it through — giving her a reason to keep moving forward.

The only thing to free a snagged log is to break it from its tethered point. What if she did that? Cut herself free of the guilt and loss and let herself float along with the world to her future?

But what about the memories and love? She couldn't let the guilt go and keep those too, could she?

Then again, logs can't stay snagged forever. Eventually, change comes.

The log breaks free or the current simply tears it apart and pulls it under.

Althea knew something had to change but had been so scared of that for so long. Yet somehow this thing with Griffen, whatever it was, felt like a good change. Felt like something different that she needed to follow through with. The only alternative was to continue being swept away and eventually sink under.

Maybe she shouldn't fight her feelings for him anymore? What if she cut the snag and simply let herself flow with the current? What if it took her somewhere close to happiness?

But for every bold thought Althea had, a much stronger jolt of fear took her.

What if this didn't work and she was more brokenhearted than before? Look how twisted up she was after a matter of barely two weeks — wouldn't more time with Griffen just leave her more exposed to hurt?

Then there was the guilt — the feeling of betrayal for wanting a future with another man. After she'd failed Jack so terribly, how could she be so selfish?

And just like that the snag yanked her back and Althea felt the waters rushing by her and life passing her by again. Disgusted with her own indecision she grabbed her purse to leave and pick up Johnny.

"Mommy, come on! We're late and I see Uncle Gwiff over with the team!"

She trotted after him, chuckling at him in his tiny football uniform, helmet and eye black under his eyes. Ever since Griffen started working with him and his team Johnny was showing real improvement in his game, and he clearly loved spending the time with him.

Johnny barreled into Griffen who threw himself back dramatically, "Great tackle man! Everybody huddle up." Griffen looked back at Althea. She waved and felt her stomach turn over at his intense gaze. He was smiling but she could see the concern behind his eyes — the worry over her.

Althea pulled her folded deck chair from its canvas bag and sat with the other mothers — who she noticed were far more numerous in number and interest level since Griffen started helping out with the team. She questioned whether some of them even had a kid in the game, or if they were just there to watch the hot celebrity writer and his muscles grace the sideline.

Several greeted her and she smiled and waved, but as with everything since Griffen entered her life, all she heard was noise. He was the only thing she could see as he coached them, the whistle bouncing against his firm chest, his strong biceps bulging out of his polo shirt, his kind eyes as he cheered up Chris after he fumbled the ball.

How could I ever let this guy go?

Althea breathed a sigh of relief when the game finally ended. Johnny's team had won and they were all ecstatic. Griffen walked over to her with Johnny, his large hand resting on Johnny's small shoulder.

"Hi," she squeaked out and looked up at him. "You did great with Johnny — with all of them."

"Thanks. Johnny means a lot to me you know. Just like his mother. This has been amazing. Coaching, being around the game without all the anger, fear, and resentment from my dad. And it's good to know what an awesome coach I can be," he smirked.

"You and that ego again," she laughed nervously.

"It's a gift." He looked down seriously at her. "Can I walk you to your car?"

"I would like that." They walked side by side silently as Johnny rattled on about the game. She reached her car and bent over to put Johnny in.

"Here, let me help," Griffen said. He picked Johnny up and secured him for her in the backseat. He turned to her after closing the door, his back blocking Johnny's view.

"I'll see you later and you'll let me know what you decided?"

"Yes. Let me drop Johnny off at the girls' house first. He wanted a sleepover there tonight. Then I'll come by and we'll talk."

"Okay."

He moved to kiss her and slowed, remembering they were in public. Althea saw the hurt in his eyes that he had to stop. That was her rule and she felt like shit about it, especially after leaving him hanging all day like this.

Althea reached up, placed her hand on his cheek and kissed him lightly just for a moment and pulled away. He smiled — a great big beautiful smile with both dimples showing, making her wonder why she was hesitating at all. Griffen pulled away, first turning to look at Johnny. "Take care big guy," then he looked back at her, running his hand down her cheek, "drive safely, gorgeous. I'll see you soon," he said, walking away.

Althea used her key to open the door to Jenna and Aubrey's apartment with one constricted hand. Johnny had worn himself out during the game and was pretty much sacked out in her arms. She struggled through the door and laid him down in the bedroom Jenna and Aubrey had designated for him, then quickly deposited her own tired body in their kitchen. After pouring herself a glass of wine she sat alone in the kitchen, no closer to resolution. It had been about twenty minutes of quiet when she heard their keys jingling and voices rising as they approached her.

"Althea, are you in here?" Jenna called.

"Back here guys," she answered with a loud whisper. They walked in and she pointed to Johnny's bedroom, placing a finger to her lips.

"Oh sorry, we'll keep it down. It's good he rests up, Johnny always has fun at Auntie Brey and Auntie Jenna's place," Aubrey smirked, probably imagining whether he was old enough to have his hair dyed blue or something.

"How'd it go last night?" Aubrey asked eagerly.

"It went well, Curt is nice."

"Forget Curt," Aubrey said. "Jenna told me Griffen came running after you at the restaurant and went all ending of a rom-com guy on you. It was even raining!"

"Yeah, he did. It was pretty intense."

"So, did Griffen spend the night?" Aubrey demanded.

"Yes," she said, his name sparking her anxiety all over again.

"How'd it go?" Aubrey asked.

Althea leaned back in her chair and looked back and forth at each of them, not sure of what to say. "He wants to stay in Pittsburgh."

"How long?" Aubrey gasped out.

"As long as I'll let him."

"What did you say?" Jenna asked.

"I told him I was scared but I'd think about it. I haven't told him anything yet, but I think I'm going to say no."

"Well, that's one way to go," Aubrey snorted at her.

"Jeez, back off Brey. I mean the whole point was an end date and I've already let myself get too close to him."

"There doesn't have to be a point. You like being with him. *That's* the point," Aubrey said to her slowly as though she was explaining something to a child that just wouldn't listen.

"That's great for Johnny, too, if he stays," Jenna pointed out. "Growing up with three chattering sorority sisters and his grandma as his only role models won't be enough for him forever."

"I don't know, I think it's best if he just sticks with the plan and returns to New York."

"Why?" Jenna asked.

"I don't know, it seemed so much easier when he was going to leave."

And take all the confusing feelings he caused with him.

"Did it ever occur to you that maybe Johnny wants a father in his life, not some memory of a man that died before he was born? A man you cry over in the dark when you think no one can hear you? Jack wouldn't want Johnny to grow up without a father figure. Jack wouldn't want you to spend your life like this — *lonely and miserable*," Aubrey demanded.

Althea bristled at her words, standing to look Aubrey in the eyes, emotion rushing through her veins, she said, "You know, everyone acts like they know what's best for me. Like they know what Jack would've wanted for me. That Jack would want me to move on. But all I know for sure is Jack would want to be *alive*, holding me and his little boy forever. That's why I'll never be able to move on."

"Bullshit," Aubrey answered.

"Excuse me?"

"I said — I call *bullshit*. Christ, you're really starting to veer into the 'girl who's too stupid to live' category. Have you thought that maybe you're just a coward?"

"I'm the coward? When you won't let any guy stay long enough for the sheets to cool down?"

Aubrey stepped closer to her and said, "I'd rather do that than spend my life hiding behind a ghost. You don't have to be a nun or a martyr to honor Jack's memory. You've cloaked yourself in so much guilt that you don't even know *what* you feel anymore!"

Althea was so angry and hurt it ran like fire through her veins, but worse, she felt ashamed. Ashamed that Aubrey could be right. For a moment she clenched her fists and gulped air like a goldfish, with the round blank eyes to match, until Jenna broke in with a shout.

"Christ, guys — stop this! Now!"

Jenna never yelled. The mere shock of it stopped the argument and began to sap the angry out of their bones.

"I'm sorry," Althea and Aubrey mumbled out to each other.

"It's just...Why do you guys keep pushing me?" Althea asked.

"We haven't pushed you enough! We should've pushed you sooner. We kept waiting and letting you wallow and be stuck. Never mentioning anything that could remind you of losing Jack. Doing anything to keep from upsetting you," Jenna said emphatically.

"But why can't you just let me do things my way?"

Jenna took her shoulders in her hands, "Because we love you, dummy! And you won't push yourself. And because we're selfish. It hurts to watch you let life just pass you by."

"For years to go by knowing you're still so afraid and we'd rather not feel like that anymore. So, *for us*, will you cut the crap?" Aubrey asked quietly.

"Seriously," Jenna said in a much gentler voice. "Why would you fight this offer? He's crazy about you and clearly loves Johnny and it would be really good for Johnny to have a strong guy around. And he grew up with Jack, it would be like having a piece of him around."

Panic started to grip Althea tighter.

Why does this offer bother me so much?

"I don't know. Griffen is great with Johnny, and I love being with him, too, but I get so scared whenever I think of him staying. And Carol will lose it if I get involved with Griffen of all people."

"Carol needs to get over it," Aubrey stated defiantly.

"I agree with Brey," Jenna said. "And I think you've used Carol as a shield for too long. She's been another excuse to hide from life. I think this thing with Griffen scares you *because* you love being with him. *Because* he makes you want to try for something real, too."

"What? That's crazy."

"Is it, Tea?" Jenna asked. "Could it be that you feel guilty because it's not just sex with him? Do you have feelings for him?"

The room began to feel small around Althea. She could taste the words in her throat, feel her belly flip-flopping. She stood there thinking silently, but to their credit, Aubrey and Jenna patiently waited for her answer. Althea put a hand on her chest, as though she could press all these terrifying emotions down and away from her. It didn't work, they just pushed up faster, out of her mouth on a quiet breath.

"Yes," she whispered, "I'm pretty sure I have feelings for him. But it's just too complicated and I'm still the same woman I was two weeks ago. I'm still Jack's wife raising his son."

"You're Jack's *widow*, there's a big difference. That's why it's a whole different word! You're a *living* woman and you need someone to share that life with. You were so quick to think Jack sent you Johnny after he died. If that's true, then maybe he sent you two to each other, too," Jenna offered softly.

"I'd never thought of it that way," she said, her voice

strengthening. "But it doesn't matter, he's not the kind of guy to want to settle down for real."

"How can you be so sure? From what he said to me last night he sounds pretty crazy about you. He thinks you want him to leave, but I know he wants to be a part of your life," Jenna said

"You're right," Althea said. "And that means I have to go."

"Good for you, girl. Now get out so we can enjoy our sleepover with Johnny," Aubrey said with a smile.

"Thanks guys. What would I do without you?"

"Well, you'll never have to find out," Jenna said, pulling her into a hug and releasing a "humph" when Aubrey roughly threw her arms around the both of them and squeezed.

Althea used the key Griffen had given her and pushed into his room on an excited breath. He must have been pacing because he was standing in the middle of the room, shirtless with only jeans on and his face was tight. God, he was so stunning. The muscles of his well-developed back were rippling with every breath. At the sound of the door, he turned to look at her and the intensity on his face floored her.

"Althea."

She took a breath and said, "Hi Griffen." He walked over and pulled her into his arms, stroking her back gently. She rested her head on his hard chest and inhaled deeply. He was so warm and in that moment she couldn't think of anything other than how wonderful he made her feel.

"Please say something. I'm dying over here," he muttered into her hair as he moved his hands lower to rest right above her bottom.

"You know you distract me when you do that."

"If it's a persuasive distraction, I'll keep it up."

"You know it is."

"Tell me what you're thinking."

She breathed again and looked in his eyes. "Griffen, I never thought of myself as a woman that would let a man take care of her and rely totally on him, but I know now that's what I did with Jack. I completely surrendered my life to him, built my world completely around 'us' — the future we were trying to build — so that when he was gone, I was lost. I can't let that happen again."

"I don't want to take over your life, Althea. I just want to be in it."

"Wow, look who's gotten so serious all of a sudden."

"You have that effect on me gorgeous. You turn me inside out. All I can think about is being with you. Seeing you again. Please tell me you're with me on this." He pulled her more closely to him, his arms wrapping around her waist.

"I'm still scared, Griffen," she said quietly, her eyes downcast.

He tilted her chin up and kissed her lips so softly it was barely a whisper of a touch.

"Because you haven't tried for more with anyone since Jack?"

"Not exactly. Everyone acts like it was a conscious decision to be alone. And maybe that was the way I looked at it at first, but it has always been pretty easy not to be with anyone. No one really appealed to me so there was no reason to question my decision to just be alone."

"But now?" he asked, kissing each of her cheeks and then her forehead.

Althea sighed and looked in his eyes, "You've turned everything upside down."

"Is that a bad thing?"

"It is if I get broken again."

"I told you. You're the strongest person I know," he ran his fingers through her hair, resting her head against his chest.

"Griffen, I feel like I'm barely held together as it is. There's just a mess of invisible strings and chewing gum keeping my heart in one piece. A stiff wind could knock it all apart and you...the effect you have on me...it feels like it could be a tornado."

"I refuse to believe you're broken. Yes, you're hurting. You've been hurting for a long time, and so have I, but I think maybe we can heal each other. Together."

"And that's what makes me want to give this a shot. Griffen, I don't know where this is going, but you're right, we can't just let it end. I know that. My nightmare last night, my day without you today, all of it just proves that to me even more. I think it's only fair for me to give this a shot until the end of the semester like you asked. I know you want more, but I appreciate you being willing to accept another baby step."

He grinned and picked her up, spinning her around until her legs were shooting out like a pinwheel. Setting her down with a kiss he said, "You've made me so happy, you know that? That you're willing to see this through with me for however long...thank you, gorgeous."

"Yes, but for how long will you be willing to wait for me? What if I'm never ready to move on for real?" she questioned softly, voicing her deepest concern.

He placed his hand on her chin, rubbing his thumb lightly back and forth across her bottom lip. "Please don't do that."

"What?"

"Think about what may go wrong. When the other shoe will drop."

"What should I do instead?"

"Be here. With me. Now. We'll figure the rest out. I promise. Just trust me."

He kissed her and it went from soft and sweet to hot and intense quickly. He palmed her ass and pulled her into his hardness with enough force to make her gasp at the sensation.

He leaned back, gripping her shoulders tightly, grunting out, "Fuck!"

Althea pulled back quickly, "What's wrong?"

"I wanted to take this slowly. Be sweet with you, but Christ, Althea. You were driving me crazy today. Not talking to me. Not letting me know if you wanted to give whatever this is a chance. I've never wanted all this before. And not knowing if you were just going to let me go. Shit. It's just..."

"I know."

"Yeah?"

"I thought about you all day. I was going crazy, too."

"A text message might have been nice," he chuckled. She laughed with him, suddenly feeling her shoulders relax a bit. "Come here," he said. He pulled her in closely and kissed her. It started sweetly, but as was always the case with them, passion and madness rapidly took them over.

They kept kissing as they walked across the suite to the window where they'd first made love. He pulled off her dress and she quickly fumbled with the zipper of his pants. Clothes were flying as they reached for each other and kissed between each garment.

Griffen suddenly held her face in his hands and controlled their kissing, saying so much to her with his mouth and tongue. He handed her a condom and she opened the packet and slid it over his length.

He pulled back, blue eyes blazing and grabbed her waist, spinning her around. He whispered in her ear, "Put your hands on the window."

She obeyed, placing her hands against the cool glass.

Griffen growled at her, "Open your eyes Althea. Watch us together. I want you to see how beautiful you look when you come with me deep inside you." She gasped as he entered her and gently smoothed away her hair so he could kiss her neck, face, and back with each thrust.

She felt him lean back from her as he ran his hand along her spine, his beautiful face reflected back at her in the glass — so intense and sexy, it aroused her even more. With each thrust, she could see her face contort with pleasure and need. His hands moved to her shoulders, using the leverage to drive more deeply into her, making her scream out. He leaned down, his hard body blanketing her smaller, softer one. One hand cupped a breast while the other reached down to stroke her throbbing clitoris.

It felt so good she thought she might shatter from the overwhelming feeling of joy that overtook her. To feel so complete with this man, after so many years of emptiness — it was almost too much.

Tears welled in her eyes but Griffen kissed them away, then licking and kissing her face, neck, and shoulders.

"Look at us, gorgeous, look at how perfect we look together," he whispered in her ear.

She forced her moist eyes open and looked at the two of them in the window's reflection as he commanded. Their joined reflection was so beautiful to her, from their faces pressed together, to their bodies joined as one, to the faintest hint of the city bustling and glowing beneath them.

He stroked her hair as she blinked her hazy lust-filled eyes.

She could barely recognize the wanton woman in front of her, but seeing them as one — he was right — they did look so perfect.

The moment finally took over as tremors started deep within her core, making her fingers almost numb and just as Griffen leaned to her ear again and whispered, "Althea, you're mine, all mine," she fell into a million pieces around him.

Yet, she had no fear, because his arms were wrapped around her and as he came with her, she knew he would be there to put her back together again.

CHAPTER NINETEEN

Griffen was jarred awake by the vibrating of his cellphone on his bedside table.

He answered it quickly, sliding his arm out from underneath Althea's warm body and breathing a sigh of relief when he confirmed she was still sleeping soundly.

He whispered into the phone as he walked to the external room of the suite. "Trey, what's up?"

"Sorry to call so late, but it can't wait. Let me warn you — you're really not going to like what I have to tell you."

"Just say it," Griffen's heart rate started to pick up, alternately eager for a resolution of his investigation and terrified at what negative information Trey was about to give him.

"You know how Jack's widow told you he got a bonus?"

"Yeah."

"Right. Well, he did get a direct deposit from an account that on first glance looked like it came from *CMU*, but when I peeled away the layers I discovered the source was actually a Chinese-based account with a fictitious name."

"How'd you do that?"

"It was surprisingly easy, let's leave it at that. Griffen, it was the same fictitious name I traced to the accounts on Jack's spreadsheet."

"Shit."

"I also checked out his phone records. Home and cell were clean, but there were multiple calls from a Chinese number to his office line."

Griffen was silent as the words felt like knives to his chest. "Shit," he whispered again.

"Griffen, I know you don't want to hear it..."

"I know. It looks really bad for Jack."

"And this is real evidence now, dude. I know I'm not usually the voice of the law, but this is the military we're talking about here. Treason type shit. I think we need to report what we've found."

"I know. Christ. But what about you? Won't you get in trouble over what you did to find this stuff?"

"I covered my tracks pretty well. Not my first rodeo dude. Besides, with what's at stake here, our use of my special skills is going to be the least of their concerns. Fact is we can't wait anymore man. When we report it they're gonna look at the timing of our knowledge. I mean, it really looks like his death wasn't an accident. These Chinese purchasers may have killed him, or he could've panicked and taken matters in his own hands and..."

"*Enough! I get it.* Look, I know you're right. Just give me until the morning, okay?"

"Sure."

"Thanks."

"Goodnight man."

"Yeah, goodnight."

Griffen felt sick. He'd hoped he'd have more time to sort

through everything, especially before telling Althea. It killed him to tell her and break her heart all over again, but it was better she learn about Jack's secret life and suspicious death from him rather than the Department of Defense.

He walked back into the bedroom of the suite and looked at Althea's lovely face and parted lips, illuminated by the sliver of moonlight peaking through the hotel curtains. Her massive fall of hair surrounded her and fanned out on the pillow.

She was so beautiful — and she could be his — but he knew telling her the truth meant he might lose her forever. He sat on a chair next to her, trying to memorize every inch of her soft skin, every eyelash, every soft muttering as she mumbled nonsense quietly in her sleep.

Griffen watched her chest rise and fall, only to feel his own constrict increasingly. Each breath she took felt like the ticking of a bomb counting down what may be the last remaining seconds of his only chance at love and happiness in life.

Althea slowly awakened to the feeling of Griffen's rough hand stroking her hip. She opened her eyes to see him leaning over her, tracing a circle around her three birds tattoo.

"Good morning, stud. You keep beating me to waking up," she said taking in his perfect bare torso, reaching up to place an open-mouthed kiss on his shoulder.

"Morning, gorgeous. I do like this tattoo, but I think you should get one of cherries, too. Maybe a cherry blossom."

He kissed her as he gripped her hip over the tattoo. She reveled in his now familiar masculine taste. His mouth tasted of bourbon and mint and she couldn't seem to get enough of it.

"Why cherries?" she asked when they came up for air.

"I always think you taste and smell like cherries, and you're so sweet. That and you look fucking smoking hot in red."

Althea preened at the compliment and curled closer into him. "Well, now that you're staying around and we're giving this a real shot, maybe you can go with me to get one."

His eyes looked haunted and he kissed her forehead then looking deeply into her eyes, "Maybe."

"Griffen, you are very bad at hiding when something's bothering you. What's going on?"

He smiled, but there was no happiness behind it and Althea started to get worried.

"Althea, I need to tell you something."

"Well, I'm pretty sure you aren't secretly a woman, so what is it?" she asked with a wink, masking her concern.

He smiled softly, but his face turned serious again. "I never told you but Jack emailed me the week before he died."

Althea straightened.

"Oh. Were you guys still close then?"

"We kept in touch on the phone and over email. He would also talk through my ideas on my books with me."

"Is that what the email was about?"

"No." He swallowed and Althea felt oddly anxious. "He asked to talk — said he needed my help with something. It was weird for him to ask for my help, but I was all wrapped up in *Sunrise* edits and put him off for a week. Then I was too late. He died."

It hurt her to think that Jack reached out to someone else for help instead of her, but the tears in Griffen's eyes pulled her back to the moment, so she reached up a hand and stroked his cheek. "It wasn't your fault. Is that what you think? What you wanted to tell me?"

"I thought it was for a long time. I don't know what I could've done, but I know it wasn't your fault either."

She looked down. "I wish I could believe that."

He pulled her close and whispered in her ear, "I *know* it wasn't your fault Althea. And *how* I know, that is what I have to tell you."

"What?" She pulled back from him and sat up, covering her bare breasts with the sheet. She suddenly felt very exposed and vulnerable and Griffen's distraught eyes weren't helping.

"After I got here — last Monday morning — I went to my mom's house where Jack and I hid a lockbox with all our favorite things — my stories, whatever we were into. I, uh, found a flash drive in there. It was Jack's from the last couple weeks before he died."

She scooted back even further. "So, after you and I started to...?"

"Yes."

"Why didn't you tell me then?"

"I thought I could figure it out. Investigate what Jack was doing. Like I'd done with my books." He was sitting on the edge of the bed now in his boxer briefs, catty-cornered to her. His muscular back was hunched as he leaned his strong arms against his knees. Even now, when she was terrified of what he would say next, she couldn't look away from him.

He turned back to her to gauge her reaction, but she didn't even know what it was herself. Everything was washing over her in nauseating waves, like she was going up a steep incline on a roller coaster, aware she would fall soon but not knowing how scary it would be — only that she couldn't stop what was coming.

"What was on it — the flash drive?"

"I couldn't tell at first, Jack had heavily encrypted each file. So I got help."

"Help?" Something clicked. "Wait, all those calls and texts you said were from your publisher. Were they about this?" He just looked at her with guilty eyes. "Who was it really?"

"Trey. He's a computer expert."

"So you lied to me?"

"It wasn't totally a lie," he said defensively, then his eyes widened, as if mortified by something he'd admitted.

"How so? So it was about your new book, too? Oh my God...you *wouldn't.*"

"I always write about my investigations. I would've talked to you before I went too far with anything bad about Jack..."

"Oh, like you're telling me now?" Her throat was tightening and she could feel her hands trembling, she pulled her knees to her chest for protection and wrapped her arms around them.

"Yes," he reached for her but she shook her head slightly and he dropped his hand.

She whispered, "What did this Trey guy do for you?"

"He examined the flash drive and..."

"And what, Griffen?" Her voice sounded harsh to her ears.

"Pulled Jack's phone and bank records."

"What! Like Jack was a criminal? What the *fuck*, Griffen? Why would you need to do that? Wait, what did you mean when you said you would talk to me before writing 'bad things' about Jack?'"

"Because the flash drive showed he was involved in something big. The robotics department was working on sensitive military contracts. Weapons, highly developed tank components. Information that was worth a ton of money on the black market. It looks like Jack had a deal with the Chinese to sell design plans for money."

"You can't be serious. Jack was your friend, how could you even think that about him?" She went to stand up and he grabbed her arm. Althea glared over at his fingers but he wouldn't release her.

"I didn't want to. Please wait and hear me out."

He kissed her neck down to her shoulder — right where he knew it drove her crazy.

"Griffen, we need to talk about this."

"We *are* talking." He pulled her tightly to him so she couldn't move. "I didn't want to believe what I was finding out about Jack. That's why I couldn't tell you before. I knew it would break your heart all over again. I want to protect you, take care of you, look after you. I don't want anything to hurt you. I want to keep all those painful things from you."

She jerked away and stood up, "Don't I get a say in that, Griffen? I had that before with Jack and it didn't work. Jack babied me and hid anything hurtful from me and he *died!* Did you ever think that maybe I want to be treated like an adult?"

"I know you do." He stood and walked to her. "But that doesn't mean I don't want to protect you. You can look after me right back."

Althea started to get dressed. She felt naked and raw emotionally already, she didn't need to add her bare ass to the equation.

She turned to him in just her bra and panties and caught him unknowingly glancing down at her breasts until she had to roll her eyes. She smacked his chest.

"Focus! If you wanted to keep this from me, then why are you telling me all this now?"

He looked into her eyes guiltily.

"I didn't know what I would find at first. I thought I was helping. That I would figure it all out and bring closure, but then all this bad shit turned up and I just couldn't tell you."

"And what about now?"

"I didn't get the most damning information until last night, after we went to sleep."

"Damning? What do you mean?"

"Jack's office line had calls from China, and that bonus he got? We tracked it to a Chinese account. It didn't come from *CMU*. Trey and I need to report what we found, I couldn't let you find out that way."

Althea flopped down onto the bed, her dress in hand. Her ears were ringing and her vision had reduced to small pinpricks of light. She could barely get air in or think around the squeezing fist in her chest. She sensed Griffen crouching in front of her, calmly telling her to breathe.

She finally squeaked out, "Oh my God. And you didn't give me any warning, why? Because I would break this off? Wouldn't agree for you to stay?"

"I didn't know what to do. I want us to be for real, Althea, so I had to wait to tell you until I had enough information...and hope that you would understand."

"That's so much better," she said sarcastically. "So when you were just screwing me it was okay to lie?" For the first time in so many years she was pissed. So pissed that she wasn't even trying to fight it anymore.

"Stop it, you know it wasn't like that for me. Ever."

"You should've told me. I deserve truth and trust." She suddenly felt like no time had passed, like secrets were ruling her life and stealing her happiness — again. Her emotions were so out of control that her fingers tingled.

"Shit. I'm handling this all wrong," Griffen mumbled.

"At least we can agree on that. I can't believe this. You begged me to trust you and take this chance with you and you were keeping this from me the whole time!"

She stood up and tugged on her dress. Griffen jumped up and was in front of her looking into her eyes and running his fingers roughly through his wavy hair. Althea hated herself for wanting to touch it herself.

"I'm so sorry, Althea. Please know I thought I was doing what was right."

"But the book..."

"Fuck the book. If you don't want me to write about all this, I'll tear it up, burn my laptop. Whatever you want." He stepped so close that he was pressed fully against her. He was almost naked and her traitorous body immediately responded to the press of his nipples and firm muscles against her. He reached his arms around her, his thumbs stroking her back repeatedly until she was almost hypnotized. "What *do* you want Althea?" he finally said. "Because I want you. Althea, I l—" Althea's eyes widened as her phone interrupted him. He rested his forehead against hers and begged, "Please ignore that."

She looked at him and her heart broke a little. "It's my ringtone for Aubrey. She has Johnny. I have to take it. I'm sorry." He leaned back.

"Aubrey, hey," she said, willing her voice to remain steady.

"How ya doing babe? Have a hot night? How'd everything go with your big talk?"

"Oh yeah, um, well, I can't really talk now." Althea was staring into Griffen's eyes as she clutched the phone.

"I bet you can't," Aubrey said lasciviously. "Look girl, I wanted to let you know I got Johnny to school on time. It was just barely though because he left his favorite stuffed animal at your house so we went to go get it. I forgot to lock up but it's okay, I saw David pulling in when we left, so he'll probably lock up after himself."

"What would David want?"

"You weren't expecting him? Gosh, I don't know what he wanted, we didn't talk, I just saw his car."

"No worries," Althea said softly, still staring at Griffen. "I need to go home to get ready for work. I can ask him when I get there." She hung up and bent over to start pulling on her shoes.

"Come on Althea, don't leave like this."

"I'm not leaving '*like this*,' Griffen. I'm just leaving."

"Let me go with you. We can keep talking."

She stood and grabbed her purse on her way out of his hotel room, sadly remembering how happy she'd been when they'd kissed so passionately that she'd simply dropped it by the door. Griffen started to walk toward her but she put her hand up. "I need to think about this, get my head around it. I don't know what I think or what is right. Just let me go right now."

He was clenching his fists, a muscle in his jaw twitching. She was half relieved, half disappointed that he let her walk to the door and open it.

"Dammit," he grunted and stalked across to her. He pushed the door shut behind her, taking her face in his hands and kissing her tenderly, his tongue stroking her lips until she finally sighed and parted them, granting him entrance. Griffen pulled away first, stroking his thumbs up and down her cheeks as he looked into her eyes. His were so intensely dark and blue. "I'm so sorry I hurt you. That is the last thing I ever want to do. I'm new to this whole sharing your life with another person thing. I'll fuck up. I *did* fuck up. But know this. We aren't done here, Althea. Not by a long shot."

"Okay," she whispered. "But I still have to go."

With that, he finally released her and her heart immediately spasm at the loss. Her mind might need some time but her heart and body had clearly made their decision. She needed space from him — and their powerful connection — if she was ever going to figure out what she was going to do next.

For the second time, Althea deserted him to a lonely hotel room. At least this time he was awake when it happened.

"Dammit," Griffen shouted, pounding his fist against the shut door in frustration. He turned and leaned back against it as he replayed the conversation over in his head.

His cell phone rang and he crossed the room to see Trey's name.

Great, just what I want to think about.

"Trey. What's up?"

"Don't sound so thrilled to hear from me."

"Sorry, Trey. It's been a shitty morning."

"Well, I wanted to tell you I made it to the last encrypted piece of the flash drive. Jack downloaded it the afternoon before he died. I've got just one more level to go through but I can't crack it for the life of me. The password requires the use of a WAV file."

"A what?"

"Basically the file won't open without the use of the correct audio WAV file as a password, you know, an MP3. It's a neat trick."

"Fuckin' Jack, always had to be so goddamn clever."

"Can you think of any song that Jack may have used?"

Griffen thought for a moment and quickly said, "Althea, by the Grateful Dead." Jack had always loved the Dead. Griffen would tease him about it mercilessly, no one would've ever guessed that Pittsburgh Catholic High School's golden boy was a closet hippie. More so than that, Jack was sentimental as hell. He probably found every book, song, and crossword in the world that invoked the name of the woman he loved. "Can you get that song off the internet?"

"Already downloaded it, dude. Let me give it a try. Holy shit, that did it! It was the opening guitar riff — sweet, I need to do that sometime."

"Focus, Trey!"

"Okay, Christ. All right, so it's more notes in Jack's handwriting — but it looks like it's just his thoughts. No specs or anything. It says he's tracked the accessing of the military files to David, but he needs to get on his physical computer to confirm before he can do anything with the information."

"What the — did you say 'David?'"

"Yeah, do you know him?"

Griffen gulped. "Jack was his research assistant."

"They would've shared a phone number, dude!"

"Yeah, and he's the one who Jack said got him that bonus."

"You mean the one that traces back to China? Holy shit, if he'd found Jack on his computer...it sure doesn't look like Jack's death was an accident."

"Not now it sure doesn't. Which means David's capable of anything. *Fuck*! And he's at Althea's house right now. I gotta go. Pull everything together, look at it all again from the view of trying to figure out exactly what David was up to and go ahead and report this to DOD. I know they aren't your favorite people, but..."

"No worries man, I got this. Go do your thing. I actually have an old friend in there and she'll be *very* happy to get my call."

Griffen figured he didn't want to know why, all he knew for sure was he had to get in touch with Althea — as soon as possible.

CHAPTER TWENTY

Althea pulled away from the hotel entrance and immediately called Jenna through the Bluetooth in her car. She needed some of Jenna's trademark sensibility to help her get her head back on straight.

"Hello?"

"Jenna? It's Tea. You got a minute?"

"Sure girly. I don't have to be on rounds until tonight, so I'm just puttering around the apartment and fixin' to clean up after Aubrey's latest arts and craft disaster with Johnny."

They always let their southern accents come through when it was just the two of them talking and it was helping to soothe Althea's nerves.

"Oh lordy, I don't wanna know," Althea chuckled, grateful for the humorous image to distract her harried mind.

"How'd it go with Griffen?" Jenna asked, bringing Althea back to her worries.

"Well, the night was great, but when I woke up he threw this bomb on me."

As she took her shortcut home, avoiding Liberty Bridge construction traffic, Althea relayed the whole story, preparing herself for an honest second opinion.

"And where are you now?" Jenna prodded after a moment of silence.

Althea sighed, "Headed home. I wasn't thinking clearly and didn't want to keep saying things I couldn't take back."

"So you ran and pushed him away?"

"I guess I know whose side you're on."

"There aren't sides Tea, honey. What he did was totally messed up. He should've been honest with you the whole time, but at least he was eventually? And don't you think he's right — would you have really wanted to know he was doing this?"

"He could've just not done it at all. Or asked for my help."

"Seriously, Tea? You would never be receptive to any bad words about Jack. You would've flipped no matter when he told you."

"Dammit, don't you ever get sick of being right, Jenna?" she grumbled. "Argh, that's Griffen calling again." She groaned. He'd been calling her throughout her conversation with Jenna, but she wasn't ready to talk to him quite yet.

"Are you just going to ignore him?"

"No..."

"*Tea.*"

"I know he and I should talk more, I just need to sort through it is all. It's a lot to take in and you know how secrecy from men really upsets me."

"Well, he just tried to call *me* now. What do you want me to do?"

"You can call him back. I'm almost home anyway. I need to see what David wants, then I promise I'll talk to Griffen. Thanks honey."

"Sure."

Griffen's head was spinning as he raced around his suite and prepared to run after Althea.

He'd been so caught up in thinking Jack was guilty, he may have exposed Althea to real harm by snooping around *CMU* the day before.

Why else would David be messing around at Althea's house without her knowledge? On this of all days?

Of course David could've heard Griffen was there asking about his star assistant. He wasn't sure why David would be at Althea's house, rather than coming straight to him, but he didn't have time to wonder about that. All he could do was whatever it took to keep her safe.

After calling to request the valet bring his car around, Griffen quickly dialed 911, giving them Althea's address and informing them an attempted murder was possibly in progress.

He couldn't rely on the police to come in time, he needed to be ready to handle this himself. It'd been years since he'd put himself directly in harm's way, but that didn't mean he didn't know how to face down a badass or two.

David may be desperate, but so was Griffen and he'd fought worse men and won.

Only difference? This time the stakes were so much higher because he actually cared about someone — about *anything*. The only thing that mattered to him was that Althea was safe.

Griffen was more than ready to lay his life down for her, even as the thought of harm coming to her twisted his heart and stomach into angry knots.

He called Althea. No answer. His pulse pounded in his ears, drowning out her voicemail greeting.

"*Althea, it's me again, Griffen. I know you need space, but it's important. David's dangerous, you need to stay away from your home. Please! God, I hope you're listening to these.*"

He cursed, knowing the chance of her hearing his messages before she walked right into danger were slim to none.

Griffen hurried to his suitcase in the closet, unzipped the inside pocket and grabbed his gun case and knife.

Griffen had done a lot of things he wasn't proud of on his investigations over the years but today he knew he'd do whatever it took to protect Althea.

He'd do it over and over again and be proud of it.

He may have failed Jack when he was alive and then doubted him in death, but he wouldn't — couldn't — fail Althea. Jack would've died for her and so would he. Griffen would rescue her for Jack, for Johnny, for the girls and *goddammit* for himself, too.

He strapped the knife to his ankle and fitted the gun in his back waistband.

With his weapons secured, he ran out of his room.

"Althea! What're you doing here?" David asked in shock as she walked in the door. He turned abruptly, his hands behind his back.

"Good morning to you, too, David. I do live here, you know," she laughed.

"I know that. I just mean why aren't you at work? Is everything okay?"

He was standing near the basement door and seemed nervous, but Althea was too overwhelmed to care. She needed to sort through all that Griffen had told her and then she would call him. That was the right thing to do. Talk through it after she had her feelings under control.

"I had a morning appointment, so I came back here to get ready. What do you need? Are you looking for something?"

"I thought I left something in the basement during Johnny's party."

"In the basement?"

"Yeah, there were those trays you needed remember?"

"Not really, sorry. What did you leave? Maybe I saw it."

"Nothing important. Just something work related."

"Oh no, that sucks, was it research or something?"

"Yeah...or something."

"I'm sorry — haven't seen anything and I don't think I can help you look. I've had the worst morning. I'll look for it later, okay? I don't mean to be rude, but..."

"Are you leaving for work soon?"

"I don't know. I may take a nap. Why?"

"Oh, so you aren't leaving?"

David's eyes kept darting around the room and he was making her very nervous.

"David. Are you okay?"

"Okay? Uh, yeah. Since you're here and not leaving, maybe we can catch up." He seemed far less casual than his words. "Were you with that Griffen guy?"

"David, it's not really any of your business." His eyes were wild and her response made him look frantic. "I'm sorry, I didn't mean it like that."

"Yeah, just wondering what's up with that guy is all. He was on campus asking about Jack yesterday. Do you know anything about that?" His eyes kept glancing around the room, still apparently looking for something.

"Well, I guess that makes sense. He was looking into Jack's last couple weeks."

"Did he have any thoughts? You know, about Jack?"

"I don't want to talk about it. I'm seriously tired."

"Oh. Okay. Uh, here, let me get you some coffee."

She plopped down in the living room, hearing the distant hiss and hum of her *Keurig*. She was frustrated he wouldn't leave, but barring her being flat out rude to David, he seemed intent on staying and finding the work material he'd lost.

David returned a minute later and handed her a cup. Althea thought it odd that his hand was trembling, but figured it was just her own nerves making her see things that weren't there.

"Thanks David." He stood in front of her as she drank it. "Aren't you having any?"

"No. I'm good, thanks," he said softly, looking at his watch.

Griffen hurried to the front of the hotel and jumped into his car, practically knocking over the valet as he stepped out of it. Feeling desperate, Griffen called Althea yet again.

No answer.

Desperate, he dialed Jenna's number.

Another no answer. *Shit!*

His mind tormented him as he gripped the steering wheel so tight his hands ached. Everything was a mess. All he could think about was getting her away from David in one piece, but he was helpless if he couldn't get in touch with her.

Each moment that passed was another second she was in danger. She could already be injured for all he knew. Griffen had to force his brain to relax as he changed lanes quickly, cutting off a slow car to his right.

With the Boulevard of the Allies suddenly opening in front of him with a series of green lights Griffen breathed a little more easily and pressed the accelerator hard as he hurried toward the Liberty Bridge to cross the Monongahela River to Althea's home.

His heart eased a little when he saw Jenna returning his call.

Several minutes had passed since Althea politely drank the coffee David had given her, yet he was still making no move to leave. Instead, he was simply staring at her in a completely unnerving way.

"David I don't want to be pushy, but I need to get a move on. I have to go to work and now I'm more tired than ever, so I really think I need to take a nap. Can you come back and look for whatever it is you need later?"

"I understand. Uh, sure. Do you want to take your nap now?"

"David, no. I really think you should leave."

"Okay, but first maybe you should talk about this Griffen thing. Do you know anything about what he found about Jack? It must've upset you right?"

"It did upset me and I *don't* really want to talk about it." Her head was swimming and simply talking to David was making her more agitated by the fog in her brain.

"Tea, Jack worked for me. It's important I know if he did something that will hurt the university. What does Griffen think Jack did? Had he talked to anyone?" His words were logical but he was edgy and it made her nervous.

"I guess you're right, it really does affect the department." She sat down in a nearby chair to ease the heaviness in her limbs. "He thought Jack stole something, he's probably going to the authorities about it."

"Oh God," David whispered. He tugged at his hair and spun around, leaning over the dining room table, eyes wild. "Oh God."

"I know it's awful to think about it, but I didn't know. How could you have?"

"How could I know?" he asked himself quietly.

"Seriously, what is wrong, David?"

He choked out a mirthless laugh and looked at her with red-rimmed distraught eyes.

"*Everything's* wrong, Tea." He pressed the heels of his hands to his eyes, leaning back in complete torment. David dropped his hands and stared at her. "How tired are you Tea?"

A wave of exhaustion hit her and she couldn't deny the swimming of her eyes. David appeared before her, kneeling in front of her face, holding her upright by her arms.

"You're pretty tired I think, Tea. Good," he whispered. "Before you doze off, please tell me where to find Jack's things? I was going to wait until you went to sleep but it's too urgent. I can't wait a second!"

"Why, what do you need?"

"A flash drive. And I need it now. Please."

"A flash drive? Of Jack's?" She squirmed away as the connections between what Griffen told her and David's mania came together in her mind. "Please let me go."

"Please, Tea, don't fight me. I need you to answer me."

"No! David, why do you need a flash drive? *What did you do?*"

He suddenly squeezed her upper arms tightly.

"Dammit, Tea. I don't want to hurt you. Just tell me if you've seen it."

"I don't know what you're talking about David," she lied.

His eyes were so wild when he looked down at her that her breath caught in her throat. He was a stranger to her. There was no semblance of the gentle man who'd helped her through years of grief. There was only the strained face of a madman.

"Look, Tea," he breathed. "I've torn apart one of your houses before. I can do it again. Everything will be easier if you just tell me."

"What? *You* robbed my house?" He lifted her off the chair and pulled her body to his. She tried to fight him, pulling away for a moment, but he only grabbed her more tightly, pulling her back to his front.

She felt so lightheaded. The fear, the confusion, was all combining to overwhelm her with panic. She wanted to fight but her muscles were feeling more and more weak.

He leaned his head on her neck and breathed deeply in such an intimate way she felt almost nauseated. With each movement of hers, he simply pulled her closer, whispering in her ear, "Jack told me he made a flash drive that night I found him on my computer. He knew what I'd done. I had to find it."

"What had you done David?" Althea asked, but she had a horrifying suspicion she already knew.

He breathed her in again, shuddering against her. "When I couldn't find the flash drive in your old place I just stuck close to you. At first I just needed to keep an eye on you, see if you knew anything." He turned her around to look in her eyes and she hoped the movement would allow her a chance to get free, but he just pulled her in more tightly. Her head was fuzzy and she didn't know why, she only knew she needed to get away from him. "But I fell in love with you Tea. I love you so much. I've waited for you. Please help me." He stroked her face but she jerked away with as much strength as her quickly weakening body would allow.

"You're not making any sense, David. Just let me go."

"I was so in love with you, *am* still so in love with you. I don't want to hurt you. If you won't help me, I need you to just go to sleep, okay?"

"Please stop, David. You're scaring me. Let me go."

She finally managed to break free and ran for the door, but her legs were so heavy that it took all her strength to make it to her phone.

"Don't do that Tea, please," David begged as she squeezed her only lifeline.

She could feel herself getting hysterical as she fumbled with her phone. Before she knew it, he had her immobilized again from behind.

He was reaching around her body for the phone. She managed to enter a "9" before he eased away from her back for a moment.

"Why won't you just go to sleep, Tea. Dammit!"

She stumbled at the newfound hope of freedom, but instead felt a swift hard pressure on the back of her head.

Then, there was nothing.

"Jenna, thank God! Have you spoken to Althea?"

"Hey Griffen. Yeah. I gotta say she's pretty worked up." Griffen made his way onto Liberty Bridge and came to a dead stop as the cars merged slowly into one tight lane.

Fucking Pittsburgh! Hundreds of bridges and half of them are under construction.

He could only hope Althea's car was stuck in this mess, too.

"Where is she? Please tell me she's still in the car."

"No. She should've just made it home."

Dammit, and I'm stuck!

Impotent rage coursed through his veins as he honked and changed lanes, desperate to get across this river that was keeping him from saving his woman.

"With David? Shit. I need to get to her. Listen to me Jenna, David's dangerous. I'm pretty sure he killed Jack."

"Oh my God! Did you call the police?"

"I did, they said they're on their way."

"I'll call Carol. She's got all kinds of connections with the cops, and fire department, too. I bet she can get someone there faster. And I'll call my guys with the paramedics, in case..."

Griffen couldn't let her finish that sentence. "Yeah. Thanks Jenna," he interrupted.

"Of course."

Griffen hung up and honked and waved his arm out of the window with all his might, his stomach flipping over itself with each inch he made it closer to Althea.

He could only hope David's apparent obsession with Althea would keep the bastard from hurting her.

Althea opened her heavy eyes, struggling to make them focus. She couldn't see David but could hear him tearing around in the study. She jumped in her seat, suddenly realizing her hands were tied behind the chair. Panic was rising in her throat and her head was throbbing so hard that she was having a hard time focusing on any thought or image in front of her. She scanned the room as she slowly wiggled her hands against her bindings. They were tight but she felt like there was enough slack that she could get one hand free — if she could only get her brain and muscles to cooperate.

Her eyes widened when she saw how trashed her first floor was. The sofa was sliced apart, papers were everywhere. Althea's brain was slow but it was processing just how desperate, crazed...and dangerous David really was. She saw the rope he'd used on the dining room table, disgusted to recognize that it had come from her own utility closet.

She started fumbling more frantically with her ropes, trying to keep her sobs in her throat, but every part of her was wrapped in terror. Just when she thought she might make some progress on her right hand's ties, her wristwatch clumsily knocked the back of the chair in such a way that the thud reverberated through the room.

She stopped moving immediately, praying it was just her fear that made it seem so loud to her, but all sounds and movement from the study stopped. David emerged and walked to her with that slight limp in his left leg that he got whenever he was really tired or stressed — another residual torment from his car accident of seven years before.

"You're up." He walked to her and knelt down with an agonized look on his face as he slowly reached a trembling hand to her cheek. She jerked away as much as her aching head and secured arms would let her.

"I'm so sorry Tea. I didn't want to do that. I never wanted to hurt you, but I couldn't let you leave. You weren't supposed to be here." He was rambling and his eyes kept darting around the room.

"What are you doing David? Why am I tied up?" she whispered as he stood and slumped down on the destroyed couch.

"I couldn't have you calling the police. You know that, Althea." His eyes were unfocused and crazed. "Why can't I just find Jack's flash drive?"

He stared at her, making nausea roll over her in waves, but she wouldn't look away. She wracked her brain to remember all her tips from the self-defense classes she'd taken.

The one that kept coming to the forefront of her mind was: *Keep him talking. Don't let the conversation stop.*

Griffen had finally made it across the river and broke about every traffic law he could think of as he sped up Mt. Washington to Althea's home.

No need to worry about stoplights or speed limits now. In fact, being followed by a cop would've been a good thing. Unfortunately, he made it there with no police escort.

The streets were quiet with everyone at work. All he could hope was he wasn't too late.

He felt sick at the time that had passed, imagining all the things David could have done to her. He pulled up to park a block down from Althea's home. There were still two cars in front of her half of the duplex and he chose to believe it was a good sign as he walked quietly closer.

"Maybe if you tell me what's on the flash drive I can think of where Jack put it," Althea choked out.

"Military information."

"Were you stealing information from the department? Why?" she slurred.

"I needed money so badly. That accident ruined my life. Even now, I still have so much pain." He stared at her miserably as he spoke. "I was totally broke, depressed, gambling. I lost everything. I couldn't research well anymore. I, uh, borrowed some of Jack's ideas."

"Oh David."

"But then we got those military contracts. And they

contacted me. They knew everything — the gambling, the drugs, the idea theft. They were going to leak it to the university. I would have nothing. Or I could take their offer and be rich. It was too easy to decide."

"Who were 'they' David?"

"Chinese black market dealers, I think. Wasn't really my place to ask." He looked lost as he rose and started to absently pour out the contents of each of the drawers in her dining room onto the ground.

"Why would you do it? You're so respected. You would always have a job at any university."

"No I wouldn't. Not when they found out." He started looking around again, but with more hopelessness. "The pain from my accident never went away. I still need the pills, Tea, even now. Oh God, but now...what am I going to do?"

"Jack wasn't helping you, was he?" The question tore at her heart, the thought of it killing her.

"Jack?" he laughed. "Never. But he did find that someone had taken the military information off the server. I had been so careful, had encrypted messages, blocked senders and receivers of messages, anything showing I had access and was making the deal. I'd worked so hard to cover my tracks, not even letting us work on the project. He just fell on it while repairing the glitches I put on there to hide my work. God, he was so smart."

"Someone would've found out, anyway, right?" she asked quietly.

"Not before I was long gone. Jack had come to me with what he was finding. He didn't know it was me, so I blew him off — told him to tell me if he found more and that I'd take it to the authorities. I had it all figured out — I'd be gone and they'd see money going to Jack and calls from China to our office line, I figured they would think it was him. I just needed more time. But he figured out someone was setting him up..."

"But he loved you, David," Althea whispered.

"I *never* wanted to hurt Jack. It all got so fucked up. I was just lucky no one looked into Jack's death. The Chinese took what little materials I'd given them and I got a small payout. Not enough for me to leave, though. I was stuck and so scared all these years." David covered his face with his hands in frustration.

"David, what do you mean, look into Jack's death... He was..."

"In the car by himself? When I saw him in my office I drugged his coffee like I did yours." Althea groaned painfully as her foggy brain suddenly made a lot more sense to her.

"I was waiting for Jack to pass out. I figured I could destroy whatever he'd found linking the Chinese to me after he passed out. Discredit him with evidence of payouts, blame him for it all and leave in time to collect my money. But he found me in the building. Confronted me. He knew everything. I was too late. Oh God, and then he told me he had a flash drive hidden somewhere safe. He refused to tell me where. I had no choice, I swear!"

"Please David, tell me you didn't."

"I didn't want to, Tea. I mean it. He was with it enough after the drugs took effect that I didn't have to totally drag him to his car. Then I drove him by your house and..."

"You drove him into the river?" Her words ripped through her like broken glass and he simply nodded.

"It wasn't easy. Luckily he was out by then. Took all my strength to put him in the driver's seat and push it into the river."

"But someone saw him alone. They tipped off the cops."

David looked at her with insane pride in his eyes.

"Anonymous tipper, right? Come on, Tea. That was me. I couldn't risk an investigation into a missing person. I needed him to be found. So you see now why I need that flash drive?"

He touched her cheek again and she jerked away as much as she could.

Suddenly calmly talking him into letting her go — connecting to him like a person — seemed impossible. She was so angry and confused and alone. Who knew how long she'd been out. No one was coming to get her and the man that ruined her life was touching her. It was all too much.

"I trusted you, David. I let you around my *son*. I treated you like family."

How could I have been so wrong about everything?

"I know. And I do love you. You know, I probably saved you. They weren't going to just let Jack get away with exposing them. You wouldn't have been safe."

He touched her face again and she wanted to scream with fury.

"Now you're going to try and make this about me. Are you insane? You hurt me and tied me up. You killed my husband!"

"I don't want to hurt you again. But I will if I have to. If I can't get away I have nothing left. Nothing but you."

Her heart started pounding when she noticed the glint of black metal on the dining room table — a gun. David picked it up awkwardly and pointed it in her direction. "I hate this thing, but I guess it's good I brought it."

"Is that what you hit me with?" He nodded and the world turned to a tiny pinprick where only fear lived. "Are you going to ki-ill me? Like you did Jack."

"Not if you get me the flash drive and come with me."

"Give me my phone, maybe I can ask someone," she proposed desperately.

"Oh no, I can't do that, but you've given me an idea. Maybe it's not with you because someone else has it. I was going to search that asshole Griffen's hotel room next, but if he likes you as much as I think he does, I may be able to save myself the trip."

David's wild eyes suddenly looked full of a disturbing glee as he grabbed her phone off the dining room table.

Griffen felt his phone vibrate. He looked at it quickly in case it was any word from Jenna or the cops.

He was shocked to see Althea's name pop up in the text message: *Please come to my house so we can talk.*

It was likely David had her phone and was setting him up. Didn't matter, he needed to get in there. At least now he didn't have to worry about making it a surprise. He felt his back to make sure his gun was secure in the waistband of his jeans, under his jacket, and headed to her front door.

Griffen walked into the house, hands up and the sight that greeted him made his stomach drop. Althea was tied to a chair with dried blood caked down the back of her neck. Though her lovely eyes were hazy and unfocused, they were marked with sheer terror.

"Oh good. There you are," David declared, still managing to sound haughty, despite the fact he was clearly hanging by a thread. "I'm looking for a flash drive and I'm hoping you have it." David's shaking hand was pointing a small revolver at Althea. He looked jittery, desperate, and capable of anything.

Althea looked in Griffen's eyes and imperceptibly shook her head and looked at the door.

Aw, hell no. No way was he leaving her here. His incessant digging got her into this mess and he needed to get her out. Even if he died doing it.

"I do, but not on me. If you let Althea go, I'll get it to you."

"No, that won't work. First, I don't believe you. Second, I'm not going to let her go. She and my freedom are all I have. So you need to give me a better offer. To start with, I need you to drop that gun you're hiding."

"Gun?"

"Don't play stupid. I know all about you asshole," he answered, his voice shaky as his hand waved the gun away from Althea toward Griffen.

"Do you think I'd just let you spend time with my Tea here — at night — without reading up on you. You fancy yourself some kind of cowboy. We both know you wouldn't come here unarmed. Now drop it."

"No problem, man. I just want to be reasonable. The flash drive doesn't mean anything to me. I just want Althea," Griffen said calmly, grateful for the press of his backup knife that was secured to his ankle. Now, if he could just get to it. He dropped the gun on the floor and watched as David picked it up clumsily and tossed it on the dining room table.

"Good, now get over into that chair." Griffen sat down and saw David pulling out more rope. Dammit, if he let himself get tied up, he wouldn't be able to help Althea, but he had faith in David's inexperience in real hard criminal activity.

David leaned over him and said, "So you're going to get your contact to leave the flash drive for us. Only after I have it in my hands will I decide what to do with you two."

Griffen sat down slowly. "Sure man, doesn't mean anything to me. I couldn't read half the shit on it anyway."

As he pulled back Griffen's left hand to secure it to the chair, one hand still pointing the gun at Althea, Griffen heard the blessed sounds of sirens in the distance. David was looking toward the window when Griffen snatched his knife from his ankle with his right hand.

"What the fuck? You called the police? Stupid. Very stupid. You know I won't let her go."

David lifted the gun pointing it at Althea. His eyes were red and full of tears. "I don't know what to do Tea. I guess it's over, but I won't go without you. I waited so long for you, don't worry. I'll be close behind you."

Those insane words filled Griffen with powerful fear as he leapt as far as he could with one hand tied up, knocking David over and forcing the gun away from Althea.

He was fortunately much stronger than David, throwing him down on the ground and slamming the knife as hard as he could toward his body. He was relieved to hear David scream, but then he heard a loud blast as the sirens grew louder.

It felt like someone had taken a red hot baseball bat to his shoulder, leading to exploding fire throughout his chest. He fought to keep awake but the pain was too much.

As Griffen's eyes slowly closed, he heard a door slam open and the distant shouts of the approaching police.

As the murky darkness descended further, Griffen heard the dull roar of nearing footsteps, shouts, shuffling, and then the sweet sound of Althea's voice in his ear and the scent of cherries surrounding him.

He tried to hold on to the glorious sensations but the warmth and blackness finally took over.

CHAPTER TWENTY-ONE

"I always knew David was a creeper, I just *knew* it," Aubrey said, letting a drop of melted ice trickle down Althea's neck until she squealed in her seat in the hospital waiting room. "Oops, sorry, Tea."

"Can you focus on my head wound Florence Nightingale and not David? I would really rather never think of him again." Althea squirmed from the next cold drop of water. "I don't even know why you made that damn ice pack, Aubrey. They said you could just monitor me."

"I want to help," Aubrey muttered. As if on cue, Althea yelped when another icy drop traveled into the back of her shirt. Aubrey cringed, "Sorry."

"It's okay. I think it's helping," Althea lied. She luckily hadn't needed to be admitted. The amount of Vicodin David put in her coffee was only enough to make her loopy quickly, not hurt her, so it wore off on its own.

Unfortunately, it hadn't kept her from comprehending the sight of Griffen unconscious and covered in blood. She'd watched as the paramedics tended to Griffen — wouldn't look away from him for a moment, even while they tried to gauge how messed up she was.

She'd still been so groggy and could barely focus, but the sight of David laying there bleeding but still alive and Griffen unconscious next to him had been almost more than she could bear. David had taken so much from her and had threatened to take even more.

Carol and Jenna had done a great job hurrying the EMTs, cops, and fire department to her house. Her heart hurt just thinking of what would've happened if they hadn't come. She was just grateful that Johnny hadn't been home. She'd had to talk to two police officers about the events, and knew that had to be just the beginning of what would be an intensive investigation into David's crimes, including what she now knew to be his murder of Jack.

Talking to the police had tormented her with the usual panic at remembering the awful night she lost Jack, but she made it through by knowing — finally — that she hadn't caused his death.

That didn't ease the frantic worry she felt at the thought of almost losing Griffen, though.

Aubrey adjusted the ice pack again, causing Althea to wince. Her head wound was more worrisome than the drugs, but she hadn't needed stitches and they said she could go home under the supervision of Jenna. All that was well and good, but Griffen had to be rushed off to surgery as soon as the ambulance got him to the hospital. There was no way Althea was leaving, which meant she had a little entourage hovering over her in the waiting room.

Johnny's head was on her lap as he slept. While Jenna and Carol worked to get help to Althea's house Aubrey had pulled Johnny out of school and rushed to their side to help in any way she could — which unfortunately involved a dripping ice bath down Althea's back.

"I can't believe Griffen rescued you. That was pretty awesome. Even you have to admit it, Brey," Jenna stated.

"Not bad. If he pulls through I'll be really nice to him." Aubrey paled when a half-squawk, half-sob escaped Althea's throat. "Oh my God, Tea, I'm such an asshole. I was just kidding, of course he'll be okay. Jenna said he would be and she knows. Christ. Oh shit, Jenna, say *something*. Fix it, please!"

Jenna sighed, "Take a break from talking, Brey, that's a good start. And chill out while you're at it. Jeez. You're the most insensitive person in the world sometimes." Jenna put an arm over Althea's shoulder and soothingly said, "Griffen will be fine. Gunshot wounds to the shoulder are tricky, but it was at a good spot and went pretty cleanly through. I know the surgeon taking the lead and he's great."

"I wish it were you doing it. You're the best."

"Oh, no way. Doctors should never operate on family or friends, or the men their best friends are crazy about. I will help him recover, though, I promise. For now, just don't listen to Brey's lame attempts at humor. I'll beat her up if you like?"

Althea chuckled. "Maybe. Let me think about it. I'm just on edge is all. Seeing him laying there in all that blood, knowing my last words to him were so angry..."

Those words were still caught in her throat, when she heard, "Mrs. Tate?"

"Huh?" Althea grunted.

"She's right here," Jenna said with her comfortable air of authority that Althea called her "doctor" voice.

"Go with it," she whispered in response to Althea's confused look. "It's the only way I could get you in there so soon after his surgery."

"That's me," she whispered on a swallowed breath. "Can you just give me one second?" The nurse nodded sympathetically.

Althea reached over and hugged Johnny closely until he woke up.

"Hi Mommy. Is Uncle Gwiff awake yet?"

"No baby, I need to go see him and wait until he wakes up." A tear welled in her eye until it threatened to break free. She breathed deeply. "I love you Johnny. Please stay here with Aunt Brey and Aunt Jenna while I visit with Uncle Griffen, okay?"

"Sure. I love you too, Mommy. Please tell Uncle Gwiff I hope he gets better soon and I'm glad he's your boyfwiend."

"What? Huh? How did you know?"

"Duh, Mom," he said sleepily. "I'm five. I'm not stupid." With that, he hugged her, then grabbed Jenna's hand and climbed into her lap.

The nurse waited for Althea and said, "Your husband's right this way."

That word jarred her almost as much as the gunshot had but she steeled herself to act normally.

The nurse opened the door and quietly said, "The doctor will be around later, but I can tell you he did well in surgery and came out of the anesthesia fine. He woke up in the recovery room, but it's common to keep resting now that he's been moved to his room. Just be patient, okay," she said with a soft smile.

Althea nodded unconsciously and looked over at Griffen lying in the hospital bed asleep. He was so beautiful and peaceful lying there, but all she wanted was to see a smirk on his face while he made some cocky comment to her. She brushed her hand across his wavy hair, trying to ignore the machines and wires all around him and the smell of antiseptic burning her nostrils.

Despite the nurse's kind words, she couldn't tamp down the stifling fear that came with almost losing him, too.

Death is permanent. It is not a fight you can make up over or a mistake you can apologize for. It's the end. And she'd almost faced that end all over again.

Maybe she would never know for sure what Jack would've wanted for her, but she really believed he wouldn't want her to be isolated forever and he would've wanted Griffen to be happy, too. Griffen coming into her life had been a gift, but she'd denied and pushed back against it for so long. Now, she simply wanted to hold onto him and never let go.

As she sat by his bed, she clutched his hand and leaned toward him, "Griffen, please wake up. Don't leave me, too. Please."

She jumped when someone opened the door and whispered, "Hi."

Althea turned to see Carol standing in the door, not missing that she'd glanced down to where she and Griffen's hands were joined. Althea's heart sped up a bit, but she swallowed and looked straight at Carol, resisting the urge to pull her hand away.

"Hi Carol. What are you doing here?" Althea winced at the harshness of the words, but she couldn't keep letting life — and this woman — steamroll her.

"I'm so sorry to disturb you. Jenna helped me get back here. I don't know if she pulled strings or has just been growing Griffen's family tree by the minute. Val wants to see him too, of course, but she was nice enough to let me come in first — because I need to talk to you."

"Okay."

She sat in a small chair against the wall and stared at Althea and Griffen for a moment.

"So, you and Griffen?"

"Yeah. We need to talk when he wakes up, but...I hope so."

Carol nodded. "I'm sorry Althea."

"For what?"

"For letting you be trapped in grief with me. For not doing anything to help either of us move on. I...I don't think I ever accepted that Jack was gone. I know that's part of what I was supposed to do, but if I did that, I knew it would really be over. He'd really be..." she gulped. "You know."

"You lost your son."

"Yeah, but I held you back in misery with me. I lost Jack's dad. Then Jack. I just needed something to stay the same. You and Johnny were a part of that, of my own way of not letting Jack go or be forgotten. I didn't even stop to think about how that would affect you."

"I didn't exactly fight you Carol. I wanted to turn back time, too."

"True, but I think I gave you another excuse not to move on, and for that I really am regretful. If I could keep treating you as Jack's wife the world would never change. I guess I thought through you and Johnny, I could keep Jack alive."

"I wanted that, too." Althea swallowed and looked down at Griffen's still hand in hers.

Carol stood and crossed to Althea, putting her hand on her shoulder.

"It's one thing to want something you can't have. It's another to let that want control you until it is all you know. Life is short. If anything, losing Jack and his father should've taught me that. Don't forget how precious our days and our ability to love are. When I heard what happened to you... What David did...it hit me how wrong I had been. I can't believe I told you I blamed you for Jack's death. It wasn't true and it was so wrong to say it. I almost lost you, too, because of my own blindness. I know it's time for me to think about some changes."

Carol stared down at Griffen, brushing his hair off his forehead. She turned to look deeply into Althea's eyes and went on. "Griffen's a good man, Althea. He was always like a son to me. He had a rough start to life. I'm not sure I'm totally comfortable with you two together yet, but you deserve to be happy. Both of you do. And I can step back while you figure things out." With that, Carol kissed Griffen's cheek and then stood and hugged Althea who held her with a fierceness she couldn't believe her exhausted body could muster.

"Carol?" Althea said before she walked out the door.

"Yes?"

"Tha-ank you." They both heard the break in Althea's voice but Carol simply nodded, one tear glistening on her cheek.

"You're welcome sweetheart."

She left and Althea simply stared at the door for several minutes before looking back and resting her head on the bed beside Griffen, letting each of his gentle breaths bring her much needed comfort.

Griffen fought the cobwebs in his brain and swallowed through a mouth so dry it felt like he'd been chewing on cotton for an hour. He wanted to fall back into the fluffy cocoon of sleep but the soft scent of cherries and jasmine started to wash across him and he fought his eyes open. He was greeted by a mass of honey hair spread across his chest, a few strands of which were tickling his nose.

"Hi gorgeous," he choked out softly.

Althea jerked awake and smiled down at him and his whole body somehow tensed and relaxed at the same time.

"Hi stud," she whispered and then started sobbing.

"Hey. Shh, come here." He reached to hold her but pain shot through his whole right side and he winced.

"Oh God. Be careful. You just came out of surgery. David shot you in the shoulder, but you did great. Let me get you some water. Do you need anything else?"

Griffen smirked at the sound of her anxious babbling. He'd been so terrified that he'd never hear it again, so he just let it wash over him, taking the Styrofoam cup of tap water from her trembling hand and sipping it eagerly.

"I'm so glad you're here," he said softly, almost afraid she'd run away.

"I think Jenna called in all her favors. You're practically smothered with attention here. She's the one that got them to let me see you."

"That's the best favor of them all. You look beautiful baby."

And she did. Her eyes were stormy, mostly green and full of emotion. She was still in the same clothes she'd worn when she'd left him, but now she was safe and with him. He suddenly felt suffused with hope.

She laughed. "Did that surgery mess with your eyesight? I'm a mess."

He smiled at her and winced as he lifted a finger to her cheek.

"You're the most beautiful thing I've ever seen. Do you forgive me?"

"I'm not happy about the secrets, but I understand why you kept it from me."

"I got carried away and should've thought about what hiding that from you would do to you."

"He was innocent, you know. It was all David."

"Right."

"But, what about your book? Will you still write it?"

"That's up to you. If you don't want me to, I won't."

"No, you should write it. I think Jack would've really liked that."

"Yeah?" he asked with a smile. It felt so good to hear her talking about Jack in a way that wasn't full of guilt and pain.

"Yeah." She rested her head into the nook of his left shoulder and they were quiet like that for a while, just enjoying the comforting feel of the other's warmth and breath.

"Althea?"

"Yes, Griffen?"

"Do you love me?"

She looked up at him and smiled softly.

"Wow, just going for the big stuff right off the bat, huh?"

"It's been a long day. I'm not into small talk right now."

She kissed him gently then pulled back and said, "I know it's crazy, but I think I've loved you for a long time now."

"Thank God," Griffen sighed.

"Seeing you covered in all that blood, thinking I may have lost you, that really drove it home for me. Griffen, do you love *me?*"

"Of course. I thought that was pretty obvious."

"I can be dense," she giggled.

"Then I'll be clear. I love you so much, gorgeous." He touched her face softly with his small amount of energy and she leaned over to brush his lips with hers.

"I wanted to feel guilty for loving you when you'd been Jack's before, and then I felt guilty for being angry that he found you first," Griffen whispered. "I keep trying to identify the moment I fell in love with you, but I can't. I think I've always been in love with you. Before I even met you. I was just waiting for you to show up. When I saw you in that bar, I knew...I knew it would be you. You know, I was thinking about your nightmares and I realized you've done the reverse to me. You took my hand and turned me from dust into a whole person. Please let me try to make you happy. Is that clear enough for you?" he added with a smirk.

"Crystal. It's just so fast it's got to be nuts, right?"

"I don't think so. All that matters is we know how we feel. Part of me would love to jump ahead in time to when we're old and have been together forever so I can prove to you what we feel is for real — but I'm just going to need to ask you to trust me. I don't know what life will hold for us but I do know when I look in the future I don't see a day without your face in it."

"Careful, you keep up all that flowery language and you may need to start writing romance novels, stud."

"Whatever you want baby," he laughed and held her hand tighter. "I think I can write a romance about you. You're so beautiful and sexy, but you're also so sweet, so smart, so very...you. I love being with you in a big room full of people and knowing you're mine. But, I'd like to feel like you're proud to be mine."

"I'm yours."

"Thanks gorgeous. And now I'm glad to say I have a bullet scar to prove it."

She winced as she came closer to him. "Don't remind me, I was so terrified. I thought I'd done it again — that I'd been so blind I let someone I love get hurt. I can't believe David fooled me all those years."

"He fooled Jack, too. But now you know you couldn't have protected Jack from what happened."

A tear started to slide down her cheek.

"Althea, what is it?"

"It's just all hitting me. What happened. I was robbed of the chance of a long life together with Jack. Christ, *any* life. Robbed of memories. What we would've had together. But I know now that was out of my control. Someone else committed that crime. Violated our trust. I know now that Jack's death," she choked on the words. "I know Jack's death wasn't my fault. But the crime I *can* prevent is abandoning this second chance with you."

"I'm not going anywhere, Althea, but you have to know, I need this to be for real. It's time for me to lay down some of my own rules. I love you too much to always be hiding who we are, what we feel for each other. I need to know that you don't feel like loving me is like spitting on Jack's grave. I need to know that you're all in, too."

"But what if something happens to you?"

"That's a risk that will never go away. Something may always happen that's out of your control, but we can't run from life because of that. I have to know you're with me on this."

"So, no more baby steps?" she asked softly.

"No. Fuck baby steps." He reached out and stroked her lovely cheek. "I want the whole big leap. With you."

"Yes. I want that, too." He hugged her fiercely, ignoring the shot of pain that ran through his shoulder. Althea grimaced and then smiled at him, "You'll keep the place in New York, though, right?"

Griffen laughed as he lay back in his hospital bed, urging her to join him in the small space by his side. "Of course, gorgeous. I'll give you whatever you want. Forever. I promise."

"How about we stick with this lifetime for now, stud?"

"Hmm, I'm pretty stuck on forever, honey."

"All right, it's a deal. You strike a tough bargain, Griffen." Althea kissed him softly, touching his stubbly cheek.

"Sounds like a good deal, gorgeous." He put out his uninjured arm and they shook on it.

"You know, right now, I feel hope."

"Me too. Now come and rest with me." He kissed her softly and sweetly, his good hand slipping around her neck. "I am so excited about this," he whispered so softly he couldn't even be sure she heard it. He reached down and began to stroke her breast. "You know what would make me feel even better right now?" Griffen asked wickedly.

"Here?" she shrieked.

"Yup."

"We could get arrested!"

"I know a great lawyer."

"You're seriously injured."

"You can be on top."

"You're unbelievable."

"Thank you."

"You're welcome, stud."

"I *knew* you calling me unbelievable is a compliment, I *knew* it." She leaned over and as he arched toward her, pain shot through him. "Maybe you're right. How about we just keep kissing instead?"

"Okay," she laughed. She cuddled up to him again after a light kiss. "Griffen?"

"Yes, gorgeous?"

"I'm so excited about this, too," she whispered against his lips.

EPILOGUE

Two and a Half Months Later

Althea loosened the wool scarf around her overheated neck before grabbing at Griffen's hand again.

It was mid-November in Pittsburgh and the remnants of leaves were still making a last vibrant gasp against the hills. In the typical unpredictable nature of Pittsburgh weather, the night was unseasonably warm. A fierce cold snap was only a day away, promising a steep temperature drop, but for that night, the air was comfortable as Johnny pulled ahead, gripping Griffen's other hand.

She and her crew were taking Johnny to *Light Up Night* for the very first time in his life and it sent a nervous thrill up her spine. This annual event was one of the biggest of the year in the city. Marking the beginning of the holiday season, downtown was overrun with Christmas decorations, parade floats, lights, and crowds of revelers on every street.

It was a huge step for her to be here. She'd avoided it every year, using the crowds or workload as an excuse, knowing it had really been her fear of all things Christmas and its painful reminder of the night that Jack had died that had kept her away.

However, tonight she was with Griffen and as with so many things, he made her feel strong enough to make a change. Usually this would be a recipe for Althea to curl up under the covers and hide, but not this year. Now she was intent on being a part of the life around her, refusing to silently mourn as it passed her by.

It was also a good opportunity to celebrate that life had finally started to settle down after David's attack. Once Griffen was released from the hospital he'd moved in with Althea and Johnny. At first it was so she could look after him as he healed but the media interest in all facets of the scandal surrounding David's crimes was oppressive and Griffen refused to leave them alone.

The government and military investigation was painful but fortunately their involvement was short lived. David and his secret allegiances were the real focus at least as far as that part was concerned. The government and the university had indeed suspected security had been compromised years before, but David had hidden the breach well after failing to execute the information sale, so nothing had come of it then. By thwarting David from following through with his plan, Jack had prevented a potential international calamity, confirming him a hero in death, just as in life.

David's trial hadn't begun, but there was talk of both the state and the feds taking a bite at the apple — the state for Jack's murder and the feds for a laundry list of crimes.

As for the press, that was a different story. Everyone seemed to want a piece of them and Griffen's fame made it only that much more salacious. For someone like Althea who'd lived an incredibly quiet and private life so far, the whole experience had been at best amusing, at worst, surreal and invasive to the point of disturbing.

Of course, Griffen wouldn't hear of her and Johnny facing it alone. Honestly, she hadn't put up much of a fight, because Althea found she loved having him close. With each day their knowledge of each other grew to match the intense connection that had hit them so hard from the beginning.

Even with all the madness around them, Griffen and Althea were enjoying their time together without secrets and finally free of the guilt over Jack's death that had plagued them both for so long.

They learned more about each other every day, and they liked what they discovered. Even their occasional quarrels — and the accompanying make-up sex — helped them to settle more easily into the hope of a future together, because they always came out the other end more intimate and connected than before.

Carol was doing better. The news about David was a shock to her but she also found relief that Jack's death was finally explained. It had also meant that *Viola* was packed with new customers hoping for a piece of the story or just to gawk. She'd even had to take on a new chef to handle all the new traffic. The new chef also acted as manager and *Viola* was running so well under her hand that Carol had been able to take a step back for once.

As Griffen wrapped an arm around her shoulder and kissed the top of her head, Althea curled into his side. Johnny was marveling at the elaborate *Macy's* store windows, each one honoring a different famous Pittsburgh sites during the holidays. It was all part of the historic opening of the Christmas season that Althea had avoided with panic and shame until now.

It thrilled her to hear Johnny rave over each window as they strolled by. He was particularly entranced by the display presenting the ice skating rink at downtown Market Square — so much so, that Althea overheard him demanding Aunt Brey or Aunt Jenna take him there as soon as possible.

Griffen looked down at her, "Are you ready?"

"So ready."

"Good," he kissed her deeply until she heard wolf whistles behind her.

"Hi Brey. Hi Jenna. Guess this means Johnny's ready to see the tree lighting now?"

"A great *G-rated* idea if you ask me," Jenna said with a laugh.

Althea hesitated for a moment and Griffen gripped her waist tightly, whispering in her ear, "Are you sure you want to do this?"

"I love that you know to ask that. But, yes, I'm sure. Just nervous and excited."

"Good," he gulped. It struck her that Griffen was acting equally skittish as they trekked deeper into downtown toward Point State Park.

Is Griffen sweating? He's definitely distracted. Is he not okay with this after all?

Althea caught his smile back to her and forced down her worried thoughts. She'd gotten much better at not wrapping herself in worst-case scenarios and Griffen was a large part of that.

"Are *you* okay, Griffen?"

"Yeah, of course." He looked deeply in her eyes, still making her weak in the knees. "I just want you to only have happy memories of Christmas from now on."

"Oh Griffen." She kissed him hard as they approached the masses of people waiting to see the lighting of the tree.

"Wow! This is so cool," Johnny cried at the sight of all the fanfare before them, only to become bored by it right away. "Mommy, can Aunt Bwey and Aunt Jenna take me to see Santa?"

"I can take you honey," Althea offered, her hand outstretched.

"No! I want my Aunts to take me, Mommy."

"What can we say? He's individuating," Jenna said with a laugh.

"Yeah. I guess you're old news Mom," Aubrey teased. "Let us take him. You know you love the fountain. Take a closer look. It *was* the site of the closest thing you two had to a first date," Aubrey offered with a wink.

"Yeah, you guys just relax. Aubrey's photographing the event for *Pittsburgh Magazine* so there's no wait to see Santa. We'll take him," Jenna said.

"What a great idea," Griffen whispered.

He took her hand and walked her to the confluence of the three rivers, where America first found a gateway to the western frontier and began a history of new beginnings for so many people. The fountain was turned off for the winter, but the memory of their picnic lunch there together still thrilled her as she leaned close to Griffen's warm body.

"Some view," she said, still overwhelmed by the symmetry of the three rivers framed by the mountains in front of them. Althea finally felt truly one with the current of the world around her and so deeply connected to this man next to her.

"Happy?"

"Yes, Griffen." She entwined her fingers in his. "So happy."

"Hopefully this will make you happy, too."

Griffen suddenly started to go down on one knee and the realization hit Althea so hard she thought her heart would burst. They were already getting attention, but she couldn't be bothered to notice. All she could feel was shock to see Griffen kneeling before her.

"Althea since the moment I met you I knew nothing would ever be the same for me. I knew that you and I were meant to ride along this life together. I want to be with you every day. To raise Johnny with you. To laugh with you. To support you. To love you."

"Griffen! What are you doing?"

"Well, I thought I was asking you to marry me. But I may not be doing a good job of it. I probably need to be more straightforward. Althea, will you marry me? I know it may seem fast, but whenever I wanted something in my life I went for it. And I want you. I love you and I want to be with you forever. And before you answer, know that I don't want to replace Jack in your heart, because he's inside mine too, just like he's in yours. So what do you think?"

Althea couldn't speak as her emotions were choking her throat like a fist.

"Please hurry up and answer, because you're starting to freak me out. If I wait much longer I think I'll have a heart attack."

"Can you never be serious Griffen?" she asked, but she was laughing now.

"I'm as serious as they come, gorgeous, what do you say?"

"Of course I'll marry you. I love you."

He stood and kissed her firmly. Cheers and hooting from their audience sounded from behind them but all she heard was their own hearts pounding. When he pulled back he opened a ring box before her.

"It's so beautiful." She looked down at a huge green stone surrounded by white diamonds. "Is that an emerald?"

"No, gorgeous. It's a green diamond. Took forever to find one but I wanted something to match the green flecks in your eyes and an emerald is too weak of a stone for you. Diamonds are forged out of great strain, pressure, and stress to emerge as something so strong, bright, and beautiful — precious — just like you. It *had* to be a diamond."

"Griffen, how long were you looking…exactly?"

"I started hunting as soon as I got out of the hospital," he cringed.

"Griffen! That was barely over two months ago!"

"What can I say? I like to push you, gorgeous."

"Oh Griffen. What am I going to do with you?"

"Wild hot engaged sex works for me. Maybe some of those tricks and treats we bought at your favorite store in New York before Halloween?"

"You're such a sentimental romantic," she said with a roll of her eyes.

"Don't let that get out. I have an image to maintain," he winked.

"So, you're all mine, then?" she smirked.

"Forever, gorgeous. All yours." He pulled her closer and sat her down on his lap on the edge of the empty fountain and kissed her deeply, just like he had on that first afternoon they'd spent alone together. She hadn't admitted it to herself, but she was pretty sure she'd already fallen hard for him even then. A light rain was falling in the warm night, but she didn't notice the spray of water on her face because she was so warmed by his kiss.

"Mommy, Mommy, did you say yes?"

Althea pulled away and looked over to see Aubrey, Jenna, and Johnny grinning at her like eager fools.

"What's that, Johnny?" she asked.

Griffen grinned at him, "I asked if Johnny would be okay with us getting married. He was cool with it."

"I said heck yeah! I asked Santa to make Uncle Gwiff my daddy, too. Just to be safe."

"And Aubrey and Jenna?"

"They tortured it out of me. And I needed to make sure the ring was okay."

"And that we approved, too, of course!" Aubrey exclaimed.

"You know, you two are owed some serious love-life meddling karma from me."

"No way, we're staying free and single forever, right Jenna?"

"Yeah, whether we like it or not," Jenna muttered as she looked down at her phone, reading something that had her face twisting into frustration.

"Jenna, are you okay?" Althea asked gently.

"What, me? I'm great! Besides, this is your night."

"Yeah," Aubrey burst in. "Enough, Tea you're killing us. You said yes, right? If not, you have a weird way of saying no."

Althea held up her hand and they squealed and jumped on her so hard she almost took a header into the concrete fountain's bed.

"Easy guys. I don't want her to get a concussion. I mean, we've got celebrating to do, right?"

Althea smiled. "Yes, we do."

Tears started to run down her cheeks and she couldn't catch her breath. She looked at this beautiful man in front of her and then back to the rivers behind her.

They call them the "Three Rivers" but it's really two rivers joining together to form the third. Each surrendering to the other to become something bigger and much more important. The rivers are not lesser for moving on and joining together, they are broader, stronger, and lead to so many more opportunities — as one.

She and Griffen were one now, but it was greater than just the two of them, because Jack would always be a part of them both. Their love for Jack would stay with them and grow as they moved forward on their own third river.

Althea smiled because she knew she was finally ready to move on.

Just as Althea felt her heart traverse this gateway to a new beginning, Griffen turned her body so she could see the massive Christmas tree explode with lights before them, reflecting the joy in her heart at this second chance at life — and love.

THE END

***Keep Reading for a Sneak Peek of
Book Two in the Gateway to Love Series:***

CITY OF CHAMPIONS
(Anticipated Release: Fall 2014)

Tragedy and betrayal taught Jenna Sutherland early on that her safest bet was to fiercely avoid any risk, whether it is in work, life, or love. Now a respected orthopedic surgical resident on the cusp of finally breaking through in her career, she's more guarded than ever.

When injured NFL quarterback Wyatt McCoy bulldozes into her life there's no denying he's cocky, selfish, and downright dangerous — everything Jenna's sworn she doesn't want.

Suddenly the levelheaded doctor finds herself facing down her greatest fear, and she's tempted to gamble all she's fought so hard to build. The two embark on an intense love affair that quickly teeters on obsession, and tempts them both to think they could go all-in on a real future together. Yet Wyatt's desperation to stay on the field — and out of the operating room — lures him to take dangerous risks with Jenna's trust.

Will they win at love or lose everything — including their fragile chance at happiness?

"I'm gonna head home after we meet the players," Jenna whispered to Tea as they followed Tom Wilkins, the assistant GM of the Pittsburgh Roughnecks, who was still chattering almost nonstop several feet ahead of them to Griffen and Johnny.

"What?" Tea whispered back more intensely, stopping suddenly until Aubrey barreled into her from behind.

"Jeez, Tea, are you trying to kill me?" Aubrey huffed at her.

"No, but I may kill Jenna. She wants to go home." Tea turned back to Jenna, glaring at her with an amount of frustration in her eyes that surprised Jenna, considering Tea was usually so nice — maybe a little dramatic at times, but always sweet. "You really can't be serious, Jenna. Not after Griffen went to all this trouble."

"I know, and I am so grateful for getting to make that connection with Tom, I had a crappy day and am totally beat. It's not like I blew this off."

"You're blowing it off now," Tea whispered angrily in response. "I can't believe you."

"Calm down, Tea…"

"Tea, ignore Jenna. She's just nervous about spending so much time with Gunslinger McCoy."

Jenna rolled her eyes at Tea but was getting no support from that member of their triad.

Instead, Tea simply glared at her.

"Hey, are you guys coming?" Jenna heard Griffen's deep voice boom back to them. He jogged in their direction and immediately looked at Tea with concern. "Gorgeous, is everything okay?" he asked her softly, as he placed his hand at the small of her back. Tea looked up at him and the two simply stared in each other's eyes for a moment. The adoration they shared for each other was almost palpable.

"I'm fine," Tea said reassuringly to Griffen. "It's Jenna, she's got a bad case of the stick-in-the-muds. She's trying to skip the tour."

"No way, Jenna, this is a huge opportunity to spend time with these players and they're expecting all of us to be there. It will look bad if one of us bails. It'll be short, I promise, and I know Johnny will be bummed if you leave. Please?"

Griffen shot his best puppy dog eyes at her, bending his head down and letting his longish, dark, wavy hair fall on his forehead.

"Uh-oh, Jenna, he's got you in his blue-eyed clutches, you're toast," Aubrey said, with a giggle, which Tea quickly joined in on with her own snickering.

Griffen wouldn't look away and threw out his bottom lip further. Jenna had to admit that he was devastatingly handsome. Yes, he was madly in love with her best friend, but she was a woman with eyes, after all.

"Fine," Jenna muttered in defeat as she started walking toward Tom and Johnny.

"Sweet," Griffen exclaimed. "Come on, hurry up, ladies, they're waiting for us."

"I win," Aubrey whispered to her.

"Grow up," Jenna said, elbowing her in the ribs.

"All right, folks, are we ready?" Tom asked when they caught up to him. Everyone nodded and proceeded to fall in behind him again like obedient puppies until they made it to the entry area in the NFL team's locker room.

Tom stood next to the three players that were pegged for the meet-and-greet portion of what was rapidly feeling like one of the longest days of Jenna's life. The sight of Wyatt McCoy was unnerving. She worked with athletes every day, but none that had intrigued her for such a long time like he did — plus, he was staring at her so intently that she began to feel downright overwhelmed.

Only one person had ever stared at her that way, or had that kind of powerful effect over her, in her whole life. Jenna wanted nothing to do with anyone who stirred up that memory, no matter how much Wyatt may have fascinated her as a player over the years.

"I have our quarterback, Wyatt, wide receiver, J.J., and safety, Trajan, here to meet you. If you're NFL fans, as I know at least a couple of you are, they won't need much introduction," Tom said, with a smooth tone suffused with authority.

Although Jenna was forcing herself to look at Tom, she was having a difficult time focusing on his words. Her chest felt oddly tight and her palms were sweating. She refused to meet Wyatt McCoy's stare or let him see that her breaths were becoming unnaturally short and sharp in her throat.

She tried next to distract herself by watching the happy response of Johnny, whose eyes were wide with excitement. Jenna couldn't help but be amazed at how he was speechless for probably the first time since he was born. She loved to see Johnny so happy and proud, knowing that his "Gwiff" had done all of this for him.

Out of the corner of her eye she could see that each of the three handsome players waiting for them had showered and seemed amiable enough. Though it was surely the annoying task of meeting "VIP Pittsburgher" Griffen Tate and his motley crew entourage after a long game and depressing defeat in overtime.

Jenna could almost feel that Wyatt Alejandro McCoy was still eyeing her like she was a glistening mojito on a hot day at the beach. He was blindingly good-looking in person. She could also tell that he'd earned the label of moody, intense, and unpredictable just by looking at him.

Every woman that saw his picture wanted him, but not Jenna, of course. She'd watched him like a hawk throughout the game — and his whole career — but she assured herself that her acute interest was purely due to her love of the game and a small concern for what looked like a subtle issue with his throwing arm.

Yet, with each moment he stared at her, her blood warmed and her ability to ignore the focused gaze of his dark brown eyes became increasingly difficult.

"What do you say, guys?"

"Huh?" Jenna muttered inelegantly. She was completely oblivious to anything in the room but the arrogant grin on Wyatt's face. She couldn't believe her own error. Aubrey had already pounced on the opportunity to torment her.

"It's time for the tour," Aubrey said brightly. "I was thinking maybe we should split up. Mr. McCoy, our friend Jenna here doesn't know much about football, could you possibly..."

"Take her on a private tour for more focused instruction?" he asked, with that same damned leering expression.

"No, that's not necessary," Jenna responded curtly.

"I insist. It would be my pleasure. Though I didn't catch your name," Wyatt inquired.

"Jenna, her name's Jenna," Tea blurted out, knocking her forward with her shoulder. "And you two should definitely split off, what a great idea," Tea crooned with a devilish grin.

"Tea, jeez," Jenna whispered, scowling at her. She should've known that Tea would get in on Aubrey's fun. They loved messing with each other. Jenna just preferred to be on the giving end of it. "Sorry for the hold up, guys, we just need to chat for a bit," Jenna said, dragging Tea and Aubrey out of earshot of the group of confused men.

"You two have got to be kidding me," Jenna whispered with irritation.

"What?" Tea whispered back innocently and then twisted her face into a scheming sneer. "Are you the only person that can pester her friends into talking to guys?"

Jenna turned to Tea and gave her a full scowl, "Seriously...jerky high-profile athletes? You know the answer to that," Jenna whispered back. "I'll just go on the tour with the rest of you guys."

"Now, Jenna, you wouldn't want to look rude after members of such an important part of your growing career have been so gracious to us, would you?" Aubrey teased.

"Dammit, Aubrey," Jenna fumed.

"You know I'm right. Now stop being such a pain in the ass and let that hot guy show you around before you offend him or anyone else here," Aubrey responded calmly.

"Fine," she huffed, turning to face Wyatt. "All right, Mr. McCoy, let's go," Jenna said, walking toward him with her toughest facial expression. It just seemed to make him more amused.

"Please call me Wyatt. How about we start with the locker room, that seems as good a place as any to begin your education," Wyatt drawled at her.

Of all the days to have to deal with a cocky self-impressed jackass... This guy can't be for real, Jenna thought to herself in frustration. It's official, I will be killing Aubrey and Tea later. But I'm stuck with him now, so my double homicide plans will have to wait.

Jenna took a steadying breath. She then steeled her nerves and schooled her face into its most confident expression before responding, "Sounds good, Mr. McCoy."

"Oh, come on, now. Don't be so formal. Don't you like me, sugar?"

"I just met you, I have no opinion of you," she answered.

"I don't think you're being honest. I think you definitely have an opinion of me, and it doesn't seem good," he responded, leading her into the expansive room lined with cherrywood lockers, benches, and various forms of equipment. Jenna had been in countless locker rooms during her life — including this one — but the nearness of Wyatt McCoy made it feel surreal and claustrophobic.

It was a dream set-up for an athlete like herself, but all she could focus on was the singing heat coursing through her from merely his fingertips on her lower back.

She turned to him to break the connection, but that only served to plant her back against a locker and her face smack dab in front of his well-built chest.

She was suddenly overcome by a terrible sense of déjà vu — the sensation that she'd been in this place before. Yet then it had all ended so very badly. Her prior sense of light irritation and intrigue from the situation was quickly morphing into an overwhelming sense of almost frantic nerves.

Jenna looked up into his eyes and immediately regretted it. Having spent so many years avoiding any romantic involvements with athletes, her instant attraction to this one was vexing to say the least. It felt like her emotions were changing more rapidly than she could process them.

Wyatt looked down at her and smiled. "Now that I have your attention, maybe we can get to know each other better, you can give me a chance to improve that low opinion you have of me. Did you like the game?"

Jenna was relieved that the conversation had turned to her favorite topic, and she immediately felt control and calm return to her.

"It was a tough loss and you seemed to be having a rough go of it."

"Ouch, that hurts."

"You keep telegraphing your throws like that and you're going to spend the rest of the season on your ass — trust me, that will hurt a lot more. You need to shorten your release," Jenna advised him.

"Um, I'm not sure I heard you right. What was that again?"

"Just critiquing your throwing style is all," she answered.

"So, you were watching me closely?"

"It's an occupational hazard."

He looked confused for a moment but quickly regained his cocky composure. Meanwhile, Jenna kept feeling hers slipping away from her.

With each unsteady breath she noticed another aspect of him that was intoxicating to her, whether it was the slight golden streaks in his chestnut hair, the matching hint of stubble on his strong jaw, or his broad shoulders — everywhere she rested her eyes on him only served to make her body more consumed with attraction and her brain more furious with that fact.

"Well, for the record, I've never heard any complaints about my release," he said, with a wink, and Jenna rolled her eyes in disgust, which only made him chuckle in amusement. "Though I thought you weren't supposed to know about football, sugar?"

"No. My ex-best friends were playing a joke. Now that you know the truth, I'll be moving along, let you get back to your life."

"But I'm having so much fun pretending to educate you. Maybe I can teach you Spanish."

"I already speak Spanish, so you've got nothing to teach me."

"Oh, I wouldn't be so sure of that. How about I teach you to relax?" he whispered in her ear — sending a shot of warmth coursing through her traitorous body.

"I'm plenty relaxed," she huffed. He smirked again, running a finger across her shoulder until she jumped.

"Relaxed, really? Hmm," he added with a cocky drawl and a slow perusal of her body that had her stomach tightening, even as her jaw clenched in irritation.

Wyatt leaned into her until she could smell his freshly-washed hair and count the beads of water on the part of his skin bared by the undone buttons at the top of his crisp Italian shirt. He was insanely attractive and far too close for Jenna's comfort. She cringed a little at her own big mouth, wishing she'd left this bad boy well enough alone. The worst thing you can do with someone like Wyatt is to engage him, and she'd done worse, she'd challenged him.

Dammit, Jenna, rookie mistake! she thought, chastising herself.

Jenna shook herself out of her hormonal stupor and stood up straight enough that he backed off a bit, "I have to ask — does this usually work?"

"What do you mean, sugar?"

"I mean this ego the size of Texas routine of yours. Calling me 'sugar' and the double entendres. I mean, come on. You want my opinion of you? Here it is. I find your little shtick — and you — exhausting and insulting. Please excuse me. I need to get back to my friends."

"I was under the impression my 'little shtick' was working," he teased, raising a hand and placing it alongside her head.

"Please. Working? Hardly," Jenna said, rolling her eyes again theatrically and ignoring the tightening in her belly and her intense desire to bury her face in his chest and just sniff him for a while.

Pull yourself together, Jenna! she ordered to herself.

"Come on, play nice," Wyatt said, with a devious half-smile, looking down at her smugly. "I mean it, you need to relax."

These simple words shook her to the core. The feel of the locker behind her and his proximity, were all too painfully familiar. Her sense of panic returned.

"Let me go. I need to go," she demanded.

"Is something wrong, sugar?"

"My name is not sugar, you jerk!" Jenna shouted, and his laugh in response had her face red in anger and humiliation.

Right at that moment, the rest of her group walked in and Jenna felt sheer mortification at her position — pressed up against Wyatt McCoy of all people, in front of a locker — practically in her place of business — screaming at him.

Everyone looked at Jenna in shock at her outburst, though Aubrey merely looked thrilled at Jenna's current predicament.

"Don't worry, folks, we're fine in here. I'll bring your friend to you soon."

"No, that won't be necessary, I can go now," Jenna said, as calmly as she could muster. She smoothed down her shirt in an effort to regain control of herself. She was about to speak when she heard, "Hey, Doc!"

Jenna looked up quickly, averting her eyes from her nosey companions and saw the kind face of one of her patients.

"Hi, Eloni!" Jenna threw Wyatt a sharp look, but he wouldn't move. He still had his hand placed on the wall next to her head and the fiery effect he had on her both her emotions and her sex drive, were quickly replaced with plain raw irritation.

That's more like it, she thought. Best to remember why you stay away from these types of guys in the first place.

She began to dart under his arm, but he only lowered it more.

"Doctor?" Wyatt asked, with a cocked eyebrow.

"Yes, Mr. McCoy, they let us little ladies be doctors now. What a world! Now, if you would please move your arm."

"Hey, Wyatt, how ya doin', man? How do you know Doctor S.?" Eloni asked, with his usual gentle giant charm. He was an offensive lineman from Samoa out of the University of Hawaii, and one of the first NFL players to give her a chance.

"Fine, Eloni," Wyatt gritted out. "I was giving her a tour."

"Oh, yeah? What brings you here, Doctor S.? Visiting a patient?"

"No, I came with some friends." Jenna breathed more easily as she turned her attention away from the incredibly unsettling quarterback. "Griffen over there is buds with your Assistant GM," she answered, jerking a thumb over to her group of friends that were now listening to a speech about on-field safety. "How's the knee, Eloni?" She could feel Wyatt's eyes boring into the side of her face, but she refused to look in his direction.

"Well, my knee feels like a million bucks. You're a miracle worker, Doctor S."

"It's all due to you and your hard work. Maybe they'll start naming the surgery after you, you keep playing so well..."

"Hey, Eloni, I think Coach is looking for you," Wyatt's voice boomed as he turned to his teammate. His nearness still overwhelmed Jenna, and she started to make her escape.

"Well, Eloni, it was good to see you. I'm heading off, too," Jenna said, and started walking toward her friends.

"Hey, where are you going?" Wyatt asked, walking alongside of her. "I wasn't done."

"I was."

"Oh, come on. What are you doing tonight?"

"I have plans," she answered, nearing Tea and Aubrey, finally.

"No, she doesn't," Aubrey blurted out.

"See, looks like you're all cleared to let me keep changing that opinion of yours about me. I won't even call you sugar, Doc."

"No need," Jenna answered, throwing Aubrey a sharp look before shouting, "Hey, Johnny, get over here." Johnny looked at Griffen and when he nodded, Johnny ran over to her.

"Hey, Johnny, Wyatt here said he'd love to watch you throw."

"Awesome! Let's do it," Johnny said enthusiastically.

"That's great, man, I appreciate it, too. Tom would that be okay?" Griffen asked his friend as he walked over.

"Of course. Come on, Wyatt, let's do it on the field. You guys can come take pictures if you like," Tom added.

"Well, y'all have fun. I think I learned enough for one day," Jenna said, as she stared in triumph at Wyatt.

He looked back at her with a challenge in his eyes and leaned down to whisper in her ear, "Have a nice night, but know that this ain't over, Doc."

A shiver ran down Jenna's spine as she watched six feet four inches of diabolically gorgeous trouble walk away from her and she struggled to decide whether she wanted to view his words as a threat — or a delicious promise.

Jenna turned and walked away, pulling herself back under control and shaking off the drugging memory of his smell and closeness with each step.

TO BE CONTINUED...

CONNECTING WITH CHLOE

Hopefully you enjoyed *Three Rivers*. If you did, please consider leaving a review so that other readers can find it.

Also, be sure to sign up for the Chloe T. Barlow newsletter. It is the best way to make sure you don't miss any deals, giveaways, new releases, or other exciting news about Chloe's creations.

Newsletter and Blog:
http://chloetbarlow.com/newsletter/
Chloe enjoys nothing more than interacting with her readers, so please keep in touch!

Facebook:
https://www.facebook.com/pages/Chloe-T-Barlow/446666692117051

Twitter:
https://twitter.com/chloetbarlow

Goodreads:
https://www.goodreads.com/book/show/18759506-three-rivers

Email:
chloe@chloetbarlow.com

Google+:
https://plus.google.com/u/0/116405903319564147007/posts

Learn More
Learn more about Chloe, *Three Rivers*, and the continuation of the Gateway to Love Series at:

Chloe's Website:
http://chloetbarlow.com

ACKNOWLEDGEMENTS

Althea has a village and so do I. The writing and editing of *Three Rivers* has been an exciting experience, but what has been the most remarkable is the generous support I have received along the way from so many great people.

My husband: I can't thank him enough for all he's done. He encouraged me to take the leap and start writing fiction again. Then he put his time where his mouth was, by doing everything he could to support me. Whether it was keeping our house intact or keeping the books, he's always there for me and I love him more than I ever thought you could love another person.

My consultants: *Janice* provided expert knowledge on the effects of grief and loss that were invaluable in the development of this book. *Bootsy* made one awesome punk music expert.

My author mentors: Author *Helena Newbury* is my savior and my inspiration. I could write an entire additional book just on how much she has helped me. If it weren't for Helena I doubt I would've ever finished this book. I was feeling discouraged and isolated and she came out of nowhere to inspire and guide me. Her insights and talents and support have been invaluable. Fate puts people in your life for a reason, and it definitely did with her. Words can't describe my gratitude to her.

That is not to diminish how grateful I am to the other wonderful women who took time out of their crazy writing schedules to help me along the way. *Julia Kent, Tessa Bailey, Seleste deLaney, Georgia Cates, Noelle Adams, Lyla Payne, Arabella Quinn, Jade C. Jamison and Denise Grover Swank* — thank you all so very much.

My Beta Readers and Early Reviewers: *Karen Marie* (of the lovely K&T Book Reviews Blog), *Summer* (of the very fun Summer's Book Blog), *Keri, Kristina,* and *Ashley* (my first

359

international fan), and the rest of my street team, "Chloe's Crew." Thank you all so very much for your input, kind words, tireless assistance, and savvy insights. There's nothing quite like the moment when other people start to believe in what you're doing and love your characters as much as you do. We were strangers when you picked up *Three Rivers*, but now I consider each of you to be very dear friends.

My team: *Eisley Jacobs* and *Complete Pixels*, thank you for putting up with me and my demanding "visions" for the cover, website, promo materials, birds tattoo, Chloe logo, and any other graphic design whim that emerged from my overactive author brain. You create beautiful things and I'm so lucky to have you on my team.

Marilyn Medina of *Eagle Eye Reads*, wow, just *wow*, you are so great at what you do and I don't know how I lucked into getting you to do it for me! Not only are you a gifted and talented editor, you are also an incredibly lovely person and I feel blessed that this process allowed me to meet you. Thank you for being you.

Kari and her gang over at *A Book Whore's Obsession,* thank you for your PR support. *Palermo Photography*, thanks for all the wonderful author portrait work you did for me.

My readers: And last, but absolutely not least, thank you to each of my readers for taking a chance on me and for sharing this world, as well as these characters with me.

THREE RIVERS SOUNDTRACK

- *River* — Joni Mitchell
- *La Vie En Rose* — Madeleine Peyroux
- *All I Want* — Kodaline
- *Little Talks* — Of Monsters and Men
- *Ol' Man River* — Ray Charles
- *Change The Sheets* — Kathleen Edwards
- *SexyBack* — Justin Timberlake
- *Last Friday Night (T.G.I.F.)* — Katy Perry
- *Blurred Lines* — Robin Thicke
- *Let Go* — Frou Frou
- *Sex On Fire* — Kings Of Leon
- *Fallen (Live)* — Sarah McLachlan
- *Sail Away* — David Gray
- *People Gonna Talk* — James Hunter
- *Love Is Blindness* — Jack White
- *Into Dust* — Mazzy Star
- *Live Like a Warrior* — Matisyahu
- *Over the Love* — Florence + The Machine
- *Things Will Change* — Treetop Flyers
- *Many Rivers to Cross* — Jimmy Cliff
- *Try* — P!nk
- *Agape* — Bear's Den
- *Stronger* — Kanye West
- *Althea* — Grateful Dead
- *No One's Gonna Love You* — Band of Horses
- *Safe and Sound* — Capital Cities
- *Reservoir* — Hem

Follow Chloe on Spotify to hear this and
other soundtracks from future novels:
http://open.spotify.com/user/chloetbarlow

ABOUT CHLOE T. BARLOW

Chloe is a contemporary romance novelist and practicing attorney living in Pittsburgh, Pennsylvania with her husband and their sweet puppy. She is a native Washingtonian that graduated *Duke University* with a degree in English and Chinese language. She met her husband at *Duke* and he brought her to Pittsburgh over a decade ago, which she has loved ever since and made her adopted hometown. She also attended the *University of Pittsburgh Law School* where she continued to be a book-loving nerd.

Chloe has always loved writing and although she does do it professionally as a lawyer, she cherishes the opportunity to craft her fictional novels and share them with the world.

When Chloe isn't writing, she spends her time exploring Pittsburgh with her husband and friends. She also enjoys yoga, jogging, and all Pittsburgh sports, as well as her *Duke Blue Devils*. She is an avid reader and wrote her debut novel *Three Rivers* in her spare time. She continues her tireless legal style of research in her fiction work as well. For example, in an effort to bring authenticity to Three River's treatment of grief and loss, she consulted with a psychologist and grief counselor during its preparation.

42568552R00228

Made in the USA
Lexington, KY
26 June 2015